Wilde
Child

THE WILDES
OF LINDOW
CASTLE

ELOISA
JAMES

NEW YORK TIMES BESTSELLER

𝒟on't miss the other novels in
the Wildes of Lindow Castle series by
New York Times Bestselling Author

ELOISA JAMES

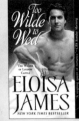
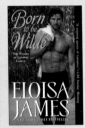

Wilde Child

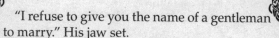

"I refuse to give you the name of a gentleman to marry." His jaw set.

Joan smiled at him. "I can find my own candidates."

"I'm one of them," Thaddeus said. He ran his hand through his hair again. Part of it was standing straight up. His gaze was unflinching. "I shall fight for you, Joan. That's what the silly girl, Ophelia, was doing. She gave back the love letters when instructed, but then she climbed in Hamlet's bloody window to make a point. To fight for what *she* wanted."

Her thoughts jumbled and her heart raced to a gallop. "I don't know what I want."

"It will come to you," Thaddeus said. He took a step forward and clasped her hands in his. "It's the middle of the night and thoroughly inappropriate, but will you kiss me? Please?"

"More inappropriate than kissing on an island?"

"Yes," he said uncompromisingly. "There's a bed behind us."

The moment he said the word, the bed loomed in Joan's view, a soft haven piled with pillows. It would be more comfortable than the picnic blanket. Heat simmered through her. Not that she meant to . . .

She rose on her tiptoes and kissed him. His lips were cool when her lips first touched them, but then they tumbled into a kiss that felt like the beginning of a sentence. A beginning to the play, to the carriage ride, to the . . .

To everything.

By Eloisa James

ELOISA JAMES

Wilde Child

THE WILDES
OF LINDOW
CASTLE

AVONBOOKS

An Imprint of HarperCollinsPublishers

WILDE CHILD. Copyright © 2021 by Eloisa James, Inc. All rights reserved. Printed in the United States of America. No part of this book may be used or reproduced in any manner whatsoever without written permission except in the case of brief quotations embodied in critical articles and reviews. For information, address HarperCollins Publishers, 195 Broadway, New York, NY 10007.

First Avon Books mass market printing: April 2021
First Avon Books hardcover printing: March 2021

Print Edition ISBN: 978-0-06-287807-6
Digital Edition ISBN: 978-0-06-287785-7

Cover design by Amy Halperin
Cover illustration by Anna Kmet
Cover image © Nisseikikaku/Shutterstock (flowers)
Author photograph by Bryan Derballa

Avon, Avon & logo, and Avon Books & logo are registered trademarks of HarperCollins Publishers in the United States of America and other countries.

HarperCollins is a registered trademark of HarperCollins Publishers in the United States of America and other countries.

FIRST EDITION

21 22 23 24 25   BVGM   10 9 8 7 6 5 4 3 2 1

*This book is dedicated to my wonderful
friend and fellow writer,
Lisa Kleypas.
Writing historical romance in the midst of a
pandemic is challenging, but Lisa's gleeful
support of this book's characters gave me
the backbone to create a joyful novel.*

Acknowledgments

My books are like small children; they take a whole village to get them to a literate state. *Wilde Child* benefited from the expertise of Carola Dunn as regards the thorny aspects of British high society. The Royal Society of Astrologers and Eton College kindly responded to queries. I also want to offer my deep gratitude to my village: my editor, Carrie Feron; my agent, Kim Witherspoon; my Web site designers, Wax Creative; and my personal team: Daniel Camou, Franzeca Drouin, Leslie Ferdinand, Sharlene Martin Moore, and Ashley Payne. My husband and daughter Anna debated many a plot point with me, and I'm fervently grateful to them. In addition, people in many departments of HarperCollins, from Art to Marketing to PR, have done a wonderful job of getting this book into readers' hands: my heartfelt thanks go to each of you.

Wilde Child

Chapter One

Lindow Castle
The Duke of Lindow's country estate
Cheshire
August 20, 1784

I need curves if you want me to play a woman's role," Otis Murgatroyd complained, frowning at the mirror.

"I'm trying," Joan said, panting as she hauled on his corset strings. "Suck in your stomach!"

"My understanding was that whalebones did the work," Otis grumbled. "Madame Turcotte's advertisements claim that her corsets can put a bend in a brick wall."

Joan, known to the world as Lady Joan Wilde, daughter of the Duke of Lindow, gave a final wrench that resulted in a slight indention around her best friend's middle. Grimacing at her reddened fingers, she tied off the corset. "Now the bustle. At least a *robe à l'anglaise* doesn't have panniers."

Otis's gown had been rescued from the attic and was out of fashion, but he wasn't going into polite society dressed as a woman, merely onto the private stage in Lindow Castle. Thirty minutes later, Joan collapsed on the sofa, worn out and vowing to raise her maid's wages.

Otis, on the other hand, looked fresh as the proverbial daisy in a green petticoat and yellow striped organdy apron with strawberry-colored overskirts and a matching bodice with a lace fichu frothing up to his chin.

"Your wig is slipping," Joan pointed out. He was wearing what her Aunt Knowe called a "gooseberry wig" with two frizzled bunches over the ears that resembled a gooseberry bush.

Otis adjusted the wig, then picked up a hat of strawberry silk adorned with a dark green bow and plopped it on top of the wig, adjusting the bow to a rakish angle. "I like wearing all these colors."

"You already aspire to the rainbow," Joan said wryly. In the three years she'd known Otis, his clothing had grown ever more outrageous, including an infamous appearance at one of the queen's drawing rooms wearing an apricot brocade coat with purple breeches.

"But now I'm curved like one," Otis said, guffawing.

"You don't sound like a lady," Joan observed.

"And I'm not very pretty."

That was true. As a man, Otis was impishly handsome, if short, but dressed in women's clothing, he became startlingly unattractive.

"Whereas you look beautiful as ever in breeches," he added.

Joan shrugged. She had always seen her beauty as a detriment rather than an asset, since her golden hair, blue eyes, and perfect skin made her the spitting image of the handsome Prussian count with whom her mother had bolted, causing a scandal.

More than one gentleman had rejected the very idea of marrying a woman whose hair color confirmed her illegitimacy.

Luckily, Joan had grown up in Lindow Castle, surrounded by a huge, loving family. She had always known who she was—a Wilde—and what's more, that the duke would murder anyone who suggested to his face that she wasn't his daughter.

Standing up and turning to the mirror, instead of a lady she saw a golden-haired, blue-eyed stripling dressed in a sober coat of dusky emerald with silver-thread embroidery down the front and around the cuffs.

Young and slender, but a man, with all a man's privileges.

She grinned at herself. "My favorite aspect of this costume is the rapier." She put her hand on the hilt and struck a pose, one knee bent before her.

"If the matrons get wind of your legs in those breeches," Otis said, "you'll be thrown out of polite society. Finally."

Joan shrugged again, having spent the last two years on the edge of being ruined. Sometimes the scandal wasn't her fault, such as when young Lord Stuckley had kidnapped her from a ball, planning a forced wedding. She had knocked him senseless with the hilt of his own sword, an action that the *ton* interpreted as unladylike. The fact that she had returned to the ball and danced the night away was ruled an even greater affront to refined sensibilities.

Her father had been livid at Stuckley, not Joan, but he wasn't happy when Joan was caught kissing a marquess in an arbor—and refused the offer to become a marchioness. A few weeks after that, she kissed the Honorable Anthony Froude on a balcony in full sight of the ballroom. That scandal burned even hotter after she informed Lady Froude that her son's kisses were only intoxicating because he had imbibed a bottle of brandy.

"Father gave me permission to wear breeches for this play. He knows I'm tired of performing damsels in distress," Joan said now. "Though I might add that I'm forbidden to leave the grounds in male attire. The duke didn't extend the command to you in a gown, though."

"I assume we're heading straight for the castle gate," Otis said, the veteran of many of Joan's schemes.

"Obviously, we need to test our costumes in public," Joan replied, putting on her wig, a small one that fit closely to her braided hair, with only two neat rolls over each ear and a short queue at the back. "Your man did a good job with your eyebrows, but you need powder and some hairpins to hold your wig."

Otis moved to sit down on the stool before her dressing table but misjudged, he and his enormous bustle ending up on the floor.

He sprawled in a jumble of skirts, looking at her. "Why would anyone in their right mind wear a bustle?"

"Up you go," Joan said, holding out her hand and ignoring a question for which she had no answer. She hauled him upright, retrieved his wig, and pinned on his hat.

"I would rather practice my lines than go for a walk," Otis said, picking up Joan's powder puff and generously dusting his face. "The only line I remember from *Hamlet* is the prince's daddy moaning *Remember me*."

"Something's rotten in the state of Denmark," Joan said cheerfully. "Hamlet's father was killed by his uncle, who took the kingdom *and* married Hamlet's mother. Hamlet scolds his mother, breaks off relations with Ophelia—that's you—and takes a trip to sea with pirates. He finally gets around to revenge, and by the last act everyone is dead."

"Including Ophelia or rather, me," Otis pointed out. "Not my sort of play, I don't mind telling you. As I recall, she goes on and on about Hamlet not loving her. Memorization was never my forte. What's more, Hamlet would have to be blind to fall in love with *me*."

He gestured toward the mirror. Joan had to admit that powder was doing nothing to hide Otis's angular jaw.

"The key to acting is imagination," she advised. "Concentrate on a sad lady. Remember how Miss

Trestle wept after her spaniel died? Imitate her facial expression."

Joan couldn't do needlework; she couldn't play the pianoforte; and she was rubbish at water-coloring. Her only skill was acting.

Unfortunately, ladies were only allowed to perform dainty, ladylike parts, and then only in the occasional private performance. She was sick of playing fair maidens waiting for a prince to save them. She wanted to play the prince who fought pirates.

Thank goodness her father had finally given in to her entreaties to be allowed to play a prince—albeit with the proviso that one of their family or friends must play Hamlet's beloved. When the females in her family had unanimously declined to act Ophelia, even for one night, her best friend, Otis, had stepped forward.

He tried out a pout that made him look as if he had dyspepsia. "I assume you're choosing some-one royal to imitate?"

"Close enough," Joan confirmed. Viscount Greywick, future Duke of Eversley, was the most pompous, irritating man she'd ever met. He had courted two of her sisters, but thankfully, both Betsy and Viola had rejected him.

She concentrated for a moment to make sure that she could picture the set of his shoulders (arrogant, of course), the turn of his lips (un-amused), and his gaze (verging on godlike be-cause he never did a single thing wrong).

According to Jeremy, one of her brothers-in-law, Greywick had even been perfect at Eton.

A paragon.

A credit to the English peerage.

Everything she wasn't.

Turning to face Otis, she let her features drop into an expression of aristocratic disdain, the air of a man who considered his bloodlines more important than his character. Or rather: considered that his bloodlines *were* his character.

Someday Greywick would be a duke, and as far as Joan could see, he never forgot that fact, even for a moment.

Plus, he and his mother were visiting the castle at the moment and would attend the performance of *Hamlet*. There was something deliciously amusing about the idea of performing Greywick before the man himself.

"Not bad," Otis said, waggling his eyebrows. "You definitely have a royal look about you. But was Hamlet so condescending? I thought he was a nice chap."

"Hamlet's a prince," Joan said. "He's been told he's better than everyone else from the moment he learned to walk."

"I'd rather be arrogant than melancholic." Otis tried pouting again. "Ho-hum, I'm such a watering pot. I think I'll jump in a brook because the prince doesn't appreciate my curves."

"Let's go," Joan said, heading for the door. "We can practice our lines in the library."

"You go ahead. I need to use the chamber pot," Otis said. "Somehow." He lifted his heavy skirts and let them fall to the floor.

Joan laughed. "It's not easy being a lady. I'll meet you downstairs."

Out in the corridor, she stopped for a moment

to readjust her rapier. The belt belonged to one of her brothers and wasn't made to circle a woman's hips.

Joan was slender, but she curved in the right places—or the wrong ones, when it came to rapiers.

She took the back stairs in a shortcut to the library, but once she reached the ground floor, the belt began slipping off again. Head bent, she was wrestling with the buckle as she turned a corner and walked straight into someone.

"Sorry!" she said, looking up.

Bloody hell.

It was he.

Chapter Two

$\mathcal{T}$haddeus Erskine Shaw, Viscount Greywick, was truly fond of the Wilde family. His mother was close friends with the duke's sister, Lady Knowe; he had been school friends with His Grace's sons and one of his sons-in-law.

But Joan was no favorite.

Her sister Betsy was clever and funny; her sister Viola was sweet and charming. He would have happily married either of them.

Joan had never been in consideration as his duchess because of her illegitimacy—but more importantly, because she was so annoying. Extremely annoying.

"Lady Joan," he said flatly.

They'd stopped bothering to greet each other with more than a modicum of politeness sometime last Season. *Sometime?* He knew to the minute when their guarded hostilities had broken into open warfare.

On April 10, he had bowed in front of her and asked her to dance—for politeness' sake, because God knew, he didn't want to spend time with her—and she had been silent for a moment and then said, "You'll have to forgive me. I have a headache and I think I'll go home." She hadn't even tried to sound convincing, and since no one in London could lie as convincingly as she, the insult came unvarnished.

He had bowed again, whereupon she walked away. Though he had the satisfaction of knowing that his face didn't change an iota, rage burned through his limbs.

A few minutes later, she walked past him, cozily arm-in-arm with the Honorable Anthony Froude. She had the damned impertinence to cast him a look before she drew Froude out onto the balcony and kissed the man senseless.

The next time they met, he didn't bow; he simply nodded. She blinked as if she couldn't remember why he was being so chilly, then gave him a scathing glance and said, "Took offense, did you? I didn't think you were sensitive. Or perhaps you view me as beyond the pale. One can but hope."

Once again, he had watched her march away.

And now . . .

Even here, in the dimly lit castle corridor, she glowed. That was the infuriating thing about her: She was exquisite. Not that beauty was unusual for a Wilde.

But she wasn't a Wilde.

She didn't have the duke's dark brows, or his black hair, or his chin. Her golden eyebrows were the same color as her hair, and her nose was a perfect replica, albeit in a feminine mold, of the infamous Prussian's.

That hair wasn't what made her exquisite, to his mind. It was the way she spoke with her eyes. And her lips: No other woman had a mouth like hers. A deep bottom lip, a lush Cupid's bow, and a natural tipped-up curve at the edges of her mouth, so she looked forever amused. Put that together with the way she laughed . . .

He shook off that idiocy.

"What in the bloody hell are you wearing?" he growled, annoyed at himself as well as her.

"Breeches," she said, giving him an impudent smile.

"I see that." Joan was a temptress at the best of times, but now? With silk tightly wrapping her thighs? "You can't wear breeches."

"It means so much to me that you disapprove," Joan said. Her smile widened, and her blue eyes suddenly sparkled with joy.

He gave her a withering look. "I've seen you practice that expression for years. Surely you know that it doesn't work on me?"

He was lying. He'd watched Joan flirt with every gentleman under sixty in London, and while he knew that it was just a performance—

Still, he *was* a man.

No man could encounter that practiced look of hers, the one that transformed her face into that of a sensual, laughing seductress whose eyes promised that he was the most desirable man in the world, and be untouched by it.

The expression wiped off her face, and she gave him an impatient glare. "Do get out of my way, won't you, Greywick? My father knows I'm wearing these breeches, and he approves. I think we'll both agree that he's the only authority I need recognize under the king."

Irritation swept up his back. He'd long ago labeled the Duke of Lindow's attitude toward Joan as permissive to a fault, but this was verging on a blasphemy. "His Grace *approves*?" He forced the words out between clenched teeth. "He approves of you being seen like that?"

"You needn't look so appalled," Joan said, obviously unmoved by a tone that he used only in the rarest of circumstances. She cast him a narrow-eyed look. "If you're not careful, you'll end up even more righteous and intolerant than you already are. You look as sour as a Quaker in a tavern."

"I look appalled because I *am*. You'll be ruined." He growled the word, leashing his temper with difficulty. Ruined meant that she'd be banished from polite society.

From . . .

From where he was. Not that he cared.

"Do you know how often I've heard that precise sentence?" She shrugged. "Pretty much every week for the last two years. Lo and behold, I am still invited everywhere. In case you're wondering why, Greywick, that would be because I'm an heiress, and a duke's daughter, at least by name. Power and money trump illegitimacy."

"You're reckless and uncaring," he said flatly.

"That too," she agreed. "Now will you move your hulking body out of the corridor? I could pull my rapier and take a first stab—ha! Get that?—at manly foreplay."

"'Foreplay'?" He heard the incredulity in his own voice.

"My goodness. I suppose I shocked the most pedantic man in London . . . *again*. Why do men wear blades in this day and age? Why, so they can excite themselves by pretending that they have a claim to manhood, skewering their opponents rather than—"

"You will be ruined," he said again, cutting her off. "Banished from polite society."

"Woe is me," Joan said. "Imagine: If I weren't forced to encounter a future duke at insipid balls and ill-tasting dinners, I might not have to endure being disparaged by him for an entire Season. When I'm not being ignored." Her voice was icy.

Thaddeus could feel a nerve twitching in his jaw. "I—you like dancing."

She folded her arms over her chest and leaned against the wall. "Only with some. Do keep talking, Your Lordship. This is an invaluable moment to gather inspiration. Memorize every nuance of an entitled royal bastard."

"I'm not—" He clamped his mouth shut.

"Oh, that's right," she said lightly. "I'm the bastard, not you. And you're not royal, but believe me, you're more royal than George himself, so I'll take it."

"What are you talking about?"

"Prince Hamlet?" she said, raising her eyebrow. "My performance thereof. Surely you know?"

Thaddeus frowned. When he and his mother had arrived the night before to stay for a fortnight, the butler had mentioned a performance by the traveling company of Theatre Royal at Drury Lane. "I thought a theater company was visiting the castle."

"I am playing the Prince of Denmark," Joan said. "My father wouldn't allow me to play a love scene with an actor in the company, so Otis will play Ophelia. Not that Hamlet shouting at Ophelia to get to a nunnery can really be termed a love scene."

"Otis Murgatroyd is playing Ophelia—in a dress?" Thaddeus asked incredulously. "Is the production akin to a pantomime, then?"

"Not a pantomime: a serious production of *Hamlet*," Joan said, her eyes glinting with mischief. "I will play the prince, in these very breeches."

"No."

"That was a good look," she said appreciatively. "I don't suppose I can manage the ticking jaw, but . . ." She scowled and lowered her eyelids to half-mast. "Do I have the air of an infuriated nobleman? Hamlet is frightfully irritable at times."

"You are performing the lead male role in a Shakespeare play in front of an audience, along with professional actors," Thaddeus said, trying to take it in. "You can't, Joan. You *cannot*."

He saw the moment when she got truly angry. Joan loved to play roles: He'd seen her switch with dizzying speed from frivolous maiden to practiced seductress. No expression she could put on affected her eye color, but now her eyes darkened to a steely blue, and her body stiffened. "I don't think of my family and a few intimates as an audience."

"Don't be a fool," he growled. "The news will

spread. What will happen to your youngest sister if you are ruined?"

She cast him a pitying look. "Artie is a Wilde, Greywick. The genuine article, not like me. No one in your precious circle will care if I don't appear in society again. 'Good riddance to bad rubbish,' they—*you*—will tell each other."

Thaddeus stared at her in disbelief. "No one has ever called you 'rubbish' in my presence," he said, hearing the menace in his voice. "They never will."

"Only because you reserve the pleasure for yourself," she retorted. "For your information, I've been called everything from 'hurly-burly hussy' to 'strumpet,' though 'baseborn' and 'love child' are perennial favorites."

"People have said these things to your face?"

"From the moment I arrived at school with my sisters," Joan confirmed.

Something in Thaddeus's chest eased at the expression in her eyes. She hadn't cared.

"I don't give a damn about the opinions of self-righteous prudes," she confirmed.

Clearly he was counted among the prudes.

"They're the only ones who will fuss if society finds out that I played a breeches role in my own home," she continued.

"You're wrong," he stated.

"You're blowing everything out of proportion," Joan said impatiently. "My sister Betsy dressed like a man, went to a public auction, and shortly thereafter married a marquess. That would be your friend Jeremy, though it's hard for me to believe that you *have* friends."

Thaddeus flinched.

"I'm sorry," she said. "That was really unkind. I'm sure you're nicer to people whom you consider to be worthy of your time, like Jeremy and Betsy. I mean, I know you are."

"I don't consider you unworthy of my time," Thaddeus said, feeling the tick in his jaw start up again. "I—don't."

She shrugged again. "You were in Wilmslow when Betsy went to that auction. It was only, what, four years ago?"

"I did not accompany your sister to the auction house," Thaddeus stated. He felt like an explosive device about to blow.

Had he hurt her feelings in the past? It was impossible to read Joan's expressions. She was like a chameleon, emotions chasing each other across her face. She had certainly never given the appearance of caring what he thought of her, or said to her.

"Because you didn't approve, I expect," Joan exclaimed. "Do move out of the way, won't you? I can't bear any more of this conversation, no matter how useful for my performance."

Thaddeus remained in place as if planted, outraged words crowding into his head. True, he hadn't gone on that particular excursion. He opened his mouth to explain—but he never defended his decisions.

A gentleman proved his worth by adhering to the rules that governed civilization and his own code of conduct. Only honor gave a man the right to term himself a gentleman. He didn't *explain*.

"You aren't taking into consideration the effect of your actions on others," he said instead.

"There won't be any," Joan replied flatly. "My family adores me, and they will still love me. They won't be stunned if I'm thrown out of society; they've been expecting it for years. I wouldn't be surprised if my brothers had placed bets on the eventuality."

"You don't understand," he said through clenched teeth. "Other people are injured by those who flout the rules. Your recklessness *will* be damaging."

She blinked at him, and her brows drew together. "Poppycock." She leaned forward, just enough so that he smelled the elderflower that she used in her hair. He'd come to expect it, a creamy, sweet honey smell that was indefinably hers.

She poked him in the chest, hard enough that he jolted. "Not everyone lives up to your impossible standards, Greywick. No one is good enough for you. Two of my sisters weren't good enough!"

"That's not true. They chose—"

"Why?" Her voice quieted, and their eyes met. "Why would they fall in love with other men when you were right there, dancing with them, playing the future duke, and generally acting like a trained buffoon dressed in a fine wool coat?"

There was a moment of silence. "I suppose you'll say that I'm not likable," he said. "Your sisters had a lucky escape, in that case."

Remorse flashed through her eyes, but before she could respond, he raised his hand. "Your opinion is valid, if not welcome. Yet I do not adhere to society's standards merely for propriety's sake. Other people are injured when selfish, careless people do exactly as they like, and devil take the hindmost!"

His last words rang in the corridor, and Joan actually fell back a step.

The air between them felt charged, like the moment after lightning struck the earth.

There are times when a lady must curtsy, and others when she should take to her heels. This occasion fell somewhere in between.

No curtsy and no running either.

Just a dignified retreat, shoulders straight, head high.

Chapter Three

$\mathcal{L}$indow Castle was well positioned on the main roads through Cheshire; as a consequence, family, friends, and mere acquaintances tended to alight at the castle steps at all times of the day or night, expecting a meal and a warm bed before they set off again in the morning for Staffordshire or, in the other direction, Scotland.

"We're no more than a posting inn," the duke had been known to growl, even as their butler, Prism, sprang into motion, making certain that every unexpected guest had a warming pan and fresh sheets.

Unlike her stepsister, Viola, Joan enjoyed the company of guests. But she also loved family nights, when the family dined alone. Or the rare times when only a few close friends were in residence. Such meals were held in the breakfast room, and the Wildes would pour in the door without ceremony, thronging in groups of six at round tables.

At the moment, she felt keenly aware that she

didn't care to sit next to, or close by, Greywick. She felt bruised enough. *Selfish* and *careless* kept racing through her head. They brought out the worst in each other. She had been unkind, saying that he had no friends. Of course he had friends. Her own brothers were among his friends!

But somehow that made his disdain for her worse. She was accustomed to scandal; her very birth was scandalous. It was absurd that this particular man's scorn would hurt.

She stayed on the other side of the drawing room before the meal, and walked into supper on Otis's arm. On family nights, the Wildes paid no attention to the social dictates ordering that the duke and duchess couldn't sit together, or that sexes must be separated. Long ago, His Grace had decreed that he would sit beside his wife. Viola was large with child, and she dropped down next to her mother with a thud. Her husband, Devin, seated himself beside her. Aunt Knowe always sat with them if given the chance, and tonight her close friend, the Duchess of Eversley, joined her.

Otis, back in a coat and breeches, led Joan to a nearby table, just as she realized that the only empty seats in the room were—

Sure enough, the brooding viscount was walking toward her.

"Has anyone noticed that modern seating has resulted in two islands?" Otis asked cheerfully. "One for the adults, and another for us. A full table of six over there, and here, only we three."

"I consider myself an adult," Greywick said, seating himself without meeting Joan's eyes.

"You are certainly mature," Joan agreed, scolding herself mentally the moment the words escaped her mouth. She refused to lower herself to another round of insults with him. "Viola and Devin are seated at the 'adult' table, so your idea doesn't hold water, Otis."

"The unmarried people are clustered here," Otis responded. "You can't say that marriage doesn't mature a person, because from everything I've seen, it's an extremely tiring state of affairs. The only part of being a vicar that I liked was performing marriages. The couples were so cheerful, whereas those who brought their baby for baptism looked as if they hadn't slept in months."

Viola caught Joan's eye from the other table and asked with a raised eyebrow whether she and Devin should join them. Joan gave a little shake of her head.

Greywick was irksome, but she was an adult, unmarried or no. They could sup together without more sharp words. She shook out the heavy linen napkin and spread it over the apricot silk of her evening gown.

"Do you miss the church, Mr. Murgatroyd?" the viscount asked Otis. As a dutiful second son, Otis had studied theology at Cambridge and joined a parish, but had left the priesthood promptly thereafter.

"Certainly not," Otis said. As he explained his reasons for leaving the clergy after a mere two weeks, Joan let her attention wander.

Something about the experience of wearing breeches was making her feel daring. What if she didn't marry a gentleman, as her family expected? What if her future was completely different from those of her siblings? What if she left the castle, the way her mother had?

Otis had overthrown his family's expectations. He'd been told he would join the priesthood since childhood, and yet after he tried the experience, he rejected it.

She looked about, trying to imagine a different life. Prism always did his best to replicate the splendor of the castle dining room, even in the breakfast room. Silver cutlery covered the tables like the scattered treasure of a king, and the gold-rimmed plates he'd ordered for use tonight merely increased the illusion. Footmen were dotted against the walls, ready to spring into action at the slightest twitch of a finger.

Her own mother, the second duchess, had turned her back on the castle, fleeing with her lover. As far as Joan knew, Yvette never regretted it. For herself, Joan was certain that she didn't need or even want the trappings of wealth. She didn't need the footmen, or a butler.

Prism reigned supreme, orchestrating every meal with the passion of a theater manager. But other people, ordinary people, cooked their own supper and dined alone with those they loved. The traveling theater troupe that visited Lindow Castle every year lived in gaily painted wagons and sometimes ate over an open fire.

"Joan?" Otis asked, pulling her into the conversation.

Greywick was looking at her searchingly. "What are you thinking of, Lady Joan?"

"Escape," she said truthfully. "It's your fault, Otis, with your talk of fleeing the parsonage. I was wondering what it would be like to flee Lindow."

"Marriage will give you that freedom," Otis said, patting her arm. "I realize that your married siblings return home as regularly as carrier pigeons, but most people consider marriage to be an excuse to avoid their childhood home except at Christmas, if that."

"I didn't know," Greywick said, a queer look on his face.

"Didn't know what?" Joan asked.

"That the two of you are betrothed."

"We're not," Joan said, at the same moment Otis said, "Not us."

"We're friends," Joan added. She reached over and gave Otis a little pinch. "Best of friends, since he agreed to put on a corset and gown so that I can play a male role."

"Very kind of you," Greywick told Otis.

"Yes, it is," Otis said. "I still can't believe I agreed to do it. I don't like the corset, and let's not even mention the challenge of using a chamber pot."

"You would never agree to such a thing, would you?" Joan asked Greywick, genuinely curious.

"Put on a corset? I hope not. And a gown? Never," the viscount stated.

"My father is wedded to his corset," Otis observed. "Given that I didn't enjoy the experience this afternoon, I probably shouldn't eat any cake."

They were well into the first course when a footman quietly entered and whispered something in Prism's ear. The butler left the room, even though he seemed to believe that the family might starve if he wasn't there with an eagle eye, noticing when a plate was empty and directing a footman by a twitch of his eyebrow.

Joan had forgotten Prism's absence forty-five minutes later, when the butler opened the doors and announced, "Lady Bumtrinket!"

Joan's stepmother sprang from her seat, followed by everyone else in the room. "Aunt Daphne, what a surpr—what a *pleasure* to see you!"

Lady Bumtrinket was the kind of well-upholstered English lady who glistens with rectitude, like a plump salmon flopping its way upstream. She was in the right, *always* in the right, even if the current appeared to be going in a different direction.

Foolish current.

A lady of her silhouette, ancestry, and education feels no need to consider social strictures that might prompt others to hesitate. Being in her eighties, or possibly her nineties, she had long since ceased to consider society's rules relevant to herself.

Because she was a relation of the Duchess of Lindow's *first* husband, Sir Peter Astley, more discerning people would consider the connection severed or at least attenuated once Sir Peter was replaced by a duke.

Not Lady Bumtrinket.

She had spent her life in the bosom of the nobility. Dukes, earls, and the occasional baron were to her as everyday as the air she breathed, and had been since she left the ducal estate where she was born.

Viola glanced over at Joan with a wrinkled nose: Great-Aunt Daphne was heartily disliked among the Wilde offspring due to her reliance on "plain speech," a phrase by which English folk often excuse rudeness.

"I'm sorry that Viola isn't seated at our table," Joan said. "She is terrified of Great-Aunt Daphne." She, Otis, and Greywick began to walk toward the door, where Joan's father and stepmother were greeting their guest.

"Last time I met her," Otis said gloomily, "she told me I was as short and round as a suet pudding. Another reason to avoid cake, I suppose."

"That is not true," Joan told him. "If it makes you feel any better, she loathes me. I believe she thinks I should have been raised in the country, or perhaps just left on the hillside, the way the Romans did with unwanted babies."

The flash of wrath in Lord Greywick's eyes startled her. "Has she been horrid to you as well?" Joan asked. "You needn't worry; the lady will certainly be seated with my parents."

In point of fact, Prism was rushing to add a chair to the right of the duke, in the place of honor.

"I think not," Lady Bumtrinket said, brushing past her niece and launching into the room. "I shall sit there, Prism." She pointed a bony finger to the seat beside Greywick's plate. "There's more space at that table. My girth is primarily the fault of the current fashion, but even so, it must be accommodated."

While Joan and Viola made their curtsies, receiving a regal nod in return, Prism summoned three footmen, who briefly swarmed the table and left a cluster of fresh china, crystal, and silver behind.

"I'll have two plover's eggs, gently coddled," Lady Bumtrinket told the butler once she was seated beside Greywick. "I'm reducing, Prism. Reducing is the bane of the elderly, a group in which I reluctantly account myself." She squinted at Otis. "I can share a recipe or two with you, young Murgatroyd."

"Thank you," Otis said.

The lady cast a peremptory eye on Greywick. "I haven't seen you in a donkey's years, Viscount. Where have you been?"

"The normal haunts," he replied. "How are you faring, Lady Bumtrinket?"

"Irritable due to reducing," she snapped. "You could use some reducing as well. You've grown inordinately large in the chest area. Or are you padding your coat?"

Greywick was apparently at a loss for words.

"I see that you are," Lady Bumtrinket said in triumph. "I suggest you dismiss your valet immediately and find one who can offer you better guidance on the art of being a duke. A future duke, I mean. We all know that your father reneged on his ducal responsibilities, running away to live in another household."

Joan blinked. She was aware that Lord Greywick's father, the Duke of Eversley, chose to live with his mistress, but she had never heard it mentioned in public.

A polite smile touched Greywick's mouth. "I assure you that the estate is well cared for in his absence, Lady Bumtrinket."

"One cannot blame you for ignorance of aristocratic behavior, given that you can hardly be said to have had a father," she continued, ignoring his comment. "Just be prudent when it comes to choosing your duchess. *Very* prudent."

Lord Greywick responded with a wordless hostility that Joan was surreptitiously finding rather enjoyable. Still, she felt a sudden urge to defend him. She was used to Lady Bumtrinket, but he might not have encountered her at such close quarters before.

"I do remember that you were trying to marry one of the Wilde girls a few years ago," Lady Bumtrinket said, without pausing for breath. "Would have been a good choice, but the youngest is still in the nursery, isn't she?" Her eyes roved the table and stopped on Joan. "Still unmarried?" she demanded.

"Yes, I am," Joan replied. She turned to Greywick. "Isn't it extraordinary how manners are changing? The ducal governess taught me never to inquire about marital status."

"Your governess knew you had to adhere to the highest standards in order to marry anyone above a grocer," Lady Bumtrinket declared. "That is not true for those of us born to the ermine. Speaking of which, I saw your father the other day," she said to Greywick. "Draped in an ermine robe in this weather. Extraordinary, even for him."

Joan was starting to feel distinctly sorry for the

viscount. No matter how much she disliked him, he didn't deserve a browbeating.

But the man had no need for her support. "My father is a duke of the realm," he stated. "If he wishes to clothe himself from head to foot in the fur of small, spotted animals, he has the means to do it."

Something about his face gave Lady Bumtrinket pause; she pursed her lips and then raised a finger. A footman sprang forward. "Three more coddled eggs," she said. "More well-browned toast. One would think that Lindow Castle was lacking in funds, given the meagerness of the dish. I'll have some of those dinner rolls as well, and just a *soupçon* of creamed spinach. Digestion requires vegetable matter, as I understand it."

She turned back to Greywick. "What are you doing here, given that the duke hasn't any unmarried daughters of age?"

Joan succumbed to a mischievous impulse and gave her a sunny smile. "Ah, but I am unmarried—as we established earlier, Lady Bumtrinket."

The lady narrowed her eyes, and then said to Thaddeus, apparently under the misapprehension that a hoarse whisper couldn't be heard across the table, "You mustn't even think of making Lady Joan—do note that I gave her the honorific—your wife."

Greywick's jaw was very tight. "I see absolutely no reason why Lady Joan should not be my duchess."

A surprising response, to Joan's mind. But then he was not a man who would welcome marital advice.

"I do," she put in cheerfully. "I hope you won't mind my comment, since you are discussing my marital fate so openly. Lord Greywick and I would not suit."

"We would suit," he replied, showing an unusual obstinacy. Of course, Lady Bumtrinket could inspire that in even the mildest of men. Joan's own father found her intolerable, and he wasn't easily enraged.

"Her golden hair isn't going anywhere," Lady Bumtrinket said with the vulgarity that only the utterly confident could wield. "Greywick, you're going to be a duke, sooner rather than later, to my mind. Something's wrong with your father. He resembled a famished rat, though I didn't say that to him, of course."

"I fail to see what my father's girth has to do with Lady Joan's hair," Thaddeus said rigidly.

"He's throwing down the gauntlet," Otis muttered in Joan's ear.

"It's nothing to do with me; Greywick is the sort of man who can't tolerate interference," Joan whispered back.

"I know," Otis replied, with a sigh. "But Bumtrinket is right that Greywick couldn't— *wouldn't*—marry you. I scarcely know him, but he's obviously as prudish as a Quaker."

"That doesn't matter," Joan pointed out. "I would never take him."

As luck would have it, her sentence fell directly into the silence that often followed one of Lady Bumtrinket's emphatic statements, while listeners sorted out whether they were offended or merely affronted.

Her eyes flew to the viscount, and to her surprise, she found a faintly speculative look in his eyes.

"I assume that the 'he' refers to Greywick," Lady Bumtrinket said. "Hardly relevant, is it, since the man won't offer for you." She fixed Otis with a shortsighted glare. "Who are you?"

"Mr. Otis Murgatroyd," Otis said.

"We both know that," she snapped. "No, I mean, who *are* you? I haven't got the gentry memorized."

"My father is Sir Reginald Murgatroyd," Otis told her.

"Second son? Third? Fifth?"

"Second," Otis said.

She squinted. "I thought he shunted the second into the church."

"I was not suited to the profession," Otis said.

Thaddeus cleared his throat.

Lady Bumtrinket whipped her head around with the intensity of a falcon on the hunt. "Are you ill?"

"No."

"Then don't cough like that. Gentlemen make their opinions known in words, not guttural utterances." She raised her finger, and a footman bounded to her side. "I would fancy one of those little squabs that I see on the sideboard. And a fresh glass of milk. This one has cooled. No, I'll have a glass of wine. And a kidney pudding, if there's one to be had."

The footman bowed. The door opened and closed behind him; at the other end of the table, the duke looked up in mild surprise. Generally, Prism's meals were precisely regimented to avoid footmen to-ing and fro-ing, as the butler described it.

"I suppose it's an acceptable match," Lady Bumtrinket said, her eyes resting on Joan and Otis. "Lady Joan's dowry must have been padded by the duke to make up for obvious . . . deficiencies."

"Precisely the same as my sisters' dowries," Joan clarified.

"Your comment is insolent and ill-bred," Lord Greywick stated, at the same moment.

"Nonsense," Lady Bumtrinket said to Greywick, with withering emphasis. "Another example of your insufficient knowledge of your status. Dukes are not namby-pamby about matters surrounding marriage, dowries, and jointures. I shall have to congratulate Lindow. A well-matched pair. A failed churchman and a . . ." Her vocabulary seemed to fail her.

"A lady," Greywick supplied, his voice hard, his expression stony.

"You're not a very cheerful type, are you?" the lady said, fishing in her pocket, pulling out a lorgnette with a long diamond-encrusted handle, and peering at him through the glass. "I suppose one might become morose, under the circumstances. That is, your father and the 'family of his heart' create a great deal of entertainment for my kitchen maids, but one would rather not find such depravity in one's family."

She paused, struck by a thought. "I gather that's why you made no progress with the two older Wilde girls, Greywick. I do hear that Lindow is an attentive father. One of the girls married a duke, but the other settled for a lord, and I heard he's a bedbug."

A moment of stunned silence followed this observation.

"None of my brothers-in-law could be described as a bedbug," Joan stated, feeling called upon to defend the family.

"Don't be hotheaded," Lady Bumtrinket said, pointing her lorgnette across the table. "You know what I mean."

"No, I do not."

"Crazy as a bedbug," Lady Bumtrinket clarified.

"No one in this family is crazy as a bedbug or any other creature." Joan was rather proud of her tone; in fact, she should probably use it when Hamlet first insists that his father was murdered and no one believes him.

"A good moment to reiterate that I'm not marrying you, Joan," Otis murmured.

"You're breaking my heart! You don't want to join a family of bedbugs?" Joan whispered back.

"Just as you say," Lady Bumtrinket stated, paying about as much attention to Joan's protest as Hamlet's mother had done. "My point is that the Duke of Lindow likely didn't want your older sisters tied to Greywick for good reason. Madness is hereditary. Do you know what your father said to me?" she asked Greywick.

If anything, his expression grew stonier.

"The Duke of Eversley sang—*sang*—'Love Divine, All Loves Excelling,'" Lady Bumtrinket exclaimed. "A mewling hymn when directed at the heavens, and even worse when the singer seems to think that I will sympathize with the idea that his mistress is divine. Imagine *that*, if you please. Unsurprisingly, the composer of that nauseating drivel was a Methodist!"

Joan felt another pang of sympathy for the tight-lipped viscount. But what could she say? Everyone knew about the Duke of Eversley's obsession with his mistress, though most didn't bring it up at the dinner table.

"Hated that hymn when I was a vicar, and I hate it now," Otis murmured. "Never thought of it being used to excuse adultery, though."

"The Wilde girls would have done," Lady Bumtrinket mused, pursuing her own train of thought. "The future Duchess of Eversley will need *gravitas*, powerful relatives, certainly an unsullied reputation, given the blemishes to the family name."

She turned to Greywick. "You'll have to wait for such a woman, or your dukedom will be forever besmirched. You might want to smile more, so that fathers don't shy away. *Love divine* indeed!" She snorted loudly.

Joan couldn't stay silent any longer. "Either of my sisters, Betsy or Viola, would have been happy to marry Lord Greywick," she said firmly. "My father, the Duke of Lindow, would have celebrated either match, as would fathers throughout society should His Lordship choose to ask for their daughters' hands. Rather, daughter, not daughters, as he'll only have to offer once because the first whom he asks will accept him, with her father's blessings."

Greywick's raised eyebrow seemed to find some amusement in her tangled speech, but she ignored him, concentrating on Lady Bumtrinket's beady eyes. Joan's acting ability came in handy, as it so often did; her voice rang with truth. "Accepting Lord Greywick's hand in marriage would make any young woman happy and her father positively ecstatic."

"Not the other way around?" Greywick murmured.

"What happened when he wooed your sisters?" Lady Bumtrinket demanded, clearly taken aback. "Everyone in society knew the viscount was courting them, one after another, not at the same time. He's so tall, for one thing. You could see him towering over the other dancers."

"As opposed to me," Otis said cheerfully. "Thank goodness, my lack of height will allow me to woo in a clandestine fashion."

"You'd have to ask Lord Greywick," Joan said to Lady Bumtrinket, turning to give His Lordship a beaming smile. "He lost interest in Viola and Betsy, as I understand it."

"Hard to believe," the lady said, squinting at the viscount. "*Very* hard to believe."

"Viola was too shy for him, and Betsy too . . . too impudent!" Joan added, since Greywick didn't seem inclined to support her story, which was entirely untrue. Betsy had fallen in love, and Viola had married quickly, after she was caught kissing a duke in plain sight.

"You'll have to lower your standards," Lady Bumtrinket advised the still silent Lord Greywick. "You should think about status, not personality. It doesn't matter if your wife is shy, as long as she's got the proper ancestral bloodlines."

"Thank you for the advice," the viscount replied. His tone was even, polite.

Joan didn't like him much, but she had to admit that he had admirable composure.

"I can see that you need guidance," Lady Bumtrinket said, warming up to the task. "Lady Joan is off the market, since she's promised to Mr. Murgatroyd—"

"No, she's not," Otis hissed.

"But let's take her as an example," Lady Bumtrinket said.

"Let's not," Greywick intervened.

"Marriage to a woman like Lady Joan would be a disaster for your children," Lady Bumtrinket said. "Her hair, the Prussian nose . . . such marked traits will carry in the bloodline. If you'll excuse my plain speaking, Lady Joan," she added, somewhat belatedly.

Joan felt oddly fascinated. Comments about her dubious parentage were made behind her back, or hissed at her in anger or disgust, but they were rarely stated in public. At her father's dining table, no less.

Otis intervened. "I believe we should change the subject. Did everyone hear that the first mail coach ran successfully between Bristol and London?"

"I would not care to correspond with any person residing in Bristol," Lady Bumtrinket said with a sniff.

"I would be honored to marry Lady Joan," Greywick said, flatly contradicting the old woman in a ringing voice.

"No, you wouldn't," Joan retorted.

But she smiled, because it was a kind gesture. He probably thought she was mortified to hear the truth about her scandalous birth spoken out loud. He had no idea how little such comments mattered to her.

"Lady Joan is marrying Murgatroyd," Lady Bumtrinket said. She was obviously unused to being challenged. Her cheeks turned a nice shade of puce, and her voice rose to something near a bellow. "Your comment indicates how little you understand the world of polite society. You cannot marry Lady Joan, or anyone like her."

"I shall marry whomever I choose," Greywick said softly but with menace.

The expression in his eyes would have made Joan think twice, but Lady Bumtrinket glared back. "I am an upright pillar of the very society with whom your children will be eager to mingle, but they won't be—"

"If you'll forgive my plain speaking," he retorted, cutting her off, "my children will mingle with whomever they choose, even more so if they grow up to be half as beautiful as Lady Joan."

Lady Bumtrinket opened her mouth to squawk a reply, but whatever she meant to say was broken off by a scraping noise. All heads turned to the head of the table.

The Duchess of Lindow was on her feet. "Great-Aunt Daphne, I understand that someone of your years needs to retire at an early hour. I shall escort you to your bedchamber."

Joan didn't allow herself to smile. Her stepmother was not imposing—yet she was a duchess, every inch of her. And now, as Her Grace walked from the other table and stood beside Lady Bumtrinket's chair, the lady rose with only a muttered grumble.

"Do excuse us," the duchess said, giving Otis, Joan, and Greywick a smile. "My aunt unfortunately must leave us early in the morning to continue her journey; we shall miss her company."

The lady opened her mouth but shut it hastily after a glance from her great-niece. The duke escorted both ladies out the door.

"The woman is a fiend," Greywick said. "I consider that a factual statement rather than an insult."

"You mustn't pay too much attention to Lady Bumtrinket's advice," Joan said, feeling awkward. Obviously, he had no interest in marrying her, so the example was irrelevant, but her great-aunt wasn't very compassionate.

"I would not term it 'advice,'" he said. "Insolence, better tolerated from an irritated coachman than a dinner companion." Greywick wore his most aristocratic expression, but this time Joan sympathized.

"I find it difficult to imagine Lady Bumtrinket as a coachman—or would that be coachwoman?" Otis commented.

"In a better world, ladies would be coachwomen," Joan said, eager to change the subject.

"Unlikely," Greywick said. He still had a forbidding look about him.

She gave him a frown. "Not unlikely but inevitable, I'd say. The world is changing, and Lady Bumtrinket clings to an antiquated past."

"You think that ladies will become coachwomen?" Otis asked. "Will *want* to drive a coach?"

"I think that ladies will become whatever they wish," Joan said. "My aunt Knowe would be a far better doctor than any who has attended the castle. Half the time she instructs them, and she won't even allow them in the room any longer during a birth." She turned to Greywick. "That is why my sister Viola is here for the last month of her confinement, so that Aunt Knowe can act as her midwife."

"The Wildes are all quite robust," Otis said. "I doubt my sister could drive a mail coach, let alone deliver a baby."

Joan patted him on the shoulder. "No need to butter me up. I won't hold you to our betrothal."

"If only I was so lucky!" Otis said. But he added briskly, raising his voice, "Just so everyone within earshot knows, I adore Joan, but my betrothal to her was of short duration."

Joan's father was walking toward his table after returning from escorting his wife and her aunt upstairs. He paused. "I wasn't aware that such an arrangement existed, even if briefly."

"To put it in context," Otis replied, "a Thoroughbred in the Newmarket Races rounds the track three times, but we didn't make it out of the gate."

Joan held up her glass. "My very first betrothal was over before I finished a glass of wine!" she laughed. "Do you suppose that's a bad sign for the future?" She caught Lord Greywick's eye.

"No," he stated.

Chapter Four

$\mathcal{T}$haddeus enjoyed the meal a great deal more once Lady Bumtrinket had been removed by her niece. He spent most of the time listening to Joan and Otis banter with each other while planning the best way to convince Joan to give up the madness of performing a play in male attire.

Whether she wished to admit it or not, someone in this castle would sell a sketch to a printer, and within a fortnight, all of England would be able to buy an image of her shapely legs, likely sold from the front window of every stationer in London.

When the Duchess of Lindow rose, signaling the conclusion of the meal, he caught Joan's arm before she could walk away with Otis.

She looked up at him, her eyes concerned. "Have you recovered from Lady Bumtrinket's objectionable behavior, Lord Greywick? I assure you that we have all found ourselves in the mouth of the lion now and then."

"The lady is an aggressive interrogator," Thaddeus said. "The Bow Street Runners would benefit from her skills in that distant future you mentioned, when a lady can choose to work for a magistrate, if she wishes."

Joan smiled at him faintly. "I would suspect you are ironic, Lord Greywick, but you show no outward sign."

"That was not ironically spoken. My mother could run an entire branch of the Runners with éclat. However, that time has not yet come, which leads me to the idea of playing Hamlet," Thaddeus said. "This has nothing to do with Lady Bumtrinket's absurd allegations—"

"Hasn't it?" she interrupted.

"No. I'm trying to protect you."

"Men say that so often." She sighed. "The result being that ladies spend their lives in padded boudoirs, surrounded by painstakingly embroidered pillows. They change their dresses four times a day because they have nothing else to do."

"My mother runs the duchy," Thaddeus said. "When I am absent from Eversley Court, she acts as justice of the peace in our shire. We employ over three hundred people in and around the duchy, and she knows every one of them."

"Brava," Joan said. "For her. The only thing I want to do is act. The *only thing.*"

"The role of Hamlet?" Thaddeus asked incredulously. He had enjoyed school, but he still remembered what a chore it was trudging through that play.

She shrugged. "It's the most significant role I could come up with that appears in the regular repertoire of the theater company that visits Lindow every year. They were kind enough to allow me and Otis to play two lead roles, but I couldn't ask them to learn a new play."

"I was under the impression that theater companies visited large towns, not private estates." The room had emptied, and out in the entry, Joan could hear the family saying good night to each other.

"The traveling company of the Theatre Royal has been coming to Lindow for years, ever since they gave us a private performance of *Wilde in Love*, the play written about my brother Alaric. I've been attending their rehearsals since I was fourteen. They know."

"They know the lines, or they know you love to act?"

"They know I *can* act," she said sharply.

"So you think that you will perform a better Hamlet than the actor who usually plays the role?"

"No, not at all! Playing the prince is a lark. If I were a proper member of the troupe, I would play roles written for women."

"You're a lady, not an actress," Thaddeus said. "Someone will sell an illustration—"

"Oh, for God's sake, don't parrot that line about me being ruined again!" she snapped.

A muscle flexed in his jaw but he held his tongue.

"Besides if I was ruined . . . if I was ruined . . ." Joan's eyes lit up. "I suppose you're right. I will be ruined."

"Quite likely."

"So I'll join the theater troupe when they move on!" she exclaimed. "Why wait to be officially thrown out of society? I'll be much happier on a theater cart than in this castle. I would be able to perform every night in front of real audiences, not just family."

"You can't do that," Thaddeus growled. "The troupe doesn't need you, for one thing."

"I'm *good*," Joan retorted, stiffening. "You have no faith—why should you?—but I assure you that I could be a lead actress in any theater in London. I'm not being boastful, just saying that my skills—and scandalous hair—would play to my advantage on the public stage. Whereas polite society simply sees me as a pariah."

"You would be recognized," Thaddeus insisted.

He had a terrible feeling that he'd made a mistake. Pushed her too far.

Joan's father had walked a fine line when he approved a private performance. Perhaps the duke understood the risk of thwarting his most obstinate daughter.

"So what?" Joan straightened. "I would be free to perform different parts, travel the country, appear before new audiences every night!"

Thaddeus's heart dropped into his stomach as he saw the excitement in her eyes.

"What if you flee the castle on a theatrical wagon, and something terrible happens to you on the road?" he demanded. "How will your family feel then?"

He watched her eyelashes flicker and added: "A woman exposing her legs in breeches will be taken to be a trollop, for sale to the highest bidder. She is at risk of rape and worse, to be blunt."

Her throat bobbled as she swallowed. He was

shocked to see a flash of despair in her eyes. The look did something to him.

Everything in his body stilled.

Joan was irritating, obstinate, scandalous—but he didn't like to see that expression on her face. In fact, his internal response was disconcertingly strong.

Her whole body looked . . . smaller. She was so incredibly brave, never allowing the taunts of women like Lady Bumtrinket to bother her, but it couldn't be easy.

"Right," she said tonelessly. "Of course, you're right. No stages other than in the castle, and no audiences other than my family." She met his eyes. "They always clap. No matter how I do. Perhaps I'm just being boastful about my skills. I might be booed off a real stage."

"No, you wouldn't," Thaddeus said.

"How could you possibly know?"

"Because I've seen you perform."

She frowned. "Were you here when we performed *A Midsummer Night's Dream* last summer?"

"No," Thaddeus said, and added, gently, "I've seen you perform any night for the last three years in London, on a public stage. During the Season, Joan."

She gave him a lopsided smile. "That's kind of you, I suppose. I just wish . . . I just wish I knew the truth about whether a real audience would clap for me. Even if only once."

Thaddeus was used to making swift decisions. "I could accompany you," he said, his voice coming out in a rasp. He cleared his throat. "Guard you. I could make sure you are safe."

Her eyes grew round. "You would join the theater troupe?"

He recoiled. "Can you see me acting a part?"

"No," she muttered. "You're too much yourself."

"One performance," he said. "One audience." His eyes searched hers. "What's the next stop? Wilmslow?" He chose the closest town, the one where the auction had been held four years ago.

"I'm fairly certain that the company continues to Wilmslow," Joan said, her eyes lightening. "On occasion, some of us have followed to see their performance, spending the night at an inn."

She caught his arm. "Oh, Greywick, would you, truly? I'd have to ask Mr. Wooty, who directs the company, but I'm sure he'd allow it. He's very kind, and fond of me."

"You are good," Thaddeus said with certainty. "And you know it, don't you?"

Her smile was not the sparkling, blinding one that she wielded to such effect. It was small, and shy.

"Mr. Wooty says that I am. My father wouldn't allow me to perform with the troupe until I turned twenty-one, but Mr. Wooty has always tutored me during his annual visits."

"One performance," Thaddeus said, shoving away his misgivings. "As Hamlet, because that's the only chance you have of not being recognized as a lady." He would have to pay every member of the troupe a bonus to ensure their silence.

"Of course," Joan said, nodding.

"After which, you must return to the castle and—and get married." The words growled out of some part of his chest that he didn't recognize.

If she were married . . .

It would be different.

"*I* have to get married!" Joan cried. "What about you? You're older than I am! In the last five years, you've courted only two ladies—both of whom happen to be my sisters—and done a pretty lack-luster job of it. I don't believe you've even tried to woo anyone since Viola married!"

"I'm aware that I need to find a bride," Thaddeus said stiffly. "I have done my best to find the right woman, though not in the last couple of years, I admit."

"You may accompany me to one performance," Joan said, a swift glance from under her lashes telling him that she had accepted his point about safety. "After which, I'll find *you* a spouse."

He opened his mouth, and she interrupted him. "You've been looking at the wrong women. My sisters would never have accepted you, future duke or no. I'll find you a candidate eager to be a duchess. Otherwise, you really may end up a withered bachelor, alone at Christmas, without children or anyone to love."

Only years of discipline kept him from showing a reaction to that prediction, or to her conviction that the only women who would agree to marry him would do so for his title. "I'll give you a list of honorable men," he said, keeping his voice even. "You'll marry one of the candidates I choose."

"I'll consider it," Joan said.

Thaddeus choked back biting sarcasm, of a sort he hadn't ever given voice to. Not even as an adolescent.

"Do you know how I can tell when you're overwrought?" Joan asked. With one of her lightning changes of mood, her eyes were amused again.

He shook his head.

"You drum your fingers on the hilt of your rapier," she said, nodding toward his waist. "You may look utterly calm and as if emotion never influences anything you do—"

"It doesn't," he said.

"Of course it does. When you're angry, your face gets even more wooden than usual, and you start thumping your fingers on the hilt of your rapier. Like this."

Frowning, he looked down and saw her long, slender fingers playing with the hilt of an imaginary rapier. His memory supplied him with the image of the plump curve of her thigh in breeches, sending a ferocious stab of lust down his groin. "I didn't realize you were so observant," he said, turning to the side so that his cockstand wasn't evident.

Her face didn't change, and he realized that she was as skilled as he at hiding her emotions. "Why should you? You consider me too selfish and careless to pay attention to others."

She curtsied. "Good night, Lord Greywick." She paused. "I just snapped at you again, but truly, I'm grateful." Again her smile wasn't the calculated curve of her mouth, but something more hesitant. "I—I have longed my entire life to perform in front of a real audience."

Thaddeus bowed and watched her go.

Why did she accuse him of calling her selfish? He remembered calling her reckless. Perhaps careless.

But never selfish.

Joan was not selfish. Over the years, he'd noticed that she spent hours in the nursery every day, telling the younger children stories and acting out plays for them.

In her first Season, he'd watched her prop up Viola, who had suffered from crippling shyness. As one of the most beautiful women in any ballroom, she could have reigned over other unmarried ladies, but instead she coaxed wallflowers into conversations that allowed them to show their best aspects to the gentlemen primarily interested in flirting with Joan, not courting wallflowers.

She was infuriating, wildly intelligent, better read than anyone he knew—at least in the genre of plays.

Headstrong. Stubborn.

Reckless to the point of idiocy.

In fact, he ought to reconsider his long-held belief that the Duke of Lindow was making a huge mistake in not reining in this particular daughter. Lindow understood that trying to curb Joan would lead to disaster.

He, Thaddeus, was the one who had provoked her to recklessness.

It was his fault Joan would appear before the public, dressed in breeches, every curve of her body open to the audience's lustful view, if for only one performance in Wilmslow.

His jaw set and he swallowed hard.

He would have unerringly pointed her out as the one lady he didn't like in all London.

Yet she was the woman he had to protect.

Chapter Five

$\mathcal{T}$he next morning, Joan made her way to the library thinking, as she had all night, of Lord Greywick. Of his proposition. Her imagination seemed to have caught on his frowning eyebrows and fierce eyes. But at the same time . . .

Of course, she *hated* him.

Loathed him.

Despised him.

She was just having trouble remembering that fact, perhaps because even given years of knowing how desperately she'd love to be on the stage, her family had always dismissed the possibility. Greywick had listened to her for two minutes and come up with a solution.

He was peremptory, and he considered her a walking scandal, and he didn't like her as a person. Yet she knew, deep in her soul, that the chance to perform on a public stage that he'd offered would change her life. Perhaps she would love the experience so much that she truly would join the theater troupe.

A cluster of Wildes could always be found in the library. Whereas the equivalent chamber in the duke's London townhouse was austere and formal, Lindow Castle's library was full of large stuffed chairs arranged in haphazard circles, the duke's weighty desk piled with unanswered correspondence, books and needlework stacked on the floor. A thick Aubusson carpet covered the floor, and tall windows leading to the Peacock Terrace were often thrown open in good weather.

Pushing open the library door, she found that Otis, dressed as Ophelia, was already there, seated on a dark purple sofa beside Viola, who was propped up with pillows, the better to accommodate her pregnant belly. Aunt Knowe sat opposite them, flipping through a copy of *Hamlet*.

"You look cross," Viola said, waving her over. Viola was the only person who was never fooled by Joan's "calm" face.

"Do tell me that your father changed his mind about your performance of *Hamlet*," Otis complained. "I feel as if I'm about to pop like a ripe gooseberry in this corset. I mourn the sea beast who gave his life to support torture-by-whalebone."

"Stop grumbling, Otis," Aunt Knowe ordered. "My brother never changes his mind, and ladies survive a lifetime in a corset."

Aunt Knowe was one of Joan's favorite people in the world: Tall, brusque, and loving, she had ruled the nursery for Joan's entire life. More than anyone except Viola, Aunt Knowe understood the limitations that made Joan feel confined, even imprisoned.

"Given my name and my current state," Viola said, "I have claim to being a ripe gooseberry, not you."

"You do seem to be on the bloated side," Otis commented, eyeing her.

"Otis!" Joan cried, sitting down opposite them. "You can't use that word about a woman carrying a child."

"This morning my own dear husband told me that I'm as fat as a distillery pig," Viola said, smiling as she folded her hands on top of her tummy.

"Since Devin adores you, I won't run him through with this useful rapier," Joan said, patting the hilt. "Though his insult bolsters the case for being an old maid, which is definitely in the cards for me." She blinked, remembering that she'd rashly promised Greywick that she would marry a gentleman of his choosing.

Surely he wouldn't hold her to it.

Yes, he would.

"What are you thinking about, my dear?" Aunt Knowe asked. "That is quite a ferocious scowl."

"Nothing important," Joan said. "Otis, do you have your script? We can work on Ophelia's scenes."

"I suppose you already have Hamlet's mawkish speeches memorized?" Otis asked, catching the book that Aunt Knowe tossed to him.

"Yes." Joan had memorized the lead parts in most Shakespeare plays years ago.

"I hope my baby comes soon," Viola said dreamily, ignoring the conversation. "I can't wait to meet him. Or her."

"At least a few weeks, my dear," Aunt Knowe said, leaning over to pat her shoulder.

Joan shivered. Babies were another reason to eschew marriage. Children were wonderful: imaginative and fun, with no silly rules about boys and girls getting in the way of make-believe and putting on plays.

But babies?

Burping, vomiting, crying, slobbering. Pooing.

"All right," Otis said discontentedly, leafing through his playbook. "When does Ophelia first show up?"

"Act One, Scene Three," Aunt Knowe said. "Her family clusters about to give her advice, as I recall."

"Ah, my father's favorite activity," Otis said, brightening. "At least I'll know how to play that scene."

Joan gave him a sympathetic grin. They were both the recipients of stifling, if loving, family advice; Otis had entered the priesthood after his father's entreaties grew to a clamor.

He found the right scene and read a few lines aloud before breaking off with a groan. "Why did you have to pick such a dreary play, Joan? If you're going to ruin yourself by performing a man's part, why not a jolly farce written in language that the audience could understand?"

"I'm likely to perform alongside a proper theater troupe only one time in my whole life, so I want to perform the most important play of all time. *And* play the most important role."

"No one could accuse you of modest goals,"

Otis said. He dropped the book and pulled up his skirts. "Look at my feet."

Joan and Aunt Knowe looked; Viola had fallen asleep.

"These shoes are *pointed*. Who invented such a monstrosity? My toes are pinched, and I'm not even standing up."

"Those are my old shoes," Aunt Knowe said. "I suppose they came from the attic."

"I can't survive an entire Shakespeare play in these shoes. The speeches are long and boring, to call a spade a spade."

"I don't think the Bard's plays are boring," Aunt Knowe said. "Mind you, I prefer romantic stories such as the one with adorable fairies. Joan was an excellent Helena."

"We've performed *A Midsummer Night's Dream* three times in the last ten years, Aunt Knowe," Joan pointed out.

"Couldn't I please take another role?" Otis begged. "I'd love to play the dead king, running around reminding Hamlet he's dead. *Remember me*," he intoned hollowly, throwing out his arm so that his wig tipped over one ear again.

"The only way my father agreed to my performing with the Theatre Royal was if you played Ophelia to my Hamlet," Joan reminded him. "Please, Otis! You were fabulous in the pantomime last Christmas."

He rolled his eyes. "I didn't have to wear a corset. Frankly, I still can't believe your father agreed, whether I play your beloved or not. One of the actors in the troupe is sure to sell an etching of you in breeches."

"My brother has given up trying to eradicate prints of his children," Aunt Knowe informed him. "Joan, my dear, I've been so careful with my knitting, and yet a hole has appeared in the middle. What did I do wrong?"

"You dropped stitches," Joan said. "Otis, let's start. I have an extra copy, Aunt Knowe. Would you please read all parts except for Ophelia and Hamlet?"

The door opened, and Greywick appeared.

"Do join us!" Aunt Knowe called to him.

"Good morning, Lady Knowe," he said, walking over and bowing. "I bring a message from my mother. She would like to walk to the village in an hour or two."

"I'll have to change to a walking costume," Aunt Knowe said, bounding to her feet. "Greywick dear, come take my place, won't you? You needn't act; just read aloud every line that isn't Hamlet's or Ophelia's."

The viscount's face was a wooden mask, but he took the book from Aunt Knowe, bowing to Joan and Otis. "Good morning."

"Good morning, Lord Greywick," Joan chirped, trying to pretend that they were merely acquaintances. "You needn't greet Viola; as you can see, she's napping."

"Morning," Otis said, glancing up from *Hamlet*.

"You have to read all the boring bits," Aunt Knowe told Greywick. "We were about to start the scene in which Hamlet and Ophelia bicker as she gives him back all his love letters. Just in case you haven't read the play lately," she added.

"I have not," Greywick said, managing to make it clear that he liked it that way.

"Better you than me," she replied with a cheerful grin. "I'll accompany your mother to the village. I'll take Viola away with me; she'll nap better in her own bed."

With that, Aunt Knowe hoisted a dazed Viola to her feet and escorted her out of the room.

"Right, let's start," Joan said. "Page thirty-eight, everyone."

The third time through the scene, Greywick lowered his book and gave Otis a direct look. "Mr. Murgatroyd, you seem to be uttering your lines with more optimism than accuracy."

Joan was sorry to say it, but her best friend was showing no sign of mastering his lines.

"You can't call me Mr. Murgatroyd," Otis said. "Not now that we've both been roped into this charade. Call me Otis."

"Very well," the viscount said.

"As far as my lines go, I only need to get a few words right," Otis said comfortably. "We've all met girls like Ophelia: brokenhearted, drifting around writing bad poetry. Her father should have locked her in her bedchamber and kept her away from the river, and she would have woken up one morning and wondered what she ever saw in the prince."

"You are rather unkind to Ophelia," Greywick observed.

Presumably he couldn't help being a pompous stick. It was such a waste, given how handsome he was.

For example, his arms were corded with thick

muscle that Joan could see through the fine broadcloth of his coat. If it wasn't for the way he looked at her, as if she were shameful—

But he did.

And had for years, what's more. The very first time they met, his eyes touched on her hair, and though he didn't move a muscle in his face, she had known instantly that he didn't approve of her parentage.

Or rather, her lack of parentage, since her parents had left her behind in the duke's nursery. She could always tell the people who thought she had inherited bad blood along with her hair, and mostly their opinion didn't bother her at all.

But Greywick?

He'd always been the exception. Something about the censorious light in his eyes just made her . . .

Furious. That was the emotion, definitely. Something about his disdain made Joan feel hot all over.

"Actually, I'm being generous to Ophelia," Otis protested. "Did you get the bit where she complains about what happened after she crawled into his bedroom window?"

"She's just singing a ballad," Joan objected. "Albeit a bawdy one."

"There's a history of such, I'll give you that," Otis said. "I like this one better than Ophelia's: *Do not trust him, gentle maiden,*" he belted out, slightly out of tune. "*Though his heart be pure as gold, He'll leave you one fine morning, With a cargo in your hold.*"

"Inappropriate in this company," Greywick stated.

"For God's sake," Otis said, rolling his eyes. "Anyone can tell that Ophelia wrote the ballad she sings. She's a silly girl with the brains of a caterpillar, and personally I wouldn't be at all surprised if she climbed in my window, likely in her nightie."

"If that is the case, Hamlet lost his honor when he didn't usher the lady promptly out the door," the viscount replied, at his most uncompromising.

"Oh, Greywick," Joan sighed, conscious that bickering with him was fast becoming one of her favorite pastimes. "You can't judge Hamlet by your own bloodless approach to life."

Something flared deep in his eyes, so she added, "Hamlet is a hero, a man who fights off pirates and is brilliant at swordplay. I expect he was overcome by desire when a beautiful woman appeared in his bedchamber."

"Since I'm playing Ophelia, let's drop 'beautiful' and think 'willing,' instead," Otis said, smirking. "I show up in his bedchamber and throw myself at him. He takes one look at my slender waist and loses his head. Unfortunately, I lose something rather more important."

"There is no excuse for taking a lady's virtue," Greywick said, with an expression that would have made a bishop proud. "Whether Hamlet's heart be 'pure as gold,' as in Otis's rhyme, or not, he ceased to be a hero when Ophelia left his room no longer a maiden."

"It wasn't precisely honorable on Hamlet's part," Joan admitted.

Otis broke out laughing. "Just look at us, engaging in deep Shakespearean commentary. If I'd had you in class, Greywick, I might have passed literature at Eton."

"You may address me as Thaddeus."

"Address me?" Otis repeated. He turned to Joan. "*He* should be playing Hamlet. You could play Ophelia, and I could play the ghost."

"I do not act," Greywick said curtly. He looked at Joan. "I would also like you to call me Thaddeus."

"Better," Otis allowed. "You sounded almost human, if you don't mind the comment."

Joan never responded to any man, including those who fell on their knees before her, offering rings and adoration. But this man? Whose eyes skated over her as if she were no more interesting than the silk wallpaper on the library walls?

This man made her body tingle, and her mind begin wondering what it would be like if such a rigid man lost control. What if Greywick—Thaddeus—dropped all the rules that had been drilled into him from birth and just let himself do what he wished?

Of course, he didn't want to do anything with her.

"Let's start over with this scene," Joan said, sighing. "Otis, do try to memorize a few more lines, so at least we understand why Ophelia is sad."

Before they could start again, Aunt Knowe erupted back into the room. "Enough rehearsing, children!" she cried. "I've just learned that Drabblefield Fair opened this morning. Greywick, your mother is eager to attend. Joan and Otis, this is an excellent opportunity to try out your costumes."

"Father said I wasn't allowed to leave the gates in breeches," Joan pointed out.

"My brother left for the tenant farms after breakfast," Aunt Knowe said, "so I'll overrule him. You can't miss the fair."

"I don't know if I'm ready to have strangers see me in a dress," Otis said, twitching his skirts.

"I wouldn't have guessed you were a man," Aunt Knowe told him. "Your features are cast in a male mode, but then, so are mine. No one has ever suggested that I am a male. You've been in this room for over an hour, doing nothing but repeat the same lines. You all need to leave the castle. Go outside!"

Joan gurgled with laughter and said to Otis and Thaddeus, "Aunt Knowe used to sweep into the nursery, find us all squabbling, and say the same thing. 'Outside!'"

"We leave for the fair in an hour," Aunt Knowe said blithely. "Greywick, you'll accompany us, of course. We never miss the fair; it's one of the high points of spending one's summer at Lindow."

Thaddeus groaned, a throaty male moan.

Joan's breath caught at a sound that he hadn't considered beforehand or delivered in a gentlemanly accent and tone. It sent a shiver down her spine.

She'd love to hear that sensual noise during a kiss.

Thaddeus was talking to Aunt Knowe so she let her gaze linger on his profile. The truth was that she liked him, which was obviously stupid and wrong in more ways than could be counted. He hadn't even smiled at Otis's ballad, whereas she thought "cargo in your hold" was rather funny. No sense of humor. But then . . .

His chin. Nose. Jaw. Other men had the same collection of features, and in fact, some of them had decidedly better features.

Not that she could think of any such men at the moment.

"There's nothing to worry about," Aunt Knowe was telling Thaddeus. "I'm well-known, and if anyone says something untoward to our Hamlet or Ophelia, I shall speak for the duke."

"I can offer adequate protection if that occurs," Thaddeus said gruffly.

Joan liked gruff.

Why, why was she unable to do things that seemed so simple for her siblings? Accepting the hand of a man who admired her, for example? Taking up embroidery or knitting instead of acting? Playing the princess, rather than the prince?

Her lips in a wry smile, Joan had to admit that she wasn't particularly startled to discover that she had a penchant for a man who disdained everything she was. Her much-vaunted independence had often displayed itself in self-defeating ways. In playing the fool, in other words.

Her heart pinched at the thought.

No wonder Thaddeus disliked her.

Continued recklessness would only bring her unhappiness. As he said, what sort of model was she setting for her little sister?

Two performances and two chances to play

Prince Hamlet, one before her family and the other before a real audience, would have to be enough.

After that, she would reform and become a proper lady. Even . . . marry.

"Lady Joan," Thaddeus said. "Will you accompany us to the fair?"

She started, realizing that Otis and Aunt Knowe had left the room. "If I address you as Thaddeus, then you must address me as Joan. But at the moment I'm not a 'lady,'" she said, getting to her feet and dusting her breeches.

"Forgive me." He bowed. "Have you chosen a name to go with your costume? I can hardly address you as Hamlet in public."

"Jack," she said, stopping just in front of him. "Not Joan."

Their eyes caught and held. "Thaddeus," he affirmed, his voice unmistakably reluctant.

"I promise not to call you by your first name when someone might hear and think we are friends," she offered. "Shall we?"

He caught her arm. "What do you mean?"

Joan gave him a wry smile. "I don't want you to feel ashamed of me, any more than you want your reputation besmirched by knowing me. I am on the verge of being ruined, as you predicted." She raised her chin. "You will be very happy to hear that I intend to turn over a new leaf. I will perform the role of Hamlet in the castle, and once at Wilmslow, and then I will . . . stop."

Thaddeus's brows drew together. "Stop what?"

"Childish things," she said. "Isn't there something in the Bible about that?"

"When I was a child, I spoke as a child, I understood as a child, I thought as a child," Thaddeus said, his hand dropping from her arm. "But when I became a man, I put away childish things."

Joan glanced down at her breeches. "Particularly apt given that these are the childhood garments of one of my brothers." When she looked back up, Thaddeus was watching her face intently.

"I just wanted you to know that I understand your reprimand," she added. "I won't embarrass you. If you'll excuse me?"

He moved to the side, and she hurried through the door.

She felt at home on a ballroom floor or a grand dinner. She liked people, and she was confident of herself and her place in society, no matter what unkind things were said to her.

But Thaddeus unsettled her. Made her want to needle him, which was obviously childish.

She would put that away too, this wish to bicker with him and cross swords.

Put that instinct in a box marked "childish things," and lock it away with her dream of being an actress.

Chapter Six

Drabblefield Fair
Cheshire

*A*n hour later, Joan ran across the castle courtyard, feeling deliciously free without heavy skirts and panniers. If women were allowed to wear breeches, even just once, there would be a revolution and they would never wear corsets and petticoats again.

"Wait for me!" Otis shouted, bunching up his skirts and trotting after her.

A large coach waited with a groom beside the door.

"My lady," the groom said, bowing, when Joan arrived.

"Peters, if you hadn't known the truth, would you have guessed me a woman in men's clothing?"

The young groom kept his eyes rigidly above her collarbone. "No, my lady."

She raised an eyebrow.

"Perhaps," he said reluctantly. "I would suggest that you lengthen your stride, my lady."

"Thanks," Joan said, grinning at him before she hopped over the mounting box and climbed straight into the coach.

Otis, on the other hand, had to be hoisted inside with Peters's shoulder braced against his bustle.

"I'm sweating," Otis moaned, collapsing onto a seat. "Melting away 'til I'll be nothing but a set of whalebones. Why in God's name do you women wear so much clothing?"

"I'm rarely overheated," Joan said.

"Because you have a grasshopper's thighs, something I know due to those indecent breeches you have on. They're a bit tighter than proper."

Before they could delve into the mysteries of fashion, Thaddeus arrived at the carriage with Aunt Knowe on one arm and his mother, the Duchess of Eversley, on the other. Her Grace was a small round woman who always wore pink and had a decidedly eccentric air. Joan had never been able to figure out how such a whimsical person had given birth to the most proper man in all the kingdom.

"Don't let me forget that Viola craves pears," Aunt Knowe said, once they were settled. "The children want new hobbyhorses, but those they can pick out themselves. My brother should be back before lunch, and he will bring the nursery to the fair this afternoon."

"I haven't been to a fair in years," the duchess said happily. "I am looking forward to Drabblefield."

"I can't imagine why," Thaddeus said. "No one

of quality or fashion would attend such a ram-shackle event."

He had clearly descended into an even worse humor than he'd been in an hour ago. "Full of the tents of the wicked," Joan said, giving him a sparkling smile, just to irritate him.

She planned to give up their childish squabbles later, when she wasn't wearing breeches any longer. Meanwhile, she might as well enjoy herself.

"Musty gingerbread, rotten eggs, and cutpurses galore," Thaddeus replied, folding his arms over his chest. "Satin waistcoats stripped from dead men and called brand-new. Malt-horses marketed as stallions, every rib showing like the tooth of a saw."

Joan blinked at him. His voice rarely changed from its civilized drawl, but the last description came out with a sharp edge.

He turned his head and looked out the window. It was annoying how broad his chest was. Her own, in comparison, was very narrow. Elegant clothing couldn't turn her into a forceful man, like Greywick.

"I'm happy that you're accompanying us, Thaddeus, even though you feel uncomfortable," the duchess said, leaning forward and touching her son's knee. "I was disappointed when you refused to come with me to the auction in Wilmslow." She turned to Joan. "You may have heard of our delightful excursion, during which your sister Betsy and I donned male clothing and went to an auction."

"I was there as well," Aunt Knowe put in.

"On that occasion, you were accompanied by

Lord Jeremy Roden and his father," Thaddeus said woodenly. "You were in no danger and did not need my company."

"I wouldn't fit into those breeches now," Her Grace said, rubbing her rounded belly.

"My father would relish this excursion," Otis said to Joan, as the duchess and Aunt Knowe digressed into a vigorous debate regarding the merits of a cucumber and vinegar diet.

"Sir Reginald seems a happy man," Thaddeus said, rather unexpectedly.

"He's lonely," Otis said. "Still misses my mother and refuses to contemplate marrying again. Now that my sister's married, if I'm not home, he rattles about in the London house like a dried pea in a pail."

Joan stopped listening and returned to secretly ogling Thaddeus from under her lashes. She wasn't in the habit of lying to herself, and it was disconcerting to realize just how much she enjoyed his looks.

Ironically, if her mother had remained faithful, Thaddeus likely would have courted her as the logical third choice after her sisters Betsy and Viola. Perhaps he would have courted her *before* Viola, because Joan was a few months older. What's more, Joan was the daughter of the second duchess, and Viola was the daughter of the duke's third duchess. Joan ranked higher, in strict terms.

The only qualification Thaddeus seemed to have in mind was "duke's daughter."

Clearly, Thaddeus had determined that Viola fit the definition, and Joan did not.

Annoying though it was to admit, she had the feeling that her acting abilities were owed to her adulterous mother, who by all accounts relished the performance required by a duchess in the public eye conducting a clandestine *affaire*.

Thaddeus's chiseled profile was so tempting because . . . why? London had its share of handsome men. His wig was perfectly positioned; his boots without a smear or speck of dust; his lips set in a firm line.

He hated being in this carriage. He loathed her breeches; he'd made that clear.

But he *was* here. She stole another look at him.

His eyes were unreadable, whatever he was thinking shuttered behind an expression of polite interest. And yet she was certain that he was brewing with anger.

Interesting.

He denied the ability to act, but she suspected he played a role a good deal of the time. A future duke, presented to the world in continuous performance.

It sounded exhausting.

Drabblefield didn't have its own fairgrounds, like Bartholomew Fair in London, or the fairs that took place on the outskirts of Bath. It was held in a large field, whose high grass hadn't even been scythed, though it would be trampled to the ground by the end of the week. One edge was marked by a thicket; another by ramshackle market stalls, some with a hastily erected wooden structure, and others making do with an old table. The third side was lined with animal pens, and the fourth by a series of tents offering refreshments or entertainment.

They were greeted by shouts from the tents and stalls: "Bottle ale!" "Cure for the pox!" "Best pig this side of London!" "Boiled eels!" "Hot tea, hot brandy, hot treacle pudding!"

Joan choked back a huge grin and set out from the carriage in a long stride.

"Wait for us!" Otis bellowed from behind her, apparently forgetting that he was dressed as a woman and ought to sound like one.

Joan wheeled about, discovering that the ladies had only just managed to clamber down from the carriage. "I'm sorry!" she cried, trotting back to them.

"Gentle ladies, the weather's hot and the fair is dusty; cool yourself in the shade!" a man bawled from one of the tents.

"I'd like a cup of Waddy's tea before venturing any further," Aunt Knowe said firmly.

Thaddeus opened his mouth. He was going to say something about unclean tin cups, or tea that was merely water colored by molasses, so Joan gave him a kick, which was pleasurably easy when unhampered by skirts.

He turned to her, his eyes like chips of ice. "Yes?"

"When you're at the fair, you're *at the fair*!" she told him.

Other than his eyes narrowing slightly, he showed no response.

She sighed. "We've been coming every year since we were wee children, and nothing's hap-

pened to us other than the odd upset stomach.
It's an adventure, you see?"

"No," he said uncompromisingly.

"Waddy's tea is marvelous," Aunt Knowe told
Otis and the duchess. "He is the one shouting
over there. He'd be hurt if I didn't visit him first."

"Excellent," Her Grace said eagerly. "I've never
had tea from a tin cup, but I understand that it
adds something to the experience."

"Will you join us?" Otis asked Joan. "Though
perhaps you should stride around the fair and
practice looking more manly." They all stared at
Joan.

The duchess shook her head. "She's too pretty."

Joan set her jaw and widened her stance.

"Pretty *and* indecorous," Her Grace amended.

Sighing, Joan adopted Thaddeus's customary
expression.

"That's it!" Aunt Knowe crowed. "Now you're
getting it. All right, my dears, tea. Joan, go forth
and polish your manhood. Otis will practice being ladylike with a tin cup while sitting on a stool."

Otis looked alarmed.

"Low to the ground in case you topple off,"
Aunt Knowe told him. "Come along!"

The three of them moved toward Waddy's tent,
followed by Peters, the duke's groom.

"You're welcome to accompany your mother,"
Joan said to Thaddeus. "I'm very comfortable at
the fair by myself."

"Is there something about the word 'dangerous' that you don't understand?" he demanded.
"Otis may be hampered by skirts, but he is a
good boxer, and they have a groom with them."

Joan took a deep breath and controlled her irritation. "Right. My favorite part of the fair is the animal tents."

He didn't move a muscle, but she could almost feel the wave of disapproval that broke over her head. "You don't care for animals?" she inquired.

A moment of silence and he said, "If you don't understand, there is nothing I can tell you." Apparently, animal shows were beneath Thaddeus's notice.

"I suppose 'no one of quality or fashion' would attend such a 'ramshackle' entertainment as an animal tent?" she asked, giving him a wide-eyed, innocent look.

"Unfortunately, they are all too likely to do just that," he answered, with a satirical twist to his mouth.

"The reptile tent comes first," she told him, not letting his disdain sink into her bones. If there was one thing that her unusual parentage had taught her, it was how to find pleasure in moments when people thought she ought to be ashamed.

Turning her back to him, she strode toward the tent marked *Leviathan: A Snake Longer Than the Thames.*

The old man at the door was missing a quantity of teeth so he burbled, "Leviathan, the Snake That Ate the World," running the words together. "Enter at yer own risk! He could eat both of you an' ask for breakfast. Loves human flesh so watch yerself near the fence. Want a ticket?"

"Yes, please," Joan said, smiling at him.

His brow puckered, but he said, "Tuppence

buys you five minutes to risk yerself alone with the giant serpent, or a penny to crowd in with others."

Joan pulled some coins from her pocket and said, "We'll take five minutes, and I'll pay for my friend as well."

Behind her shoulder, she caught a sharp movement. It seemed that Lord Greywick didn't care to have a woman pay his entry fee?

Ha! She was already enjoying herself.

The tent was shady after the bright sunshine outside. A picket fence in the middle was shaped in an octagon. In Joan's opinion, the boards were rather flimsy, given the purported appetite of the snake.

The reptile was truly huge. Coils and coils of fat, glistening snake wound on each other, moving from bigger to smaller until at the very top the snake's head emerged from his grotesque body. He was a gray-green color, with black markings.

He looked at her unblinkingly and then raised his head, tongue licking at the air.

She drew in a breath and caught Thaddeus's arm. "Do you see that? I think it scents prey!"

He lifted her hand off his arm, replaced it to her side, and said curtly, "I doubt it."

His touch sent a shiver down Joan's spine, which was particularly humiliating given that he acted as if she had contaminated him by her mere touch. "Don't you ever get tired of sneering at people?" she asked, before she thought better. "That behemoth of a snake is terrifying, but you won't allow me to touch your arm?"

"You're dressed as a *man*," Thaddeus said. "Gentlemen don't clutch each other in alarm."

"I paid tuppence for privacy," Joan reminded him. "What did I ever do to you?" she demanded, putting her hands on her hips.

His face registered boredom, although his lips were tight. She glanced down: yes! His fingers were thumping the hilt of his rapier.

"Well?" she insisted, when he didn't respond.

"I don't know how to answer that question," Thaddeus said. "I have a constitutional dislike of questions that are no more than clever traps without a genuine request for information at the heart."

"Mine is a genuine question. I don't understand why you look at me with such dislike." She raised her hand when he opened his mouth. "Please do not prevaricate. Clearly you disapprove of my mother's infidelity, but I am doing you the courtesy of assuming that you do not blame me for the sins of my parents."

He still didn't speak, just stared at her, so she cleared her throat. "I gather gentlemanly decorum dictates your silence."

She could feel her face getting red as common sense intervened. Plenty of people in society considered her a disgraceful hussy, even without reference to her mother's behavior. Why was she pushing him to be truthful?

So he didn't like her.

Why should she assume that everyone would like her? Any number of people thought she was reckless, scandalous, and on the brink of ruin.

But inside, she had thought he liked her, even though he disapproved of her.

The Wilde family was so large, and so loving, that each of them had been told over and over how adorable they were. Lack of confidence didn't come naturally to her, but hell's bells, she felt it around Thaddeus.

She turned to watch the snake as it tasted the air until she was absolutely certain that she had her expression under control. Then she turned her head and found Thaddeus was looking at her, rather than the snake. "So what do you think?" she asked lightly, her tone perfect.

"Two minutes left!" the man outside bawled.

His eyes bleak, Thaddeus asked, "What do I think of Leviathan or of you?"

"We have concluded the discussion of your dislike . . ." She stumbled to a halt, feeling like a fool. "I mean, your lack of affable feelings toward me, which is absolutely your prerogative, because I know that I am . . . that I irritate people."

A splintering noise drew her eyes, and she looked down to find that Thaddeus's hand had cracked the flimsy board topping the fence.

"Careful!" she said, summoning a smile. "You don't want to allow Leviathan to escape and come after us!"

He let go of the board, stepped toward her, and tipped up her chin. "*You*," he growled.

Joan stared at him.

His mouth came down on hers hard, and her lips instinctively opened to his silent demand. Thaddeus's tongue met hers, a silky, erotic stroke that made her pulse speed to a gallop. This was no gentle buss or courteous peck, such as she was accustomed to.

Joan had been kissed more times than she could count, in private and in public. She had kissed men out of boredom and out of curiosity.

She had never kissed, or been kissed, in a blaze of passion like this. Thaddeus shifted infinitesimally closer to her, making her fiercely aware of the subtle movements of his body, the possessive warmth of his spread fingers on her lower back, the taste of peppermint and strong tea on his tongue.

She wouldn't have imagined that Viscount Greywick, the man famed for his faultless behavior, would give her this particular kiss. Not this rough, demanding kiss that made her blood heat and her heart throb against her ribs. Her skin prickled all over as she swayed even closer to him.

He lifted his head, and she made a small sound in the back of her throat, an urgent, embarrassing plea for more, that came from some part of her that she'd never known before. Their eyes met, and his mouth crashed down on hers again. She opened to him eagerly, her arms going around his neck—

"*Zounds!*"

The curse made them jump apart. The startled expression on Thaddeus's face evaporated in a moment, and he turned toward the old man who had interrupted them, every lineament of Thaddeus's body as regal as Hamlet at his best.

Joan couldn't help herself; she memorized the way outrage translated to Thaddeus's entire body:

his stiffened shoulders, frigid gaze, hand on his rapier . . . the general air of menace that descended into the tent.

Perfect for Hamlet, for a prince outraged by murder.

And for a viscount interrupted in a kiss.

The man opened his mouth, but Thaddeus held up his hand. "I have no interest in your opinion. Do you understand?"

The man's cheeks had turned a ruddy color. "I'll have—the parish constable—my tent!"

"I collect that you are outraged."

Joan could feel herself blushing when she caught the man's scandalized gaze.

"I shall kiss my wife in any dwelling that I choose," Thaddeus announced, at his most imperious.

Joan's blush got hotter as the man's eyes skated from her head to her feet. Who would have thought that Lord Greywick could lie, let alone lie with such conviction?

"*What?*" The man gaped at her. "That ain't—"

"My wife chose not to wear a gown to the dusty environs of a public fair," Thaddeus stated, with an air that suggested ladies often made that choice. "I trust you aren't questioning the sartorial preferences of my viscountess." He withdrew his hand from his pocket, and a guinea caught a ray of sunlight coming in the tent door.

"No, sir," the man said, his face suddenly wreathed in smiles. "I'd guess that my wife, bless her soul, would have thought it a frolic herself, when we were young." He accepted the coin and nodded to Joan. "I thought when you came to

my tent that you were the prettiest young gentleman as I ever did see, my lady. And I say that as
sees everyone who comes to the fair, from across
the whole of England. Now I see why you're so
fetching!"

Joan cleared her throat. "I appreciate that.
Thank you."

She walked out of the tent, her mind reeling,
knowing that her cheeks were flaming red. What
just happened?

Thaddeus had kissed her. He *kissed her.* A smile
trembled around her lips because for once she
hadn't invited the kiss with a temptress's smile.

She'd spent years practicing her smiles in a
glass. Without being overly prideful, she thought
she could entice almost any young man in the
kingdom who wasn't promised or in love with
another woman to kiss her, if they found themselves away from prying eyes.

And yet she hadn't even been thinking of kisses.
In fact, hadn't she been scowling at Thaddeus?
She thought she had. All the same, he had kissed
her. Her smile spread, which made her realize
that her lips were swollen, and her fingers were
trembling. She'd like to do that again. Kiss him.

She turned around, curious to see if Thaddeus
shared her inclination.

He was walking from the tent, his expression
bleak and icy, his eyes like chips of blue stone.
Her heart sank.

Apparently not.

"That was unforgivable on my part," he stated
tautly, when he reached her side. "I beg your par-
don. I have no excuse."

In other circumstances, she would have made a laughing rejoinder, but nothing came to mind. Instead, she just stared at him, trying to figure out if he was angry with her. He looked as stiff and pompous as she'd ever seen him.

But she thought the expression in his eyes was self-loathing.

"It was only a kiss, for goodness' sake," she exclaimed, before she thought better of it. "It isn't as if I climbed in your bedchamber window, and you failed to push me back out the door!"

If possible, his expression shaded even cooler. "It wasn't the act of a gentleman," he explained, with the odious air of one teaching ethical standards to a felon.

She could agree with him . . . or she could provoke him. "Oh, I don't know," she said, deliberately giving him a dimpling smile. "I've found that many a *gentleman* snatches a kiss upon occasion."

"Despicable," he said curtly. "A weakness."

"One you share, apparently." It wasn't possible to make her tone sunnier, but she put in a good-faith effort. It was sad just how much she was enjoying the raw discomfort she saw on his face. "Weakness or not, I've been kissed by many gentlemen. I would never judge you by a kiss in a snake tent, of all places! It was nothing. Think no more about it. So what do you think of Leviathan?" she asked over her shoulder, beginning to stroll to the next tent.

There was silence, and then: "Leviathan is a barred grass snake," Thaddeus stated.

"What? No grass snake is that big," Joan objected, stopping in her tracks.

"*Natrix natrix helvetica.* At most, it can grow to twice your arm length." He cast her one of his condescending looks. "That poor fellow was perched on top of a clay snake fashioned from unconvincing coils."

Joan was silenced. She had been entirely duped. Of course, she loved make-believe and theater.

"I thought they may have pinned his tail to the clay but he showed no signs of distress. I expect he was tied down," Thaddeus continued.

She raised an eyebrow. "What would you have done if he were pinned?"

His face was inflexible, his mouth a thin line. "Set him free."

Of course he would have.

The fact that Joan's heart thumped to think of Thaddeus saving a grass snake was a further demonstration of the fact she'd lost her mind. At this rate, she'd find herself mad as poor Ophelia, but Thaddeus wouldn't be writing her any love letters that she could return to him later.

She considered his expression as he strode beside her, glowering at the beaten grass. His cold eyes had made it very clear that the knot of longing she felt in the pit of her stomach was felt by her alone.

She refused to feel humiliated. He had kissed her, not the other way around. She had always declined to be pushed into marriage due to mere kisses—as when she kissed poor Anthony Froude just to irritate Thaddeus.

Whispering matrons thought she should be humiliated that Froude didn't offer marriage, not knowing that he had done so, three times.

And been rejected each time.

She wasn't humiliated by their sympathy, and she refused to be humiliated by Thaddeus's glower.

"The next tent, the rabbit hutch, is my favorite," she told him, speeding up as they approached it. This time she paid only for herself. Perhaps Thaddeus wouldn't want to enter, given his response to Leviathan.

"Careful going in, lad," the man at the door told her. "They'll be all around your feet."

Lad!

He didn't think she was a woman.

"What is this?" Thaddeus asked a moment later, folding himself almost in half to get in the door, then standing up and rubbing the back of his neck.

"Bunnies," Joan said happily. She crouched down, waiting. Sure enough, an inquisitive brown baby bunny hopped over and sniffed her shoe, so she picked it up and held it in front of her face. "Oh, you are adorable," she crooned, sitting down. Another baby hopped over and soon she had three funny, sweet balls on her lap.

"Look!" she cried a moment later. One of her bunnies was standing up on his hind legs and rubbing his nose. "Isn't he sweet?"

True to form, Thaddeus hadn't picked up a single rabbit, or even bent over, though a baby had perched itself on top of his shining black boot.

"Your valet is not going to thank you," Joan pointed out, nodding at his foot. "Rabbits poo all the time. Speaking of which . . ." She gently put the bunnies down and stood, giving her hips a wiggle that made tiny pellets fly into the air around her.

Thaddeus gently nudged the little rabbit from his boot. "Whenever you're done cuddling dinner, I'll meet you outside." Without waiting for an answer, he ducked through the door and left the tent.

Joan crouched back down, running a finger over a bunny's fluffy coat and admiring her pale pink ears. "He's a mean man," she told her. "Calling you dinner! He's a stewed prune. A loon. A fopdoodle."

The sound of a throat clearing made her glance up. Thaddeus was looking in the door. "The next tent features a truth-telling piglet. The show begins now."

Joan got up, trying to feel bad that he'd heard her call him a "fopdoodle" and not succeeding.

This time he walked ahead of her, and when she reached the tent door, the man said, "Your uncle already paid for you, lad."

Joan grinned at him and walked into a considerably larger tent set up with rows of chairs facing a stage, and a crowd waiting restlessly for the show. Thaddeus had seated himself at the front, so Joan chose a seat in the back. To her annoyance, he glanced around, saw where she was, and came to join her without a comment.

"What is a truth-telling piglet?" she asked.

"Didn't you read the sign?"

She paused just long enough to suggest the silliness of his question, and said, very gently, "No."

"Percy Piglet answers any and all questions with yes or no," Thaddeus said, folding his arms over his chest and staring at the empty stage. "According to the man at the door, pigs are more intelligent than humans, and Percy Piglet is the smartest swine of them all."

"What fun! I have questions!" Joan cried.

He glanced at her. "You can't possibly be taking this seriously."

"Did you *ever*, in your whole life, have *fun*?" Joan demanded. "Let yourself believe."

"Of course I have fun," he said, without hesitation.

"Outside of the nursery?" she prompted.

"Life, adult life, isn't about make-believe," he retorted. "It isn't about feckless pleasure."

"Then what is it about?"

In front of them, two men began having a loud discussion about the fact that pigs preferred ale to slop, which apparently proved their intelligence.

Thaddeus paused, taking her question seriously, rather to her surprise. "Caring for one's family. Ensuring that England's citizens are prosperous, healthy, and happy. Defending the country abroad, if need be. To sum it up: proving that inherited honors are deserved." The challenge in his voice prickled down her spine.

"Well, I can't run the country, I'm not a soldier, and I didn't inherit any honors," Joan said. "So I guess that means that I can simply enjoy myself.

I have nothing to live up to, and no one to bully."
She gave him a beatific smile.

He made a low sound in his throat.

"Did I say 'bully'?" she asked. "I meant 'command.'"

Luckily, because his eyes had become even flintier than usual, a cheerful fellow in a rusty red coat bounded out from the curtained area of the tent. "Welcome, one and all! I am Mr. Numps, owner of the finest piglet in all the king's lands. Prepare to meet the best pig in the fair, a sincere swine, a bold boar, an honest hog, an unspoiled pigling, the most perfect little suckling pig in the world: Percy Piglet!"

Joan began giggling, wishing that Viola was with them.

"He'll answer any and all questions that you propose! As the most intelligent of his kind, he satisfies the ignorant and the innocent. The price of your admission introduced you to this fine swine, but I'll need another tuppence before Percy will answer your particular question. Think of your queries while I fetch the authentic, brilliant Mr. Percy Piglet!"

Thaddeus muttered something, leaning back and crossing his arms over his chest again.

Joan cast a glance at his biceps because why deny herself the pleasure? And then looked at the stage just in time to see Mr. Numps return from behind the curtain with an endearing piglet in his arms, still a little fuzzy, with large floppy ears and a sweet expression.

"Aww," Joan whispered, elbowing Thaddeus.

"You have to admit that Percy is adorable. Just look at his curly tail. He's so pink!"

Thaddeus grunted and didn't take his eyes off Mr. Numps, who was challenging the crowd to ask him questions.

He pointed to a cleric in the front row. "You're wondering how Percy will give me these miraculous answers? With the help of God, who endowed this piglet with astounding talent. He answers with a squeal, Vicar. One squeal for yes and two for no. And since you're a man of God, I won't charge you for a question."

Beside her, Thaddeus stiffened.

"What's the matter?" Joan whispered.

"The squealing," he growled. "He'll be twisting that adorable tail, I'll bet."

But he didn't. The cleric declined, but Numps accepted tuppence from a lady in the front, who asked whether her daughter would be married in the coming year or no.

Numps raised the piglet to his face, just as Joan had raised the bunny. "Well, Percy?" he asked. "Shall this fine woman's daughter find herself wearing wedding gloves?"

Joan watched Percy's curly tail, but Mr. Numps didn't touch it at all. Percy gave a loud squeal.

"Yes, your daughter will be happy by this time next year," Mr. Numps said, tucking Percy back against his chest and beaming at the audience. "Who has another question for my magnificent piglet? He's never wrong, has *never* been proven wrong."

Thaddeus leaned forward, arms on his knees. Joan glanced at him, wishing that Aunt Knowe was in the tent. They would be taking out pennies and planning their questions, but instead disapproval fairly radiated off Thaddeus.

"Of course it's a hoax," she whispered to him, "but a fun one!"

He turned his head slowly, and the words dried up in her mouth. "Do you know anything about pigs?"

She shook her head.

"They can't answer questions, and they don't squeal on command." His tone was caustic.

"Perhaps Numps trained him to squeal," she suggested. "Have you been to a circus and seen trained dogs? They're frightfully clever."

Mr. Numps had accepted another question, a more serious one, since a surly fellow in the back wanted to know whether his wife had played him false.

"Percy doesn't care for that sort of question," Numps said, "but even so, his answers are as true as Holy Writ and will put your mind at ease, one way or the other."

Joan was pricklingly aware of the leashed strength and narrowed eyes of the man beside her.

"Come on, Percy," Mr. Numps said, holding him up, "has this charming gentleman been done wrong by his lady wife?"

There was a second's pause, and then Percy squealed loudly once and then again, and started vigorously kicking as well.

Mr. Numps wrestled with him. "I did tell you, Percy doesn't care for indecent questions—"

He never finished the sentence because Thaddeus was out of his chair and in the front of the tent before Joan realized what was happening. He grabbed the piglet with one hand and smashed Mr. Numps in the jaw with the other.

Joan gasped. The tent filled with exclamations.

"Here, you!" Mr. Numps cried, scrambling to his feet. "What are you—"

Thaddeus turned and held up the piglet so the audience could see. "For your entertainment," he said scathingly, "this animal has been pierced in the belly."

Even Joan in the back could see three wounds with little trickles of blood.

"Ew!" the lady in the front cried.

"He's my piglet," Mr. Numps said shrilly. "I can treat him as I like. He's mine, and that's the law."

"But he isn't no truth-telling pig," someone bellowed.

"Could have told you that," the surly man in the back row snarled. "My wife left home two days ago, and she ain't coming back."

"I want my money back," a stout matron declared, getting up and heading for the door.

"What right have you got to interrupt my show?" Mr. Numps barked at Thaddeus. "Here, you, give me back that pig. You might be a fine gentleman, but I know my rights." He balled up his fists.

"You can sell me the piglet, or I can knock you down again," Thaddeus said, looking unmoved. He tucked Percy under his left arm.

Joan ran to the front and said, "Give me the pig!"

He raised an eyebrow. "Why?"

"So you can knock him down, obviously."

Numps was reaching for Percy.

"I don't need both hands for that," Thaddeus said, as his right fist shot out and caught Numps under the chin. The man actually rose off his feet before he crashed into one side of the tent, making the entire edifice tremble.

Behind them, the remaining audience shrieked and scrambled for the door.

Thaddeus stepped forward and stared down at Numps. "How much do you want for the pig?"

"That a fine suckling piglet, that is," the man said, rubbing his jaw and not moving a muscle to get up. "At least a crown, a low price only due to the good of my heart because it doesn't take into account all the pennies you lost from me show. He was a good one, with a strong squeal."

Thaddeus dropped a coin in the dust by Numps's head, turned on his heel and walked out, the piglet tucked under his arm.

Joan ran after him. "What are you going to do with Percy?" she asked, somewhat breathless by the time she caught up with him. Thaddeus was marching back to the carriage, ignoring people trying to sell him everything from ballads to baby rattles.

"He's a pig," Thaddeus said, striding even faster, so she had to run again to keep up. "I shall hand him over to my swineherd."

"His name is *Percy*," Joan cried. "You saved him from being poked to death. You can't turn him into pork dinner!"

"The animal was being tortured, not poked

to death," Thaddeus said. "Once he lost heart and refused to squeal, he would have been sent to the pork tent to be roasted as a suckling pig and made into luncheon. They would have killed him, not Numps."

"You can't give Percy to your swineherd!" Joan said, putting on a burst of speed so she came around in front of him and stopped, blocking his way. The piglet obviously felt safe and comfortable under Thaddeus's arm. He was looking about inquisitively, his pink nose in the air.

Thaddeus looked down at her with an inscrutable expression, which she was beginning to find really irritating. "His name is Percy," she said, catching her breath. "He's a person, I mean, he's got a name. I can take him back to Lindow. Viola used to have two cows—"

"I've been introduced to Daisy and Cleopatra," he said.

"Of course you were, when you were courting Viola," Joan said, feeling a little pang at the thought. "When Viola married, she took Daisy and Cleo to Devin's country house, so Percy can live in their empty cowshed at the castle. Please, Thaddeus."

"He's not a pet. He's an animal that should be treated with respect and kindness. Before being served for dinner."

Her gaze locked with his, and she held out her arms for the piglet. "*Please.*"

"If I give him to you, you have to wear a different coat for the performance. One of my choosing." It was a curt command, not a question.

"What?" Joan pushed away the unwelcome realization that she *loved* it when his voice dropped
to that gravely tone. "What's the matter with my
coat?"

"It's too short in the rear."

"I needn't worry about being *à la mode*," Joan
explained. "Most theater companies buy their
costumes from the aristocracy. They wear coats
that may have been sitting in someone's attic
since the Stuarts were on the throne. It's all about
the pretense, not the fashion of the moment. This
coat belonged to my brother Alaric when he was
a boy, so it's at least twenty years old."

He looked at her. "Do you want this pig?"

"Yes."

"Then you'll wear a different coat for *Hamlet*,
one that covers your rear."

"But this is perfect for a prince," she objected.
"The silver thread embroidery, you see?"

Silence.

Joan shrugged. "I'll have to fish around in the
attics and get dusty, but it will be worth it to save
Percy."

It looked as if Thaddeus rolled his eyes, but
she must have been wrong. The oh-so-pompous
viscount would never lower his countenance to
make such an impolite gesture.

"I'll bring the pig to your coachman," he said,
nodding toward the carriage.

"I'll find Aunt Knowe meanwhile," Joan said
and then caught his eye. "No, I'll come with you
because the fair is dangerous," she said with a
sigh.

They walked in silence back to the coach. "Give this piglet some water," Thaddeus instructed the coachman. "He's had a difficult morning."

"Yes, Your Lordship," Mr. Bisquet replied.

"Bisquet, the piglet's name is Percy," Joan added. "He's going to live in Cleo's old cowshed and never be served for dinner, so be sure not to let him go free accidentally. He's just a baby."

"I see that," Bisquet said, taking the piglet. "We can try giving him to a nursing sow, but I think he'll have to be fed with an old glove."

Percy made a soft grunting noise.

Joan scratched his forehead. "Be a good boy, Percy, and I'll be back soon."

"Oh, for God's sake," Thaddeus said next to her. "Try to look at least boyish, if not manly. Men don't moon over baby swine."

"How sad for your sex," Joan said. She bent over and gave Percy a kiss on his forehead. "I suppose they don't kiss them either. Be a good boy, Percy. You are going to love the nursery!"

"The nursery?" Thaddeus asked as they walked back into the fair. "Surely you don't mean the castle nursery?"

"Of course I do. The children will adore him."

"Couldn't they visit him in the cowshed?"

"Well, yes, but we often bring animals to the nursery. Sometimes they spend the night. Viola has a pet crow, you know. He's living in the nursery since she's visiting. We also have two pet rats at the moment. Unusual pets are a tradition, ever since Willa—that's my brother Alaric's wife—lent us her skunk when I was fourteen, and we took care of her for three weeks."

"By skunk, you refer to the animals from the Americas with a powerful odor?"

Joan nodded. "Willa adopted her as a baby."

Thaddeus had probably never had any pets. Most people didn't approve of skunks, rats, and crows as pets. Let alone pigs.

"I'm guessing that you won't want to visit Carmela, the camel who comes from deepest, darkest Sahara?" Joan asked, changing the subject. "Her tent is down there at the end."

"If you wish." It was amazing how unenthusiastic he made that simple statement.

"You probably won't enjoy her," Joan admitted. "Carmela doesn't have the best costume in the world. Her hump is perched on top of a saddle, and over the years, the fur has started molting. But we adored Carmela when we were small."

She happened to glance at him just in time to see a smile quirk the corner of his mouth. "You smiled! You didn't used to be so grim. I remember when you were courting Betsy, four years ago. You were cheerful, but now you seem to glower most of the time."

His jaw tightened. "I do not glower."

"Perhaps not so that most people would notice," she allowed. "But you don't smile much, do you? What happened? Your mother and father are still alive . . . It's not because you were disappointed in love, is it?"

Unaccountably, that idea made her gut squeeze. It would have been Betsy who broke his heart, if so. She had almost married him, as Joan remembered it.

Thankfully, Thaddeus laughed. A deep, rumbling laugh that sounded a bit rusty, but was still a laugh.

"I'm glad to hear you laugh," she said, skipping a step before she remembered to stride, not walk. "I would hate to think that one of my sisters drove you into a melancholy, like Ophelia."

"Finding a wife is a necessity, a pleasurable one. But the task would never put me into a melancholy." His tone was matter-of-fact, without heat.

"I gather you believe that romantic love is fiction?"

"A fairy tale to please silly girls like Ophelia," he confirmed. "In my experience, people use 'love' as an excuse for shameful behavior."

Well, that summed up Joan's parentage. She couldn't think of anything to say in response.

"There you are, my darlings!" Aunt Knowe caroled, waving at them from a stall. "Come help me pick one of these hats." She wore a wide-brimmed blue one, and she was holding two more.

The hat stall was one of the largest at the fair; it even had a tall glass in which buyers could view themselves. Otis was trying on a large hat encircled with unlikely purple peonies.

Joan reached for a rather darling bonnet with a bunch of roses, before she remembered, cleared her throat, and asked, "Do you have macaroni hats, my good man?"

The stall owner looked at her, his brow knitted, and Thaddeus said in his calm, deep voice, "My younger brother would like to see a hat with a feather."

Flustered, the man bustled to the cart behind

his stall and emerged with several. Joan took a black felt hat with a matching feather and stepped in front of the glass. The stall owner left for the other side of the stall, where the duchess was fingering a bonnet adorned with a plush rose over one ear.

"What do you think?" Joan said, pulling the point of the black hat low over her eyes and turning to Thaddeus.

To her surprise, he had a dusky color in his cheeks and he looked . . . something.

"What?" she demanded.

"Nothing."

She glanced behind her, and then froze. Her back was clearly visible in the glass. The green coat clung to her narrow shoulders—and ended in a boyish flounce at her hips. Which left her silken-clad, round bottom open to view.

"Oh."

He nodded. Arms folded over his chest again, Thaddeus's eyes glinted at her. "See what I mean?"

Joan squinted at him and twirled her finger.

He didn't move.

She sighed and walked around to his rear. His frock coat was made of the finest wool, naturally. It strained over his broad shoulders, and then followed the line of his back in two precisely stitched lines that emphasized his lean waist. At that point the coat spilled into disciplined pleats hanging to his knees, so his arse wasn't exposed for the world to see.

"All right," she said, feeling suddenly as if she were half naked. "I take your point."

"Also, that hat is too large for you. Gentlemen's hats are made for the shape of their head. One doesn't buy them in a fair."

Joan sighed and edged around until her bottom was hidden by a table piled with hats. She took off the macaroni hat and put it to the side, picking up Alaric's old one again.

"I've chosen three hats," Aunt Knowe said gaily, coming over to them. "Nothing for you, my dear? Thaddeus, your mother is contemplating buying a pink hat, although I told her she has enough pink headgear to last out the century."

He gave her a wry smile. "My mother adores the color."

"That is not news to me," Aunt Knowe said tartly. "I've known Emily since she was a girl, when her affection for the color was charming."

Thaddeus raised an eyebrow. "It still is."

Not many people dared to reprimand Lady Knowe, twin sister of the Duke of Lindow. Joan watched with fascination as her aunt barked with laughter. "You raised your son well," she called over her shoulder.

The duchess smiled widely. "I believe I'll have these two, Thaddeus, dear. What do you think? This good man has silk roses in the back and tells me that it would be the work of a moment to change the violets to pink roses."

"Certainly," Thaddeus said. He nodded to the happy stall keeper and took out his purse. "These two, and three for Lady Knowe."

"Mine too," Otis cried. "You know that scene when Ophelia is tossing flowers around the throne room? It will make far more sense if I'm wearing this hat!"

The brim of the hat was topped by a huge puff of cherry-striped fabric adorned with a profusion of multicolored posies, a good many ribbons, large bows, and six curly ruby-colored feathers. It was easily twice the width of Otis's head, even given his gooseberry wig.

"To be sure," Thaddeus said, his expression not changing.

Joan began giggling. Something about the combination of Otis's homely face topped by so many flowers and flounces was irresistibly funny.

Otis narrowed his eyes. "What?"

"You look like an animated mushroom!"

"Only if a window box fell onto the mushroom," Aunt Knowe put in, huffing with laughter.

"This is my finest hat, straight from Paris," the stall keeper protested. "The young lady has exquisite taste."

Aunt Knowe and Joan laughed even harder.

Otis fixed them with a glare, caught sight of himself in the glass, and broke into a reluctant smile.

The duchess cocked her head and said thoughtfully, "I think you look like a fancy chicken that I once saw at the Tower of London."

"I shall wear it home to the castle and directly pay a visit to the nursery," Otis said airily. "I don't want to deny anyone the pleasure of seeing the fanciest chicken who ever pranced through Drabblefield Fair."

They were walking back to the carriage, laden

down with everything from pears to a baby rattle for Viola's unborn child, six cutwork handkerchiefs, and a great quantity of gingerbread, when Thaddeus said to Joan, "To return to our previous subject of conversation, I am not melancholy."

"Then why do I feel as if I should mark on a calendar every time you laugh?" she asked. "On the rare occasions when you do laugh, I mean."

She had the hang of striding now. Swinging one's arms was important too. In fact, being a man was an all-body endeavor.

"I suppose you laugh many times a day?" There wasn't anything wistful about Thaddeus's voice; it had the same pleasant, courtly timbre as always.

"Of course," Joan said.

"Joan is a great laugher," Aunt Knowe said from behind them. "The boys used to adore making her giggle long before she could speak a word. The nursery would have been much less jolly without her."

"As polite society will be if anyone catches sight of you in that coat," Otis said, poking Joan in the back. "I don't think it's appropriate. I hadn't caught sight of you from the rear before."

Joan felt herself turning pink. "Lord Greywick has already expressed his opinion of my coat. I know it's too short."

"He's right," Otis said firmly. "Just think of that scene in which you have to wave a dagger about. *Is this a dagger that I see before me?*"

"Wrong play!" Joan cried, turning around and walking backward because she felt so self-conscious. "That's *Macbeth.*"

"Hamlet waves around a rapier in Act Five, when he's dueling everyone, right? My point is that the audience is going to be watching your arse instead of the dagger," Otis said.

"You shouldn't mention private parts in front of ladies!" Aunt Knowe exclaimed.

Thaddeus mumbled something.

Joan looked up. "What did you say?"

Their eyes met, and she felt herself growing even pinker.

Aunt Knowe was bickering with Otis and not listening.

"I don't read much Shakespeare," Thaddeus said, a shade of apology in his voice.

Joan waved her hand. "Most of my family agrees with your poor opinion of the Bard."

"I said that your arse might make that wretched play palatable," he said, his voice low but perfectly clear.

Joan's mouth fell open.

"Not that you will ever wear that coat in public again," the viscount decreed.

Chapter Seven

On return from the fair, Thaddeus stripped, tossing his garments on a chair and stepping into the bath his valet had prepared.

"Your clothes are filthy," Pitcher said with distaste. "If you'll forgive me, my lord, I'll take them directly to the laundry." He bundled them, and then wielded a feather duster on the chair.

Thaddeus relaxed into the steaming tub with a sigh of relief, tipping his head back to stare at the ceiling. He had eaten many meals in company with the Duke of Lindow's family. He had played billiards with the duke's sons in the middle of the night; he had gone sledding with the children and trounced the duchess at archery. He had attended balls and country house parties.

Lindow wasn't home, but it wasn't foreign to him either. He'd always been comfortable there, knowing his place and feeling among friends.

No longer.

Now he felt as if he were in the grip of emotion— a condition he detested—and what's worse, he wasn't even certain what the emotion was. One moment he was angry, and the next he found himself with a cockstand such as he had scarcely experienced in his life, which would not go away, no matter how hard he contemplated the plight of the poor or the hairy wart on his late grandmother's chin.

Joan was the obvious catalyst.

She kept looking into his eyes, as if she guessed the feelings he had hidden from everyone, including himself.

Not to mention that kiss.

Bloody hell.

He had looked down at Joan and realized that she'd taken his refusal to answer her question as confirmation that he disliked her—and completely lost his head. Even the memory of that kiss made a rush of lust overcome him with the ferocity of a wildfire.

Given another half hour, he would have propped her against that wretched fence and lost his head entirely.

God help him, when she was trying on a hat with that impudent smile, he actually glanced at the thicket and contemplated ducking behind it accompanied by a lady dressed as a man and kissing that lady to a standstill.

It was even worse after Joan peered at her bottom and then turned to him with a flush in her cheeks. All he could think about was what she would look like after coming in his arms.

He wasn't the sort of man who was ever taken by surprise by lust. Desire had its place; he enjoyed respectful exchanges with women who cheerfully welcomed him into their beds with no expectation of money or a future.

Picturing intimacies with one of them had never caused him to shudder so deeply that he felt it in his backbone.

He felt unmoored.

It took an effort of will to admit that he had fallen under the spell of a woman who had been practicing her wiles on London society for three years. He had watched Joan do it. He *knew* what an amazing performance she put on.

That poor dupe, Anthony Froude, had told him months after Joan kissed him at the ball that he'd never be happy with another woman.

Succumbing to her, *kissing* her, made him as foolish as Anthony.

He shook his head and reached for a ball of lemon soap—which put him in a direct eye line with a glass that hung over the dressing table. He watched himself run the ball over his arms and chest, soapy water sliding over his muscles.

He'd never given any thought to whether his future wife would dislike his burly frame. It hadn't mattered, to be frank. But now he wondered what Joan would think. Several times he'd caught her peeking at his chest.

Irritatingly, his veins were on fire, unable to stop imagining her as a lover. He had a feeling she'd be nothing like the women he'd made love to over the years.

He could imagine her: sweaty, bossy, sparkling, requesting more than he wanted to give, and getting it. She would demand more of him than any woman had before. Not that he'd left a woman unsatisfied.

But it would be different with her.

He rubbed soap in his hair, watching his biceps bulge in the glass. He hadn't realized how muscled he'd become, even given Lady Bumtrinket's unwelcome comments about his supposedly padded frame.

The pinnacle of gentlemanly form was a slender man, graceful in the ballroom, willowy and aristocratic.

In the last two years, he'd repeatedly taken out deep frustration in the boxing salon, and his body had changed, growing thicker and more masculine, for want of a better word. More rugged, as befit someone who walked in the door of the salon six days of the week and paid for the privilege of pummeling the strongest men in London.

Sinking back under the water, he rinsed the soap from his hair and braced his hands on the sides of the tub. It was time to rise, to put on the garments and the comportment of a viscount bade to dinner in a castle, in company with a duke and two duchesses, one of whom was his mother.

As well as Lady Joan.

The image of her flickered in his mind, and he let out a groan before he slid back down into the tub, and watched his right hand slide down his wet chest and disappear under the sudsy water.

The moment he took hold of his cock, his head arched backward, and a rough sound broke from his lips.

Five minutes later he was forced to accept an unpalatable truth: The orgasm that tore through him like fire, that convulsed his body, had left him unsatisfied. Perhaps, like poor Anthony Froude, he would never be satisfied again.

At least, not by his own hand.

An hour later, he escorted his mother into the drawing room and discovered Joan standing before the great fireplace, reciting one of Hamlet's soliloquies to an audience of her parents.

Except she'd mixed up the skull and the soliloquy. Joan was talking to a skull—albeit a stuffed one—but it wasn't human. In fact, it had originally belonged to an alligator, given its pronounced snout. He recognized it as part of the stuffed alligator that normally resided in a corner of the drawing room after having been sent home, as he understood it, by the famous explorer Lord Alaric Wilde, though he hadn't realized that the head could separate from its body.

The alligator's eyes had been replaced by shiny green marbles, and his jaw hung open in a way that made him look as if he were laughing.

As Thaddeus remembered, Hamlet's speech addressed to a skull was about the brevity of fame. But Joan was performing *To be or not to be*, and the way she was talking to the alligator had the duke and duchess in gales of laughter. Instead of delivering a profound treatise on suicide, Joan was poking fun at a rich and privileged prince, absurdly self-indulgent in his moaning.

"Oh, my goodness," Thaddeus's mother whispered, bringing him to a halt. "Let's not interrupt her! I'd have never thought Hamlet could be funny."

"Neither had I," he said.

Joan's low bodice framed breasts so plump and delicious that his knees felt weak at the sight— and yet, at this moment, she *was* a man.

Not any man: a prince. She was dressed as a woman, but her expressive face was that of an arrogant young man indulging himself with long-winded speeches.

The duke and duchess stood with their backs to Thaddeus and his mother. His Grace, the Duke of Lindow, was a tall, well-built man who carried his years lightly. His duchess was smaller, tucked under his arm. The soliloquy over, they both clapped wildly.

"Brava!" His Grace said, still chuckling.

"The most enjoyable Hamlet I've seen!" the duchess crowed.

Thaddeus and his mother began to walk toward them.

He felt like a moth drawn to a flame. It was a disconcerting feeling because—he reminded himself—he didn't like Joan as a person. She was reckless. Scandalous. Her attitude toward Percy Piglet hadn't made a difference in those essential traits.

"You were brilliant," the Duke of Lindow told his daughter. "But I still don't understand: Why *Hamlet*? Why not perform one of the great comedies? You stripped that prince to the bone; your version is an extremely foolish, funny prig."

"I'll be serious in performance," Joan promised, leaning back against the stone of the unlit fireplace. "I chose *Hamlet* because the play has everything in it: tragedy, deaths, disclosures, ghosts, love and despair, illusion and disguise. Not too much comedy, but I couldn't resist it to-night."

Her eyes landed on Thaddeus's mother, and she suddenly threw off Hamlet and became a young lady. "Your Grace," she said, stepping forward to drop into a graceful curtsy. "Lord Grey-wick. Good evening."

The duke and duchess turned to greet them. Sometime later, Thaddeus found himself seated beside Joan on a small settee.

No, he seated himself beside her. She hadn't given him even an inviting glance. It was as if they had never kissed.

Which was precisely what he wanted, of course.

"Champagne, Prism," the duke said, nodding to the castle butler.

"Where is the rest of the family?" Joan asked.

"Devin will eat with Viola, who can't bear the idea of dressing for the evening meal," her mother said. "The children are in the nursery, exhausted by an afternoon at the fair. I'm not sure where Aunt Knowe or Otis can be found."

"Otis is always late," Joan remarked. "It's a habit of mind. I know he was only a vicar for two weeks, but I'd bet my dowry that church services, even weddings, never began on time."

"I have so many children, and yet the castle seems terribly thin of company," the duke said, accepting a glass of champagne from the butler.

His wife smiled at him and took his hand. "You

are never happier than when all are safely in the castle." Then she leaned over and kissed him on the cheek. "We all wish that Horatius could be here as well."

It took Thaddeus a moment to remember that Horatius was the duke's eldest son, who had died in an accident in the bog east of the castle. "I knew the Marquess of Saltersley when I was a schoolboy," he said. "I'm very sorry for your loss."

His Grace threw back his champagne, and a footman stepped forward instantly to refill his glass. "He was a troublesome heir, pompous and always right. One of the last things he said to me was that I should spend more time in Parliament, and dig more canals. Who would want to be around an heir who was convinced *he* would make the better duke?"

"You," his wife said affectionately, kissing him on the cheek. "We all would. I knew Horatius for only seven years, but he was deeply lovable, no matter how bombastic."

Thaddeus's mother straightened. "It's the anniversary of his death, isn't it?" she exclaimed. "I'm so sorry, my dears. If I had realized, I would have delayed our arrival."

"He's been lost to us for a long time," the duke said. "He died eleven years ago, in '73. I took a long walk in the Moss today to commemorate him." Lindow Moss was the bog where Horatius drowned.

"I think we should be very grateful that Horatius isn't haunting the castle bellowing *Remember me* like Hamlet's father," Joan said, injecting just the right amount of humor into her voice. "He would frighten us to death. He was brilliant at playing pirates. Some of my earliest memories are the happy afternoons when he would come to the nursery and act out long adventure stories. Sometimes he would take us out to search for treasure."

"That's right," the duke said. "He was obsessed with the lost treasure, wasn't he?" He turned to Thaddeus and his mother. "One of my ancestors was besieged by Oswald of Northumbria back in the 600s. Family lore has it that he took a fortune in silver and buried it."

"Not buried it," Joan corrected. "He *sank* it. That means either the bog or the lake."

"The boys used to dive in the lake," the duke said. "There's nothing there: It's a shallow lake that my great-grandfather widened into a circle, turning its island into a garden retreat."

"Which means the treasure has to be in the bog," Joan said. "Even Horatius never looked there. Too dangerous. On special occasions, he would fetch us from the nursery. We'd dress in old clothing, and collect spades, and go dig a hole in the apple orchard, or the banks of the lake. It was glorious."

"Horatius condescended to everyone under the king," her father said with a wry smile, "but never to his siblings."

"Nor to me," the duchess put in. "I was ill prepared for the role of duchess, having never had the ambition to marry a duke, nor to have more children. Horatius was endlessly kind."

"I was younger than he, but I remember that

quality from our schooldays at Eton," Thaddeus said.

"What do you remember?" the duke asked, bending toward him.

Thaddeus realized that His Grace was brimming with emotion, longing to talk of the son he lost. "Lord Saltersley was kind, if somewhat arrogant, if you'll forgive me."

Joan cast him a look under her eyelashes that he interpreted as "Pot, meet kettle."

"He had reason to be arrogant," Thaddeus clarified. "He was the best at almost everything, from cricket to oratory."

The duke's forehead crinkled. "Didn't he bring you to join us for luncheon?"

"Yes," Thaddeus said. "It was half term. My mother generally paid me a visit, but on this occasion, my father had expressed interest."

"Your thirteenth birthday," his mother murmured, sounding pained.

Thaddeus nodded. "Lord Saltersley saw me waiting long after most children had been fetched by their parents and realized that my father had changed his mind. If he had shown pity or sympathy, I would have refused to accompany him. But he snapped his fingers at me in a superior manner, and ordered me to go with him. As a younger boy, I had no choice but to obey him."

"I remember the afternoon. Tea at the Crown & Cushion," the duke said, a smile playing around his mouth. "Horatius could eat a leg of mutton at a sitting."

"As could I," Thaddeus said. "We were always hungry in those days."

"I used to send you boxes of food," his mother recalled, patting his knee.

Otis burst in the door, wearing an aubergine coat with a frothing neck scarf. "Good evening!" he called, stopping to accept a glass of champagne from Prism, before he seated himself across from Thaddeus and Joan. "Where's Lady Viola? Has a new member of the household joined us?"

"My new grandchild shows no imminent signs of arrival," the Duchess of Lindow said, smiling at him. "Good evening, Mr. Murgatroyd."

Thaddeus nodded to Otis. "If you'll forgive me, I'll just finish a tale from years ago." He turned back to the duke. "I was so grateful not to be left in the reception chamber, pitied by all the boys who knew my father's absence from my life."

By which he meant his father's well-known adoration of his mistress's family.

The Duke of Lindow nodded. "Thank you for telling me that story." The quiet rumble of his voice showed how much he still grieved for his late son.

Otis was chattering away with Joan, who began chortling with laughter. Thaddeus watched them with the odd feeling that the two were a different species from him. Where did that joy that bubbled up so easily come from?

His mother's hand tightened on his knee. "It was kind of you to tell that memory," she said quietly. "I'm sure you wish to forget the afternoon."

She had guessed the truth. He had loathed the demoralizing experience of being surrounded by a loving family. It was particularly horrible to sit at a table headed by a father who was eager to hear the result of every cricket game, the reason for a failed examination paper, the intricacies of surviving Eton.

His own father had no interest in him and never had, no matter how many cricket runs he made, or examinations he took.

He had spent the entire afternoon wishing to be anywhere but the Crown & Cushion, but that didn't make Horatius's gesture any less kindly.

Joan was looking at him, eyes bright and interested. "If you don't mind my asking, did you ever learn why your father didn't arrive to collect you?"

His mother turned away, blurting out a compliment about Otis's cravat.

"The birth of my half brother," Thaddeus said, pitching his voice so that only Joan could hear him. "I already had two half sisters, but as it turned out, my half brother and I share birthdays." He didn't enjoy the revelation, but frankly, the details of his father's second family could be seen in any stationer selling scandalous prints.

"Your father is pestilent," Joan said fiercely. "So once he knew he had a second son, he felt free to neglect you?"

"I was scarcely neglected," Thaddeus pointed out. "I was relatively happy at Eton, certainly well fed and well clothed. I had spending money, and my mother regularly sent boxes of food. I didn't need him."

"Perhaps not," Joan said. "But I'm sure you *wanted* him. One always—" She stopped. "I was so lucky in my parents, but even so, I sometimes wonder about the two who left me behind as a baby." Her eyes narrowed. "I gather we have that in common. Oddly, I thought we had *nothing* in common!"

Thaddeus didn't know what to make of that comment. "We share a piglet," he said. "I checked on Percy just before the meal, and he is happily sharing a stall with a friendly cow."

"Who is Percy?" the duke asked, breaking in.

"Our new piglet," Joan told her father, smiling. "Lord Greywick saved him from being stuck with pins at the fair. I was worried Percy would miss his mother, but he has been joined by a young heifer rejected by her mother. When I visited, she was licking his face, so I think she'll keep him from being lonely."

"'Our new piglet,'" Thaddeus's mother said, her voice thoughtful. "As in yours and my son's?"

"No, no, the castle's new piglet," Joan explained. "Lord Greywick granted me Percy in exchange for . . ." She faltered, and a faint wash of pink showed in her cheeks. "He gave me the piglet, after I most earnestly asked for Percy to return home with me."

"I would guess that Percy had to be rescued," the duchess said.

"A sapient pig," Thaddeus told her. "Who was being stuck with a pin to prove his unlikely intelligence."

"I am grateful to you for taking Percy, my dear," his mother said to Joan. "Our house and grounds are full of rescued animals, from donkeys to cats. We have no room for spare swine."

Thaddeus's mouth tightened. He would have preferred to keep that information to himself.

"Really?" Joan asked, flicking a surprised glance at Thaddeus. "Because I was under the impression that Percy would be handed over to the swineherd, only to reappear on the breakfast table as bacon."

"More likely on a platter," Thaddeus said. "Suckling pig is a great delicacy in these parts."

"We live with two donkeys, one missing a rear leg, rescued after being ill-treated," his mother retorted. "A sheep named Petra who was kicked by a horse, convalesced in the stables, and was never made into mutton. A whole barnful of horses too old to be ridden. Some exotic chickens who aren't even penned. The rooster is particularly annoying, having a tendency to crow just outside my bedchamber window."

"I see," Joan said, one eyebrow raised. "I wouldn't have imagined it, given Lord Greywick's disdain for the animal tents at the fair."

"I dislike seeing animals abused for human entertainment," Thaddeus said, knowing how woodenly he spoke. He tried to smile, but it probably looked more like a grimace.

"We could give you a couple of peacocks for your zoo," the duke suggested.

"No, we couldn't!" Joan said indignantly. "Fitzy and Floyd aren't going anywhere."

"They scream at each other," His Grace told the duchess. "I'm sure you've already been an unwilling audience to their nightly battles."

Joan laughed. "Parth always says that when the

day of Revelation arrives, we will miss the announcement, because Fitzy and Floyd are louder than angelic trumpets."

When the gong rang for the meal, Thaddeus, as the second-most highly ranked gentleman in the room, ought to have escorted his mother to the dining room. But she attached herself to Otis, which left Joan.

Tonight she was dressed like a perfect lady, a member of the peerage. Her gown was yellow, paler than a lemon, with skirts embroidered in golden leaves. The sleeves ended at her elbow with fine pleats falling away from her arm.

She looked like a lemon ice, one of his favorite things in the world.

As they followed the others from the room, Joan slipped her hand into the crook of his arm. "I've been trying to think how to break the news to my father that I plan to perform *Hamlet* on a public stage in Wilmslow," she said thoughtfully.

A curse escaped his lips before he could catch it back.

"Goodness me," she said, laughing. "I can scarcely believe what I heard, Lord Greywick. The paragon of English society indulging in disrespectful language!"

He stared down at her, lips pressed into a line, and then made himself open them to say, "You called me Lord Greywick."

She smiled up at him, and he realized with a jolt to his gut that she didn't wear a scrap of face paint. Nothing on her lips. No beauty patch, nothing.

She was ordinarily, intrinsically this beautiful. Every day.

Thanks to the Prussian, a voice in his head pointed out, but the words meant nothing. Except they did.

A future duke couldn't consider marrying a woman whose bloodlines weren't impeccable. Something he knew long before Lady Bumtrinket began handing out her unwanted advice.

"I was shielding your reputation," Joan explained, her eyes earnest. "Your mother may be within earshot."

"My mother," Thaddeus repeated, trying to pull his thoughts together.

"The duchess?" She looked at him inquiringly. "Your mother, that duchess. I'm sure you don't want her to think that we're on intimate terms."

"In case she assumed that we were courting?"

"Well, she wouldn't assume that, would she?" Joan said matter-of-factly. "No one above the rank of squire has properly courted me, unless I forced the issue. I enticed a few aristocrats into kissing me, but that was just to see the panic on their faces when they realized that honor obliged them to propose. My father would have enforced marriage, even over their parents' strenuous protests. I enjoyed terrifying them into proposing, but I never wished to marry any of them."

He frowned at her. "Conversation with you is trying. I generally follow the subject, but I find myself at sea. Are you talking about kissing that poor fool Anthony Froude?"

"I had reasons," she said secretively.

He waited.

"One of my sisters overheard him telling a friend that I gleamed like false gold," she admitted. Any other young lady would be unhappy, recounting the tale. But Joan merely sounded a trifle disgruntled and broke into a smile. "It took me a mere twenty minutes to bring him to heel and then kiss him in full view of his mother. I wanted him to panic."

"About marrying you? A few days later, he told me that he'd never be happy with another woman."

Joan shrugged. "He was just embarrassed and making up for his flirtation with gilt, not gold."

"No," Thaddeus stated. "He's not. You are gold. You brought him to his knees, and he stayed there. As did the others, Joan. Their proposals had nothing to do with honor, and everything to do with desire."

Joan looked up at him with a faint smile. "I don't believe you, but I think it's kind of you to suggest it."

Prism bowed as they passed the butler to enter the breakfast room, where only one table was set this evening. The butler ushered Joan to a place, and an odd possessive twinge went through Thaddeus like a shrill noise when he realized she wouldn't be beside him. He drew out her seat, and she happily settled between Lady Knowe and Otis.

For his part, he moved around the table to sit between the Duchess of Lindow and his mother, two charming ladies.

But . . .

Not what he wanted.

That was such an odd thought that he spent most of the meal wrestling with it. He never bothered about what he "wanted." In fact, the idea was anathema. Only weak people had "wants" and "desires," impulses that they put ahead of gentlemanly conduct.

Like his father, for example.

He hadn't seen his father for over two years, not since His Grace made such a horrendous suggestion that Thaddeus nearly threw a punch at his sire, barely restraining himself in time.

They existed in a state of frigid warfare. The only engagement he had with his father was missives from the duke's solicitors.

The very thought of those letters put Thaddeus in a foul mood.

From the moment he was born, he'd been molded to become a duke. His nanny, his tutors, his schools, his friends, his mother . . .

All of them.

They looked at him and saw a title, and a man who needed to be shaped to live up to the honor.

At some point he glanced to his left and right, just to make sure that he could keep gnawing over his childhood. His mother was happily chatting with Lady Knowe, and the duchess was flirting with her husband. The Duke of Lindow looked ten years younger than his age, and his duchess was beautiful.

Why the hell shouldn't His Grace give his wife a smoldering look, particularly since Thaddeus had the distinct impression that the Duchess of Lindow would do everything in her power to distract her husband from his lingering grief over Horatius's death tonight? Hell, he envied the man.

He wanted the same in his—

The idea startled him so much that he physically jolted and then snatched up his wineglass and emptied it.

"Is everything all right, dearest?" his mother asked, turning to him with a look of concern.

"Of course," he said, summoning a smile from somewhere. "Do return to your conversation."

"If you don't mind," his mother said. "Lady Knowe is telling me about some fascinating cures for a cold."

Thaddeus went back to brooding. He'd like to have a healthy, satisfactory intimate life even at the age of fifty. Or sixty. He wasn't actually sure of the duke's age.

Of course, he had to marry for that to happen. He would be a duke someday, and that required a duchess.

The problem was that if he thought about marriage, the sound that echoed in his ears was the sweet, throaty moan that Joan uttered when he was kissing her.

Just like that, his cock went from placid to hard as a rock, straining the front of his breeches, so sensitive that he could feel the weight of the napkin that covered his lap.

His lips moved, uttering curses that he would never say aloud. He glanced up and met Joan's eyes across the table.

She raised an eyebrow, letting him know that

she could read lips, and his silence hadn't protected her sensibilities.

Thaddeus raised his shoulders just a fraction.
Merely meeting her blue eyes made his cockstand harden until he had to clench his teeth to
get himself under control. He ended up scowling
at her.

True to form, Joan didn't flinch or look startled
by his bad temper; instead she began chuckling,
and a moment later the table was laughing with
her, not even knowing why.

That's what she was like. Wherever she was,
whether in the bosom of her family or a ballroom, people laughed with her.

Thaddeus couldn't stop looking at her lips. The
sweets course included a marbled confection
made of chilled rose-colored jelly. Watching Joan
slide a spoonful of jelly through her lips made
his pulse thrum through his body.

It wasn't until he caught her glancing at him
with a mischievous glint in her eyes and then
slowly taking another spoonful that he realized
she was performing for an audience: *him*.

He froze.

Was this one of her tricks, like that practiced
smile? He narrowed his eyes in a silent question,
and she smiled at him blithely.

No.

It wasn't practiced.

All the same, she knew what she was doing to him, and she was reveling in it. Even as
he watched, the tip of her tongue stole out and
lapped up the last of the jelly on her spoon.

Unforgivably gauche.

Any governess would rap her knuckles for being so unladylike. And Joan would only laugh, he realized, because all the people who had informed her that she was illegitimate?

They had told her over and over that she was no lady.

They had given her freedom that no other woman in the aristocracy had. No wonder she confidently strode onto a private stage and showed nothing but excitement thinking of a public one. No wonder she pranced through the fair in tight breeches.

As he watched, she took another bite, her lips closing lovingly around her silver spoon. She wasn't just beautiful; she was like one of the ancient Greek sirens, created by the gods to bring a man to his knees whenever she chose to unleash her joy and sensuality.

"My dear," his mother said, interrupting that rather grim train of thought, "Mr. Murgatroyd says that the two of you plan to accompany Lady Joan to a public performance of *Hamlet* in Wilmslow."

Joan's head jerked up, and sensuality slid off her face like water.

It seemed that Otis had come up with a plan that would allow Joan to perform the role of Hamlet in Wilmslow without her father's knowledge.

"I thought it'd be amusing to see someone perform Ophelia better than I," Otis said, giving Thaddeus a look that directed him to support the scheme.

"I gather the troupe will continue on to Wilmslow after their performance here in the castle," Thaddeus said, playing his part. He flicked a glance back at Otis. "I, for one, would like to see an Ophelia who knows her lines."

"I don't mind admitting that it strains belief to think that I'm attractive enough to catch the eye of a prince," Otis said.

"You have winning attributes," Joan said, leaning over to kiss him on the cheek. "Plus I truly love you, so our relationship will feel real on the stage."

"It's not the same," Otis pointed out.

"What's this?" the duke asked, turning away from a conversation with his duchess.

"We're planning a trip to Wilmslow to see Mr. Wooty's troupe perform *Hamlet* without Otis in the role of Ophelia," Joan explained.

"Not in your breeches," her father ordered.

She stilled, and Thaddeus learned something very important about Lady Joan Wilde: She didn't like to lie, even by omission.

"Lady Joan will travel to Wilmslow as herself," he said, cutting in. "I feel certain that Mr. Murgatroyd would rather not don his corset under any circumstances, so I can assure you that he will be in breeches."

"I would chaperone you, but I can't leave Viola," the Duchess of Lindow said.

"I'd be happy to accompany you," Thaddeus's mother said. "Although I may stay in the inn that evening rather than see *Hamlet* yet again. The Gherkin & Cheese has an excellent kitchen, as I remember."

"Thank you, Your Grace," Otis said, beaming at her.

Thaddeus watched as Joan let out a soundless breath of air.

"If Viola's baby is on the way, you must remain in the castle," Aunt Knowe said, eyes on Joan. "She will want you nearby."

Suddenly, Thaddeus was quite certain that Lady Knowe had guessed that Joan and Otis would play their roles before a public audience. Presumably she approved, or didn't disapprove to the point of disclosing the truth to the duke.

"Of course," Joan promised. "I would never leave Viola if there is even a sign of the baby coming. We'll only be gone for a single night."

"You are lucky," Thaddeus said, breaching the strict etiquette that governed conversation, which occurred only to the left and right, and never across the table.

She raised an eyebrow at him.

"In your friends. Viola and Mr. Murgatroyd."

"I keep expecting my father to be at my shoulder when you address me so formally," Otis said. He looked around the table. "Since Lady Knowe saw fit to rope the inestimable Lord Greywick into rehearsing this wretched play with us, Joan and I are addressing him by his first name. To answer your question, Thaddeus, yes, Joan is extremely lucky to have me as a friend. And Viola as a sister."

"Speaking of which, I should go back upstairs and check on how Viola is doing," Lady Knowe said.

"Have there been any signs of the baby?" Viola's

mother asked, a flicker of anxiety going through her eyes.

"No," her sister-in-law said with a reassuring smile. "But your daughter ate four Williams pears this afternoon, which was three too many."

"Ow," Otis said, obviously impressed. "My stomach hurts at the thought."

"Another two weeks," Lady Knowe advised. "First babies often linger."

"We're performing *Hamlet* in six days," Joan said, "so that would be perfect timing."

"That play has too much death and not enough life," the duke said, giving Joan a wry smile. "It would be enlivened by the arrival of a new family member. Are you both ready for the night?"

"The only part of the performance that worries me is the sword fight," Joan said. "I've been practicing walking about with Alaric's rapier, but that's not the same as pulling it out and trying to kill someone with it."

"All I have to do is practice throwing flowers," Otis said smugly. He plucked some violets from the blue finger glass before his plate and offered them to Joan with a smirk. "Violets for . . . for . . . don't tell me! For thoughts?"

"You really need to memorize your lines," Joan told him. "Ophelia says she can't give out any violets because they all withered when her father died."

"She's mad as a March hare, so what does she know?" Otis muttered, shaking water from his hand.

"When will the theater troupe arrive?" the Duchess of Lindow asked.

"In three days," Joan said, excitement shining from her eyes.

Lady Knowe rose, so all the men did as well. She skirted the table and stopped at Thaddeus's shoulder. "I trust you know what you're doing," she said in a low voice.

He bowed.

In the old days, he probably would have met her eyes and said, "Always."

Not true any longer.

Thaddeus had lost his unshakable understanding of the world, rooted in his birth and his title. He'd never understood how much he leaned on his birthright before the prospect of it being torn away was presented to him in no uncertain terms by his own father.

He had no idea why he was supporting Joan's mad adventure either. He wouldn't have done it two years ago. He had considered himself a lion in his den, or an eagle in his aerie: solitary due to birth rather than choice.

Condemned to solitude by his title. Virtuous to the bone.

But now?

Chapter Eight

Three days later, they were running through the scene in which Ophelia, in the grip of madness, strews flowers around the throne room. Thaddeus was reading the extra male roles, and Aunt Knowe the queen's.

"Why does Ophelia have to pass out flowers?" Otis complained, dropping his book. "I feel like an oyster woman at Billingsgate handing out samples. And what's more, I don't even believe Ophelia *is* mad."

"I do," Thaddeus said. "The person she loved had no honor, and it broke her spirit. We don't have words for that betrayal in English, so she's talking with flowers instead."

"You really think Hamlet betrayed her?" Joan asked uncertainly. Her vision of Hamlet was more heroic, using his rapier to conquer pirates and avenge his father.

"The man was obsessed by revenge and ruling the kingdom," Thaddeus said. "He threw Ophelia to the side, because she was secondary to his ambitions. He didn't care what happened to her."

Looking at Thaddeus's hard jaw and flinty eyes, Joan had the distinct feeling that she had misunderstood the man. He wasn't cold, but rather explosive. Not uncaring, but caring too much.

He wasn't a stick.

"Nasty," Otis said, twirling the flower he was holding. "I still think she should have had more backbone and just kicked him in—" He caught himself. "Sorry, Joan. You're dressed in breeches, and it's inspiring me to ignore the niceties."

"*I* am here, and wearing a gown," Aunt Knowe observed.

Otis hopped to his feet and bowed, ignoring his skirts. "How could I possibly ignore the sparkling, sinful queen, Hamlet's mother?"

"You are no Shakespeare," Aunt Knowe laughed. "Shall we continue?"

"I think I know enough of my lines," Otis said, plopping down again. "For God's sake, no one needs me to be letter perfect. Joan, we want your little siblings to understand what's going on, right?"

"You're skipping almost everything Ophelia says," Joan protested.

"You can't want me to repeat, *By cock, they are to blame,* in front of your little sister. We can give the nursery a heads-up: When I begin throwing flowers around and bleating about true love, I'm heartbroken. If I go on about it too much, they'll want to throw me in the brook themselves."

Thaddeus cleared his throat, but the family

butler, Prism, appeared at the door of the sitting room before he could speak.

"The baby!" Aunt Knowe cried, jumping up and throwing her copy of the play to the side.

"No, my lady," Prism said, bowing. "Not the child, but the theater troupe. Their wagons are drawing up in the usual place behind the stables. I have informed them that the west ballroom is theirs for rehearsal."

Aunt Knowe dropped back into her seat with a thud. "Thank goodness! You can rehearse with them from now on. I am worn out, having to read through this wretched play so many times."

Joan gave her a beaming smile. "You are free, oh best of aunts. Otis and I will rehearse with the actors."

From the corner of her eye, she saw Thaddeus's eyelashes flicker. Never mind the fact that she had haunted the ballroom during the troupe's visit every year since she turned fourteen. He wouldn't—

"I shall join you," he stated, his voice as uncompromising as his expression.

"I don't need a chaperone," Joan said, impatience leaking into her voice.

"I do," Otis said, grinning. "What if one of the actors is overcome by lust for my flowery self and can't restrain himself? Thaddeus can put a rapier through his gizzard."

"Do not even think of it," Aunt Knowe advised Thaddeus. "If you stab an actor, the cast would be short a body, and I, for one, refuse to spend more than another hour or two with this wretched play."

"Presumably two actors normally play Hamlet and Ophelia," Thaddeus pointed out.

"They'll have to remain in the audience, overcome with envy when they see my dashing performance of the mad miss," Otis said.

Joan got to her feet. "Let's go meet the troupe. Thaddeus, if you're certain you want to join us, come along."

He rose without a word and paced after them. The ballroom was filled with a crowd of familiar faces, since the theater troupe came every year. Stagehands were briskly stringing a green velvet curtain to the rear of the low stage, creating a dressing area.

Mr. Wooty, the head of the troupe, bustled toward Joan, a welcoming smile on his face. He was well over six feet, with a tapering shape, like a bass viol turned upside down. His shoulders were broad, and everything from there dwindled down to his feet. For all the oddity of his physical appearance, he managed to play a majestic king or a loathsome thief, whichever was required.

"My lady!" He stopped and gave her a sweeping bow, the sort that befitted a queen.

She laughed and swept him a curtsy, even though she was in breeches. "How are you, Mr. Wooty? And the rest of the troupe?"

"We're in the pink, my lady, in the pink."

"May I introduce our Ophelia, Mr. Murgatroyd?" Joan asked. "Otis, this is Mr. Wooty, who has visited the castle once a year since I was a girl. He taught me everything I know about acting."

Otis began to bow, caught himself, and managed to sink into a curtsy only to have to catch his hat before it toppled to the ground.

Mr. Wooty's mouth opened and shut, before he said, "That is a most remarkable headpiece, Mr. Murgatroyd."

"Very Ophelia," Otis told him proudly. "The girl liked flowers, after all."

"When it's not on your head, it can double for a fairy hill," Mr. Wooty said. "You're not beautiful, sir, but you'll do, especially if the family squints. Lady Joan, you are looking quite royal."

Joan grinned. "I also brought a friend along to enjoy our rehearsals, Mr. Wooty. Lord Greywick, may I introduce Mr. Wooty, the amazing and talented impresario of the Theatre Royal?"

"So you play the part of Shakespeare, running the company?" Thaddeus asked, nodding to the director.

"I do indeed," Mr. Wooty said. "Without the playwriting, of course. We'll start proper rehearsals tomorrow morning, but for the moment I'd like to introduce Hamlet and Ophelia to the cast and just run over a few lines."

"May I speak to you afterwards?" Joan asked. "I have a favor to ask. Another favor, that is, because I am so grateful that you are allowing Otis and me this opportunity."

"For you, anything," Mr. Wooty said.

He turned to Thaddeus. "From the moment Lady Joan walked into one of our rehearsals a decade ago, I realized that she has a rare talent. It's a shame that she was born to the castle. I know most wouldn't agree with me, but that's the truth of it."

"We don't always fit the mantles we're born to," Thaddeus said quietly.

Joan thought that was an interesting comment, since of all the gentlemen whom she'd met in her life, Thaddeus was the one person most suited to his position in life.

Mr. Wooty clapped, and the cast clustered around.

Joan couldn't stop smiling as she greeted old friends and was introduced to new faces. Otis kept doing a reasonable job of curtsying.

A young woman with wheat-colored hair and eyes the color of dark jade came to join them. Otis promptly forgot to curtsy and bowed instead.

"My niece, Mademoiselle Madeline Wooty," Mr. Wooty said. "She grew up in France with my brother, God rest his soul, and joined the troupe a month ago. Madeline inherited a flair for the dramatic from her mother."

Just as I did, Joan thought.

Although Madeline was presumably not illegitimate.

Madeline curtsied before Joan. "How do you do, Lady Joan?"

Joan bowed. "It's lovely to meet you, Miss Wooty. Please call me Joan. After all, we're going to be rehearsing for long hours, if nothing has changed from previous years."

Madeline giggled. "That is true. My uncle never seems to think that a scene is perfect, even if we all know our lines."

"Every single line?" Otis said, looking alarmed. "I shall disappoint him, I'm afraid."

"I have been playing Ophelia in the last few weeks, sir," Madeline said to Otis. "Perhaps I can be of assistance."

"I would be most grateful," Otis said, giving her a smile so lavish that Joan blinked.

"We might practice your lines while the cast rehearses other scenes," Madeline suggested. "Ophelia is rarely on the stage, after all."

"Let's begin," Mr. Wooty bawled, turning toward the stage. "We'll run through the play with properties, no lines, so we begin to master the entrances and exits. Mr. Garnish, you're playing Claudius and the Ghost, so I'd advise you to be quick in putting on the Ghost's armored headpiece. Mrs. Wooty, you're Hamlet's mother. You'll need to paste a few more jewels on your crown, or Ophelia's hat will steal your thunder."

Mrs. Wooty had once told Joan that it was better to be a lady than an actress, as acting was backbreaking labor. Yet she climbed onto the stage with a cheerful wave, popped a tarnished crown on her head, and transformed into a queen with the flick of an eyelash.

Joan marched toward the stage. For the first time in her life, she was *part* of the troupe instead of being a bystander, longing to be on stage. She couldn't stop smiling.

Thaddeus crossed to a chair by the wall and sat down.

Mr. Wooty called the characters to the stage, one by one.

Hamlet was last.

Joan walked forward, hand on her rapier, and put on her "Lord Greywick" expression. She couldn't think of it as Thaddeus's any longer. He had become a far more complicated person to her.

"Not bad," Mr. Wooty said, narrowing his eyes. "You'll need a codpiece, though. Dunny!"

The stagehand stuck his head from behind the curtain where he was organizing important properties—like the skull Hamlet talked to. Joan couldn't wait to do that scene.

"Fit Hamlet with a codpiece!"

"No," Thaddeus said, from the side. He didn't raise his voice, but the word reached every wall of the ballroom, and they all froze.

"Right!" Mr. Wooty said. "No codpiece."

"She may wear a codpiece, but it will be fitted by her maid," Thaddeus clarified.

Wooty nodded. "Moving on."

The afternoon seemed to pass far too quickly. Joan had never felt so happy. She felt self-conscious launching into her first speech, but it wasn't about *her*. The important thing was the play as a whole.

Thaddeus didn't go to sleep, or even look bored. He sat at the side of the room watching closely. He didn't say anything, but she could feel his gaze, like a warm blanket around her shoulders.

When the stagehand passed her a skull—a *real skull!*—she felt an incredible thrill, holding it up to the late afternoon light. Afterward, she couldn't stop herself from glancing over at Thaddeus.

He gave her a small, secret smile, and warmth poured down her back.

When the ballroom began to grow dark, Prism entered and asked Joan whether she would like the great chandeliers lowered from the ceiling so the candles could be lit.

"Mr. Wooty?" she asked. Even deferring to her theater director was a thrill. It meant she was part of something other than the Wilde family.

He shook his head. "It's been a long day." Mr. Wooty turned to the troupe. "We'll start at eight in the morning, everyone in costume." He pointed to Otis. "You, young Ophelia, I'd like you to stay in your women's garb night and day until the performance. Practice walking like a woman, thinking like a woman. Speaking might be too much to ask."

Otis nodded.

Mr. Wooty turned to Joan. "The fencing scenes are a problem. Is there someone in the castle who can give you some basic instruction in dueling? As you saw, our Laertes is a hearty lad, and it strains belief to think that you could offer him a match, let alone kill him."

"I can teach Lady Joan," Thaddeus said, moving forward.

"Excellent," Mr. Wooty said. "Put the stage back in order, everyone!"

"Are you comfortably situated?" Joan asked him.

"Entirely," Mr. Wooty said. "We like to sleep in our wagons, as you know, my lady. Mr. Prism has promised us a fine feast tonight, which we've been looking forward to since we left London."

From the corner of her eye, Joan saw that Thaddeus had turned away to chat with Otis and Madeline.

"May I speak to you for a moment, Mr. Wooty?" she asked.

"Of course, my dear."

She led him to the other side of the room, and they sat down on two of the chairs lined against the wall.

"Now what can I do for you?" Mr. Wooty asked. "Your command of the text is perfect, as I would have expected. It's unusual to have a woman playing the role, but I reckon that you'll manage it in such a way that no one will feel anything missing."

"That's what I wanted to talk to you about," Joan said. "You see, Mr. Wooty, my family will clap no matter what I do, even if I forget all my lines."

"That's a good thing," Mr. Wooty observed. "Young Mr. Murgatroyd has a willing heart, but memorization appears to be a challenge."

"Otis was a vicar for two weeks, but only after six years of preparation," Joan confided. "It took him a month to memorize the doxology."

"Madeline will improve his grasp," Mr. Wooty said. He gave Joan a direct look. "My niece is a good girl, and I'm pleased to hear that Mr. Murgatroyd was a man of the cloth, albeit for a short period."

"Otis is very honorable," Joan assured him. Then she just burst out with her request. "Mr. Wooty, do you suppose that Otis and I could come along to your opening in Wilmslow and act our parts again? I have always longed to perform in front of a real audience."

Mr. Wooty frowned. "As if you were a member of my troupe?"

"Who's to know?" Joan asked. "I'm not well-known in Wilmslow, and Otis has never been there in his life."

"My understanding is that a lady's reputation is all important," Mr. Wooty said. "What of your gentleman?"

"What?"

"Lord Greyslick," Mr. Wooty said, jerking his head toward the other side of the ballroom.

"Grey*wick*," Joan corrected. "He's not *mine*! He simply volunteered himself to be a chaperone. You needn't worry about my safety, because he volunteered himself to come to Wilmslow as well, and between him and Otis, I shall be perfectly safe."

"Not yours?" Mr. Wooty asked, chuckling. "He didn't take his eyes off you, Lady Joan."

"He could never marry me," she said, telling him the truth because. . . . why not? "He'll be a duke someday." Then it occurred to her that perhaps Mr. Wooty wasn't aware of her irregular parentage, but he merely nodded.

Because, in case she had ever wondered, the truth was that all of England knew of her Prussian father and adulterous mother.

"We don't even like each other," she continued. "He is simply a friend of the family, with an oversized sense of responsibility. He's afraid that I'll be ruined by playing the role of Hamlet, even here in the castle, but I think he's far too old-fashioned."

"It is a bold move," Mr. Wooty said, looking up and over her shoulder. "Your marital future is no concern of mine, Lady Joan. I've told you before, and I'll say it again; you're a rare actress, and if you have a mind to leave the castle—and your father agrees—I would take you with me in the blink of an eye. I would build you a new wagon, fit for my lead actress."

"She is a lady, a duke's daughter, not an actress," a deep voice said.

Joan turned. Thaddeus was staring down at them, wearing his most enigmatic, judgmental expression. She sighed. "You really must stop popping up, looking as if you'd like an excuse to stab someone with a rapier."

Thaddeus glanced down at his drumming fingers and stilled his hand. He looked back at Mr. Wooty. "Lady Joan will never sleep in a wagon, new or not."

"Just as I thought," Mr. Wooty said, nodding.

"Thaddeus, stop being so difficult," Joan said. "Lord Greywick will accompany me and Otis to Wilmslow, Mr. Wooty."

"As will my mother, the Duchess of Eversley," Thaddeus said.

Joan threw him a grateful look; his phrasing was so wily that she might have constructed the sentence herself. She had a constitutional dislike of lying, but she found that any number of uncomfortable truths could be blurred with the correct wording.

"My mother complains that standards have fallen since the days of Good Queen Bess," Mr. Wooty mused. "I can scarcely believe that the duke will allow his daughter to perform on the public stage, let alone in breeches. And yet a duchess will accompany you, as if to no more than a May outing!"

Joan didn't correct him, and Thaddeus held his tongue as well.

"Mr. Murgatroyd as Ophelia poses something of a drawback for the Wilmslow performance," Mr. Wooty pointed out. "Not, I hasten to add, in the bosom of the family, but before a general audience."

"Surely, not an overwhelming problem," Thaddeus said. "One performance, and you're on your way, with no one the wiser for one regrettable evening. Surely, such irritating issues crop up frequently? I would, of course, insist on offering compensation for any losses."

"'The show must go on' is a rule that has resulted in any number of lackluster performances," Mr. Wooty agreed. "A drunk Hamlet is sad to see, especially during those fight scenes. A colleague of mine had an even worse situation: His Macbeth was having an affair with Malcolm's wife, and so he skewered his fellow actor in Act Five. That company won't say the name of the play aloud as a result."

"Otis is not violent," Joan said encouragingly.

"I'm worried about vegetables," Mr. Wooty said.

She knit her brow. "In what sense?"

"Audiences sometimes entertain themselves by throwing tomatoes if they're not enjoying the performance," Thaddeus explained.

"Even a marrow, now and then," Mr. Wooty said resignedly. "Though Wilmslow has not proved an excitable crowd in the past."

"We'll hire people to stand at the door and remove any marrows that an audience member might have on their person," Thaddeus said calmly.

"Excellent," Mr. Wooty said, looking relieved.

"Those men can't be in livery," Joan told Thaddeus. "That might lead to someone suspecting the Wildes are somehow involved."

"Certainly not."

"This brings to mind another problem," Mr. Wooty said. "The fencing. In Act Five. You'll have to be even more convincing than I originally thought. Our regular audiences love derring-do far more than long soliloquies."

"Lord Greywick will help me," Joan said.

Mr. Wooty's brow wrinkled. "You'll need to fight a proper duel in Wilmslow. Much of the audience gets through the language just waiting for the swords to come out."

"I will instruct Lady Joan in the art of dueling," Thaddeus said.

She glanced up at him. "You've never been in a duel in your life!" Thaddeus seemed so in control of his every movement and word; it was hard to imagine him feeling the need to do more than glance down his nose at a miscreant who dared insult him.

"At Eton, we were forced to perform plays," he said. "I learned how to slide a sword beneath an armpit, for example."

"Teach Lady Joan how to fall," Mr. Wooty said to Thaddeus. "You can work with her the next two afternoons, and I'll start her with Laertes the day after." He bounded to his feet. "I'll agree to Wilmslow. But I won't tell the troupe until that night, in case you change your mind after playing Hamlet. It isn't the easiest part."

"Will the person who normally plays Hamlet mind?" Joan asked. If she were in the troupe, she would spend all day longing for the moment when she stepped on the stage.

"Not he," Mr. Wooty said. "He's still in London flirting with any pretty girl who will give him the time of day. He has a fine royal nose, and ladies admire it."

"But I'll be on the stage in his place," Joan said.

"He won't care," Mr. Wooty said with finality. "You're thinking the life of an actor is all about the passion for the role, my lady. It's brutal work, and Caballero—as plays my Hamlet—isn't the sort of man who does more than what's required."

"How disappointing," Joan sighed.

"Why?" Thaddeus asked.

"I imagine actors, especially lead actors, relishing a cloud of Shakespearean language. A sour prince one night, and a villain the next."

Mr. Wooty smiled wryly. "It's a hard life, my lady. For those of us with the passion and the backbone for it, there's nothing else. Caballero is a brilliant actor, but he will walk out on me one of these days. He's just biding his time."

"Not fair," Joan said. "So many people would like to be lead actors!"

"Presumably he has the talent, and the others do not," Thaddeus said. "He's playing the roles for money, one would assume."

"That's it," Mr. Wooty said. "Caballero is impatient with applause, if you can believe it. Another actor can wither if an audience doesn't like his performance, but he just laughs. All right. Enough of him!"

He clapped his hands. "Time for dinner!"

Chapter Nine

*W*here shall we practice dueling?" Thaddeus asked Joan the next day, when Mr. Wooty dismissed them after a morning of rehearsal. Otis would be drilled in his lines by Madeline all afternoon, a fate he seemed to welcome.

"Outside, don't you think?" Joan asked. "So I can learn how to fall. Also, so that no one can see me make a fool of myself."

Thaddeus agreed. To learn how to fence properly, she'd have to take off her coat. And he'd be damned if anyone ever saw her rear again.

Except for him.

But he didn't count. *Friend of the family*, she had called him.

"I'm hungry," he said.

"We can stop by the kitchens and ask Cook for a picnic," Joan said.

Thaddeus had been thinking along the lines of several courses, eaten comfortably at a table. Instead, he was handed a weighty basket.

"I know just the place," Joan said, heading

down one of the castle's many narrow corridors. "There's a lovely spot on the island, on the other side of the apple orchard."

To his surprise, the corridor led to the library. Lindow was so sprawling, and had been added to and elaborated upon by so many owners, that once inside a person could lose his sense of direction altogether. They walked through the library onto a terrace.

"We call this Peacock Terrace. There's Fitzy!" Joan said, trotting down the marble steps to the lawn.

Fitzy—an aging but still majestic peacock— paced toward them, dragging his tail in the grass.

"He's frightfully old," Joan said. "Drat! I usually have bread in my pocket, but these breeches are hopeless. The pockets are terribly small; I can't imagine how you gentlemen manage."

The peacock came a few steps closer and flicked his tail, as if to suggest that he could raise it if he wished, but they weren't worth the trouble.

"Don't step forward, because he'll realize you're a man and become exceedingly annoyed," Joan said. She'd taken the basket from Thaddeus and was rooting around in it. "He loathes the male sex."

"Every one?" Thaddeus asked, rather startled.

"He tolerates my brothers," Joan said. "Isn't it interesting that he doesn't mind me, even though I'm in breeches? I gather he responds to something more innate than clothing."

Fitzy gobbled up the bread she threw, but Thaddeus noticed that he cocked his head to the side, keeping a close watch. Sure enough, when Joan stepped back onto the path, leaving Thaddeus in clear view, Fitzy's head jerked up.

His tail followed: a magnificent fan of blue and green feathers, waving in the breeze caused by displaying all that plumage. Fitzy's shining eyes bent on Thaddeus, he scratched one claw in the dirt and opened his beak very wide, throwing his head back.

"Time to go," Joan said. "He'll be cross at me for two days for bringing a male into his territory."

Sure enough, Fitzy's curses followed them across the lawn. When they plunged into a wood, they could still hear him issuing challenges.

Thaddeus followed Joan's slender, upright form out the other side of the wood and into an apple orchard.

A white goat gamboled toward them, some strands of grass sticking to his whiskers, a frayed rope at his neck. "Gully! I'm happy to introduce you to Gulliver, who likes to travel, obviously," Joan told Thaddeus, scratching the goat's forehead. "Gully mostly spends his time in the orchard, but always goes home to the stable at night, so we don't worry about him."

"Goats are herd animals," Thaddeus said. "Is he entirely alone?"

"He's a Lindow castle goat," Joan explained. "Not your ordinary type. He seems to disdain his fellows. The stables were built for one hundred and twenty-two horses, but we have far fewer these days, so Gully has a group of friendly nanny-goats who reside with him. Most days he escapes and spends the day in the orchard or the back lawn."

"One hundred and twenty-two horses," Thaddeus said, struck by the number.

"The stables were meant to hold about that many hounds as well, and then there's the cow barn and so on. Gully is not fond of other goats, and certainly not cows or hounds. He prefers to be alone."

Thaddeus nodded. "He has magnificent horns." They rose in an extravagant twist above Gully's head before they curled backward.

"Apparently he was dangerous before his horns grew backwards. Now he can't poke them into anyone. Father says he's a ducal goat, too ornamental for ordinary company."

"That's a rather sad characterization of a duke's life," Thaddeus said, taking his turn scratching Gulliver, who had sidled up to him and began sniffing his shoes in a way that suggested he would be happy to start chewing leather rather than grass. "No," he told him.

Gulliver obediently raised his head and rubbed it against Thaddeus's coat, demanding petting in lieu of leather.

"Father claims it's a lonely business being a duke. Aunt Knowe just laughs and says that without the family, his head would swell like a bladder," Joan said.

"From compliments?" Thaddeus inquired.

"All the people bowing and scraping."

"Not an attractive vision but perhaps accurate," he admitted.

"Gully will keep you scratching his head all day," Joan said. "I'll distract him with luncheon."

She took the basket again, knelt, and pulled out some grapes. "Luncheon, Gully!"

Gulliver deserted Thaddeus and trotted over to her. They left him meditatively eating grapes under an apple tree, and continued through the orchard until the path wound down a gentle slope to end at an ornamental lake.

At some point in the past, the lake had been turned into an artistic refuge for gentlepersons to enjoy nature without a hint of nature's irritating irregularities; the round lake was dotted with a round island, punctuated by a marble cupola with a round roof.

"This is the lake that your great-grandfather dug into a circle?" Thaddeus asked.

Joan nodded. "My grandfather built that temple thing for my grandmother," she said, waving at the island. "The one that looks like a third of an eggshell with legs."

"A monopteron," Thaddeus observed.

She raised an eyebrow.

"A circular temple supported by pillars, without a cella, or an enclosed portion."

"My father says the island was grassy and perfectly tended when he was a boy, but since he doesn't care for pleasure gardens, the children took it over years ago, before I was born."

"By 'took it over,' you mean that they banished gardeners?" Thaddeus inquired. The environs of the lake were overgrown, with huge willows trailing in the water all around the shore, where wild cherry trees stood cheek by jowl with beeches. Reeds grew in profusion, and the lake itself was covered with a carpet of water lilies.

"Exactly," Joan said, heading down the low mound that led to the lake. "Apparently, the second duchess—my mother—wanted to clear the nettles and cut the weeds, but my older brothers kicked up a fuss. My father overruled her. The boys were always searching for lost treasure back then, and he thought the pond was safer than the bog."

"In lieu of silver, there might be good fishing in the pond," Thaddeus said, staring down at the water. They were close enough that he could just see a small frog sitting on a lily pad, using its white flower as a parasol.

"Carp," Joan said. "Alaric complained last time he was here that the water was choked, and they weren't growing very large. I'm going to presume that since you do everything well, you row as well," she said, giving Thaddeus an impudent look.

He'd captained his rowing crew at Cambridge. "I can row."

"Excellent," she said happily, toeing off her shoes. "Be sure to leave your wig here. And your shoes. One of my sisters-in-law, Diana, still complains about losing one of her shoes in the lake. Now we all drop them here, on the grass."

Thaddeus lifted off his wig and placed it on the slope, running his fingers thankfully through his hair.

"And your stockings!" Joan added. "Just think about how long it will take to get grass stains out of white silk. Your valet will have hysterics."

Thaddeus paid his valet well over the normal wage expressly so that the man would never speak of uninteresting topics, such as stain removal. But he obediently removed his stockings.

Joan's stockings were clocked up the side and elegant enough for a prince. Her legs were slender and touched with gold hair that glinted in the sunlight. Her toes curled in the grass, and she looked up at him with a smile that swept him into its joy. "I am having a wonderful day. Even though—"

She broke off.

"Even though you're stuck with me," he supplied, turning to put his folded stockings on top of his shoes.

"You have to admit that we haven't been friends," she said defensively. "That is, we aren't friends now either. You are doing a favor to the family, and I realize that."

"Why would you say that we're not friends?"

"We're far too different."

He glanced down at himself. He had always been tall, but he'd never felt more of a hulking beast in his life. His legs were hairy and bulged with muscle.

Her eyes followed his. "No, I don't mean the fact that your legs could provide the supports for a bridge. Nor even that you are a man, and I am only pretending to be one."

He raised an eyebrow.

"Just what do you mean by that?" she asked. "I feel as if we communicated without words over dinner the other night. It's a new language for me, so I can't be expected to interpret your every expression."

While he tried to think how to answer her, Joan wriggled out of her tight coat. "Luckily, you won't be shocked by the sight of my rear end," she said blithely.

She was wrong. Before he could avert his eyes, she bent over to put her coat down beside her shoes and her wig. Her bottom was surprisingly plump and round for such a slender woman; like her breasts, it seemed to be designed to bring a man to his knees.

The shock that jolted his body definitely wasn't horror. It was a tide of lust over which he had absolutely no control. His cock fought the restriction of his breeches, which meant he could not remove his coat.

With another young lady, perhaps.

An innocent maiden who wouldn't have any idea what was straining his breeches, or wouldn't dream of glancing below his waist. But Joan? With her jests about foreplay and penetration? She might guess that his desire for her was nearly out of control. The very idea was horrific.

Luckily, Joan didn't even glance at him. She quickly unwrapped her neck cloth, dropped it, and pulled off her waistcoat.

He had joined the hordes of men who couldn't control themselves around her. Who proved their idiocy by succumbing to her smile or the way she touched their arms.

One would think that depressing realization would make his cockstand go down, but no.

Joan scrambled down the bank. "We're lucky because sometimes the boat drifts under the willow," she said, bending over to untie the rope from the gunwale of the rowboat. "It's hard to pull through the reeds."

Thaddeus remained where he was, willing himself under control and failing utterly.

"Aren't you coming?" she asked, straightening and turning back to him. Her cheeks were flushed with exertion.

He caught back a groan by the slimmest of margins.

She cast him a narrow glance but apparently saw nothing, as her dimpled smile appeared again—not the seductress one, but the smile she gave family—and she pointed at the basket. "I'm ravenous, and there should be a few scraps of food left that we didn't give to Fitzy or Gully. Come on, let's get over to the island. Aren't you going to take off your coat? You'll be as hot as a black pudding by the time we get to the island."

Thaddeus gave a firm shake of his head. Another woman might have argued with him, but he was coming to know Joan: Perhaps because of her unusual background, she was remarkably accepting. She offered advice; he refused; that was the end of it.

"I'm nominating you to row," she announced.

Thaddeus untied and unwound his starched white neck cloth and added it to his belongings.

"Don't forget to remove your rapier before you get into the boat," he said, picking up the basket.

"Why?" She began obediently fumbling with the buckle.

"Always put it to the side in a carriage—or a boat."

"All right." She nodded, and he recognized with a bolt of something very like shame that he felt happy whenever she listened to him, when he was able to protect her from some danger.

His deep-seated happiness was entirely inappropriate. Unfounded.

Joan clambered into the boat, put her hilted rapier on her lap, and watched as he stowed the basket at her feet and sat down. "You look as proper as a gentleman in Hyde Park." Then she glanced down and broke into giggles. "Even your feet are elegant for a man. Does your valet put wax on your toes?"

He was concentrating on his grandmother's wart so that hopefully, by the time he got to the island, he could remove his blasted coat. "Wax? Why?" He put the oars in the water and gave them a powerful wrench that sent the rowboat skimming through the water lilies.

"To remove hair, of course," Joan cried. "Haven't you ever discussed hairy toes with other men?"

He glanced down at her delicately shaped ankles and slender feet as he pulled the oars again. "Your maid waxes your toes?"

She laughed. "Not women's, *men's*. Gentlemen's, to be precise. My brothers once had a lively conversation about their disdain for such gentlemanly practices. You haven't a single hair on your toes. So, Thaddeus—"

With another silent groan, he acknowledged the fact that his name on her lips was more powerful than the memory of his grandmother's wart. At this rate, he'd sweat through his coat before he could take it off.

Whatever she meant to say was thankfully interrupted when they bumped into the shore of the island. He had managed to maneuver the boat so they arrived at the dilapidated landing, scarcely visible through mounds of water-crowfoot and lilies so thick that he upended the oar and stuck it into the muck to guide the boat through them.

Joan climbed forward and then scrambled off the boat, giving him a marvelous view of her rear.

Again.

Thaddeus stowed the oars while she was tying up the boat and took the opportunity to give himself a lecture.

She wasn't for him. He wasn't for her.

Given his father's stated wish to disinherit him and, even worse, declare him illegitimate based on a wedding that supposedly occurred between the duke and his mistress prior to his documented wedding, Thaddeus had to marry in the very highest rank of society in order to fight off challenges to his dukedom.

Lady Bumtrinket didn't even know that scandalous detail, nor did anyone else in polite society.

The last thing he could do was marry a woman who blithely flaunted her irregular birth.

Not that he wanted to marry Joan.

This flaring, mad desire was part and parcel with the confusion in his life. No one knew about his father's claims, which meant that no one except solicitors knew that his father had gone stark raving mad.

He preferred to think of the problem as madness, rather than acknowledge that his father disliked him so much that he would do anything to disinherit his eldest in favor of his first "real" son, in the duke's words. His "real" wife.

That did it.

Thankfully, his cock lay quiescent as Thaddeus hoisted the basket and followed Joan out of the boat. She seemed to dance through the reedy shrubbery, but he found himself walking slowly, his bare feet prickling with the strange feeling of being shoeless. It wasn't unpleasant, but it was new.

A boy who is a future duke hardly touches the ground; he'd had no one to play with, and his nursemaids, and later his tutors, preferred improving activities to mucking about barefoot. He swore silently when he trod on a briar but all the same, the feeling was exhilarating.

At the top of the mound, he put down the basket and wrestled off his close-fitting coat. Sure enough, the lining was soaked with sweat.

"The boys used to play in the temple," Joan said, waving at the simple structure made from white marble with airy columns and a round roof. "The mono-whatever-you-called-it. I'll show you my favorite place that they don't even know about." She threw a conspiratorial glance over her shoulder.

Bloody hell.

He lost control again. He slung his coat over the basket and held the two of them in just the right position as he followed her.

A narrow path wound around the side of the temple and wandered off through honeysuckle bushes thick with blossoms. A heady perfume hung in the air as his shoulders brushed flowers on either side.

"Did you know that if you plant honeysuckle around the door of your house, a witch can't enter?" Joan tossed over her shoulder. The path bent right, and she disappeared around the curve before he could think of an answer. Was there an answer?

If she hadn't disappeared, he might have dropped the basket and kissed her, by way of answer. Thaddeus stopped for a moment to collect himself. The last two years had been horrific. That was no excuse to lose his mind now.

Taking a deep breath, he followed the path again.

Joan's favorite place on the island turned out to be a small, weedy clearing marked out by a few yellowing larch trees and enough honeysuckle shrubs to crowd out sprouts that might have sprung from larch cones. A bee swooped by his head, and he realized the air hummed with the sound of industry.

"Isn't it wonderful?" Joan asked happily. "Here, let me have the basket. We can eat before we practice fencing."

Thaddeus put the basket down, and she unlatched the top, revealing a sky-blue cotton cloth that billowed as she shook it out. He caught the far side while she ran about and pinned down the edges with four large stones left there for the purpose.

"Viola and I have come here for years," she explained, poking around behind a tall larch and pulling out a waxed cloth bag. "I was a horribly demanding sister. I made her read parts in Shakespeare plays over and over, until she detested the man and all his works." She untied the bag and tugged out two shabby pillows.

"Here's yours. That tree can be your chair. Viola would sit there, and I would make this space my stage."

"Every day?"

Joan nodded. "I'm afraid so. I would rush through lessons, waiting to grab Viola's hand and disappear. Our governess never found where we were going, though I don't suppose she tried hard. There are so many Wilde children, you see. Later, when we went away to school, we'd come here during school holidays unless it was too cold."

"Can you swim?" Thaddeus inquired, thinking that he would want to know if his little daughters were launching themselves in a rowboat across a lake.

"Oh, yes. We fell out of that boat a hundred times and quickly learned to paddle back. Sometimes we had to leave the boat behind and make for shore, and beg one of our older brothers to rescue it."

She knelt beside the basket and began pulling out wooden boxes, one with an elaborate glass painting on top, others with simple latches, one with an elaborate gilt design.

Thaddeus crouched beside her and picked up the glass-topped box.

"From China," Joan explained. "Alaric brought it back. The lady is painted in reverse on the back of the glass."

Thaddeus turned it over. "A beautiful piece. Oughtn't it to be residing in a cabinet somewhere?"

"My father doesn't believe in useless decorative objects," Joan said. She began to flip open the boxes. "None of us take snuff, so we use the boxes for picnics. We must have thirty or forty waiting in the kitchens. Sometimes the staff prepares three or four baskets in a single day."

"Even the stuffed alligator has its use," Thaddeus said, remembering Joan's soliloquy addressed to its disembodied head.

"The poor fellow is among the least practical objects in the castle, I have to admit. We're lucky! Cook's given us meat pies. Would you like one?" She held up a small, beautifully browned pie. "Or three? We had six, but we gave one to Gulliver. I don't want more than two."

"Three, please." He hesitated. "No fork or knife?"

"No need." She put his pies in a napkin and handed them over. Then she took a bite of the pie she held, and grinned at him, her lips shiny.

Thaddeus turned to the tree she had designated as his chair. He put down his pillow and sat on it.

Joan burst out laughing. "You don't sit *on* the pillow!" she cried. "You lean against it. Like this." She moved to lean against a tree opposite, her half-eaten meat pastry in her hand, looking indescribably lovely.

"You're very bossy," he observed, moving his pillow to his back.

Joan shrugged, eyes happy. "I was born to play Prince Hamlet."

"I believe that the French king and queen hold elegant picnics with china and silver cutlery, while sitting on silk-fringed pillows," Thaddeus said.

"Poppycock. Picnics are for friends and family, ants crawling in your food, and drinking wine in the open air. Everything tastes better outside. Aren't you going to eat? Cook's given us a feast. These pies are excellent."

Instead, he reached over and grabbed the wine bottle whose stem was peeking from the basket.

"Cups should be in the basket along with a corkscrew," Joan said lazily. Out of the corner of his eye, he saw her wiggle down into a more relaxed position as she began on a second meat tart.

The basket held two rather battered tin cups. He uncorked the bottle and poured wine into the cups and gave one to her. He wanted to ask how many men she'd shared a picnic with . . . and how many *here*, in her favorite place?

It wouldn't be polite.

"So picnics are a regular practice at Lindow," he said instead, wondering if his country estate had ever hosted a picnic. He doubted it very much.

"Of course," Joan said, sliding down onto her back and stuffing the pillow under her head. She crossed one leg over the other. "There's nothing better than grabbing a basket and heading out of the castle. The boys spent years of their life in the bog, Lindow Moss. Viola and I mostly came here."

She wrinkled her nose. "The bog smells like peat."

"I see." He had finished his pies, so he picked up a piece of crusty bread and looked over the open boxes. He put a slice of roast beef on the bread, and then a salty pickle, and leaned back against the tree trunk.

The bread was warm and fragrant, and the rare beef tasted better than anything he'd eaten in his life. The pickle exploded in his mouth. A blackberry bramble must be nearby, as he could smell berries, so warmed by the sun that they smelled like a pie in the oven.

"Did you have a special place on your estate for picnics?" Joan asked. "I don't believe I've ever visited Eversley Court, although I remember your mother inviting the family a few summers ago. That was very brave of her, given how many of us there are."

Thaddeus swallowed his bite. "I've never been on a picnic before."

Joan blinked at him. "That's so sad."

"Future dukes don't share meals with ants. Like French royalty, they don't eat without silver cutlery, and they drink from crystal goblets, not tin cups."

"Enough," she said, sighing. "My brother North is the ducal heir, if you remember, and he's been on a hundred picnics. I'm already sorry for you. You needn't beat the drum about the deficiencies of your childhood."

Sun filtered through the trees, bouncing off the honeysuckle flowers and spangling Joan's hair and face with dancing flecks of light. Thaddeus swallowed his bite and took another, suddenly aware that he'd never been so happy in his life.

On the other side of the blanket, Joan finished her second meat pie, shielding her eyes from the sun's glitter and staring into the oak leaves overhead. She started humming rather tunelessly, waggling the bare foot on her crossed leg. "I wish I had a more melodic voice," she said.

Happiness was not a manly pursuit. Thaddeus hadn't been taught to venerate it, chase it, or even acknowledge it. Dukes didn't care for such frivolities as feelings.

To be fair, he had hardened that concept into armor as he watched his father dive deeper and deeper into behavior dictated by feelings—his love for his other family. Perhaps his aversion to his father had turned an implicit lesson into a rigidly held rule.

And yet, here he was.

Happy.

He finished his wine and leaned over to splash more into Joan's cup. "Have you brought other men here for a picnic?" he asked, the words slipping out because he couldn't contain them.

She turned her face toward him, golden wisps of hair floating in the air, looking like a princess, albeit in breeches. And snorted again.

"You're jesting, right?"

He shook his head, thanking God that his napkin covered his lap. Her blue eyes didn't help his control. Or her delicately curved calf. Or her toes. God help him, he would like to nibble on her toes and then kiss his way up her leg.

"Forgive me if the question was too gauche."

"You really aren't from this century," Joan said, looking back up at the trees. "I couldn't possibly bring a man here. He might lose his head and molest me, to be blunt."

Thaddeus finished his wine. He could feel a lazy, sweet intoxication at the base of his neck, not so much from the wine as the air. At least, that's what he told himself. He had always been capable of matching gentlemen tossing back glass for glass of the best brandy and yet walking away steadily. But now . . .

"I am a man," he observed, picking up another piece of bread and putting a slice of chicken on top.

"Try it with a slice of plum," Joan ordered, pointing.

"Plum? One doesn't eat plum with chicken."

"Just try it."

She truly was bossy. But he tried it. The sweet, slightly bitter plum perfectly married the juicy chicken.

"Have you ever had plum jerkum?" Joan asked. She had rolled over on her side so she could reach the boxes and was making herself a bread stack like his.

"No."

"It's a local drink that goes straight to your head," she advised. "Makes me giggle like a chimney with a draft. Viola and I used to sneak it sometimes."

Instantly he decided that plum jerkum was in his future. With Joan.

"I *am* a man," he repeated, once she was settled on her back, one knee braced over the other, toes waggling.

"You know what I mean."

He didn't.

If he was less of a gentleman, he would be next to her in a flash. Or on top of her. Braced on his arms over her, swooping down to kiss lips that glistened with plum juice.

She waved her bread, and drops of plum juice flew into the air, one landing on her cheekbone. "I mean that you're a duke, well, not quite a duke yet. But the key thing is that you're not interested in me."

She took a huge bite, and he had to wait until she finished chewing. Which was good, because it gave Thaddeus time to collect himself.

The hell he wasn't interested in her. He had *kissed* her. Kissed a marriageable young maiden: his first, since he had never approached her sisters in that fashion.

Had she no idea that he was staring at the drop of violet-colored plum juice on her cheek and thinking about licking it off?

"I could never bring any of my suitors here because they would take it as an invitation," Joan continued.

"You're certain that *I* won't?" His voice had dropped an octave, but she didn't seem to notice.

"Never."

She was right, of course.

The truth of it rang dully in his soul. He was bloodless, as she herself had said. She glanced sideways, and whatever she saw in his eyes made her sit up.

"Look, you don't understand. Two types of men court me."

"Yes?" He didn't care about her suitors, but it wouldn't be polite to say so.

"The first are those who are at the rank of squire or below: in short, from the gentry. For them, my beauty and dowry, combined with connections to a dukedom, are more than enough reason to write me worthless poetry and fall on their knees at any opportunity. They tend to court me with enthusiasm, expecting me to be fervently grateful that they are lowering themselves to a woman known to all as illegitimate."

Her tone was wry, but not bitter.

"I see," he said.

"The second aren't courting me. In fact, their mothers have explicitly warned them to stay away from me. For mothers, my hair is a version of the flags that the peat farmers erect near a marshy area."

"What sort of flag?"

"Danger." She moved forward and examined all the boxes again before she pulled out a ripe strawberry and bit it. "Men from the nobility don't want to marry me, because I am infamous, no matter what my father—to clarify, the duke—says." Her eyes sparkled with mischief. "Except sometimes I cannot stop myself from teasing them, as I told you before."

"By enticing them to kiss you," he filled in. "They then offer marriage, which you refuse."

"Exactly." She leaned over and patted his knee. "You are safe, as you yourself told me that you are invulnerable to my most enticing look. This one." She cast him that melting look, the one that announced he was the only man in the world whom she desired.

His cock responded with a jerk, so he snatched the napkin and wiped his mouth, sticking it hastily back in his lap.

The expression peeled off her face like water.

"You're immune to my charms, such as they are," she said. "Being a future duke, you can't marry me, and there's no pleasure in tormenting you by enticing you to kiss me. You're not afraid that my father will force you to marry me."

"I kissed you."

She shrugged. "Not because I invited it." She lay back down, apparently considering the subject closed.

He hated to admit it, but her reasoning was sound. He wouldn't take advantage of her. He couldn't marry her. They both knew it.

Still.

He tossed his napkin to the side and moved so that he was braced over her, knees on either side of her hips.

Her mouth opened, but no word escaped.

"You informed me that you wouldn't judge me based on our kiss in the snake tent," he said, scowling down at her.

She reached up and ran a finger over the crevice between his brows, forcing him to stop frowning. "So I did."

"You were not trying to entice me to kiss you then, or now."

Her face stilled, amusement gleaming in her eyes, not the carefully manufactured desire that she used as a weapon against unwary gentlemen. "No, I am not."

The drop of plum juice was high on one cheek, a violet shadow. "Perhaps I won't kiss you." He lowered his head and licked her cheekbone instead. The juice on his tongue was tart and sweet, like Joan.

She sucked in a breath.

"I don't care to be judged," he said silkily. He licked her other cheekbone, because he wanted to.

His heart was thudding in his chest. She lay under him, quiescent, blue eyes wide. Would he ever believe her if he saw desire in them? Yet he wanted to see that emotion in her eyes, more than anything.

"You should never bring any man here," he said, his voice harsh to his own ears. "The fallacy in your argument is your assumption that a man has to be enticed in order to want to kiss you."

"I trust you."

"You shouldn't."

Joan laughed at him. "You just informed me that you won't even kiss me! The gentlemen who were horrified at the idea of being forced to marry me were lower in rank than my father. You'll be a duke someday. You're the only man who's ever kissed me who's had *no fear* of my father!"

That wasn't entirely true.

In Thaddeus's estimation, the Duke of Lindow was a reasonable and calm man. But if Thaddeus injured one of his children? His Grace would slice him into ribbons, and no hereditary degree would prevent the ensuing bloodbath.

"If you won't kiss me," Joan said suddenly, "perhaps I will kiss you."

He stared down at her. "Why?"

Her cheeks turned rosy, and she fidgeted beneath him. No one can feign a blush.

"I've never kissed anyone," she admitted. "I've been kissed."

He waited.

Thaddeus was good at waiting. He stared down into her eyes, realizing something very important: Lady Joan Wilde made sure that people around her danced to her bidding.

He had every expectation that her father was privately flummoxed by the fact that he'd given permission for her to play the role of Hamlet. And then there was her close friend, Otis. Some men enjoyed dressing in women's clothing; Otis was not one of them.

With a sudden movement, Thaddeus straightened and moved back to his side of the picnic cloth. Joan turned her head and watched him. Then she sighed and looked back up at the sky. "Well played, Thaddeus."

His erection jerked against his stomach because—she said his name. If that reaction wasn't the stupidest thing he'd ever experienced, he didn't know what was.

Cleavage was enticing. Less so than when he was fourteen, but still delectable.

A delicately turned ankle, a shining pair of eyes, a slender waist.

But his name?

Simply his name, shaped by plush, laughing lips? From her, it was like a kiss.

"Would you like any more to eat?" he asked, leaning over to give her more wine.

"I'm starting to feel muzzy," Joan said. "I shouldn't drink too much. What if I skewer you by accident, once we begin practicing?"

"I brought these," he said, putting his hand in his pocket and pulling out the tips that were used in training.

"I'm afraid to pull this rapier from its scabbard," Joan confessed. "In the nursery, we had wooden swords. May I have a jam tart?"

He inspected the boxes and handed over a jam tart, the dough shaped into a blossom, with a ruby-red center. He took a couple for himself and sat back against the tree.

Joan was humming again.

Thaddeus was always thinking. He considered it intrinsic to his personality. When other men remarked that they hadn't bothered to follow a lecture, a speech, or a sermon, Thaddeus was always faintly surprised.

It wasn't in his power *not* to follow, to analyze, to dissect an argument.

Yet here, in a bee-loud glade, he just let himself be.

Taste jam. Watch a lovely woman hum to herself.

Be happy.

Chapter Ten

*J*oan was completely out of her depth. In the years since she debuted, she had happily played with fire, enticing boys to kiss her. She'd always made certain that they couldn't possibly take advantage of her.

And yet . . .

Here she was.

Thaddeus Erskine Shaw was no "boy." He was a man, sitting on the other side of the picnic cloth, eating a jam tart with as much enjoyment as if it were caviar. She had to swallow just looking at him.

A lock of dark gold hair kept falling over his eyes. His lashes were brown and very thick. Perhaps that was one reason why no one seemed to really know him; they were rarely able to meet his eyes.

Now she thought about it, she hadn't seen much of Thaddeus in the last two years, ever since Viola chose Devin. He had gracefully bowed out of that courtship when Viola married, of course.

In the last two years?

There was the ball when he finally asked her to dance after ignoring her for a month. She'd been too irritated by his neglect to dance with him.

Which led to the foolishness with Anthony Froude: not one of her finest moments, she had to admit.

"What have you been doing the last two years?" she asked, licking her fingers. "I've only seen you occasionally at balls and the like. You haven't been courting anyone, as far as I know?" She turned her head, raising an eyebrow.

"No."

"Here, is that your fourth jam tart?" she asked, sitting up. "I'd like another one, you greedy piglet."

He laughed, a sound that was deep and relaxed. She liked it.

Joan held a finger up in the air. "Stroke one on the calendar: future duke laughs. Or is that stroke two?"

"Three," he confirmed, handing her two tarts.

"In a week," Joan said. "Likely a record."

His mouth twisted in a wry smile that had nothing to do with humor.

Something was wrong. Thaddeus was so self-contained that she had the idea none of her brothers would know the problem, nor her brother-in-law Jeremy either, for all they'd been friends at Eton. Thaddeus wouldn't share problems with his mother, because he was instinctively protective. He adored the duchess, that was clear. He would never worry her.

Joan finished one of her tarts, thinking hard.

He wouldn't respond to a simple question. There was a cloak of self-possession around him that seemed to be part of his character. Maybe future dukes were taught to be prudent in that respect.

But no, her father had once told her that he assessed a man's strength by whether he was confident enough to admit he needed help. "Never choose a man who thinks he can rule the world," the duke had told her, years ago now. "Your marriage won't be a partnership."

Not that she had any intention of marrying Thaddeus, of course.

For one thing, it wasn't up to her.

He had cheerfully accepted her statement that he had no interest in marrying her. When she offered to kiss him, he promptly removed himself to the other side of the cloth.

The idea pinched, somehow. But what could she expect? He was so honorable that if they behaved improperly, he *would* feel obligated to marry her. Nothing to do with her father, and everything to do with honor.

He didn't want to marry her, of course.

He didn't want to.

It was odd how much she disliked that thought.

"So, the last two years?" she prompted, pushing away a train of thought that was likely to make her unhappy.

"I've engaged myself in the activities of a gentleman: nothing more, nothing less."

His voice was flat. Joan was more and more certain that something was wrong. But she had to be careful. Thaddeus would never answer a straightforward question.

"I've often wondered what gentlemen do all day," she said, changing the subject. She pointed at his chest. "You seem to have grown several inches around since I debuted, and not in the waist area. Since your coat is off, Lady Bumtrinket is wrong about your valet padding your garments. Have you been working with horses? My brother North complains that it's made him burly."

He glanced down. "Burly, I take it, is not a positive attribute."

Joan decided not to answer that. As far as she could see, Thaddeus's life had been a parade of one compliment after another. He didn't need any shoring up about his looks. He generally looked so immaculate and handsome that he could be mistaken for a porcelain statue of a duke.

Not at the moment, though. She stole another look at his legs. There was nothing soft about him. Burly was a definite compliment, not that she had any intention of telling him that.

"Gentlemen are by definition willowy," she said, instead. "Delicacy advertises high rank: white gloves, silken stockings prone to snags, towering wigs, cucumber diets even as others struggle to buy bread. A member of the nobility is a person who needn't work with his or her hands and advertises that fact."

"You would work as a stage actress, if life had dealt you a different hand of cards?"

"Yes. Even though being an actress is apparently brutally difficult work. Mrs. Wooty hopes for better for Madeline."

"What would that be?"

"Marriage to a man of business, perhaps." She looked at him over the rim of her cup. "Or to Otis. Did you notice how he brightened when she offered to help him learn his lines?"

"I did."

"I suppose you would consider it a terrible *mésalliance*. A diluting of noble blood. Or gentry blood, in this case."

"I have long believed that it is my responsibility to marry a woman from the nobility," Thaddeus responded, dodging the question. "Marriages should never be enacted on the basis of rash emotion. Marriage is a contract entered into for the betterment of an estate."

"That's cold," Joan said, thinking that she had to squash any weakness she felt for him *now*. Thaddeus truly was a bloodless fellow. The woman who married him would wither, given his general perfection, combined with lack of affection.

She got to her knees and began latching the wooden boxes that had held their lunch.

He immediately started helping her, and they closed the boxes in silence. "Napkin," Joan asked briskly, holding out her hand.

Thaddeus neatly folded his.

Awkward silences didn't happen often in Lindow Castle. There were too many people with big opinions, Joan among them. She had to accept Thaddeus's fencing lesson and then go home.

His hand brushed hers, and she caught a scent of him: citrus with a touch of starch. It was pure stupidity on her part that her knees went boneless.

Go home, perform Hamlet twice, keep away from Thaddeus thereafter.

Once they returned to the castle, she could cling to Otis, who tended to control all conversation. Thaddeus was his opposite.

Yet the sight of him did something to her equilibrium, so she looked away, fast, before he could notice. Thaddeus was fitting the boxes into the picnic basket as if that were a new kind of puzzle. She opened her mouth, about to say something cheerful about pulling out their rapiers—without the *slightest* sensual innuendo—when he abruptly spoke.

"My father fell in love when he was eighteen."

Her hands stilled.

She knew, of course. They all knew, all of England knew, that the Duke of Eversley had rebelled a month or two after producing an heir, and moved away to live with his "true love."

Some people called it the greatest romance of the era. Others said His Grace was a degenerate beast.

Joan had never met the Duke of Eversley. He eschewed London and polite society, and lived in retirement with the woman he had chosen.

Thaddeus seemed to have lost track of where he was going.

"I actually know that," Joan prompted.

"Everyone knows," he said unemotionally. "A stationer once told me that prints of His Grace with the 'family of his heart' outsell every image but those of the Wildes and the royal family."

"Ha! We rule!" Joan cried.

His eyes flashed to hers, startled.

"You can't be taking that metric seriously," she said to him, certain that if she offered even a hint of sympathy or pity, he would be completely mute on the subject thereafter. "Your father is portrayed all over England as a middle-aged Romeo not quite stupid enough to kill himself for love."

Something eased in his shoulders.

"You do acknowledge that he's a rum duke? My father calls him an addlepate, and generally he's not harsh about adulterers." She sighed theatrically. "For obvious reasons, given that my mother, his second duchess, is a famous member of that circle. What's more, Aunt Knowe told me that your father is a debauchee, and your mother was well shot of him."

Thaddeus was staring at the blue cloth, his brows knit.

"Are your feelings hurt?" Joan asked.

"Not at all." He sounded unruffled, but when he looked up at her, his eyes had darkened to stormy blue. "I've spent the past two years fighting off my father's determined attempts to ensure that his other son—the one whose birthday I share— can inherit."

Joan's mouth fell open. "Is he cracked? That's impossible."

Thaddeus's mouth twisted. "You'd be surprised."

"But—but the English inheritance system is all about marriage. Who was born first, who was born in wedlock. You were born first, and the other son, whoever he is, is the product of an illicit liaison between a duke and his mistress!"

"Perhaps," Thaddeus said. He reached for the bottle of wine and splashed more in his cup. "My father believes the system is immoral, and he is bringing everything he has to the fight. Luckily, the estate is entailed."

"*My* father's right," Joan exclaimed. "*Your* father is a chuckleheaded fool." She paused. "Actually, it is rare that my father isn't right. It's one of the most annoying things about being a member of the Wilde family."

Thaddeus looked at her, and she was shocked by the intensity in his eyes. "But as I understand, your father is a Prussian."

She shook her head, smiling. "Oh, no. My father is Hugo Wilde, Duke of Lindow. There's never been any doubt in my mind."

"I see," Thaddeus said.

"Not that the Prussian in question didn't make a contribution," she offered. "The second duchess and he left me in the cradle and ran away together. But my father and Aunt Knowe loved me twice as much. I always knew I was loved, and that was enough. Really, that's all a child wants to know."

Thaddeus drank his wine. Joan watched his powerful throat move and pushed away an inconvenient wish to misbehave.

"Isn't it odd that both of our parents behaved like lovelorn fools?" she offered. "I should have chosen *Romeo and Juliet* for my debut on the stage. The bottle's empty, so if you hope to drown your sorrows, we'll have to row back for another."

"My mother loves me," Thaddeus stated.

"Obviously."

"My father can't bear me." His voice was utterly flat. "The feeling is mutual. He's an emotional clown, who cannot believe I refuse to stand aside and allow true love to win. He accuses me of greed, intolerance, and far worse."

"I actually don't believe that you *can* simply give up a dukedom," Joan said, frowning. "North wanted to do it, you know. I can't remember how he's getting around it, but Aunt Knowe said something once that made me think his plan was impossible. More importantly, even if you did give up the title, it would never go to a bastard child. Given your lack of siblings, the title would revert to a cousin."

Thaddeus's lips thinned. "My father claims that he married his mistress before he married my mother, which would make me illegitimate."

Joan sucked in a breath. "No!" She instinctively moved toward him and put a hand on his arm. "Does he have any proof?"

"He says that he could present the proof if necessary," Thaddeus said, "but to this point he has declined to do so."

"Absurd!" Joan cried indignantly. "Make him show you those marriage lines, because I'd guess they're forged."

Thaddeus's mouth eased into a smile. "My solicitors agree. Unfortunately, the claim, and the process of disproving it, would be dreadful for my mother."

Joan thought of the dear, pink-clothed duchess. There was nothing strong about her. She was Aunt Knowe's closest friend, but they couldn't be more different.

Aunt Knowe faced the world like Joan's own namesake, Joan of Arc. The Duchess of Eversley was quiet and shy. She still giggled like a girl.

Joan hadn't known her long but she knew instinctively that the duchess would be devastated if her estranged husband told the world their marriage had never existed.

"That's horrible," she breathed.

"My mother wouldn't leave the house again," Thaddeus said flatly. "Not even once the courts proved his claim to be a lie, which it certainly is. The humiliation would be too acute."

"He must be mad," Joan stated.

"Indeed, he might have an illness of the brain. He is obsessed. Ruining his bloodline, squandering the duchy: none of it matters more to him than legitimizing my half brother."

Joan knew about that type of illness. When she was a girl, one of her brother Alaric's admirers had become dangerous in her passionate pursuit of him.

She cleared her throat. "Aunt Knowe still visits a family acquaintance who lives in retirement, due to her inability to recognize reality."

Thaddeus raised an eyebrow.

"The lady in question firmly believes that she's married to Alaric, and they have a child on the way. Meanwhile, my brother hasn't seen her in four or five years. Aunt Knowe says that she lives in a fantasy world, more pleasant for her than the ordinary one in which we are forced to reside. Is that what your father is doing?"

Thaddeus shook his head. "Not precisely. My father is both cunning and unscrupulous. He knows I'll do almost anything to stop my mother from being hurt by his allegations that their marriage was not legitimate."

His mouth twisted. "My mother is a gentle person, yet he told her on their wedding night that he would never love her, and moreover, that he had a disdain for her figure, her face, and the color pink, which she had worn to the altar."

"She's worn it ever since," Joan murmured.

"Revenge can take quiet forms."

"How have you managed to stop him from releasing this so-called evidence so far?"

"I allowed him to believe that I am considering stepping aside in favor of my half brother. That I am thinking about it."

She opened her mouth to say, again, that "stepping aside" wasn't allowed, but Thaddeus raised his hand. "I know. But he thinks that I will finally recognize that his opinion is the most important. And he feels that as a duke, English law doesn't apply to him."

"So he doesn't believe in the laws of primogeniture. The eldest son doesn't get everything."

"He says it is a foolish rule and every duke— every man—should be able to choose his successor."

"How does that make you feel?"

She wanted to take back the words the moment they left her mouth. Of course, he felt unloved. Rejected.

"Like a fool," Thaddeus said unemotionally.

"*He's* the fool," Joan cried. "He's the one going against British tradition back to, back to, well, not the Roman times, but a long time ago. Inheritance is all about marriage. And blood, the right blood. As you said earlier, with future dukes marrying noblewomen."

"Which you know all too well, given most gentlemen's rejection of you as a possible spouse," Thaddeus said grimly.

"That's an exaggeration," Joan said, giving him a mischievous smile. "I don't know how many British men are in the gentry and below, but I haven't met with any particular reluctance from the larger group."

He rolled closer and ran a finger down her nose. "You laugh at the very things that would destroy a woman such as my mother."

"I'm not laughing," Joan protested. "I'm just making my point. If you add together the men whom I've kissed in order to prove that point—"

"Let's not," Thaddeus murmured. He bent his head and feasted on her mouth, letting himself kiss her slowly and thoroughly. She gasped, then murmured something and put her arms around his neck.

Long minutes later, they were still kissing, occasionally breaking apart for air. He was so thirsty for her: for the sweetness of her lips, the sauciness of her tongue tangling with his, the way her slender body trembled against his.

Though he hadn't allowed himself to touch her, other than to cup the back of her head with his hand, protecting her from the ground.

More kisses . . . He became aware that he was shaking too.

"Are you making a point of your own?" she whispered against his lips, opening eyes drenched in desire. Real desire, not the kind she displayed at balls.

He felt a throb of triumph go through him, and then registered her question.

"No." He took her mouth again. Joan's lips were pliant and sweet, but she'd asked a question that ripped the erotic haze from his mind.

So he pulled back, ignoring the needy pulse in his body. "What point could I possibly be making?" he asked in a husky voice, tracing her rosy bottom lip with one finger.

Joan looked up at him. "That I shouldn't have brought you to the island. Or that I'm attractive, even though I'm illegitimate. Or that . . ." Her voice trailed off. "I'm not sure, to be honest."

"I would never hurt you," Thaddeus said. The words sounded like a vow; he watched her eyelashes flutter as she looked away. "You're not merely attractive; you're the most beautiful woman in the world."

She flinched, a small movement, but he saw it. Then she pulled away and scrambled to her feet. "Enough of this foolishness," she said, her voice gay. "We really ought to fold the cloth and practice fencing now."

Thaddeus got to his feet, knowing that his cock was straining his silk breeches.

Her eyes flew to his crotch and away. Oddly, Thaddeus found himself grinning. His cheer felt like part and parcel of the afternoon: He'd shared his father's claim of a wedding to his mistress with someone other than his solicitor; he'd had his first picnic; he'd kissed a gentlewoman . . .

With no plans to offer marriage, and she knew it.

He rolled up his sleeves. The light linen of his

shirt was not overly warm but he'd seen Joan looking at his arms. On the other side of the glade, Joan rolled up hers as well. His arms were burly, roped with sinew and muscle. Hers were slender but not frail.

Mind you, she was gripping her rapier as if it were a cricket bat.

He strode across to her and adjusted her grip, then backed up again. "*En garde*," he said, bending his knees slightly. "No, no, look at my hands." He held his sword lightly before him. "You must always know where your opponent's sword is."

"First, you stop *that*," she said, her voice rising.

He frowned.

Rosy color poured into her cheeks. "*That!*" She waved her fingers toward his waist.

Thaddeus looked down. His cockstand was as evident as it could be, given the silk breeches he wore. He was well-endowed, and every inch was proudly displaying itself. A smile spread across his face, and he found himself laughing.

"Laugh number four," Joan said crossly.

"I'm choking back any number of boyish jests about swords," he told her, and then took pity. "It's not in my command. Nor that of any man."

She scowled at him.

He straightened. "I want you, my body wants you, and my mind can't control that."

The sentence interrupted the bees, the quiet, the birdsong.

"You can't have me," she replied, eyes meeting his. "Not just because you're a future duke, but because you will need to fight a battle in the court of public opinion, if your father has his way. Lady

Bumtrinket is right. You have to marry someone of irreproachable, noble birth."

"I know. But my body doesn't." He paused. "I suspect that my body will always want you, Joan. Forever."

"Nonsense," she said. "Remember your father? He should have cleaved to your mother, as it says in the Bible. Put his mistress to the side."

He felt his brows drawing together. "Are you suggesting that I will long for you my whole life? Find myself berating my legitimate son, wishing to disinherit him in favor of a child of yours?"

"For God's sake," Joan said blankly. "You're suggesting that *I* might become your mistress?"

"You brought up the simile, not I," he said.

Her turn to laugh, startling the birds. "The role of courtesan doesn't interest me, Thaddeus. Even for you."

Then she bent her knees and gripped her sword. "*En garde!*"

He shook his head and walked behind her, putting his arms around her from the rear. His body fired to even keener attention, but he forced himself to breathe evenly. "Hold your rapier like this. Now dodge and twist, like this."

His arm curled over hers, the foil pointed at an imaginary Laertes, he showed her how to thrust while turning, and finally to plunge forward with a straight lunge under the armpit of her imaginary foe. "Pull back your blade with a shuddering motion, as if withdrawing it from flesh," he advised.

"You learned to do this in school?" she asked.

"Play dueling in the bedchambers. We would

drive each other back and forth, leaping on and off the bed."

Two hours later, as Thaddeus was rowing them back through the weedy lake, Joan was tired but happy. She was hopeful that she could fool the eye enough to please an audience. Thaddeus had taught her some flashy moves with her sword, while cautioning her that they would get her killed in a real duel.

She was going over the moves in her head, when she heard a loud curse and jerked up her head.

Gulliver was waiting for them on the bank.

Joan's clothing was untouched, in the same heap where she left it. But Thaddeus's clothing had been scattered. A white stocking hung from both sides of Gully's mouth, as if he had suddenly grown a long, snowy mustache.

Thaddeus bounded to the bank and tied off the boat, shouting, "Bloody hell, Gulliver!"

The goat looked at him inquiringly and cocked his head.

"He's never done that before," Joan said, giggling madly as she made her way off the boat. "I am truly sorry."

Thaddeus turned around, crossing his arms over his chest. "You know why he did this, don't you?"

"No idea," Joan said. "Oh, dear, I'm so sorry about your shoe. Perhaps it can be repaired." She picked it up. "No, I'm afraid not." She started giggling again.

"That bloody goat is in love with you," Thaddeus said bluntly. "He was marking his territory, letting me know that I'm not welcome. Not unlike the belligerent peacock. I suppose I'm lucky the bird didn't follow us down here and piss on my wig."

He bent over and picked up his coat from on top of the picnic basket and pulled it on. "You're his owner; you owe me a forfeit."

"Fitzy wouldn't have done that," Joan protested. But she broke out into giggles again as Thaddeus tugged on one side of the stocking hanging from Gulliver's mouth. She ended up laughing so hard that she bent over.

"Forfeit," a voice repeated just in front of her.

She straightened and found herself in Thaddeus's arms. He was warm and hard, his mouth capturing hers, a sensual hint of pressure telling her to open her mouth to his.

Joan wound her arms around his neck and let his tongue tangle with hers. She felt like a teakettle on the boil, bubbles fizzing through her veins. As soon as they started kissing, it was if they had never left off.

Her attention was entirely on Thaddeus, so much that she stopped smelling Gulliver's odiferous presence, or feeling late afternoon sunshine slanting onto her neck. The world shrank to Thaddeus's lavish, passionate kisses.

She didn't hear a breathy snort that resembled a protest issued by an ancient relative of a minotaur, removed two or three hundred times.

But she certainly felt it when Gulliver's solid—if elegant—horns butted Thaddeus directly in the rear end. He lurched forward; she fell backward onto the grass. He went down after her, catching himself on his hands before he flattened her.

A thought that sent a stab of lust through her.

"Are you all right?"

She looked up at him, blinking. "Yes."

Thaddeus turned to his side and pointed at Gulliver, who looked as close to laughing as a goat could look. "You," he said, in a calm but authoritative tone.

Gulliver cocked his head.

"Drop my stocking."

To Joan's shock, Gully's mouth fell open, and a mangled, wet stocking plopped onto the grass.

"Now go back to your orchard," Thaddeus said, keeping his eyes on Gulliver.

"I can't believe it," Joan exclaimed, propping herself on her elbows to watch Gulliver trot away. "You bested him!"

Thaddeus turned back. He was lying half over her, the weight of his body a heady pleasure.

"Gully isn't defeated," he said, a wry smile playing on his mouth. "Did you catch the moment when he dipped his head? He took my other shoe with him."

"It's not as if you could wear only one," Joan whispered, curling one of her hands around the back of his neck. Not to pull him toward her, because that would be frightfully unladylike. Her fingers played along the strong cords of his neck.

"I'll have to return to the castle with no stockings and no shoes," Thaddeus said, looking unperturbed by this prospect.

"It doesn't bother you?" she asked, realizing when she spoke that her voice had dropped to a husky tone that she'd never heard before. "Such a state of disorder isn't very ducal."

"I find it does not."

He was looking down at her, eyes intent.

Damn it. She was going to have to kiss him this time. She moved her head just enough to nip his lower lip.

In response, he dropped to an elbow. One of his hands slid underneath her and cupped her bottom. "These breeches will be my downfall," Thaddeus said.

A conversational comment, except that if her voice had been husky, his was a rasp.

She wiggled against his hand, grinning at him. "I rather like your . . . breeches as well. Or what's inside them."

He went still all over. "Do you?"

"I've seen such things on babies and in books," she said, laughter swelling up inside her again. "Never in the wild, so to speak."

Only one leg lay over her, but holding her gaze, he shifted just enough so that his warm tool pulsed against her thigh.

"Yes," Joan said, her mind so fogged with desire that she couldn't think of anything to say. "That."

"Yes, *that*," Thaddeus said. Leaning his head down, he nipped her lower lip.

But Joan couldn't play this cat-and-mouse game of desire any longer. She opened her mouth with a soft sound from the back of her throat and whispered, "Thaddeus."

"God, I love it when you say my name," he groaned. His mouth came down on hers again, urgent and possessive.

They kissed until the sunlight slanted so low

that Thaddeus's hair turned from barley to gold, until the grass lost its sunlit warmth, until Joan's whole body was pressing against his, wanting to feel more, know more.

"Time to go," Thaddeus said in her ear as she caught her breath.

"No." The word was plaintive, because desire was filling her lungs, and her blood, and every bit of her.

His weight lifted, and she choked back another protest. "Joan," Thaddeus said, brushing a lock of hair away from her eyes. She had braided it to fit under a man's wig, but many of the pins holding her braids in place were lost.

The world snapped back into place around him: the sky, the grass, the castle off in the distance, out of sight. The *world*.

And she, on her back, pleading with a man who couldn't marry her to ruin her instead.

"I suppose I can't take your virtue," she said, sighing, instinctively avoiding anything serious.

She would die before she would let him know that she was in love with him.

Hopelessly, foolishly, completely in love with him.

She'd laughed at Anthony Froude for protesting how much he loved her after they shared a few kisses. Now she wasn't so sure the man was shallow. Thaddeus's kisses were potent. She felt as if he spoke to her of love in every kiss. Which he didn't.

So kisses were lies, which she should have known since her own kisses—those she offered to Anthony Froude, for instance—were false.

"Desire is a potent emotion," Thaddeus said,

his thumb rubbing against her cheek. His eyes looked as if he knew what she was thinking. "Easily mistaken for another."

The words sent cold water down her spine.

Perhaps he was guessing that she had fallen in love with him. Perhaps he could—a humiliating thought—see a besotted expression in her eyes. She rolled on one side and summoned up the expression that he claimed didn't affect him.

Ha!

It did affect him.

His eyes darkened just a fraction, and he leaned toward her an infinitesimal amount.

"Don't worry," she said, keeping her tone perfectly light. "I told you how many men I've kissed, Thaddeus. I think . . ." She paused teasingly and tapped her chin with one finger. "I think that I'll judge you on the basis of *this* kiss, rather than the one we shared in the snake tent or those on the island."

His expression was impossible to decipher. "And?"

Her mind spun, finding the best answer, the most cautious answer, the one that would cause her the least humiliation.

"Very good," she said in a confiding tone. "Excellent." She met his eyes and let clear honesty shine in her own. "You kiss marvelously, Thaddeus."

It worked.

Lavish praise did for him what gushing acknowledgments of her beauty did for her.

The edges of his mouth tightened.

"We should return," she said. "I enjoyed rolling in the grass with you, Thaddeus, I truly did, because your kisses are *wonderful*. Better than Anthony Froude's by far."

With a sinking feeling, she watched as he stood up and then held out his hand to help her to her feet, the very image of a proper gentleman once again.

In case the compliment wasn't enough to squash the idea that she was besotted, she put a hand on his arm and looked up at him, giving him a frank look. "I haven't hurt your feelings, have I?"

"Certainly not. Why would you think that?"

"I just wanted to make sure." She hesitated, counting the seconds, and then added, "You *are* finding me a husband, after all."

His eyes were completely shuttered by his thick eyelashes. "I had not forgotten."

"Of course not." She smiled. "I have several candidates in mind for you as well. We shouldn't frolic about in the grass again, though. It isn't proper for two people of our age."

"Of our age?"

"I didn't mean to say that we shared our birthdays. I meant for two people such as we, who have made up our minds to seriously commit to a future life," she said. "I consider my days of kissing random gentlemen to be in the past."

That did it. His eyes narrowed.

Thaddeus didn't like being compared to a random gentleman. Why would he? He was a future duke, no matter what his father had to say about it.

They walked back to the castle side by side, bare

feet scuffing through grass. Gully was nowhere to be seen as they walked through the orchard.

"I fear your shoe has been taken to the stables," Joan said.

Thaddeus was staring ahead; he didn't even turn his head. "A gift to the castle goat."

They crossed the lawn in silence; presumably Fitzy was dozing somewhere in the shade.

Thaddeus pulled open the tall double doors that led to the library. "I will return the basket to the kitchens."

"Thank you," Joan said quietly.

She'd fallen in love, and that love felt like a millstone around her neck. He wanted her, but didn't love her. She wasn't even certain that he *liked* her.

And she loved Thaddeus, every inch of his disagreeable, composed, ducal self, from his hairless toes to his tousled head. She wanted all of it. Even the moments when he made his face unreadable and yet disdainful.

She walked past him, her bottom prickling at the idea he might be watching her. She could still feel the warm imprint of his hand clasping her rear.

Leaving the library, she paused and looked back, but Thaddeus hadn't followed. He was crouched down at the side of the room, staring into Aunt Knowe's knitting basket. There couldn't be anything very interesting there; her aunt never got farther than creating squares or rectangles, all of them adorned with holes, because she couldn't seem to avoid dropping stitches.

But Joan had a sudden thought and turned

back. "Is it a nest of mice again?" she called, stopping about halfway back and making sure a chair was between them, in case a mother mouse was about to make a break for freedom. "You could bring them outside. Or ask Prism to do so. I'm afraid that the castle is very old, and mice are inevitable."

Thaddeus looked up at her, and to her relief, the wary look had disappeared from his eyes. "I am starting to believe that Lindow Castle is akin to a menagerie."

Joan took a wary step backward. The last time a family of mice were born in Aunt Knowe's basket, she had decided to let them be. Joan had avoided the library for a month, until the babies were deemed old enough to be moved to the stables.

"No mice," Thaddeus said. "It's Percy. Our piglet has apparently been transported to a somewhat cramped bed in the castle."

"Percy?" Joan frowned. "Percy sleeps in Cleopatra's cowshed. I visited him there this morning." She walked back. Sure enough, Percy was curled in a tight ball, napping peacefully. He barely fit into the round basket, but he looked comfortable enough at the moment. "He can't stay there," she said unnecessarily.

Percy opened sleepy, long-lashed eyes, so she crouched down and gave him a rub. Her knee touched Thaddeus's, sending a pang through her body. "Hello, Percy, old fellow," she said, shifting away.

The piglet grunted in a welcoming sort of way.

Joan was tinglingly aware of Thaddeus crouching beside her. He turned his head, and their eyes met. Joan caught her breath. His eyes were so beautiful: grave, honorable, everything she could ever want in a man.

Facts tumbled through her mind. She was smitten. He couldn't know she was smitten. She wanted to kiss him. He couldn't know she wanted to kiss him.

They were still looking at each other, speechlessly, when the library door opened with a bang, followed by the sound of running footsteps.

"Joan!" a voice shrilled. "It's me, Artie. Did you see Percy? He's my baby now, and I'm bringing him supper."

Joan turned around with a huge grin. Her six-year-old half sister trotted toward her, a cream puff in each hand.

"Hello, darling," Joan said, holding out her arms.

Artie swerved past her. "Hello!" She dropped to her knees by the basket. "Are you quite fine, Percy?" she asked breathlessly. "See what I brought? Cream puffs! You love cream puffs!"

Thaddeus was chuckling on Joan's other side, his big body vibrating slightly. Sure enough, Percy thought a cream puff was a very fine gift. He uncurled himself with some difficulty, stood up, and snuffled one up. It wasn't the neatest meal in the world.

"I hope your aunt doesn't value her knitting," Thaddeus murmured.

"Those are her scraps and remnants," Joan

said. "We should take Percy back to his shed, Artie," she added. "Percy is not an indoor pig."

Artie's eyes narrowed. "He could be."

"Your mother has already said no, hasn't she?"

Artie's mouth pressed together.

"And your governess?"

"They will never know he's here," the little girl argued. Her brows drew together. "What are you wearing?"

Joan glanced down at her breeches. "A costume that your uncle North used to wear when he was a boy."

"What will Percy eat besides cream puffs?" Thaddeus asked. "He doesn't have a trough in the library."

Artie cast him the same narrow-eyed look. "I'll bring him carrots every morning and cream puffs in the afternoon."

"That sounds like a pleasant repast, but not enough for a growing piglet." Thaddeus scooped up Percy, tucked him under his arm, and rose to his feet. "Lady Artemisia, Percy needs to sleep in his own sty." The piglet grunted, looking longingly at the second cream puff clutched in Artie's fist, threatening to spill cream on the Aubusson carpet. "Let's give him to a footman, so he can sleep in his own bed tonight."

Joan held her breath. Her half sister Artie hated her full name, but all the same, she scrambled to her feet.

"Percy isn't going to be bacon when he grows up," Artie informed Thaddeus as they walked from the room. "Erik said he is, but that's because Erik is mean and *bad*!"

"Erik is not mean," Joan said from behind them. "He's just twelve years old, Artie. It makes him want to tease you."

"That's bad," Artie repeated. She looked up at Thaddeus. "Did you tease your brother when you were twelve?"

He shook his head, looking down at her. "I don't have a brother."

"You can have my cream puff," Artie said, holding out the battered puff. "Percy doesn't need two." Her tone was appalled, as befitted a young lady who'd grown up in a nursery full of children.

"Thank you," Thaddeus said, accepting the puff and promptly taking a bite. "It's excellent."

Artie was silent as they left the room. Then, once they'd handed over Percy to be returned to the shed, she asked, "Did you have a piglet when you were a little boy?"

"I had a donkey," Thaddeus replied.

Apparently suddenly remembering that she was a duke's daughter, Artie bent her knees into an approximation of a curtsy. "Good afternoon. I would like a donkey," she told him. "For my birthday, which is happening soon. Percy would be happy too."

"I'll consider it," Thaddeus said gravely.

Artie turned to Joan. "And those—" she said, pointing to Joan's breeches. "I want *those*."

Joan could just imagine the Duchess of Lindow's face when she heard that her little daughter wanted to wear breeches.

"I'll consider it," she said, stealing Thaddeus's line.

Artie squinted at them, and then, in a magnificent approximation of Aunt Knowe's voice, said, "See that you do."

Joan was still gaping after her little sister, who was dashing up the stairs to the nursery, when she realized that Thaddeus was laughing again. Bellowing with laughter.

"She's the picture of your aunt Knowe," he said, when he caught his breath.

"I agree," Joan said. And: "You're laughing again!"

Thaddeus glanced over her head, but the footman usually stationed in the entry was still delivering Percy to his stall. Before she could say another word, he caught her up in an openmouthed, rough kiss.

"I laugh around you," he said, his voice as rough as his kiss. "*Damn it.*"

Joan knew when to extract herself from a man's embrace, even if she wanted nothing more than to kiss this particular man again.

"Thank you for the fencing lessons," she said, stepping away. She turned and followed Artie up the steps, impatient to be upstairs and away from the onslaught of emotion that Thaddeus was causing her.

If they were alone together again—if they practiced dueling again—they couldn't go to the island. It was too tempting.

He was too tempting.

Damn it all.

Chapter Eleven

*J*oan strolled into the drawing room that night and realized instantly that Otis, who was usually of a sunny disposition, was not happy. He was seated on a sofa beside Aunt Knowe, his brows meeting above his nose.

"What's the matter?" she asked.

"My father arrived this afternoon and will join us in a minute!" Otis hissed. "Prism didn't warn me, and *here I am*." He plucked at his gown with an expression of extreme distaste. "My father is going to be shocked, if not apoplectic. The only thing worse would be if Lady Bumtrinket made an appearance."

"I told him that it would be better to get explanations out of the way now," Aunt Knowe said, smiling broadly. "It's good for a man to experience a surprise now and then."

Joan opened her mouth, but before she could speak, the drawing room door opened. "Sir Reginald Murgatroyd," Prism announced, nodding to Otis's father. And, "The Duchess of Eversley." Thaddeus's mother.

Watching them stroll across the room was like waiting for the storm to roll onto the coast from the sea.

Otis seemed frozen. Sir Reginald was walking slowly, with Thaddeus's mother on his arm. Speaking of whom, where was Thaddeus?

Otis tottered to his feet; Joan had to grab his elbow to keep him from falling over as his father and Her Grace appeared.

"Good evening, Lady Joan. What a pleasure to see you," Sir Reginald said, bowing as deeply as his corset would allow.

"Good evening, Sir Reginald, Your Grace," Joan said, dropping into a curtsy.

Otis's father straightened. "And who is . . ." His voice died out, and Joan watched his face fade to the color of overcooked oatmeal. "Dear me. It seems to be . . . Otis. I didn't—"

"I would curtsy," Otis said, "but I find a corset to be confining. This is merely a jest, Father. You know I didn't care for wearing a gown as a vicar." There was a note of desperation in his voice.

"I find your son's attire very amusing, Sir Reginald," the duchess put in. "He's been such a good sport, playing the role of Ophelia in *Hamlet*."

"My father asked Otis to play Ophelia as a special favor. He didn't want to. I am playing Hamlet," Joan rattled off.

Sir Reginald blinked.

"In breeches," she clarified.

"I wouldn't be wearing this gown other than in rehearsal," Otis added, "but the director feels that I do not appear sufficiently feminine. He asked me to remain in costume for the remaining days before the performance."

"Instruct your man to shave you thrice before you go on stage," his father said, his eyes resting on Otis's chin. He turned to Joan. "Did you say that His Grace asked my son to play this role? Why, in God's name? I am inordinately proud of my children, but Otis cannot be described as an attractive young lady."

"I begged to play Hamlet," Joan explained, "but my father insisted that Hamlet's beloved, Ophelia, could not be a professional actor. I assure you that Otis was my last resort. I asked every lady in the castle. My sister Viola would have done it, albeit unwillingly, but she is expecting a child in a week or so."

"An Ophelia ripe with child might actually have made sense," Sir Reginald commented.

"Joan was beginning to despair before Otis agreed to play the part," Aunt Knowe put in. "She even begged me to take the role, but I am no nubile maiden."

"Neither am I," Otis said, pointing out the obvious. "Father, I thought you planned to stay in London and would never learn of my less-than-glorious acting career. If you'll forgive me, I shall sit down, as I find high heels uncomfortable, if not dangerous."

They all seated themselves. Joan cast a desperate look at the door. Where was Thaddeus? He had a way of soothing things over that would be helpful at the moment.

"I found London somewhat lonely," Sir Reginald said, "but my dear friend the duchess wrote me that she was visiting you, and suggested I join you." He gave the Duchess of Eversley a wry smile. "She neglected to tell me that I would find my son wearing a gown!"

Her Grace broke out into a musical fit of giggles. "It was meant to be a surprise! If only you could have seen your own face!"

"I was definitely surprised," Sir Reginald allowed.

"That's what's so much fun," Aunt Knowe said, grinning widely.

Otis clamped on Joan's arm. "That was very nearly a disaster," he breathed, as Sir Reginald began chatting with Her Grace and Lady Knowe.

"Your father was quite courteous," Joan said. "Some men would have become inarticulate with rage."

"Father's not like that. My guess is that he's mostly hurt that I didn't invite him to the performance," Otis said glumly. "I was hoping he'd never find out. Now he'll tell my sister, and she'll plague me to death. I'm a rotten Ophelia, Joan."

"I know, and I'm sorry."

"And I *hate* wearing this godforsaken garment," he added.

"I'm sorry," Joan said again.

"But, on the other hand, I can introduce Father to Madeline." Otis brightened and turned toward Sir Reginald and the Duchess of Eversley. "Tomorrow I shall introduce you to Mr. Wooty, the manager of the Theatre Royal."

"We shall invite Mr. Wooty to dinner tomorrow," Aunt Knowe said, smoothly picking up her cue. "Including his wife and lovely niece Madeline, of course."

"Mr. Wooty has been extremely accommodating," Otis told his father. "His theater company is one of the best in England, and I'm sure my portrayal of Ophelia gives him dyspepsia. Joan and I and the duchess plan to visit Wilmslow the following evening for the performance, if only to see what true Ophelia looks like on the stage— one who can remember her lines, for example."

"I recall your first celebration of Mass as a vicar," his father replied, wincing. "Memorization is not your forte."

"Loyalty is one of my favorite qualities," the Duchess of Eversley said diplomatically. "No one can doubt the deep friendship between Lady Joan and your son."

"When in Wilmslow, will you stay overnight at the Gherkin & Cheese?" Sir Reginald asked Joan. "They have an excellent cook."

"Yes, of course."

"Perhaps you would accompany us," the duchess suggested. "I'm afraid that I cannot countenance two performances of *Hamlet* in a row, so I should be very glad of company during the evening."

"Of course!" Sir Reginald cried.

Joan was fascinated to see how friendly the two of them were. Sir Reginald's wife had passed away years ago, and the duchess's husband had left her when Thaddeus was only a small boy, as she understood it.

But of course nothing could happen between them. The Duke of Eversley might flaunt his mistress, but Joan had no doubt but that the duchess would remain faithful to her marriage vows.

Just then her father and mother strolled into the room, followed by Viola and Devin . . . but still no sign of Thaddeus. Not that she was watching for him in particular, of course.

"How did your lesson in fencing go this afternoon?" Otis asked.

Joan very nearly opened her mouth to say something absurd: *It was the best afternoon of my life*. But she caught herself. "I feel much more confident about Act Five. How is your grasp of Ophelia's lines?"

"Madeline tested me over and over," Otis said.

He didn't sound disgruntled. In fact, he was turning a little pink.

"You like her?" Joan whispered.

"She's a lovely young woman. But I was *in a dress* all day," Otis hissed.

"Madeline is not a lady," Joan pointed out, somewhat hesitantly.

Otis shrugged. "I have my own estate. Why should I care about that? Society will accept my wife, or I will go my own way."

At that moment Thaddeus appeared in the door of the drawing room. She jerked up her head, and he strode toward them, his eyes on Joan's face. She didn't know how she felt about the instant bolt of happiness she experienced when he entered the room.

But it happened. She felt it.

"I should practice walking," Otis said, mischief deep in his voice. "Father dear, won't you walk me the length of the drawing room?"

His father snorted. "I most certainly will not!"

"But I need practice walking," Otis complained, getting to his feet, wobbling slightly, and then swishing his skirts. "I have to trot all around the throne room throwing flowers at people."

Aunt Knowe jumped to her feet. "I'll walk with you, dear."

They set off, and Thaddeus took Otis's seat beside Joan. "How are you, Lord Greywick?" she asked, ignoring the fact that they had parted a mere two hours before.

"Very well, thank you."

But he wasn't. His eyes were shadowed.

She waited until the rest were engaged in lively conversation and then she dug an elbow into his side. "What happened?"

He glanced down at her arm and then at her face, eyebrow raised. "Can I do something for you, Lady Joan?"

"What's the matter?" She watched his face closely, because it was the most fascinating puzzle she'd ever encountered.

His thick eyelashes fluttered, and his jaw was tight.

"It's your father," she breathed. She stood up. "I believe that I too should like to stroll before the meal," she announced. "Lord Greywick, won't you please escort me?"

He muttered something, rose to his feet, and held out his elbow. "What did you just say?" Joan asked.

"Bossy," he said.

She rolled her eyes at him. "What happened?" she repeated. She saw the moment he gave in, when the proudest, most solitary man she'd ever known decided to answer.

"The duke's solicitor wrote—"

"He cannot win this ridiculous suit!" Joan interrupted. "My father will make certain of that, if no one else."

"Why would His Grace do that?" Thaddeus asked, his face at its most impervious.

"Because you're—you're a friend of the family," Joan said, feeling a prickling embarrassment at the back of her neck. She loathed the idea that he might think she was making some claim on him due to all that kissing.

He was silent as they crossed paths with Otis and Aunt Knowe, heading back down the long drawing room. Thank goodness, he was looking down, because those two were bent on mortifying her; their faces were wreathed in suggestive smiles, and Otis was waggling his eyebrows like a satyr in a dress.

Joan narrowed her eyes and warned them silently to keep their silly ideas to themselves. Just because she and Thaddeus were . . . whatever they were . . . friends, perhaps, didn't mean her family should jump to conclusions.

"It appears my father is dying," Thaddeus said abruptly. "Not today, but soon."

Joan let out a soundless gasp. Thaddeus's jaw was so tight that she was surprised the words made it to the open air. "I'm sorry for your loss," she offered.

He looked at her.

"Or not," she corrected herself.

"First, he isn't a 'loss' yet. But second, he will

never be 'my' loss. He's absented himself from my mother's and my life long ago. On the few occasions I met him before his second son was born, he was uninterested and uncaring."

"A weasel," Joan stated.

He cast her a quick glance. "Not a loon or a fopdoodle?"

"Shakespeare's insults run the gamut from gentle to fierce," Joan told him, glad to see no sorrow in his eyes. She added, cautiously, "Do you wish to visit your father before he passes away?"

"His Grace has not issued an invitation," Thaddeus said, a tick starting in his jaw. "In fact, my mother and I are explicitly not invited to pay him a call, not that she would care to see him."

"So the letter was a notification?"

"An announcement."

"I've never heard of announcing one's death," Joan said.

"He embraces the dramatic," Thaddeus said, his dry tone making it clear that he abhorred histrionics.

Not that she had any illusion that he enjoyed the character trait. Unfortunately, she shared it. She *was* it. Dramatic, that is. Theatrical.

"My father has apparently written a letter declaring that he had married his mistress before he was forced to marry my mother," Thaddeus continued. "He is leaving instructions for this 'confession' to be published in the *Morning Post*, and for a petition to be presented to Parliament, overturning the laws of primogeniture, in honor of his chosen family and his beloved son."

"If he had a marriage certificate, he would publish it," Joan said, coming to a halt. "Oh, Thaddeus, this means that your title is secure!"

"I always knew that," Thaddeus said, his voice grating. "Just as I knew that my father is a discredit to his country and family, with no more conscience than a caterpillar."

They reached the end of the room and turned about. From this vantage point, she could see the duchess laughing as she talked to Sir Reginald and Viola. "You must warn your mother," Joan said.

"She'll never leave home again," Thaddeus said tonelessly. "She's shy, and while another woman might have gained confidence upon marriage, my father did his best to tear her down on every occasion, so that she wouldn't complain about his rampant infidelity."

Joan bumped him with her shoulder. "I am sorry."

He looked at her.

"Your father is a coward, an infinite liar, an hourly promise-breaker," she said, quoting Shakespeare. "And an ass," she added.

Outside the door, Prism rang the gong for the evening meal.

"If it was up to me," Thaddeus said, "I'd burn the letter, laugh at the confession in the paper, and continue with my life. I agree with you: If he had a marriage certificate, he would have waved it about years ago. But my mother will be devastated. What am I going to do, Joan?" His voice grated.

If she had been able, she would have cupped his cheek and brushed a kiss on his lips. A kiss that said, *You are a good man, no matter your father.*

Which struck her as ironic, because she told herself that same thing daily.

The party was making its way out of the drawing room door.

"We can—we can figure it all out tomorrow afternoon," she promised. "There's a solution. We simply have to find it."

He smiled faintly. "While we're supposedly practicing fencing?"

"Exactly. Less kissing, more policy."

Thaddeus sighed. "A plan for my life, I'm afraid."

Chapter Twelve

$\mathcal{T}$haddeus watched the rehearsal the following morning through unseeing eyes. He hadn't slept well, and in the middle of the night, he'd narrowed his choices to two: He could travel to the estate where his father lived with his mistress and children, and wrench the letter from his dying hands by force. Or he could warn his mother of the announcement without mentioning her husband's imminent demise.

He was leaning toward the first choice. With an option for patricide, though he knew he'd never actually murder his father.

Didn't even want to.

His father was an unkind, dishonorable man. But in a twisted way, Thaddeus respected the way his father had single-mindedly tried to turn over the English inheritance system in favor of the heir he preferred.

Unfortunately for the duke, the entire estate was entailed, from the country manor house and its surrounding lands to the townhouse. Thaddeus himself paid the bills associated with his father's second establishment. He had never wanted his mother to see those details.

He looked back at the stage where Otis was throwing flowers around. Murgatroyd would never look like a woman, nor sound like one either, but he seemed to have the lines memorized, helped by the fact that Miss Wooty stood to the side and prompted him whenever he looked at her.

Which he did, frequently.

She was a very pretty young woman.

Not a lady.

Thaddeus was abruptly caught by a bolt of jealousy so intense that it felt as if it cut through his gut. Otis could choose the woman he wished to marry. He knew the man well enough to be certain that he wasn't casting looks at a woman whom he wished to make into his mistress.

No, Otis Murgatroyd was contemplating a *mésalliance*. He planned to introduce Miss Madeline Wooty to Sir Reginald at dinner, which would take the question past contemplation into reality.

If only his own father had had the courage to marry his squire's daughter when he first fell in love with her. Now the duke's claims to have married his beloved before making a society marriage had the hysterical edge of a man whose entire life has been predicated by regret.

Act Five began, and Thaddeus was gratified to see that Joan's fencing had improved. If it had been a real duel, Laertes would be in no danger, but she'd stopped wielding the sword like a battle-axe.

Thaddeus rose to his feet when the cast hopped up from their varied deaths and descended from the stage, milling about while they waited for afternoon orders.

"Dress rehearsal tomorrow morning; performance in the evening," Mr. Wooty called. "Look sharp, all of you. Claudius, don't forget to exit right rather than left from the prayer scene. Hamlet, you're better on the fencing, but I'd like you to practice dying this afternoon."

He looked to Thaddeus, who nodded.

"Ophelia, your grasp of the language has improved although I would suggest less simpering." He looked at his niece. "This afternoon, let's run Ophelia through his longer scenes. Here, where I can be of help."

Thaddeus smiled faintly. He wasn't the only one to have noticed that Miss Wooty had caught Otis's eye.

"I can't believe he wants me to work on dying!" Joan said indignantly, when they arrived at the island two hours later, having divested wigs, coats, waistcoats, stockings, and shoes on the bank. "I thought I died *very* well."

This time Thaddeus hadn't hesitated; he too had stripped down to his linen shirt and breeches. "Perhaps too much moaning?"

"Only a reasonable amount," Joan protested. "Nothing like the exhibitions my brothers would put on in the nursery. They used to writhe all over the floor, after 'dying' in a duel."

Thaddeus tried to imagine that, and failed. The Wilde men whom he knew showed no signs of dramatic ability, and in fact, tended toward the type of man whom one would think completely practical, if anything.

You could trust them, and their judgment, without question.

He was still thinking about that when he carried the picnic basket up the bank, following Joan. Once in the clearing, they put down the cloth—flowered yellow cotton, instead of blue—and pinned it to the ground with rocks.

"Are you hungry?" Joan inquired. "I'm sorry I took so long after the rehearsal, but I wanted a bath after collapsing onto the stage in death throes. It was frightfully dusty."

They began to pull the boxes from the picnic basket. Today's offerings were different from yesterday's.

"Mmmm," Joan said, appreciation a purr deep in her throat that made his nerves tighten. "Cook sent along pot pies, and they're still warm. And lemon tarts!" Her delight sent flecks of sensation down his spine.

She rooted out a corked earthenware jug and gave him a mischievous grin. "Plum jerkum!" Pulling out the cork, she poured a rosy liqueur into the tin cups.

"How intoxicating is it?" Thaddeus asked.

"Very," Joan said. "Viola and I tried it neat once, and later we threw up. This, however, is Aunt Knowe's version, which is mixed with cider and should be no stronger than wine."

Thaddeus looked down at the fizzing cup and saluted her with it. "To your performance of Hamlet."

Joan grinned at him. "Thank you."

Sparkling, tart liquid slid down his throat. Even though he knew perfectly well that brandy hardly affected him, he chose to interpret the heady feeling that spread through him as inebriation rather than—

Than some sort of illicit emotion inspired by Joan's eyes.

And her smile.

Joan took two small pot pies and a napkin and lay down on the opposite side of the cloth, propping up her head with a pillow.

He started picking up the boxes that were between them and placing them to the side.

Joan was on her back, ankle crossed over her knee, staring at the shifting leaves overhead. When she noticed what he was doing, she turned her head lazily. "I'd like more to eat, even if you don't."

"I'm not packing away the food. The boxes are in the way of my pillow."

A smile played with the corners of Joan's lovely mouth. "I see."

He placed his pillow, very precisely, next to hers. "If you don't need a tree to lean against, neither do I."

When he had lain down next to her, not touching but close, Joan said, "You haven't truly experienced a picnic until you watch the leaves."

Thaddeus stared up at them. They were leaves. Shifting into patterns that sorted and resorted in symmetrical patterns—mathematics had been one of his favorite subjects in university—but ultimately, just trees.

A plump tail flicked across a branch and then

scampered down the tree on Joan's right. At the bottom of the trunk, the squirrel stopped and sat up.

"He'd like pie," Joan said softly.

The young squirrel had an extraordinarily fluffy tail that curled up and over his head in an exuberance of fur.

"Why isn't he more afraid of us?" she asked.

"He's too young," Thaddeus answered, equally quietly. "He's no more than a baby." Cautiously, he came up on one elbow and rolled some crumbs not toward the squirrel, but off to the side.

The baby gave them a look, scampered over, snatched up the biggest crumb, and left with a flip of his tail.

"You like animals, don't you?" Joan said, turning her head to look at him. A ray of sunlight caught her hair so it glowed amber.

"Yes."

He couldn't look at her any longer without kissing her, so he rolled onto his back and put an arm over his eyes.

A rustling suggested Joan had inched closer to him, but she didn't touch him. He could smell her, though: She smelled like sparkling plum cider, a hint of buttery pastry, a touch of something indescribable that was Joan.

"Are you all right?" Her breath touched his ear.

He discovered he was holding his breath as if she were a shy forest creature whom he was trying to coax closer. He let the breath out. "Of course."

"Your father's unkindness must be very hurtful."

"I wish he had simply run away years ago, the way your mother and father did," he said, keeping his voice even. "But he's not brave. I realize now that he probably began to feel ill two years ago, when he started badgering me to give up the inheritance. Any courage he has is fueled by knowledge of his imminent demise."

"Here, have a bite." A warm, flaky pastry touched his lips, and he took a bite without moving his arm from his eyes.

"My father, the duke, told me that my mother's courage came from being unloved," Joan said. "He didn't love her, and he said that no one in her family had cared for her either. So when she met the Prussian, her life reshaped itself around that one fact: love. At least, I hope the Prussian loves her."

"If she looked like you, he is probably prostrate at her feet," Thaddeus said wryly.

He *felt* her withdrawal even though she wasn't touching him. She was on her side, head propped up on an elbow.

"I hope for her sake that he cared for more than that," Joan said. "Beauty is fleeting, skin-deep, etcetera."

"Only if you think of 'beauty' as encompassing merely physical traits such as hair and skin. That squirrel had a beautiful tail, by any measure."

"A royal tail," Joan said, her voice softening.

"But his face is *beautiful*," Thaddeus pointed out. "The way he turned his head slightly away and still watched us, the scrappy shine in his eyes, four long, springy whiskers on each side of his mouth."

"Hmm." Pastry touched his lips again. He took another bite. "I would give you jerkum but I'm afraid to spill plum-colored liquid on your shirt. Down in the laundry, they'd have to lather it over and over."

"How do you know?"

"Aunt Knowe had each of us, the boys too, work in the laundry room for a day. We did the same in the buttery—she finds new beer fascinating—and the stables, and the kitchens. We learned how to lay a fire and scrub a hearth. How else could we run our own households someday?"

He absorbed that in silence. To him, running a household was a matter of giving orders. He learned that lesson at his mother's knee. The Wildes obviously had a different concept. Likely a better one, he admitted.

Everything he knew was learned by rote. A rule, memorized, like a part in a play: *The Duke of Eversley*.

Something sharp poked him in the side. "Time to sit up," Joan said cheerfully. "You can't watch the leaves—"

He rolled over, his mouth coming down on hers without opening his eyes. It was as if he had mapped her territory in space. He knew where her body was in relation to his. Joan's mouth opened to him as naturally as if he were a flaky pastry, but the sound she made in the back of her throat? That raspy note of excitement? No pastry was worth that.

Thaddeus sank into their kiss as if nothing else existed but the moment and the lady. Their tongues curled around each other, dancing in a rhythm that turned the desire in Thaddeus's body into a thunderstorm that blotted out *rules*.

All of them memorized, not learned.

He pushed the thought away. He was drunk on Joan's taste and smell, the sunlight, perhaps even the sparkling drops of plum liqueur.

He finally opened his eyes, rearing back his head, and ran a hand from her waist to her ribs. "May I?" Her eyelashes fluttered open. Thaddeus's mind reeled, trying to find names for that blue. "In the 1100s, the color blue was considered divine," he added.

Her lips tipped up. "Consider me your neighborhood goddess. Yes, you may."

His hand slipped around her ribs and cupped one breast, their eyes still locked together. Her mouth formed an almost comical circle as breath slipped soundlessly from her lips. He didn't have to ask if his caress felt good: She instinctively arched into his hand.

His thumb rubbed across her nipple, and he felt the shudder through her entire body.

"You're not wearing a corset." His voice had dropped at least an octave.

She shook her head. "My corsets are built to make my breasts look larger than they are. That is not the effect I wanted when playing Hamlet."

He took up a gentle rhythm and watched as pleasure rippled over her face. "Hamlet with breasts. I would like to see that."

"You would?" The silky invitation in her voice was unmistakable.

They kissed until everything faded from the little glade: the song of birds, the skitter of the squirrel, back for more crumbs. Nothing existed but Joan and the involuntary sounds she made.

Until she tore her mouth away, panting, and cried, "Bloody hell, Thaddeus!" Then she froze, eyes on his, obviously waiting to see if he was shocked.

He *was* shocked, but by himself, not her. He came up on his knees, a bellow of laughter coming from his chest such as he hadn't experienced in years. More than years. Perhaps since childhood.

"It's long been an ambition of mine to see a Hamlet with breasts," he said, eyes on hers so he could see the faintest sign of hesitation.

None.

She smiled, but it wasn't the practiced sensuality that she'd wielded like a weapon against unthinking mankind. This smile was joyful, a little shy, mischievous, desirous, *sweet*.

The real Joan.

The realization rocked him to his core.

"As it happens," she said with an enchanting giggle, "I can help you with that ambition."

She untied the simple knot at her neck. And began pulling handfuls of linen from her breeches.

He watched, unmoving. No gentleman would disrobe a lady. But if a lady disrobed herself? There was nothing he could do in the world, at this moment, other than watch Hamlet disrobe.

Some part of his mind was dimly aware that he wasn't acting like himself. That the whole being whom he'd crafted—the future Duke of Eversley—had deserted him, leaving:

Thaddeus.

Thaddeus, his inner self, sprang to life with the same joy with which he used to argue about astronomy in school, certain that individual stars hid galaxies behind them. The way he used to dedicate himself to an injured animal, nursing it, coaxing it to live, no matter how abused it had been.

Only Thaddeus, not a future duke, watched Joan pull her shirt up until a pale band of skin showed at her waist, the color of new cream. She crossed her arms, ready to pull it over her head. "Shall I?"

He swallowed hard.

Her smile widened, and she took his silence for an answer, because the shirt made the squirrel jump as it thumped the ground. Out of the corner of his eye, Thaddeus saw the young fellow take an enormous leap in the air and then settle back down, coming up on his back legs to launch into an angry monologue.

"He's cross," Joan murmured. She reached slender arms up in a casual manner, and crossed them behind her head. She looked mischievous more than anything—but he saw a pulse beating in her neck, and her breath was unsteady.

His hands came out, hovered in the air. "You're the most beautiful—" He caught the words back. She hated empty compliments, even when they were true. "Did you know that every star is unique?" he asked instead.

She shook her head.

"They look the same from our vantage point. But were we able to approach them, we would see that each flames in its own way. Men compare breasts to apples or melons."

Joan quirked up one side of her mouth. "I'd put my own in the apple category."

"You're like a star: so perfect that you are dangerous to the naked eye." The curve of her breast looked like a mathematical theorem, the explanation of the universe.

Or of man's desire.

"May I?" he asked, desire pumping through his blood, his voice a rumble. She raised an eyebrow, so he ran a finger along the curve of her mouth. "Touch you? Caress you?"

"Yes." It was a simple word, but with independence and confidence behind it. Something in him calmed. He wasn't taking advantage of her, because Joan considered herself his equal.

Perhaps it took a woman with no claims to birthright to dismiss his title, to view him as a man and nothing more. Everything in him rejoiced.

His hands rounded her delicious curves as if his fingers had grown to this size in order to caress her. A shudder went down her spine, and she closed her eyes, holding her breath. Thaddeus bent down, watching Joan's silky skin quiver when he gently blew on her nipple. Hearing a squeak when he licked her for the first time. Feeling her slender body shake as he closed his lips around her nipple.

"*Hell*," Joan breathed.

He stopped kissing her in order to laugh. Her eyes popped open and she stared at him, annoyed. "That wasn't a reproach. Feel free to return to your former activity."

"I was told, growing up, that cursing was a sign of lack of control."

"Me too," Joan said. She squinted her eyes. "Pretend I am Miss Whittier, the most proper governess of all who entered the castle."

He teased her nipples, one with each hand. "Never a fantasy of mine, but all right, Miss Whittier."

Joan's breath caught. And then: "I didn't mean that!" Her face changed and somehow, improbably, she looked older and very stern. "Lady Joan, I pray that I never hear such an exclamation from your lips again. Such a one as you must be even more prudent with your language than must a true lady."

Thaddeus's hands stilled and his brows drew together.

"My father sacked her," Joan said cheerfully. "I didn't tell, but Viola did. My stepsister may seem shy, but she's a fierce protectress. From that moment, I decided that the rules governing 'true ladies' didn't apply to me."

She wiggled, arching her back into his hands. "You might continue what you were doing before."

With no hesitation, Thaddeus bent to the highly enjoyable task of driving his lady, "true" or not, from hoarse noises to the occasional unladylike exclamation. By then, his erection was straining the front of his breeches, and he could feel sweat on his back.

The world had closed to her curves, her body,

her smell and taste. He felt as if he were snatching a moment from time, dizzyingly heady, impossibly delicious. Forbidden.

"I never thought you . . . Who *are* you?" Joan murmured at some point. Her arms were over her head, her creamy breasts spangled by sunlight.

Whoever he was, he was following instinct rather than rules for the first time in his life. Thaddeus moved from kissing her lips again to kissing her breasts, and again, until she was shaking beneath him, her nipples hard, her fingers tugging at his hair.

Instinct.

It wasn't something that dukes were encouraged to think about. Who needed instinct when he had generations of tradition to follow?

Instinct told Thaddeus how Joan wanted to be kissed, when she would welcome a nibble, how to turn his thumb in order to create a rougher stroke. She felt sweeter and more delicious than anything he'd ever tasted. He kissed his way over a taut expanse of pale skin, and dusted her belly with kisses.

When he spoke, his voice came out in a rasp. "I want to touch you." Following his instinct, he slid a hand between her legs, clasped her tightly, and felt her body quiver. She was hot and soft through the silk breeches, naked flesh waiting for his caress.

Of course she wouldn't wear a pair of drawers under her breeches.

"Only a touch," he added.

Joan had turned rosy pink. "You are so much

more adventuresome than I would have expected."

He pressed his fingers slightly and her breath caught.

"With you," he said wryly. "My second picnic."

"Family picnics are never like this!"

He tapped his fingers, and she drew in a breath with a little squeak. "That feels so *good*."

Thaddeus was dimly aware of all he'd forgotten: manners and civilization, for one. His father and his title, for another. Gone, as lightly as if they were garments that a man put on in the morning and took off in the evening.

Life, real life, was here, with Joan, whose eyes were not dazed but sparkling, whose mouth was red, who arched into his hand and then looked surprised at herself.

"I trust you," she told the open air, before throwing one arm over her eyes.

Her breeches were made from silk grown fragile from age.

He dragged his hands over the curve of her hips. "Tsk, tsk. These breeches cover your knee-caps. Quite unfashionable, Hamlet. And ribbon garters?" He snorted.

"Hair ribbons," Joan said, peeking at him. "Hush with your criticism. Even as children, my brothers had stout legs. The breeches flap at the knee without ribbons."

Thaddeus pulled free the second ribbon, and ran his fingers teasingly down her calves and then under the breeches to cup her knees. "Are you quite certain, Joan?"

"Touching only," she commanded, moving her arm so she could see his face.

Until the past two years, Thaddeus had considered himself a lucky man. Fortunate. Privileged in every way possible, barring his father's absence from his life.

Now he knew that he hadn't even understood what *could* have been in his life, were he truly fortunate.

This, *this*, sunlit glade. He glanced up and found the squirrel, having tamed them with a scold, was busily investigating the open boxes on the other side of the cloth.

"Yes." He ran his hands over her calves again. "If you'd prefer, we can stop here, Joan." He heard the intimate note in his own voice with wonder.

Intimacy was . . . Intimacy was like laughter. Something other people did.

"I'm curious," Joan admitted, her cheeks stained red.

Her head sank back, arm over her eyes again, and he breathed a silent prayer of gratitude—and pulled her breeches gently down her rounded hips, slender legs, off her feet. Put it away, carefully, so he didn't incur another scolding from the squirrel.

Before he did anything else, he moved forward so he could gently lift her arm and kiss her mouth, smiling down at her. "It's just me."

"You're clothed, and I'm not. *Outside*."

"If we were both unclothed, I might abrogate the rules that have governed my life." His voice was wry.

"Perhaps that was Hamlet's problem," Joan murmured. "Ophelia climbed in his bedroom window when he didn't have a barrier of clothing to protect his honor."

Thaddeus shrugged. Personally, he considered Hamlet a scoundrel who wandered around braying *Revenge*, breaking Ophelia's trust and her mind—and what about when he ordered his two best friends killed?

Yet Joan admired the prince, obviously, so he held his tongue.

He kissed his way from her breasts, down the gentle curve of her stomach, nibbling to hear her giggle again, down one leg to her knee, starting back toward the soft thatch of hair between her legs.

Joan seemed to be holding her breath. He eased her legs apart and dropped kisses on her thighs, loving the creamy skin that felt like finest silk.

He heard a noise. Throat clearing. He raised his head.

Joan was looking down at him with desire, curiosity, interest. Her cheeks were red as fire. "Touching does *not* include kissing."

He pressed a kiss on one thigh. "Yes, it does."

"Nor looking. You're *looking* at me," she pointed out.

He ducked his head and dropped a kiss on her other thigh. "Yes. You smell so good, and you are beautiful, like the most beautiful flower in the world."

"You—"

"I want to kiss you everywhere, Joan." The words hung on the air like the lazy chirp of a sleepy bird.

She swallowed. "I've heard of that," she whispered. "Read about it, I mean. In a book of etchings."

"So have I."

"But you haven't done it before?"

"No. I offered, once, but the lady in question declined." He brushed his lips against her thigh again, followed with a tiny stroke of his tongue.

She startled and gasped.

He followed his kiss with a lick to the delicate crease of her leg, nestled beside a soft thatch of hair. It was natural to turn his cheek, to nuzzle her. She smelled like a perfume that would cost a fortune.

"Breathe," he murmured.

The air whooshed from her lungs.

"I love your smell," he said, his voice rough, nuzzling her again. "Lavender, sweetly feminine. Vanilla, jasmine, lemon."

He looked up to meet her wide eyes. "What?"

"I've never heard anyone talk that way."

"I want to taste," he said, his voice dropping below a growl.

"I feel *so naked*," Joan whispered.

Thaddeus forced himself to move away.

She met his eyes and, to his shock, a smile lit her eyes. Lazily, she reached above her head again and stretched. Her body lay before him, gleaming, as if one of the stars he dreamed of had fallen to earth.

"It's unnerving, but I like it," Joan announced. Her eyes shone like starlight.

"I—" But the words didn't come to him.

Her lips curled. "You may."

"May?"

"Continue," Joan said, laughing. "You may continue."

Despite himself, Thaddeus discovered he was smiling too. "Continue what?" he asked, making his tone innocent.

Joan put her hands behind her head, and now she was grinning at him impishly. "Kissing me," she said baldly.

He didn't wait for clarification but eased her legs farther apart. He understood, dimly, that he'd been given the first gift in his life that truly mattered. For this moment, she had given herself into his care. His own fallen star.

A kiss on her thigh, a lick, a kiss, another lick . . .

"Bloody hell!" the gentlewoman in question gasped.

Thaddeus caught back a grin. Then he settled into the task, letting the warm sunshine and birdsong become part of a tapestry of desire he was building, reminding himself that he wouldn't take off any of his own clothing: He hadn't lost his ethical compass.

She tasted delicious, tart and sparkling as plum jerkum.

"Are you . . . are you bored?" Joan gasped at some point, shivering hard.

"I could stay here all day," Thaddeus said, hearing the happiness in his voice. "I could kiss you like this for a year." He bent his head, just to make sure that she didn't stop shaking, and brought a hand into play. "A century."

She gasped something, unsurprisingly a word that would never cross the lips of a gentlewoman. But that lady wouldn't lie fearlessly before him, divested of her male attire, crying out when he sucked hard, nearly sobbing when he gripped her thigh.

"Thaddeus!" Joan reached down with one hand. He curled his fingers around it, at the same time that he applied himself.

And when Thaddeus Shaw applied himself . . .

He succeeded.

Always.

Joan yelped, and then—true to form—threw back her head and screamed as her body caught waves of passion that rippled through her.

Thaddeus got to see all of it. Her silky, wet flesh, the arch of her throat, the glittering sunlight bathing her in diamonds.

As he eased away, he was certain of one thing.

He had just experienced the happiest moment of his life.

Chapter Thirteen

 *J*oan stared at the leaves above her, feeling as if she'd never seen a tree before. Her first tree.

Her legs felt boneless and empty, as if she lay on the surface of the earth so lightly that she might float into the air, a spent dandelion.

"That . . ." she murmured, and forgot what she meant to say.

There had been so many firsts that her mind actually danced away from the idea of listing them. She was *naked* outdoors. Her skin was damp, and Thaddeus Erskine Shaw, future duke, friend of her family, was casually stroking her thigh, looking at her skin with as much absorption as if she were . . . as if she were a book that he was reading.

She'd seen him in the library over the years, reading with complete attention, eyes on the page, not even aware of her presence.

Now?

She had the feeling that, for him, there were

only the two of them in the world. She propped herself up on her elbows, feeling her breasts shift. As she watched, Thaddeus leaned over and placed a kiss precisely where he had been caressing her.

"Thank you," she breathed.

His head jerked up: She was right. He had been absorbed in *her*. Thaddeus's mouth widened into a smile. He was a beautiful man, fifty times more beautiful when he was happy.

She sat up and reached for her shirt. Instantly he caught it up and handed it to her. She froze. "Ants?"

Thaddeus took it back and gave it a vigorous shake. "If there was an ant, it would be unlikely to bite you."

"It would *crawl* on me."

"Like this?" One hand teasingly skittered up her calf.

She squeaked and jumped. "You!" She pulled the shirt over her head. "You are not supposed to have a sense of humor."

"I don't," Thaddeus said, his eyes utterly sober. Then his other hand crept up her other leg, making her squeak again. He broke into laughter.

Joan hopped to her feet and looked about. Her breeches were off to the side, so she shook them out and stepped into them. She felt embarrassed.

His fingers circled her bare ankle as she was buttoning up her breeches.

"Joan?"

She looked down at him, realizing with a sudden thump of her heart that the worst possible thing had happened to her. She truly was in love with a man whom she could not have. With a future duke.

Deeply in love.

With *Thaddeus*.

If she wasn't careful, she would begin hoping. She would rather die than long for a man who didn't love her.

Oh, Thaddeus liked her. And he liked kissing her.

But love?

He didn't even believe in the emotion, and she had a feeling that when this particular future duke made up his mind, he didn't change it. What's more, as they'd both agreed, he needed a woman from the nobility, not an illegitimate woman on the edge of being thrown from society.

Thaddeus looked up at her and then wrapped a second hand around her other ankle. "Sit down?"

"We should . . . we should practice dying," she said. She realized what she'd just said and felt herself turning pink.

"*La petite mort*," Thaddeus said, his accent perfect, naturally. "The French think an orgasm is the closest to Paradise that humanity can reach, so: a little death."

Joan sat down before him. His hands slipped from her ankles. "That was wonderful," she said bluntly. "I can't imagine what got into either of us. Perhaps Aunt Knowe made the plum jerkum stronger than it normally is."

He shook his head. "I had only a swallow." He leaned forward and brushed her mouth with a kiss. "I don't want to drink anything because I can still taste you on my tongue. Essence of Joan, far more sparkling than plum jerkum."

Color flooded Joan's cheeks yet again. She cleared her throat and looked away.

He caught her chin with his hand. "Never come here with another man. Promise me, Joan."

Joan stared at him. Where did that come from?

Thaddeus stared into her eyes as if he were asking for a vow.

"No. I won't promise."

He winced, and his brows drew together.

She forced the words out of her mouth. "I don't break vows, so I won't make that one. I might bring my husband here someday, Thaddeus." She paused, curving her hand around his strong jaw. "That doesn't mean I will ever forget the pleasure you gave me."

Her heart was thudding a heavy rhythm, because she loved him. She didn't want to hurt his feelings.

She didn't.

He nodded. "I asked you an ill-phrased question. I simply worried that another man would take advantage of you if you brought him here."

Joan felt a drop of ice down her back. Her hand fell from his cheek. Did he think that because she let *him* take off her breeches, she would do the same for any gentleman with whom she picnicked?

Perhaps . . . why wouldn't he think that?

"A husband by definition can't take advantage of me," she pointed out.

"I am finding you a husband," Thaddeus said.

Hatefully, he looked relieved at the thought. Happy, even, to be handing her off.

"You seem to think that"—she swallowed hard—"that this experience will lead me to escort gentlemen to the island on a regular basis."

He looked appalled. "I didn't mean to give you that impression."

"Good," she said evenly. "I shall wait for that husband you've promised. I *will* bring him, if you don't mind. This afternoon has been a revelation."

Thaddeus was good at controlling his expression, but something flashed through his eyes, and she caught it.

"After all, I might wish to unclothe him," she added.

She let her eyes deliberately fall down his front, straight to his crotch where a large bulge inflated his breeches. "I would like to see a man in the sunlight, rather than only under the bedclothes. I gather that is the practice of most married couples."

He nodded, and fury marched up her back because Thaddeus showed no sign of caring in the slightest. It was as if she'd told him that she would give her future husband an engraved snuffbox for his birthday.

"Perhaps I could return the pleasure that you taught me," she added. "To him."

Out of the corner of her eye, she saw a throb in his breeches. It was comforting. He might not want to marry her, but he did *want* her. That had to be good enough, when it came to Thaddeus Shaw.

All this emotion she felt for him had sprung from nothing, and surely it would go away just as easily.

She got up and pushed a few more boxes off the cloth, then reached over to grab her rapier, still kitted out with training tips. To her dismay, bending over made her private parts brush against the seam of her breeches, sending a pulse through her body.

"So how should I die?" she asked, turning to him.

He had come to his feet, of course. "Quietly. A prince dies without vulgar moans or groans, and certainly without writhing."

"How do you know?" she asked rebelliously. "I think my family would enjoy seeing Hamlet take his time to die."

Thaddeus shook his head. "The man has spent his entire life training to be king. A king dies in silence, without displaying pain or fear."

She stilled. "Is this what you meant when you said your father is a coward?"

"To some extent. In my father's case, impending death has reminded him of the mistakes he made in life. In Hamlet's case, although Ophelia is dead, he seems to have few regrets."

Joan scowled. "I'm starting to dislike Hamlet, which is unfortunate, since I have to play the fellow tomorrow."

"Let him die like a prince," Thaddeus said. "He lacks dignity throughout, with his uncle mocking his black clothing, a ghost bullying him, his wretched behavior toward a young lady exposed to her brother and the whole court. His own mother says he's fat and short of breath. Give him back that, at least."

Joan sighed. "Your version of Hamlet is so much less heroic than mine."

Thaddeus stayed silent.

For the next hour, they practiced death: dignified, quiet collapses.

"I have it," Joan said. She fell back a step from his sword and collapsed in a gentle heap, slow and silent. "He was a prince forced to be a puppet," she said, looking up from the ground. "I shall play him as a man grateful to be freed."

Thaddeus stared down at her, looking struck.

"You agree?" she asked, poking him in the bare ankle. His ankles were as strong as the rest of him. If things were different, she would roll to her side and . . .

"I think Hamlet was trained for the role of king, not prince," Thaddeus said. "His uncle stole the title, and he lost his compass."

Joan thought about answering, but the parallels were all too obvious. Thaddeus was losing his compass with her, but he would find it again. Without her, obviously.

For the first time, she thought about which woman she would recommend that he woo. The very idea sent a pang of fury through her and she leapt to her feet. "Let's practice the duel this time."

A half hour later, they were lying beside each other on the flowered cloth, panting. Thaddeus as well, Joan noticed with pleasure.

"You've improved," Thaddeus said, his chest

rising and falling. His arm brushed hers. He was hot as a coal.

She hadn't really improved, but it was amazing how a flash of anger could fuel a counterfeit duel. She had to remember that for the performance: Imagine Thaddeus courting a lady. A gentle, sweet, well-bred lady.

Over the years, she'd learned how to put away painful thoughts, but this one was hard to banish. There was no woman in all of England whom she could happily envision as his future duchess.

"Have you decided what you wish to do about your father?" she asked, trying to change her train of thought.

Thaddeus shook his head. His hair was the dark gold of ripe wheat.

She rolled onto her side and touched a thick lock. "Do you hate wearing a wig?"

He was staring up at the leaves. "Does it matter?"

"Yes."

"I've never given it any thought. Why entertain the question, if a gentleman must by definition wear a wig in public?"

"Because a gentleman is not always in public," Joan pointed out. "My father rarely wears one in Lindow Castle. My brothers used to share a few wigs and jam one on only when forced. Of course, my oldest brother, Horatius, was always immaculate before he passed away. Powdered and bewigged."

"I remember," Thaddeus said. "Do you miss him?"

"Yes," Joan said. "He was stuffy, but we adored him in the nursery."

"He wasn't stuffy as much as perfect," Thaddeus said.

Joan laughed. "A fault you share, then." She twisted the lock of hair she held, making it glimmer. "What does your father gain by publishing such a letter if he can't back it up with a marriage license?"

"His family will launch a legal claim on the estate," Thaddeus said tonelessly. "They'll try to break the entail by making an appeal to Parliament."

"But they won't succeed."

"He's mad," Thaddeus said, squinting at the leaves. "I am certain his solicitors have told him repeatedly that he has no claim. This is a last, desperate attempt."

"To destroy your lives? To spend absurd amounts of money on lawyers? There has to be more to it!"

"I don't believe so."

"It's stupefying," Joan argued. "Nonsensical."

"He's enraged that he married the wrong woman," Thaddeus said. "He told me once that his parents forced him to marry my mother, even knowing that, according to him, he was secretly married to another. He firmly believes that the law of primogeniture, giving everything to the eldest son, is evil. This is his last attempt to change English traditions going back hundreds of years."

"So the letter will launch a moral campaign?"

"Backed by selfishness," Thaddeus said wryly. "As is so often the case."

Joan caught up his hand. Thaddeus's fingers curled around hers, but he didn't turn his head.

They lay in silence, their fingers linked. Off to the side, the squirrel was chattering to himself, busily going through every one of the open boxes and selecting items to put to the side.

"He's making plans for the winter," Joan said softly.

"My father is doing the same," Thaddeus said. "He's afraid that I'll throw out his other family and refuse to support them. He thinks that if the court of public opinion is brought into play, I'll be shamed into supporting them. Or perhaps his solicitors will ask for a settlement in lieu of withdrawing the petition to Parliament. I wouldn't be surprised if his letter implied that I had found and destroyed his first marriage license."

"Hell." Her fingers tightened around his. "That's absolute rubbish. He doesn't know you, does he?"

"No." Finally, Thaddeus turned his head. She felt the shock of his gaze down her back. Into . . . perhaps into her heart. "He doesn't know me, and he has never cared to. I represent his life's greatest injustice, not that he ever gave my mother a chance."

"If he *did* know you, he would realize that you would never throw your own family onto the road, especially because that family had the worst of a very poor bargain."

"What bargain?"

His eyes crinkled a bit at the edges. A smile wasn't visible, but it was there. "You smile with your eyes, did you know that?" Joan asked.

"What bargain?" he repeated.

He was a stubborn man, she could see that. It was absurd to fall in love with someone so unyielding and pedantic and—and ducal.

Too late, too late.

They had to leave. Even holding his hand made her feel slightly dazed.

"You have your mother; your half siblings have your father," she said. "The duchess is wonderful, and he is selfish, peevish, and now, demented."

Thaddeus smiled wryly.

"We should return to the castle," Joan said.

Thaddeus helped her collect the food that the squirrel had rejected, and they walked back down the path to the boat waiting in the reeds, across the water . . .

Back to the castle.

Back to reality, Joan told herself.

Chapter Fourteen

The Lindow Castle ballroom didn't have a curtain to fall before the stage, nor trumpets to signal the entrance of the king, nor the cannons called for in the script of *The Tragedy of Hamlet, Prince of Denmark*.

But as Act Five drew to a close, Joan was certain that Lindow Castle had hosted an excellent *Hamlet*. Certainly, the audience had loved it. Everyone attended: the family and guests, all the household staff who could be spared.

Mind you, there were hiccups.

Otis uttered his lines perfectly until the scene in which Ophelia enters in a mad state and tosses around flowers. At that point, the giggles of the younger Wildes and kitchen maids infected him, and he tossed not only the flowers mentioned in the script, but a few from his hat as well.

Joan fancied she did Hamlet a disservice in the famous *To be or not to be* speech. She wasn't a suicidal person—and as the play progressed, she began to suspect that she wasn't an actress either.

In fact, after spending her entire life longing to be part of a theater company . . . she wasn't sure any longer.

To play a role, you have to *be* that person.

Be Hamlet. *Love* Hamlet.

She didn't love Hamlet. In fact, the last two weeks had taught her that he was pretty *un*lovable, and he should have counted his blessings when Ophelia wrote him adoring letters and climbed in his bedchamber window.

Her favorite part of the performance came when she was drumming her fingers on Hamlet's sword, and she glanced at the audience (seated all of two feet away) and saw Thaddeus's eyes narrow. Everything in her wanted to give him an impudent smile, but she didn't.

She was professional, if only for that night.

The mood after the performance was celebratory, with champagne circulating around the ballroom.

"Bravo, Hamlet!" Mr. Wooty cried, coming up behind Joan. "You did the prince proud, Lady Joan, you truly did."

She smiled at him. "I am so grateful that you allowed me to perform with your troupe, Mr. Wooty. And that you took on Otis as well."

"Mr. Murgatroyd has a rare hand for the comic," the director said. "He could make his fortune on the stage. He knows the mood of an audience. Even if he forgets his lines, it wouldn't matter. Mind you, no more lady's roles. I'd give him the part of a Fool."

"Yet after tonight, I believe that I could not make my fortune," Joan said, coming out with it. "Could I, Mr. Wooty?"

There was a brief silence, and then he said, "A woman as beautiful as yourself would always be welcome in a theater company. It's a difficult life, Lady Joan."

"That's not what I meant," Joan replied.

"You are very much yourself," Mr. Wooty said apologetically. "A great lady, the daughter of a duke. That lady shone through Hamlet's complaints, I'm afraid."

"Good evening, Mr. Wooty," Thaddeus said, strolling up. "May I offer my congratulations on a stellar Shakespeare performance?"

Mr. Wooty turned to him with a distinct air of relief. "You may!" he boomed. "This young lady had a great deal to do with it, of course."

"Lady Joan was a brilliant Prince of Denmark," Thaddeus stated.

Joan saw complete sincerity in his eyes. She sighed. "No, I wasn't."

"Of course you were," Thaddeus declared, a ferocious scowl uniting his eyebrows.

Aunt Knowe joined them. "I was eavesdropping," she said without a drop of remorse. "Am I to understand that you didn't care for your own performance, Joan?"

"I was fine," Joan said, a curious sense of freedom blooming in her chest.

Aunt Knowe wrapped an arm around her waist. "Dear one."

Joan rubbed her ear against her aunt's shoulder. "Mr. Wooty, you are so kind to have given me this opportunity."

"It was my pleasure, my lady, and I would disagree with your assessment."

"What's your Hamlet usually like?" she asked. "I mean, as performed by the actor in your company?"

"Every Hamlet is different, my lady. My current Hamlet plays the role with bravado. The actor has a past, which helps."

"Surely most actors have led interesting lives," Aunt Knowe said. "What sort of a past?"

"On the high seas," Mr. Wooty said, looking disapproving. "Grew up a lad on the ships, and I've chosen not to inquire too closely into the circumstances of his father's naval career."

"Black sails?" Joan cried. "The skull and crossbones, together with *Walk the plank, lad*?"

"Could be," Mr. Wooty said. "Could be."

"Or he could be a tailor's son who dreamed of running away to sea, but joined a theater instead," Thaddeus said dryly. "The life of many a pirate is cut short by violence."

"Or drowning," Aunt Knowe put in.

"My Hamlet's not dead," Mr. Wooty said. "My point is that he plays a different Hamlet, Lady Joan. Yours is thoughtful, dignified, and regretful. His is bursting with life and infuriated that the kingdom was snatched from his hands by his uncle. He plays the outraged heir; you played the grieving son."

Joan elbowed Thaddeus, and then said in a low voice, "I *told* you that you should have played Hamlet, rather than me!"

Thaddeus flinched. "Never."

Mr. Wooty glanced over his shoulder and realized that Otis was talking to his niece in a low voice at the side of the room. "If you'll excuse me," he said, bustling away.

"I enjoy watching those two," Aunt Knowe said, nodding toward Otis and Madeline. "She was in the corner acting as the prompter, and he played his part mostly for her."

"Except for the mad scene," Thaddeus said dryly. "I fancy Otis came into his own when inspired by the nursery."

"Did you act at Eton?" Aunt Knowe asked.

Thaddeus shook his head. "Not unless forced to do so."

"You preferred mathematics?" Joan asked.

"Astronomy," he said. "Which is close to mathematics."

Thaddeus had no particular expression, but as he began to explain the theory of galaxies to Aunt Knowe, Joan saw his eyes brighten. If he hadn't been born to be a duke, he'd be a scientist. He would be writing about the stars, a member of the Royal Society, spending his evenings peering at the sky.

Or perhaps he would study animals, she thought, remembering the squirrel.

"Do you have a telescope?" Aunt Knowe asked him, obviously coming to the same conclusion.

"No need," Thaddeus said. "I outgrew the interests of my boyhood."

Joan stood quietly, watching his face as he explained the mysteries of the universe to her aunt. She was in trouble.

She felt far too much.

A dangerous amount. She had instantly decided to give him a telescope for his birthday.

Ladies didn't give gentlemen gifts . . . unless they were married to them.

She shouldn't have taken off her shirt on the island, let alone allowed the intimacies that followed. She should have guarded her heart.

Even looking at him made ripples of feeling wash through her body. Followed by a wave of panic. She had to cancel the trip to Wilmslow tomorrow. She didn't particularly want to play Hamlet again, to be honest.

Her fervent wish to play before a public audience?

Not gone, but definitely muted. She'd learned something about herself in the course of the evening, and prudence suggested that she wave goodbye to Thaddeus Erskine Shaw and set about getting herself into a sane frame of mind.

Plus, there was the bargain she'd struck with Thaddeus: She would perform for a live audience, and he would find her a husband.

No performance, no husband.

That was a double no when it came to finding him a wife. He could find his own wife. She wanted nothing to do with it.

A flurry of movement caught her eye, and she realized that Viola was waving at her from the other side of the room. Her stepsister was seated in a large chair brought into the ballroom especially for her, as the imminent arrival of her child, despite Viola's small frame, had made one of the flimsy gilt ballroom chairs an impossibility.

Joan dropped a curtsy to Thaddeus and Aunt Knowe, still talking of stars, and headed over to Viola. "Hello, V," she said, sitting down and realizing (for the thousandth time) how comfortable she felt wearing Hamlet's breeches rather than a voluminous gown.

"You were marvelous!" Viola said, beaming at her. "Wasn't she, Devin?"

Devin was standing behind his wife, a hand on her shoulder as if he were poised to snatch her into his arms and head upstairs. "Yes," her husband agreed, his eyes warm. "You were an excellent Hamlet."

Joan grinned at her brother-in-law. He was a man of few words, but she had come to treasure every one. "Had you seen the play before?" she demanded. "Mr. Wooty just told me that my interpretation of Hamlet is the opposite of the Hamlet he usually stages."

"A first encounter is the best way to judge a performance," Devin countered. "I hadn't realized Hamlet was such a dislikable character, but you were entirely believable."

"He was so mean to poor Ophelia," Viola said, squeezing Joan's hand. "She was always my favorite character in the play. Shy, you could tell. At least, until she became mad."

Devin cleared his throat. "I'm not certain that Otis deserves the same accolades as does Joan."

"He doesn't care," Viola said, giggling. "Who is that extraordinarily pretty girl he eyed throughout the performance? He nearly fell off the stage at least twice."

They looked across the room to where Otis and his father were talking to the Wooty family. Everyone was smiling.

"Dear me," Devin said. "I believe that Otis has fallen in love."

Joan managed a smile. She was happy for her friend. But she was jealous too.

She didn't get a chance to talk to him for quite a while, until the theater company had retired to their wagons, the nursery had been ushered off to bed, Viola had departed on her husband's arm, and everyone else was quietly leaving for their rooms.

"Otis!" she cried, catching his arm.

He turned to her with a beaming smile. "I'm betrothed!"

"I thought so." She leaned in and kissed his cheek. "Madeline is a lovely woman."

"She's beautiful, but most of all, she's funny. I realized within an hour of talking to her that I couldn't possibly marry anyone who didn't make me laugh. She does."

Joan kissed him again, and then said, "Otis, I'd rather not do the performance in Wilmslow tomorrow night, if you don't mind."

To her surprise, his brows drew together. "We're traveling there tomorrow with the Wootys. I've talked them into staying at the inn with us."

"I don't want to do it," Joan said, unable to explain that she didn't want to spend time with Thaddeus.

"Is it because I'm such a bad Ophelia?" Otis asked. "Madeline said that I was fine until the mad scene in the throne room, but tomorrow I won't let the absurdity get to me. I promise."

"You were quite good," Joan said, feeling even more crushed. "Especially when you gave a flower to my stepmother. And when you threw flowers to the children. They loved that."

"Your stepmother's name *is* Ophelia," Otis said smugly. "I couldn't neglect her under those circumstances."

"I don't want to do a public performance," Joan said starkly.

"You weren't a terrible Hamlet," Otis protested.

"I knew the part. But I wasn't a *good* Hamlet, Otis. And don't try to tell me that I was. I've been going to plays for my entire life."

"I thought you were excellent," Otis said.

"I was adequate," Joan corrected him. She had never been the sort of woman who lied to herself, not about her parentage, her prospects, or anything else.

"You can't back out of tomorrow," Otis said, abandoning the question of her acting skills. He crossed his arms over his chest, looking unusually stubborn. "The performance in Wilmslow has already been advertised. My future father-in-law can't cancel it with no notice."

"You could pay him to do so," Joan suggested. "Buy out the theater."

Otis rolled his eyes. "I'm not nearly as knowledgeable about the theater as you are, but even I know that the show must go on."

Joan opened her mouth, but Otis raised his hand. "I would rather that my future wife has made her last public performance, because Madeline doesn't care for the stage. When her parents died and she came to England, she had no choice. Therefore, I play Ophelia tomorrow night."

"I feel for Madeline," Joan said, "but I don't want to play Hamlet again."

"Your Hamlet was unusual," Otis said encouragingly.

"Not heroic," Joan said flatly.

"You certainly brought forward the prince's less

valiant side, but it's there on the page. I was startled when Hamlet casually announced he'd had his two friends killed. I don't remember that detail from when we read it at school."

He caught her arm. "*Please*, Joan. I promised Madeline that I would take her part and I can't do it without you."

"I suppose I owe you, since I forced you into a corset in the first place," Joan allowed.

Otis gave her a kiss and started to go, before turning back. "Don't forget that my father and Thaddeus's mother are accompanying us tomorrow, and they have no idea about the public performance. My man will sneak a trunk with your breeches onto the coach at first light tomorrow."

"All right," Joan said. She'd never been so exhausted in her life. *Hamlet* was a long play, including the sword fighting. Even a dignified death was tiring.

"I hate these skirts more every moment," Otis grumbled.

Joan followed him out the door.

She only had to endure one day and evening with Thaddeus. She'd put on her breeches for the last time, and then return to the castle and don her skirts. She could tell him tomorrow that the bargain was off. It had been an absurd idea, anyway. She was no matchmaker, able to conjure up a future duchess.

She could find her own husband, a kindly fellow with no ambitions to a dukedom.

Someone who would adore her unconditionally and always agree with her.

Chapter Fifteen

$\mathcal{A}$s the next day wore on, Thaddeus felt himself growing more and more angry, an emotion he abhorred at the best of times. It seemed impossible to maintain his usual equanimity.

He was trying to decide if he should inform his mother about his father's threat. The quandary nagged at him in the middle of the night until he gave up the idea of sleeping. What if the duke had already died, and the bloody letter appeared in the morning paper?

The worst of it was that Joan had . . . left. She was in the castle, but it was as if she had walked out of the room, as if the intimacies they'd shared had never existed.

Oh, she smiled at him, laughed at the right moments, carried on conversations over breakfast . . .

But it wasn't *Joan*.

His Joan.

He had always known that she was a brilliant actress. But he didn't understand just how much self-control she had until she started playing the part of a perfect young lady: docile, cheerful, kind.

After a morning of relentless cheer, he caught his mother gazing at Joan with a pleat between her brows.

People tended to ignore his mother because she was shy, eccentric, and always wore pink. Yet she was one of the most perceptive people he'd ever known.

She'd known for the last two years that something was wrong with him, for example, though he'd managed not to confess.

"Otis traveled to Wilmslow with the Wooty family, in their wagon," Joan said as luncheon drew to a close. "I've never been invited inside one of the wagons." Her voice had a distinctly wistful tone.

Sir Reginald nodded. "My son is now a member of that family. I apologized to Miss Wooty for not coming to the theater to see her Ophelia tonight. Seeing *Hamlet* two nights in a row is too much Bard for me."

As Thaddeus watched, Joan gave him a charming smile. "I understand," she confided. "The play is long and rather tedious."

"Playing the title role didn't infect you with love of the play?" Sir Reginald asked.

Joan shook her head. "No. Instead of being infected with a love of performance, I believe my reaction to performing the part was the opposite."

"Done with breeches parts?" Sir Reginald asked.

"I'm not as mad for performance as I thought I was. I pictured *myself* as an actress. What I was not picturing was myself playing Hamlet, or Ophelia, or another role, if that makes sense."

"It does," Thaddeus's mother put in. "I know exactly what you mean. I frequently remind myself that I'm a duchess when in public. It's a role I assume when needed."

Thaddeus would never have made a distinction between himself and the dukedom—until his father began to insist that his younger son ought to be the duke.

"In fact, I think I shall put theatricals to the side for the time being," Joan said. "After my sister's baby is born, my stepmother and I have promised to attend a country house party given by Lady Ailesbury."

Sir Reginald smiled at her roguishly. "The bachelors will be very happy to see you."

Thaddeus's heart sank.

"I gather that Otis will travel from Wilmslow to London with the Wootys," Joan said. "Will you join them, Sir Reginald?"

"I scarcely arrived, so I plan to stay at the castle for another fortnight," Sir Reginald said, his eyes sliding to Thaddeus's mother's face.

The meal concluded, and the ladies rose to their feet. "Lady Joan, what time would you like to travel to Wilmslow?" Thaddeus asked, coming around the table to meet her. "As I understand it, the building is on the opposite side of the town."

She looked up at him with utmost friendliness—and not an ounce of intimacy. "That would be very kind of you, Lord Greywick. Are you certain that you can bear to see the performance twice?"

"I could accompany you, my dear," the Duchess of Eversley said. "To tell the truth, I always fall asleep in Shakespeare plays, so I don't mind seeing *Hamlet* twice."

Out of the corner of his eye, Thaddeus saw Sir Reginald's face fall.

Interesting.

For the first time, it occurred to him that perhaps his mother wouldn't wish to remain a duchess after her husband died. Perhaps she would remarry.

"If you are tired in the evening, Mother, you would do better to have a quiet supper with Sir Reginald by the fireside," he suggested.

"Your mother will do precisely as she wishes!" Joan flashed. "*You would do better* indeed!"

He watched with amusement as Joan remembered the reason she didn't want his mother in the theater. As dismay flashed through her eyes, he turned to his mother. "I apologize for my presumption," he said, bowing.

"Don't be silly, dear," his mother replied. "I would enjoy staying in the inn. Perhaps my old friend will match me in a game of chess."

"You always wallop me," Sir Reginald said, his face wreathed with smiles.

"True," the duchess said. "But I enjoy doing it."

"Why don't we travel to Wilmslow immediately? We could visit St. Bartholomew's, which is justly famous, as parts of it date back to the 1240s," Sir Reginald suggested.

To the best of Thaddeus's knowledge, his mother had never shown the slightest interest in antiquities, religious or otherwise, but now she agreed with enthusiasm.

"We can travel in my carriage," Sir Reginald said, offering his arm.

There was a pause—and she agreed.

As far as Thaddeus was concerned, that settled it. The only question was whether his mother would observe a mourning period after her husband's death. Why should she?

The older couple strolled from the room. Joan followed, her skirts the width of the door frame, so Thaddeus walked in the rear.

Seen from behind, Joan was so entirely a woman that it was impossible to believe that anyone would think her a man. And yet—they would. He would bet the estate that he didn't yet have that no one in the audience would imagine that a woman was playing Hamlet.

A few hours later, when his carriage door closed behind Joan, she threw off her cloak and hissed, "Undress me!"

Thaddeus found himself laughing. "I can think of no command that I'd prefer, but is this the time? The place?"

"Bloody hell, Thaddeus," she snapped, looking over her shoulder at him. "I have barely an hour to get out of this dress and into my breeches. I can't arrive as Lady Joan and reappear as Hamlet. My maid did everything she could; I am dressed in a simple gown. But I need your help."

"Of course."

Never mind the fact that for one crystalline moment he was filled with joy, as if everything that was wrong in his world had suddenly sorted itself out.

The idea was so surprising that he began unlacing her gown without a word.

Meanwhile, Joan was flinging hairpins to the floor until she threw her wig on the opposite seat and pulled a smaller man's wig from a travel case. Her dress fell forward, baring her slender shoulders, now clad only in a shift so transparent that he could see the delicate knobs of her backbone. She snatched her breeches from the bag and hopped to a standing position in order to pull them on.

Thaddeus froze, watching as no gentleman would while she hauled them up her legs. For one glorious moment, as she pulled the chemise off, he saw her bare back. Then she pulled on a shirt and began stuffing it into the top of the breeches. "You're going to have to manage my neck cloth," she said, not turning around.

"I'd be happy to," Thaddeus said, reaching out to steady her as they went around a corner. His hands curved around her waist, and happiness flooded him again. As a child, he'd learned that ignoring an irritating emotion—such as missing his father—would diminish the feeling.

He had an odd sense that it wouldn't be true this time around.

Another problem to solve.

Joan threw herself onto the opposite seat and began hauling stockings up her legs. "Can you pull out my knee ribbons?" she asked, nodding at the bag. "I have my garters." Thaddeus wrenched his eyes away from the lacy garters that Hamlet would apparently wear under his breeches.

He poked around in the bag and found two hair ribbons.

"Here," Joan ordered, straightening one leg while she pulled on the other stocking. "Double knot it, please. These ribbons have to survive the sword fight."

Thaddeus grinned. "I never anticipated the need to learn a valet's tasks."

"You should have," she retorted, adjusting her breeches over a garter. "What good is a man who can't tie his own neck cloth?"

"I do tie my own," Thaddeus said. He leaned over and pulled the ribbons tight, knotting them more than twice. No one was going to see his lady's leg—

His lady's leg.

The lady in question was pulling on her coat. "Shoes!" she said urgently.

Thaddeus turned to the bag and pulled out shoes. "Diamond buckles," he said, raising an eyebrow. "You didn't wear these last night."

"I need to look like a prince," Joan said. She slapped her hat on top of her wig. "Last night, the costume was irrelevant, but tonight I have to actually look royal. Otis is going to meet me and escort me to his dressing room so I can fix anything that is out of order."

"Give me your Hamlet look," he said.

Instantly her face dropped into lines that signaled a bone-deep feeling of superiority. "My rapier!" she cried. "I almost forgot it."

Thaddeus pulled it from the bag and helped her buckle it on. Suddenly he remembered something from the night before. "Hamlet appears to have a propensity to drum his fingers on the hilt of his sword when worried."

She flashed him a smile. "As do you. This is your look as well." The bored, condescending look of an aristocrat settled onto her face.

Thaddeus blinked, appalled. "I?" The word came out in a rasp.

The carriage was slowing to a halt. Joan leaned forward and patted his arm. "I told you that I was mimicking the habits of a duke, remember? You don't look like that when we're in private."

"I didn't think I looked like that ever." He thought of the expression as ducal composure, but apparently more emotion leaked than he had imagined.

Joan almost patted his arm again, but he drew back before he could stop himself. She had a sympathetic, nearly regretful, look on her face. "I apologize, Thaddeus. I didn't know you when I planned my Hamlet. Now that I know you, of course I feel differently."

So he *did* wear that expression.

"I didn't realize that you were playacting," she went on awkwardly, as silence grew between them. "As when your mother described herself playing the role of a duchess. I had no idea. I have always known that I, in particular, must play the part of a lady, and sometimes I have chosen not to comply. I didn't think of others faced with the same conundrum."

"I don't *play* the part of a duke's heir," Thaddeus stated. "I am a duke's heir." He deliberately made his expression mimic Hamlet's. "I assure you that I haven't homicidal feelings toward the boy who may usurp my title."

"Of course you don't!" Joan said. She picked up a small glass and poked at her wig, making sure there were no stray tendrils showing. "By the way, I've been meaning to tell you that I shall not need your help choosing a husband. My mother is quite willing to take on the task, now that I've promised that I will take it seriously. Which I shall."

"When you travel to Lady Ailesbury's house party," he said, knowing his voice was wooden.

She smiled at him as cheerily as if they were discussing the weather. "I also want to get my part of the bargain out of the way. I suggest that you avoid dukes' daughters; you need someone haughty but not *too* haughty, if you see what I mean. I've given it some thought, and I suggest Lady Lucy Lockett. Her mother was a marquess's daughter, and her father is an earl. She has excellent connections, admirable composure, and no one will question whether she is fit to be a duchess."

For a second, Thaddeus felt as if someone had drenched him in privy water.

Joan babbled on about the virtues of Lucy—who sounded like an excruciating bore—while Thaddeus ordered himself to show no signs of anger. Ducal composure.

"Her face is a perfect oval," Joan told him. "She's very dainty, if you know what I mean.

I expect you can put your hands around her waist."

Thaddeus knew exactly what Joan meant: no picnics for him. No ants, no rolling in the grass, no vengeful goats. One heir and a spare, because his dainty wife wouldn't want to spoil her figure.

Perfect. Lovely Lucy.

"And," Joan wound up with a brilliant smile, "your mother will like her. Lucy often wears pink." She blinked. Her smile faltered.

Thaddeus clenched his teeth and kept his composure by counting to ten. It seemed that the woman he loved had suddenly remembered that people weren't chess pieces to be moved about the board and matched due to superficial traits such as birth and clothing.

The fact that he himself had declared an intention to marry a duke's daughter was of no consequence. He'd been a fool.

He couldn't bring himself to look at her as they descended from the carriage, which had drawn up behind the theater. "Good luck with the performance tonight," he said, with a curt nod. It would never do to bow to an actor, a male actor, in case anyone was watching.

Otis was waiting at the theater door, so Thaddeus got back into the carriage without another word.

The door closed and he took a deep breath. He was about to rap on the ceiling and tell the coachman to take him around to the front of the building, when the door swung open. His head jerked up, but it wasn't his groom.

"Vanity and pride are not inherited along

with a title!" Joan flashed. Then she slammed the door shut.

Thaddeus's jaw tightened, and he could feel a nerve ticking in his jaw. He banged on the roof. "Around the front."

"Yes, my lord," the coachman shouted.

The coach lurched slightly as his groom jumped onto the back, and the horses began clopping over the cobblestones. The carriage looked as if a trunk had exploded in it. Thaddeus began picking up her garments and folding them.

Stockings, light as air and marked with clocks on the side. Delicate straw-colored shoes, curiously embroidered. A white and gold fichu, subtly anointed with fresh scent that made his heartbeat speed up because he would always associate elderflower with Joan. A tall wig, though not large for a woman.

By the time the carriage rounded the front of the theater, he had Joan's belongings folded on the opposite seat or tucked in the traveling case. He stepped down to the street and paused. The Wilmslow theater wasn't what he had imagined.

He had been to the great London theaters throughout his life. He was particularly fond of the Haymarket Theatre. Like many others, he would arrive by boat on the Thames, escorting his mother up the steps and into the elegant stone building. He would stroll into the theater, nodding to gentlemen, most of whom he would recognize, feeling every inch a future duke. His knee buckles were adorned with rubies, if not diamonds. His frock coat was elegant; his silk waistcoat likely trimmed with gold.

He would join his fellow noblemen, who were ushered to the upper regions via private doors, while apprentices crowded the pit just below the stage.

Damn it, the cursed memory made him feel as if he *had* donned a costume and strolled through the Haymarket Theatre as an actor playing a duke. And his mother on his arm, playing the duchess.

But this was no London stage.

With a sinking feeling, Thaddeus realized that Joan's sensitive, melancholy prince would tread the boards—of a *barn*. The people crowding in the entrance, throwing ha'pennies in the general direction of the man collecting fees, were not wearing diamond buckles.

Some of them were obviously inebriated, and since large flagons of fortified ale were being sold at the door, others soon would be. No wonder Wooty was worried about flying vegetables.

The ale sellers weren't the only people at work; boys were pushing their way through the unruly crowd, likely collecting purses as they went, and women with garish lip color were plying their trade as well, ushering men around the side of the barn.

Unhurriedly, Thaddeus walked forward, flanked by two grooms who sprang from the carriage. He glanced over his shoulder at the coachman. "Don't loosen the harnesses, if you please. The grooms can stay with you."

The man nodded, his eyes scanning the unruly crowd.

A brightly painted woman stepped into Thaddeus's path. "Time and enough to go round behind, sir," she said, jerking her head toward the side. "You smell that good." She leaned in and took a loud sniff.

"Thank you, but no," Thaddeus replied, giving her a coin.

The crowd pulled back as he approached the door, watching him, not silently but with cheerful interest. Comments flew among them, comparing him to a local squire, and then rightly guessing that he must be a swell coming from Lindow.

"One of them at the castle," he heard distinctly. "Not a Wilde, though. Them Wilde eyebrows is unmistakable."

"Didn't you see the coach?" another asked. "That's a Lindow coach. I seen the picture on the door."

Thaddeus handed over a ha'penny coin.

"All standing tonight. Only seating's on the stage," the doorkeeper told him. "Additional sixpence for a stool."

Thaddeus gave him sixpence.

"Haven't seen anyone else wanting to pay," the man said. "Don't have the missus with you? You might be on your own to the side of the stage, but you'll blend in, I'd wager. The play is about kings, as I heard."

"I heard the same," Thaddeus said amiably.

"I hope there's something to keep the crowd happy," the man confided, dropping the money into a leather bag tied with strong cord to his belt.

"Last thing I want is my barn burning down, as has happened in other places when the play doesn't please."

"The play is *excellent*," Thaddeus said, raising his voice so that all behind him could hear. "It has everything: tragedy, deaths, disclosures, ghosts, love and despair, illusion and disguise."

"Hope you're right," the doorkeeper said, turning to holler, "Jehoshaphat, get yourself over here. Get a stool and take the gentleman up on the stage."

An eight- or nine-year-old boy led Thaddeus to the back of the barn where a crudely built stage jutted at waist height. Thaddeus put a hand on the boards and leapt up.

"Are you looking forward to the play?" Thaddeus inquired, as Jehoshaphat fetched a stool.

"I heard there's a king," the boy said. "I'm named after a king. And swords! I like swords. Plus, there's juggling in between every scene, not just the acts." He hopped down from the stage and disappeared into the crowd milling about in front of the stage.

Thaddeus positioned his stool off to the side, where the wings would be in a London theater, close enough so that he could snatch Joan from the stage if need be, but not awkwardly in the way of the action.

He sank onto the stool. He was used to being alone, seated above the crowd. Walking through the world in a duke's costume. He barely suppressed a grimace.

Rather than survey the crowd—many members

of whom showed a ready willingness to engage
in fisticuffs if they took affront—he sent those
closest a silent warning that had them turning
their backs, and then stared across the stage at
the barn wall.

He didn't have to live in costume. He was no
Hamlet.

Yet somehow he had become Hamlet: emotional,
uncontrolled, desperate.

His reaction felt primitive and entirely ungentlemanly. No subtleties. He wanted—he wanted her.
Joan. No Lucy Lockett for him.

He would have her, his unladylike, dramatic,
illegitimate . . . love.

He turned the statement over in his head until
he realized that reason played no part in it. He
had fallen, not for feminine wiles, but for something altogether more powerful and honest: a
woman who made him laugh, who made his
heart pound with a mere glance, who seduced
him with a spoonful of rose jelly.

He was still mulling over what in the hell had
happened to him when Jehoshaphat came back
with two more stools, and a couple in tow. They
ponderously mounted steps to the stage that he
hadn't noticed.

"Mrs. Meadowsweet," the lady told him, when
he rose and bowed.

She had a faint resemblance to a gladiator: well
fed and possessed of a remarkable breastplate.
"Mr. Meadowsweet and I were just married this
morning, so we thought we'd have a bit of fun to
celebrate. I told Mr. Meadowsweet that I wouldn't

tolerate being down among the groundlings." She sat down heavily, teetered, and managed to keep her balance on the stool.

"Mrs. Meadowsweet is worth three times as many sixpences," her husband announced. He bowed. "Mr. Meadowsweet, at your service."

Thaddeus bowed. "Lord Greywick."

Mrs. Meadowsweet turned to her husband. "A real lord! Now aren't you glad that we chose the theater over a trout stream? You can see trout any day of the week!"

Before her husband affirmed the paucity of lords as opposed to fish, an actor sprang out from the curtain at the back of the stage and blew a trumpet, signaling the beginning of *Hamlet, Prince of Denmark*.

Joan's Hamlet paced across the stage, looking like a melancholy warrior, ready to draw his rapier and stab someone in the heart. The crowd didn't seem too impressed, but they liked the Ghost and squealed every time he boomed his famous line, *Remember me*.

Thaddeus watched Mr. Wooty, positioned directly across from him on a prompter's stool, glance repeatedly at the crowd. It didn't take theatrical experience to realize that the crowd wasn't following Hamlet's convoluted speeches and didn't understand much of what was going on.

The biggest cheering came for the juggler who followed the first two scenes. Thaddeus watched him for a moment before he nodded to the Meadowsweets, rose, and walked off the back of the stage to the area where the actors were entering and exiting.

Mr. Wooty was coaching Otis in his lines, while a laughing Madeline dusted some rouge on his cheeks.

Joan was practicing yanking her sword from its hilt. She jerked her head up as he walked over and to his enormous pleasure, her eyes lit up. "Thaddeus!"

He bowed. "Hamlet."

He turned to Mr. Wooty. "It's not working," he said bluntly.

"I shouldn't have done it," Mr. Wooty admitted. "I wouldn't have, but we had to rehearse for Lindow, and I didn't want to lose a day rehearsing a different play."

"Do it as a comedy," Thaddeus said bluntly.

"*What?*"

Thaddeus turned to Joan and Otis. "Do it the way you played for the children. Make it funny. The audience will love it."

"But the other actors—" Joan protested.

"They'd just as soon not be plastered with tomatoes," Mr. Wooty said. "But I've never heard of a funny Hamlet. Now this particular Ophelia . . . certainly. Last night I laughed myself into stitches, watching her pull flowers off her hat and offer them to the queen."

Joan was shaking her head, so Thaddeus took a step closer. "You're *funny*, Joan. The funniest person I know. Everyone laughs around you."

"It's *Hamlet*," she whispered. "A classic of English—"

"A boring play about a fretful prince," he interrupted her. "All these people paid for a night's entertainment, and you can give them that, Joan.

Just play the Hamlet who gazed at the alligator head."

"I don't think I can," she said, winding her hands together.

"I know you can."

"I agree," Otis said. "Look, I'm about to go in there and have my big scene where I give you back my love letters, right?"

"First, your father tells you to give back the letters," Joan told him.

"I knew that!" Otis said, making a quick recovery. "Anyway, as soon as I walk out, they'll begin laughing. Just play along."

"I know that you wanted to play a serious part," Thaddeus told her. "I'm sorry, Joan. I'll arrange for you to play Hamlet in London, if you wish."

"God, no!" she cried. Her face expressed utter conviction.

Thaddeus had to stop himself from kissing her.

"More lip color," Otis said to Madeline. "More rouge too. And can you throw a few more flowers onto my hat?"

Up on the stage, the juggler caught his balls, blew a kiss to the crowd, and jumped off the back. Thaddeus made his way to his stool, where Mrs. Meadowsweet leaned toward him. "We've been discussing you," she announced. "Did you write this play?"

"No, I did not," he answered.

She looked relieved. "Mr. Meadowsweet feels it's right rubbish and not worth the money."

Her husband muttered something that sounded like, "A trout stream is free."

"The play will get better," Thaddeus promised.

"Was that ghost the king who's dead?" Mrs. Meadowsweet asked.

Thaddeus nodded. "Thus he's a ghost."

"Twisty," she said. "I expect the queen's new husband killed him. He looks a fair rotter, like my second, as died last year. Not that Mr. Meadowsweet killed him, of course."

Mr. Meadowsweet put on a stern look. "I certainly did not."

Luckily, the trumpet sounded before Thaddeus had to comment on the homicidal propensities of Mrs. Meadowsweet's third husband.

Otis was a huge success. The audience began laughing immediately, not bothering to pretend that Ophelia was actually a woman, but recognizing one of their favorite pantomime characters: Cinderella, or Patient Griselda, or any other character, played by a man.

Ophelia complained to her father that Hamlet seemed to have gone mad, and acted out the madness herself. The audience roared with laughter.

It was even better when Hamlet and Ophelia were on the stage together. The tense, agonizing scene in which Ophelia gives Hamlet back his love letters turned into a raucous conversation, and when Hamlet told Ophelia she should enter a nunnery, the audience screamed with laughter.

This Ophelia? In a nunnery?

Not the way she was strutting around the stage, swishing her hips and poking Hamlet in the stomach when she got cross.

"He's better off without her," the woman to

the front of the stage told her husband in a loud voice. "She's no better than she should be. A nunnery indeed!"

Thaddeus couldn't stop himself from laughing, watching Joan play the audience like a virtuoso. When she acted Hamlet the night before, she had pretended the audience wasn't there and performed as if they were recreating history. But tonight?

She held them in the palm of her hand.

To be or not to be was hilariously received, and Otis's mad scene, when he gave away all his flowers and then began plucking them from his hat and throwing them into the audience, was cheered so loudly they must have heard it in the center of town.

He was slightly concerned how Joan would handle the dueling, but he shouldn't have worried. From the moment she had trouble pulling her rapier from its hilt, to the point at which she collapsed on the stage, employing every technique her brothers had taught her about long, dramatic deaths, the audience adored her.

Cheering brought the company back on stage three times to take bows.

Thaddeus watched his neighbor clapping and then leaned in. "So you enjoyed it?"

"The best was that lady with the jaw like a frying pan."

"A man," Thaddeus confirmed, tucking away the "jaw like a frying pan" to amuse Otis.

"She climbed in the prince's bedroom window," Mrs. Meadowsweet said. "No better than she should be." She leaned in closer. "Don't believe that she drowned herself, though. That sort would have paddled off downstream, and the family buried an empty casket to keep themselves from being mortified." She narrowed her eyes with a vigorous nod. "Aye, that's how it went."

In London, the audience clustered around the stage door, wanting to meet their favorite actors. Here, they poured into the street and left for the public house. The Lindow coach was waiting, so Thaddeus instructed the coachman to go around to the back and pick up Joan and Otis.

She jumped into the coach, beaming. "I saw you laughing!" she cried breathlessly.

Thaddeus's hands actually twitched; he was about to pull her into his lap, but Otis fell across his knees, having been given a vigorous shove by the groom; his heavy hat and wig fell off and hit the floor with a thump.

"I am *never* putting on these garments again," Otis said, pushing himself upright with a grunt as the carriage door closed behind them.

"I can't imagine why you would want to," Joan agreed.

"You were both marvelous," Thaddeus said. "Are you worried about being seen by your father, Otis, or my mother, as we enter the inn?"

Otis shook his head. "I told my father and swore him to secrecy. He said if it was another play, he would come along but he can't bear *Hamlet*."

"I'll just wrap up in my cloak and sneak down the corridor," Joan said, pulling the garment from the other seat. "Did you really think we were marvelous?"

Thaddeus reached out to steady a lamp, swaying as the carriage rounded a corner. "Yes." Ridiculous twaddle flooded his mind. *Your eyes looked like forget-me-nots. I want to kiss you. I want to tear off your clothing.*

I want to marry you.

You are my duchess.

Joan was fidgeting with the fold of her cloak and finally looked up at the two of them. "I find myself grateful for my birth."

"So you're no longer pining to tread the boards of London's finest theaters," Otis exclaimed, while Thaddeus was still trying to figure out whether she was talking about the Prussian or the duke. Illegitimacy or privilege?

Privilege, it seemed.

"This evening and the last were exhausting," Joan said. "My hip hurts from falling onto the hilt of my rapier. I felt like a drunken swallow swooping back and forth across the stage. My arm aches from all the twirling I did with my foil at the end."

"That was the funniest part," Otis said. "We were all howling with laughter behind the stage."

"I'm so grateful that I had the chance to act before an audience," Joan said, looking at Thaddeus. "Thank you. I shall . . . I won't be longing for a life that I wouldn't have enjoyed. You've taught me so much."

In her eyes he saw a future in which she would serenely circle ballroom floors, laughing up at the husband she chose while he—

Until this moment, the whole of it had been hanging in the balance. He hadn't let himself plan ahead.

But in the shadowy carriage, the swaying lamp striking sparks on Joan's hair—for she'd thrown her wig to the side—Thaddeus realized something.

He was far more like his blasted father than he would have thought.

There was only one woman for him, and she wasn't appropriate for the dukedom. His father had surmised that about his love, and succumbed to his parents' urgings to marry another.

His beloved—the mistress with whom the duke had spent his life—had been a baron's daughter before her family cast her off for the crime of living in sin with a married duke.

Lady Joan Wilde was far less eligible than his father's inamorata had been.

Yet Thaddeus refused to make his father's mistake.

Lady Joan, illegitimate or not, fathered by a Prussian or a baker, was the only woman he would love in this life.

She was leaning forward, teasing Otis about his come-hither look. "No one was surprised to learn that your Ophelia climbed in Hamlet's window!" she chortled.

Thaddeus's eyes rested on her shining head and bright, laughing eyes. She hadn't taken any other man to the island.

She would marry him.

Chapter Sixteen

*J*oan crept into the Gherkin & Cheese and made it to her bedchamber without misadventure. After a bath, she bade good night to her maid and sat down by the window to eat a thick, rich piece of plum cake. It had been a magical evening.

A life-changing one.

She had spent her girlhood railing against the fate that had put her in Lindow Castle rather than in a theater troupe. After the last two nights, she felt as if a burden had fallen from her shoulders.

She *was* in the right place.

She *was* a lady, albeit one with a penchant for private theater.

The inn had fallen silent. Her room looked onto a Wilmslow street, rather than the inn yard. The air was clear and crisp, with the August heat blown away. Somewhere a chaffinch was singing to his mate.

The babies would have been born by May, and had flown away. But still he tinkled on like a silver bell in the darkness. Joan sipped a rapidly cooling cup of tea, thinking about chaffinches mating for life, when she heard something else: a scrabbling noise, like a dog turning around before he sleeps, or . . .

She stood up, went to her window, and looked out.

Nothing.

Wilmslow lay before her, a cluster of rustic cottages and shuttered shops tiger-striped by moonlight, St. Bartholomew's church tower triumphantly rising above them all.

Then she glanced down.

A dark head was making its way up the vine-covered wall of the Gherkin & Cheese. A man was climbing silently, his hands moving unerringly from brick to brick.

"I always wondered how people could climb ivy," she said, leaning against the window frame and taking another sip of tea. "Now I see that bricks are the true ladder."

Thaddeus grunted. He had cleared the first story but her room was on the third.

"Do you propose to sing a ballad about this tomorrow?" She put her tea aside and shifted so her elbows were on the windowsill. With anyone else, she would have been frightened that they might tumble to the ground—but not Thaddeus.

He was climbing as easily as if the wall were horizontal, strong fingers reaching up, disappearing in the vines, and pulling his body up. It was enthralling, even more so because he wasn't wearing a coat. His white shirt caught the moonlight as it molded against the muscles of his shoulders and arms.

When he almost reached her windowsill, she drew back in case he tumbled through the frame. But that would be far too ungentlemanly. He reached high enough to swing his legs through and landed with a gentle thump on her bed-chamber floor.

"Hello," she said, smiling at him. "Would you like a cup of tea? I don't have another teacup, since my maid didn't anticipate midnight visitors, but I could give it to you in a glass."

Thaddeus shook his head and pulled a bunch of purple thistles from his pocket. "For you."

"Globe thistles," Joan said, enjoying herself hugely. It seemed that midnight callers brought flowers, just as did morning callers: Who would have thought?

"They are the color of your eyes," Thaddeus said. He was standing beside the window still, his large form outlined against the moonlight.

He followed her gaze down his body to his bare feet. "Shoes might have impeded my way up the wall. I haven't been outside my bedchamber or bath barefooted in years, except on your island."

Joan swallowed because for some reason, strong male feet—his feet—made a pulse run through her body that started at her loins and spread slowly through her like warm honey. She turned away, feeling herself blushing. He hadn't asked for tea so she poured water from the pitcher into a glass and stuffed the purple thistles inside. They had long stems and prickly, beautiful globes on top.

"Thank you," she said, trying to think of something to make his visit less awkward. "Would you like to sit down? That must have been a strenuous climb."

Thaddeus moved forward but didn't seat himself. Instead, he stopped just in front of her. Joan's smile trembled because his eyes were dark and intense, with an expression she'd never seen before.

Her heart sped up, and she rushed into speech. "If you're climbing into my window like Ophelia, I suppose that your flowers have meaning?"

His eyes searched her face. "They mean that I want to marry you." He shoved his hand through his hair. "Probably some other things too, but that's the most important one."

Joan was rarely silenced, but she was now. In fact, she only realized she was gaping at him when she snapped her mouth closed. "You do?"

Thaddeus nodded.

"But you can't—"

He made an abrupt movement. "Don't. My father made that mistake, and wretched though he was as a parent, I can still learn from him."

Joan felt dazed, as if she were in a play but had lost the script. Never read it, in fact. "I didn't know."

"Of course you didn't." He stared down at her, tall and intimidating, though she felt entirely at ease in his presence. "Our bargain is fulfilled. You performed in public. I refuse to marry Lucy Lockett."

"I see," she said, feeling very happy.

"I refuse to give you the name of a gentleman to marry." His jaw set.

Joan smiled at him. "I can find my own candidates."

"I'm one of them," Thaddeus said. He ran his hand through his hair again. Part of it was standing straight up. His gaze was unflinching. "I shall fight for you, Joan. That's what the silly girl Ophelia was doing. She gave back the love letters when instructed, but then she climbed in Hamlet's bloody window to make a point. To fight for what *she* wanted."

Her thoughts jumbled and her heart raced to a gallop. "I don't know what I want."

"It will come to you," Thaddeus said. He took a step forward and clasped her hands in his. "It's the middle of the night and thoroughly inappropriate, but will you kiss me? Please?"

"More inappropriate than kissing on an island?"

"Yes," he said uncompromisingly. "There's a bed behind us."

The moment he said the word, the bed loomed in Joan's view, a soft haven piled with pillows. It would be more comfortable than the picnic blanket. Heat simmered through her. Not that she meant to . . .

She rose on her tiptoes and kissed him. His lips were cool when her lips first touched them, but then they tumbled into a kiss that felt like the beginning of a sentence. A beginning to the play, to the carriage ride, to the . . .

To everything.

She pushed the thought away and concentrated on running her hands over his head, feeling strong, silky hair curl around her fingers. He would hate a true curl, she thought dimly, but his hair had life.

A long time later, perhaps five minutes, more likely an hour, she stumbled backward, bringing Thaddeus with her, and managed to get him onto the bed. "I'm tired," she said, when he looked as if he might disagree.

Instantly, his brows drew together.

She kissed the corner of his mouth. "Not that I want to sleep at the moment." She wound her arms around his neck and ran her tongue along the seam of his lips.

He succumbed with a grunt, digging his elbows into the bed, kissing her again, deeply. His chest touched hers but the rest of his body angled to the side, and for the life of her, Joan couldn't figure out how to pull him on top of her.

Not for . . . that.

But it had felt so good on the island. It would feel even better now, with a mattress beneath them. Finally, she resorted to her favorite tool: speech. "Up here," she gasped, breathless, tugging at him.

"Bossy," Thaddeus muttered, but he shifted. It felt so good that the air swooshed from her lungs, and a nakedly desirous noise came from her throat.

Thaddeus stared down at her, his eyes intent and grave.

"Don't tell me that doesn't feel good," Joan said, playing with his hair again and dusting his chin with kisses. "I can *feel* you."

He rocked his hips forward. "Improper."

"We've been more improper. Besides, you're Ophelia, trying to change my mind about you."

"I never simply *try*," the future duke stated.

"No?" Laughter was burbling up in her chest, joy making itself known in liquid syllables.

"I succeed." Flatly said, with total confidence.

She nipped Thaddeus's lip. "How would you define success at the moment?"

"I want all the love letters you write in the future." He said it even as his eyes asked a question about the past.

She snorted. "You must be joking. To whom could I possibly have written love letters? Although I was deeply taken by a dancing master when we were girls. My father had to send him away because I would lurk in the corridors to give him roses. I found out later that the poor fellow begged to leave the castle."

Thaddeus paused in the act of kissing her chin, one hand making delicious circles on her hip. "Fled, did he?"

"I gather my courtship was overly fervent," Joan said, her eyes glinting with laughter.

"I won't mind," Thaddeus said, "if you wish to court me."

"I shan't," Joan stated. "I—"

But he was kissing her again, and she lost track of the sentence. By the time he drew back, her body was alive, and her mind was silent. Need was coursing through her, making it impossible to think. His hand was still on her hip, so she slowly bent her knee, causing her nightgown to fall over his fingers.

"That's an invitation," she whispered. Everything in her was clenched, tight with longing.

"To touch you?"

She could feel herself turning pink. "Or . . ."

"Or?"

"You could kiss me," she said in a rush. "The way you did before. *Not* that it means I agree to marry you, because I haven't."

"No?" The word was a drowsy murmur on the silent air.

She eased her legs apart. "No. Not—not yet."

His hand moved in just the right way, caressing her thigh, his powerful fingers stroking her skin. Her breath caught, and she let her knee fall to the side. "Please," she whispered. "Thaddeus."

He groaned. "I love it when you say my name." His voice was rough and low.

"I love it when you touch me," she breathed, arching into his touch. "Oh, yes, like that."

His other hand did no more than encircle her breast, rub his thumb once across her taut nipple, and she began to tremble. He moved his fingers and an embarrassing squeak came from her throat. Her eyes flew open, and he laughed silently, his mouth drifting over hers. "Like this?"

"Yes," she choked.

"Joan," he whispered, and then he plundered her mouth at the same moment that his hand played her like a stringed instrument. She convulsed under his touch, squeezing her eyes closed and crying out.

Feeling rippled through her again and again: It would begin to subside, and Thaddeus would languidly move his fingers again, and new sensation would roll away from his touch, making her gasp for air.

When she finally lay back, shuddering and

catching her breath, he smiled down at her. "Success," he said cheerfully. He kissed her, his mouth warm and strong, but she could feel a farewell. He intended to return to his bed.

"Ophelia didn't leave so soon," Joan said.

"Hamlet was a fickle prince," Thaddeus said. He drew his hand away from her and lazily licked his fingers, grinning at her. "You taste like summer, like clover and lemon."

"I want you," Joan breathed. "I want more." She reached for his shoulders. "Please."

He was silent, his eyes on hers. Whatever he saw there pleased him; Joan registered the smile in his eyes with relief.

"I suppose Ophelia removed her nightgown," he said. He moved backward, hauled his shirt over his head, and draped it over the bed knob.

"And her breeches," Joan prompted.

"Ophelia definitely removed her breeches," Thaddeus agreed. He swung his legs off the bed and pulled them down.

Her eyes followed his every movement. "You wear smalls under your breeches?"

"It's more comfortable, especially with buckram."

"Ophelia removed her smalls."

"Naturally." Thaddeus drew them down his legs. His hips were narrow, given how strong his legs were.

"My goodness," Joan exclaimed, disconcerted. She'd seen illustrations, of course. There was that naughty book that she and Viola had found in the library. There were illustrated ballads of the more bawdy sort that the boys sometimes left in their rooms when they went away to school.

But.

Shocking, but very desirable.

"This gives a whole new meaning to Ophelia's *By cock, they are to blame*," she murmured, tapping one finger against her lips.

Thaddeus burst out laughing. "I thought maidens didn't know what 'cocks' were."

"I'm a Wilde," she said, grinning. "We are the more knowledgeable kind of maiden. You didn't think that Aunt Knowe would let us go to a ball without a thorough knowledge of male anatomy, did you? Albeit through book learning."

Thaddeus stood before her, hands at his sides, a lopsided smile on his mouth, letting her look her fill. Joan cleared her throat. "May I?"

Thaddeus looked down at her. "May you?"

She scowled at him.

He stepped closer, laughter glinting in his eyes. Teasing her. She sat up and pulled off her nightgown too, and as she knelt on the edge of the bed, the laughter fell from his eyes, which made her feel unreasonably triumphant.

Joan crooked a finger and he moved forward, his thighs bumping the side of the bed. She wrapped her fingers around his private part—his cock— and it moved in her hand, with a restless power that made her melt in her legs and her arms and everything in between.

"I want you," Joan said, her voice coming out as low as his. "Now, tonight. Now," she repeated. Then she lay back, because she trusted her instincts.

His mouth opened and closed, brows drawing together.

"You didn't truly think that you'd leave my bedroom without 'doing,' as Ophelia describes it?"

Thaddeus looked down at his future wife smiling at him impishly, his heart filled with the joy of his good fortune, and his body filled with quite another pleasure.

He knew his Joan. She wouldn't promise herself to him in marriage yet. She would lead him on a merry chase, because she deserved it, and she was worth it—

But she had made up her mind.

In fact, he'd bet that the moment he set foot on that island for the very first time, she had already made up her mind.

"I'm yours if you want me," he said, the sentence a vow in his mind and heart.

"Oh, I want you," Joan said, reaching out her hands. "Come here."

The night flew by. To this point, Thaddeus's erotic experiences had been enjoyable for both parties. They had never involved gusts of laughter. Or squeals. Or commands.

And yet later, when he leaned over her, arms braced against the mattress, and slid his cock through her silky, wet folds, Joan cried, *"Thaddeus."*

A command. Definitely a command.

He eased forward, thinking to give her time to adjust to him. But this was Joan. Her hands tightened around his forearms, and she looked up at him, her lips deep red from his kisses.

"More," she gasped. "Please?"

Thaddeus dipped his head and kissed her deeply, letting his recognition of who she was to him fill his lungs and sink into his skin. He moved slowly, letting her set the pace, reining in his senses because the slick glide threatened his control, narrowing his vision to her lips and her eyes.

He didn't seat himself entirely because he was large, and she was very, very small. When he'd slipped in as far as he judged possible for her first time, he moved to his elbows and nipped her ear gently. "All right?"

Her fingers moved up and wound through his. "Thaddeus . . ."

The word caught at his loins and made him shake.

"More," she commanded. And: "Please."

The word echoed around his head for a moment, because he was so busy controlling his movements that he'd forgotten its meaning.

Hovering his lips over hers, their breath intermingling, he did his lady's bidding. When a little pinch appeared between her brows, he kissed her back into pleasure, until her breath sped up again, making her breasts rise and fall, her nipples begging for his attention.

After that, he memorized every telltale sign, the catch in her breath when he altered an angle, the involuntary cry when he brought his hand into play, the low moan when he lowered his head to her breast. It became harder and harder to control himself as he was enveloped by the tightest, warmest cunny he'd ever known. And when the woman he loved was beneath him, her skin dewy, her eyes squeezed shut, her hands closed around his arms.

She wasn't watching, so he let his face express everything he felt: how precious she was, how exquisite, erotic, beloved.

She, on the other hand? Looked frustrated.

"It's your first time," he said, his voice a rough whisper. "Maybe everything won't happen at this moment?"

"It's just there," Joan cried, longing and annoyance threaded together. "I just can't reach it, Thaddeus!" She opened her eyes, bluebells drenched with tears—and desire. Real desire because it wasn't about him, but about *her*.

Her practiced glances were about the man she enticed, but this one?

It was pure, raw desire.

"Are you sore?" he asked gently, nipping her earlobe.

She shook her head. "The pain went away. After that, it felt so good. But somehow I simply can't *do* it."

He stopped, arms braced, dipped his head to kiss her. "There's time, Joan. Tomorrow, and the next day, and the year after that."

"I don't want time," she said, arching up. "I want to come! There are women who can't . . ."

"Not you," he said with certainty. He moved his knees forward, altering their joining and making her gasp. "You're a bossy lass," he said, dipping his head to nip her lip. "I love that about you. You'll teach me how to please you."

Her cheeks turned even rosier. Thaddeus marked the fact that she had silently accepted their future together. "Have you looked at the two of us joined?"

She shook her head, a lock of damp golden hair falling over her forehead.

Tenderly he pushed it behind her ear, and then pulled away, sliding partly out of her. She came up on her elbows and looked down her body.

His tool was dark red and stiff, and they watched together as he pulled all the way to the broad crown, then stroked slowly forward, parting the tuft of buttery curls that protected her. A rough sound broke from her throat as he breached her, and he grunted in response, pulling back again and thrusting forward a trifle faster. "Do you like that?" he rasped.

"Bloody hell," Joan whispered, her eyes fixed on his rod. She bent her knees and arched up. "Oh." She blinked.

"Better?"

He pulled back again, bringing his free hand to her nipple in a rough caress, and then timed a pinch to a deep thrust. "Watch," he growled. Her eyes flew back to where they were joined.

Her mouth opened, so he raised his free hand and rubbed a finger along her lush lips, then tucked it inside. "Lick," he commanded.

She sucked, her eyes heavy-lidded, and he had to take a harsh breath and regain control. Then he ran his finger down her silky cleft, pausing over a swollen nub masked by curls to swirl his finger.

Her hips strained up to him involuntarily, and her eyes flew from where they were joined, to his face. "Thaddeus," she said. "*Please*, Thaddeus." She stopped biting her lip. "Could you come deeper?"

Could he?

Damned right he could.

He dipped his head again and kissed her. "Not too tender?" he asked huskily. She shook her head wordlessly. "Are you sure?"

She gave him a look. She was a born duchess, and duchesses knew what they wanted.

Thaddeus pulled back again and then thrust until their bodies joined as deeply as possible, his rod buried in her heat. He sucked in another breath.

"Yes," Joan panted. Her eyes were blissful.

He pulled back, thrust again, starting an insistent rhythm that threatened to destroy his control. Threatened to?

Did.

Joan's knees pressed against his sides as she arched again, urging him on. Her hands slipped above her head, and she clenched his arms. "More, Thaddeus," she commanded. "More."

He bit back a smile. "Joan."

"Yes?" she whispered. "Is there something I should do?" She ran her hand down his back and onto his bottom, making him shake. "You like that," she said in a pleased voice.

His answer was a dazed grunt accompanied by a forceful thrust that made her eyes glaze with pleasure and hands fly back to his arms. "I love how thick you are," she gasped.

Thaddeus managed to grin, even as he clenched his teeth. "I have heard a complaint once or twice, so I'm glad to hear it."

She somehow managed to turn even brighter rose. "I didn't mean!" Her fingers curled into his biceps. "I meant—" But she gasped as he plunged into her. "I like that."

Her smile went to his heart.

"Joan," he growled.

"Hmm?" She was near, her eyes wide, her brow dewy, her fingers biting into his arms. "This is me, claiming you," he grunted, the ungentlemanly words slipping out of him. At this moment, he wasn't a duke. He wasn't a nobleman at all.

He was a man, a sweaty, panting man, making love for the first time in his life.

Joan's eyes fluttered half open. "I'll claim you later," she gasped. She tightened on him and threw her head back, a throaty scream breaking from her throat.

Thaddeus's heart almost stopped from gratitude.

He swallowed hard and dropped to his elbows, bucking into her once, twice, then exploding as her body pulsed around him.

While he was trying to catch his breath, Joan's hands slipped from his arms, fingers caressing the marks left by her grip, and wrapped around his neck. He opened his eyes, dazed, almost dizzy, sleepy, loving.

Hers were glinting at him, shining. *Not* sleepy. "How soon can we do that again?"

His tool twitched, signaling its willingness. "Five minutes for a second bout, ten for a third."

Joan captured his mouth with her own, her lips lingering on his, eyes open. "I see. Thaddeus?"

He was half erect already; in some distant part of his mind he wondered if he would have to go through life hiding an erection every time his wife said his name.

"Yes?"

Her smile covered her whole face. "This is me claiming you," she whispered.

Thaddeus looked down at her steadily. "'Til death do us part."

She wrinkled her nose. "Do we have to be so grim?" Her brows drew together. "Because of your father?"

"It gives one a reminder of mortality," Thaddeus said. "Damn it."

Joan raised an eyebrow.

"How am I going to preserve my righteous anger against my sire, since he taught me what matters most in life?"

Her body went still under him. "Not . . . me?"

"You. You, Joan. With your breeches, and your joy, and your wit. The way you playact through life, making everyone laugh with you. The fact that you can't sing. The fact that I have never felt as possessive about anything in the world, including my title. Don't tell me that our children won't be terribly naughty because I'm certain they will be."

She didn't say anything, her eyes fixed on his. "Are you . . . are you saying—"

"That I love you?" He kissed her nose. "I love you, Lady Joan, the best Wilde of all, the wildest of the Prussian offspring that might exist in the world, the perfect gentlewoman, the best Duchess of Eversley."

"I gather we're at a crossroads," Joan said.

Thaddeus shook his head, certain of her. "You claimed me, remember?" He moved to lie on his side next to her, one hand curved over her hip.

"In the heat of the moment." But she was smiling. "On that subject, who knew that 'doing' was so hot and sweaty? And"—she peered down her body—"messy?"

Thaddeus took a fold of sheet and gently patted between her legs. Getting up, he poured water into the basin and washed himself. Then he threw it out the window, and brought over fresh water and a linen towel. "My lady?"

"I can do it myself," Joan said, looking embarrassed.

"Please?"

She nodded.

Thaddeus washed her with the same fierce attention he brought to almost everything in his life, washing a blur of blood from her inside thigh, making certain every fold was clean, rinsing the towel and then washing her beneath, below . . . everything.

They could have no secrets from each other. He smiled when he saw Joan turn red. "I am a perfectionist," he told her. "I am looking at perfection."

"I see," Joan said, wiggling because he tucked a dry towel under her bottom and started dripping water down her cleft, drop by drop. "Why are you doing *that*?"

"For fun. When you are aroused, your cunny turns plump and even pinker," he said, with all the gravity of a schoolmaster. He touched her gently. Her eyes turned smoky and she fell back against the pillows.

"And I'm thirsty," he added, sliding farther down, so he could lap water.

Chapter Seventeen

*L*ater, much later, Joan found herself wide awake while Thaddeus slept.

He looked like one of those medieval knights, burly legs meant for coursing up and down the field, shoulders topped with muscle, the better for hoisting a heavy jousting stick.

Were they jousting sticks? Jousting rods? Lances?

Speaking of which . . . his rod lay on its side, still thick but not erect. The sight made a happy thrum run through her body.

She felt as if sparks of pleasure were still flying around her body, following the path of a shock that had curled her toes. Who would have thought the act of bedding was so sweaty and breathless? The illustrations seemed cold-blooded in comparison; a man positioning his tool in just such a way while his partner looked on approvingly.

She'd once seen two june bugs, entwined but still flying, gripping hard to stay together as they lurched up and down in the air like drunken mates leaving a pub. It was like that: mad or drunk with the act.

Thaddeus's eyes opened up again, not even dazed: clear and wide awake. "What are you thinking about?"

"Our resemblance to mating june bugs," she told him, propping her head up on her hand.

He nodded, seeming unperturbed by being compared to an insect. He rolled to his side and glanced down at himself. Sure enough, his tool had become even thicker and showed signs of stiffening. "It's been eight and a half minutes, or thereabouts."

She tipped toward him and rubbed his nose with hers. "Can you count moments internally? I have to look at a clock."

"Minutes range themselves up in my head if I wish to pay attention," he said.

"You're frightfully intelligent," Joan said, feeling quite pleased. She'd never been more than mediocre in school, so it behooved her to find a man who could give her children a dose of powerful brains.

"So are you."

She wrinkled her nose at him. "In a different sort of way. My own way."

Thaddeus nodded, accepting that.

"Do you care to discuss how to approach things with your father? Because it seems that we are going to—" She floundered to a stop.

"Marry," Thaddeus said helpfully, obviously enjoying himself. "Claimed and reclaimed, remember? And will be once again, but with a ring."

She couldn't help noticing that his tool was announcing its readiness to go another round, a whole minute early.

Thaddeus smiled at her wryly. "Even the subject of my father doesn't seem to dampen my enthusiasm for you."

"First, we should discuss your father," she said. "We both agreed that marriage was an impossibility, due to the fact that you may have to defend your dukedom in the courts, as well as polite society, and with particular attention to the latter, you ought to marry a lady of untarnished reputation."

He shrugged his free shoulder.

"No, don't shrug," she said. "It's important, Thaddeus. I can't marry you if you're not going to be a duke."

He flinched.

"Don't be silly. The title doesn't matter, but *you* do. You're a duke."

"Not intrinsically," he said slowly. "A duke is a role, like Hamlet. One of the reasons the man is so cross is because his uncle stole his crown."

"Well, you can't kill your half brother the way Hamlet did his uncle," Joan said. "We have to figure out something else. Some way to make your father change his mind."

"I don't care," Thaddeus said, looking peaceful. "I tarnished your reputation. We'd better marry immediately so that I can make you an honest woman."

Joan rolled her eyes. "Are you trying to tell me that we should marry in order to head off a scandal, as if that would bolster your claim to the dukedom? Because I'm afraid I'm always going to be a scandalous choice."

"I will marry you even if you are great with child on the way up the aisle," Thaddeus said.

Joan felt a jolt of unfamiliarity, and then she realized what his expression was: happiness.

Thaddeus Erskine Shaw, future Duke of Eversley, was happy.

Because of her.

Because he loved her.

The words tumbled in her mind like tufts of wind-blown dandelion.

"No," she said, clinging to the truth as she knew it. Thaddeus, *her* Thaddeus, would be lost without the dukedom. Perhaps he would blame her someday. "We have to work out the problem with your father before I'll marry you."

His eyes darkened. "You'll marry me no matter what happens because of this evening."

Joan sat up. Aunt Knowe had told all of the Wilde girls years ago that they had to make certain that their future husbands understood that they were not namby-pamby weaklings. The best marriage was a partnership, not indentured servitude, albeit at a ducal level. "I do not agree to marry you until I know that you will be a duke."

His jaw was tight. "I wasn't aware you were so interested in the idea of being a duchess."

Joan looked down at him and felt a surge of love. Thaddeus was so wonderful—albeit dense, like all men. "Think whatever you like," she told him kindly. "My point is that your father and his lies hang over us like a storm cloud."

The look in Thaddeus's eyes might have made a

lesser woman quail. One who hadn't been raised by Aunt Knowe.

"Why don't we pay him a betrothal visit?" she asked, inspired.

"Oh, so you'll agree to be betrothed to me, but not to marry?"

"Well, perhaps," Joan said. "Although as I said, I refuse to be responsible for your losing the dukedom."

"Do you think that I couldn't support you without the estate?" he growled.

She gave him a sunny smile. Marriage was going to be fun; she loved fencing matches, albeit verbal ones. "Horse training? My brother North makes a great deal of money that way."

Thaddeus narrowed his eyes at her. He was watching her the same way that he'd perused the skies the other night. Curious and purposeful.

"Or would you become a stargazer," she asked, inspired. "What do they call them . . . an astronomer?"

"No money in that," Thaddeus said flatly.

"Is that what you would have done, in a different world?" she asked, reaching out and linking their right and left hands together.

"Studying the unattainable," he said wryly. "What's the good of it?"

"Knowledge is a good of its own."

He nodded in acknowledgment. "True. My tutors were fully cognizant of the depth of experience it takes to manage three estates, and all the souls who live in and around them, so they made certain I learned useful information, such as accounting."

"Perhaps you will encourage your son to love knowledge for its own sake."

"Which brings us back to the question of marriage," Thaddeus said.

Joan got up on her knees, loving the way his eyes caught on her breasts. She grinned at him, seeing his tool jerk against his stomach. "No marriage until you know you're going to be a duke," she said cheerfully. "Think of your future wife as a mercenary wench with a passion for titles." She sank back on her heels. "She has a passion for other things too. May I touch?"

His gaze went from hard to molten, and he rolled onto his back. "All yours."

Joan moved forward on all fours and stopped. "Thaddeus."

He instantly turned his head.

"I really mean it about marrying you. I don't care about being ruined. I don't care if there's a scandal. I believe that our marriage might be destroyed if your father carries out that campaign. It would cause an explosion, whether or not you won the law case, which I'm sure you would."

"I understand your point of view," he said.

They stared at each other mutely, a distant creak from a wooden floor and a loud cricket making themselves heard. She swallowed. "In that case?"

His face had gentled, his eyes far too knowing. "I'm still yours."

Something had happened between them: some line crossed or breached, she wasn't sure. By declaring herself—and she *meant it*—a new cord bound them together. They were closer, rather than farther apart.

But just at the moment there was another world to discover. She edged closer and put a hand on his ribbed stomach. Just below his navel, his tool thumped against his skin again. "Out of your control," she said, letting her fingers slide in that direction.

"Generally speaking, yes," he agreed.

Obviously, there were nuances to the situation, ones she could learn later. She moved her fingers sideways, like a crab dancing.

"What are you thinking?" he asked.

"That my fingers are crablike." She glanced up; his eyes were surprised. "I'm sorry, that wasn't very romantic, was it? Seductive, I mean."

Delight spread over his face. "It didn't live up to all those pouts by which you ruled the ballroom, no."

Joan had forgotten that she wasn't wearing clothing, but suddenly she was achingly aware of the weight of her own breasts. Her legs were tucked to the side, like a mermaid, but the pressure of her legs together made her private parts flare with heat. As if, having been introduced to the act, she . . .

No, that was ridiculous. She could feel herself growing pink.

"I'm going to assume that your thoughts have moved from animals to humankind," Thaddeus said. He picked up her hand, hovering just above his belly button, and released it squarely on top of his cock, as Ophelia would have called it. Or rather, as Shakespeare apparently called it.

Her hand closed greedily to see if what had felt thick and strong was—

It was. He was. His gasp was the most delicious thing she'd ever heard.

Joan discovered she was smiling.

Had she claimed him before? Not like this. Here, this moment, with Thaddeus's head flung back and his intent eyes closed in pleasure, all because her hand slid over satiny tender skin?

Claiming.

Chapter Eighteen

The following evening, back in Lindow Castle, Joan asked her maid a precise series of questions about pregnancy. She knew the basics, of course.

But nine months? Ten months? Time had a different rhythm at the moment because deep in her gut, in some knowing part of herself that she hadn't been acquainted with before, she was certain she was with child.

In nine or ten months, there would be a little girl or boy who needed married parents. She knew that much, if only because of her own childhood. The errant Duke of Eversley, Thaddeus's father, needed to be taken in hand.

Thaddeus was made to be a duke . . . it was his destiny, to be grandiose about it. The question of the dukedom had to be settled now. Lady Bumtrinket's grim predictions floated through Joan's head and she pushed them away. Thaddeus had to become the man he was meant to be, because if marriage to her lost him the dukedom, it might destroy their future.

Joan descended the staircase in her favorite gown, silk dotted with exquisite hand-painted flowers. The bodice was very low, and trimmed with a pleated silk ruffle starched to frame her neck.

Thaddeus waited for her at the bottom of the steps. He looked up at her expressionlessly, but the stillness of his face was no longer imperturbable to her. He would always be there, waiting for her.

"Don't look at me like that!" she exclaimed, reaching the bottom step.

A smile reached his mouth, this time. "How so?"

"As if you've seen me naked," she whispered, so that the two footmen Prism had assigned to the entry wouldn't hear her.

Thaddeus shot them a look, and they melted back through the green baize door.

"I *have* seen you naked," he pointed out. "I would rather lose every memory I've ever had than the memory of last night."

Joan's smile wobbled.

Thaddeus's sultry eyes were intent on hers. "I would give up every single memory, Joan. But not those that lie in our future." He drew her against his body and tipped up her chin. "May I?" His voice was an erotic murmur.

She nodded, and his mouth came down on hers. He took his time, lavishing her face with kisses so that by the time he breached her lips, she had her arms wound around his neck, and she was on her toes.

When his tongue finally slipped between her lips, she whimpered, a small sound that died in the large entryway but burned between them. He hardened against her, and memories of the night before rushed through her head, making her shiver. "Me, also," Joan whispered.

Thaddeus pulled back, his eyes the dark blue of twilight and slightly dazed. "You what?" He sounded short of breath, and Joan let herself savor the triumph of it for a moment.

"I wouldn't ever want to forget last night," she told him.

They were kissing again, hot and fast. "I can't get enough of you," Thaddeus growled, tearing his mouth away.

The baize door opened, and a footman diffidently reappeared, sidling along the wall.

Thaddeus ignored him. "You won't allow me to announce our betrothal?" His voice was achingly soft. "I haven't yet asked your father for permission to marry you, but I believe he will not cavil."

"Absolutely not," Joan replied. "No dukedom, no wife." Then she kissed him again because she couldn't stop herself.

He took her arm and drew her toward the great doors to the drawing room. The footman sprang forward and pulled open the door; Prism, standing just inside, bowed.

Thaddeus looked at her. "Truly, no?" He sounded surprised, nonplussed. Likely no one said no to him.

"No," Joan said, enjoying the moment.

"Damn."

Prism announced them as they walked into the room.

"We're like an old married couple, speaking in one-word sentences," Thaddeus murmured.

"I will help you with your father," Joan said. "I can help."

"I'd like to kiss you again," Thaddeus remarked. "By way of thank you."

"Absolutely not!" Joan replied. "And I said it before: Don't look at me like that!"

She turned away, willing away a blush. For such a proper future duke, Thaddeus had remarkably suggestive eyes. More of her siblings had descended on the castle during the day. Her older brother North and his wife, Diana, were talking to Sir Reginald, and her parents were chatting with her adopted brother Parth and his wife, Lavinia.

"There's Jeremy," Thaddeus said, a happy note in his voice, looking to the other side of the room where Lord Jeremy Roden, who was married to Joan's older sister Betsy, was talking to Aunt Knowe.

"You are an odd pair to be such close friends," Joan said. "Jeremy is so grumpy—well, not when he's with us, of course, but in general. I always feel as if he's on the edge of an outburst. And you're so calm."

"He is a good man," Thaddeus said. "The best."

A half hour later, when everyone had been greeted, curtsies and hugs exchanged, Joan found herself on a sofa with Betsy. "Thaddeus, huh?" Betsy said, giving her a wicked smile.

"He oughtn't to marry me," Joan said. Thaddeus was across the room talking to Jeremy. "Didn't he once tell you that I was ineligible?"

"He did. Several times." Betsy chortled with laughter. "Obviously, he's changed his mind."

"I won't make a good duchess," Joan said, smoothing her blue skirts. She wasn't certain, though, and Betsy just smirked at her, amused and unbelieving. "A duchess oughtn't to be illegitimate."

"You don't care who your father is," her sister pointed out. "You never have. If you don't care, society won't either."

"They have, and they do," Joan retorted.

"But *you* don't care. Duchesses set the tone," Betsy said. "I didn't understand it myself, but now I do. It's a person's inner confidence that matters, Joan. No one can say that you weren't raised to the role. Aunt Knowe made sure every one of us could run Lindow Castle."

Joan chewed her lip. "That's true."

"I was invited to Eversley once but didn't pay a visit. Have you?" Betsy asked.

"The Duchess of Eversley," Prism announced.

Thaddeus's mother paused in the doorway, looking somewhat stricken. Thaddeus was far down the room, so Joan said, "Excuse me, Betsy," rose, and went to meet Her Grace, who was wearing a gown of changeable pink silk taffeta, with a pink-tinted wig.

"Good evening, Your Grace," Joan said, dropping into a deep curtsy.

"Goodness me, I didn't realize so many people were joining us," the duchess said, looking uncertain.

"Not people, only Wildes," Joan corrected her. "You're wearing an enchanting gown this evening."

"I thought I had a distinct resemblance to a rose beetle," Her Grace confided.

Joan laughed before she could stop herself. "I don't see any beetlelike characteristics! Where is your hard shell?"

"I am short and round," the duchess said. "Rose-colored, obviously. I have antennae." She gestured upward toward three ostrich feathers that had been painstakingly hand-painted in shades of pink.

"Mother, I believe that rose beetles are colored a metallic green," Thaddeus said, appearing at Joan's shoulder. "They are named for the food they prefer, not for their appearance."

"Disappointing," the duchess commented.

"On the other hand, the elephant hawk-moth is England's most common moth," her son said. "Its coloring is distinctly pink to allow it to blend in with willow herb plants."

"Willow herb is a weed," his mother said. "I don't like to compare myself to an elephant. Round and small is acceptable; but an elephant's girth is disheartening."

Percy the pig, who was a beautiful, distinct pink, came to mind, but Joan thought better of mentioning it, only to find the duchess looking at her and bursting into laughter.

"We had the same thought, didn't we, Lady Joan? My girth does remind me of that delightful piglet of yours. I visited Percy this afternoon, and was somewhat surprised to find him wearing a pleated collar that gave him a fetchingly Elizabethan air."

Joan grinned at her. "My smaller siblings decided that he needed adornment. Percy is a great favorite in the nursery. I do hope that Diana brought her son Peter along with her. He's three years old and the right age to appreciate an affectionate piglet."

"Your gown is lovely as well," Her Grace said.

"It was made from one of my stepmother's favorites," Joan told her. "The fabric came from France, before she married my father. One of the earliest memories I have of my stepmother is the first ball held at Lindow Castle in her honor, when she wore a sack gown in the French style, this gown. When sack gowns went out of fashion, we had it remade into a *robe à l'anglaise*."

"How prudent," the duchess murmured, her eyes approving. "Dearest, do bring me over to greet the new guests," she added, turning to her son.

Joan curtsied and returned to the seat beside her sister, who gave her an impudent wink. "'Her Grace' has a nice ring to it," Betsy mused. "I should talk to your darling Greywick. After all, I do know him. A bit. He courted me for at least two days."

"Don't embarrass me," Joan said.

"Would I ever do such a thing?" Betsy asked demurely.

"Yes, you would," Joan replied.

Betsy had the knack of behaving like the most proper lady in the room, but she could also pivot straight into mischief. Just now she was looking across the room with a distinctly naughty glint in her eye.

"Have you seen Viola?" Joan asked, catching her sister's arm before she launched across the room.

"We only arrived at Lindow in time to bathe and change for the evening meal. Why isn't she here? Prism told me that the baby hasn't arrived yet. Everything is all right, isn't it?"

"Aunt Knowe wants her to rest because her ankles are swollen," Joan said. "I'm sure she's hoping to see you; she's frightfully tired of being confined to her bedchamber with her feet up."

Betsy squinted at her. "That was positively Machiavellian, Joan. But successful." She got to her feet. "Tell everyone where I am, won't you?"

Later, after Betsy sent a message down saying that she would dine with Viola and Devin, Joan walked into the dining room on Jeremy's arm. Betsy's husband was one of those tall, brooding men whom Joan found frightfully attractive in the abstract.

But not compared to Thaddeus.

He walked ahead, his mother on his arm. She'd seen those shoulders unclothed. And his back, the way it narrowed to his hips. And then . . .

An elbow bumped her, and she turned to meet the amused eyes of her brother-in-law. "Does Greywick know your—ahem—appreciation for his figure?"

She elbowed him back. "I have no idea what you're talking about."

"Jests aside, you couldn't do better," Jeremy said. "He's a good man to the bone. I suppose if you take him, I'll feel a little less guilty about stealing Betsy from under his nose."

"You don't feel guilty," Joan retorted. "I wasn't out yet, but I wasn't blind. You hid out in the billiard room because you knew how much Betsy loves the game. You could find her there day and night. Likely unchaperoned."

"Something like that," Jeremy said, a contented, tender look on his face. "I give you fair warning, young Joan. I remember Thaddeus from our schooldays. If that man wants something, there is no stopping him from getting it."

Joan thought about that and then smiled up at Thaddeus. "Sometimes I think the Wildes were brought into the world for one thing."

"Which was?"

She waited until he had seated her in a chair before she said, "Convincing would-be spouses that *their* opinion is not irrelevant, exactly, but . . ."

"Immaterial?" he suggested. "I will admit that Betsy took a great deal of convincing. Luckily, I knew how to play billiards, or I might never have succeeded. I'll advise Thaddeus to find your fatal flaw, the billiards in your life."

Joan laughed. Thaddeus had already found it: He had instantly supported her foray onto the public stage.

"I gather he's in no need of advice," Jeremy said, a wry crook to his mouth.

"Hush," Joan said. A footman shook out her napkin and handed it to her. "Thank you, Putter."

A chair scraped beside her, and she turned, startled to find that Thaddeus was seating himself beside her. Shouldn't he be seated beside his mother? "I like the remade gown," he said, as if they had never been parted. "Does scarcity of fabric explain the fact that your nipples are very nearly exposed to the air?"

"I'll have you know that some *robes à l'anglaise*

are designed precisely for that reason," she said loftily.

Behind his shoulder, she saw Prism leading one of her brothers-in-law toward her, only to find the seat occupied so he veered away. "You aren't supposed to sit here," she told Thaddeus, a giggle escaping her.

He raised an eyebrow. "I want to sit beside you. What if someone tried to paw you under the table?"

She laughed outright at that. "The room is full of Wildes."

"They're very inspiring," he said, leaning over to murmur in her ear. "Gentlemen by training but . . ."

Joan followed his eyes and saw that Parth was seated beside his wife, and not only had an arm around her, but had just dropped a kiss on her ear. North was similarly entranced by his wife, who was impishly scolding him while he smiled down at her.

"Do you suppose that North knows what a fool he looks?" Thaddeus asked.

Joan glanced at him. "He doesn't care."

"True."

"I have an idea of how to deal with your father," Joan said.

"What?"

"We'll travel to the estate. Then I'll dress all in white, tiptoe into his room and inform that I'm his guardian angel, and he's risking damnation."

Thaddeus broke into laughter. "You refused to marry me, and therefore you cannot travel to my father's house. You can't have it both ways, Joan.

The only way to perform the role of an angel is to marry me, or at least accept my proposal."

"Nonsense, I could bring a chaperone," she said. She poked him. "We're partners."

He blinked, as if the concept hadn't occurred to him. Hadn't she told him that already? But she couldn't remember exactly whether the concept had been aired.

"Where does your father live?" Joan asked. The very idea of letting Thaddeus out of her sight made her feel restless and unhappy. Infatuated. In love.

"One of our estates," Thaddeus said. "Eversley comprises three estates, not counting a vineyard in Portugal that makes terrible wine and a fishing retreat in Scotland."

"I've never been to Portugal," she said.

"No traveling together unless you marry me." Thaddeus turned to his left, edging his chair back so that Joan could see across him. "Lady Knowe, I have a question to ask you."

"Are you certain you want to ask *me* this question?" Aunt Knowe said, twinkling at him. "I can think of a question or two you might want to ask my brother. I couldn't help overhearing snippets of conversation."

Joan felt herself turning pink. "I haven't agreed to marry him."

Her aunt Knowe had the winged eyebrows of the Wilde family, and they flew up. "You surprise me, dearest."

"Joan will accept my proposal soon," Thaddeus said, sounding completely unperturbed.

"Pride goeth before a fall," Joan remarked.

"My father, the Duke of Eversley, proposes that I give up the dukedom in favor of my younger half brother," Thaddeus said, pitching his voice beneath the hum of conversation.

Aunt Knowe glanced down the table at her closest friend, the duchess.

"My mother shares a passion for dyeing cloth with Lavinia," he said. "They are completely absorbed."

"Sometimes I find myself wondering whether I have finally lost my wits," Aunt Knowe commented. "Did you just say what I thought you said?"

"I did," Thaddeus replied.

"Where on earth did Eversley get such a tom-fool idea?"

Joan reached out and took Thaddeus's hand under the table.

He curled his fingers around hers and smiled wryly at Aunt Knowe. "I'm afraid that it springs from this family. It was widely reported some years ago that North intended to renounce his title, when the time came."

"I knew we should have kept that idea to ourselves," Aunt Knowe said with a gusty sigh.

"My solicitors strongly feel that renunciation is not legal."

"Ours agree. Luckily, my brother seems remarkably healthy," Aunt Knowe said, waving her hand. "The Wildes will make it work, if need be; the family has a knack for getting what they want, legal or no. Witness my brother's divorce, for example. Rarely granted, but he got one."

Joan was rather glad that the footmen arrived

with the first course. Her father's divorce from Yvette, her mother, was indeed unusual. But so were flagrant exhibitions of adultery.

Thaddeus edged his chair back to the table and they spooned up a delicious *potage au lait d'amandes*, chatting of this and that.

Joan noticed as Prism moved unhurriedly to her father's side and bent to murmur in his ear. That was unusual; the duke greatly disliked being interrupted during a meal. Hopefully, Lady Bumtrinket hadn't paid them another visit or, if so, her stepmother would imprison her in a bedchamber.

As it turned out, the duchess had no say as regards their guest.

The great double doors to the dining room flew open. Prism straightened in outrage, his eyes bulging like a surprised frog in livery, but before he could march back and reassert his command, four men walked through the door carrying a litter.

Thaddeus made a sudden jerky movement, but Joan didn't turn to him; the scene before her was too fascinating. The litter bore a gentleman with a full head of unpowdered yellow curls. He was lying on his side, propped up on white velvet pillows, his face gaunt and ashen. The remnants of great beauty could be seen there too, in the jaw, the hawkish nose, the commanding, heavy-lidded eyes.

Joan was irresistibly reminded of a performance of Shakespeare's *Antony and Cleopatra* that she'd seen in London. The Egyptian queen had been carried across the stage while supposedly floating down the Nile on her pleasure boat, dressed from head to foot in cloth of gold, servants fanning her with peacock feathers.

This entrance could definitely compete with Cleopatra's.

The man lay on a bed of glistening white silk, the velvet cushions nestled around his head. Despite the August heat, a magnificent white ermine robe had been thrown over his lower half, below which his toes could be seen, garbed in pointed white silk slippers adorned with pearls.

His servants weren't fanning him, but she recognized the livery they wore. Slowly she turned her head to Thaddeus. He was watching tight-lipped, his arms folded over his chest.

"Thaddeus," she breathed.

Except for that word, the Lindow Castle dining room was completely silent, which never happened in a chamber that held more than one family member.

The man said, "So many Wildes in one room. I am near to overcome by the brilliance of it all." His eyes moved from person to person, as commandingly as if he were royalty. Yet there was nothing regal about his expression. He had the peevish, ripe look of a man who put his own welfare above that of all others.

"And my wife." His voice was melodious and deep, much larger than his wasted body suggested. To Joan, it sounded like the drone of bees.

He was looking at the Duchess of Eversley, so Joan was right about the livery. The grooms on Thaddeus's carriage wore the same colors.

The Duke of Eversley—dying or not—had arrived at Lindow Castle.

"Along with my inestimable elder son," Eversley rumbled, his eyes moving to Thaddeus. "Trying to wrangle a permanent berth in Lindow Castle? Third time's the charm, eh? Good thing that Lindow has so many daughters."

Thaddeus stared back at him, utterly expressionless.

With a scrape of his chair, Joan's father rose from the head of the table. "Eversley," the Duke of Lindow acknowledged, strolling forward. "Your dramatic arrival irresistibly reminds me of theatricals at Oxford."

"How would you know? You never took part in them, and I cannot recall seeing you in the audience," Eversley retorted.

"It's true that I generally found better things to do. You seem to have taken those days to heart," Lindow said agreeably. "To what do we owe the pleasure of your company?"

"Necessity," Eversley said, running a hand through his curls. "The castle housed two people whom I need to see before I die, so I made the journey. A good thing too, because my doctor tells me I have little time."

Joan would have thought it pure dramatics, but the hand he had languidly raised into the air was faintly blue. As were his lips, when she squinted.

"I cannot imagine that you wish to see me, Eversley," his duchess said, rising from her chair. "You have made no such request in over a decade or more. We have nothing to discuss."

"To be truthful, you weren't on my list," the duke said nonchalantly. "Didn't even recognize you at first, but I guessed when I saw a fat rose-bush sitting up at the dinner table."

Joan registered that comment with a shock of rage that went right down her back. The sweet, shy duchess didn't deserve this from her adulterous husband.

Sir Reginald, seated next to the Duchess of Eversley, looked as if he were on the verge of stabbing Eversley in the heart.

Thaddeus was on his feet. "I would gather that the pleasure of speaking to you is to be mine." His voice was hard and dry, without a shade of other emotion. "Would you prefer to retire and speak in private?"

"Don't see any reason for that," Eversley replied. "The world will shortly know everything, so we might as well begin with the Wildes."

His duchess walked around the end of the table and approached the bier. "This has been such an unexpected pleasure, yet I believe I shall retire for the evening. Farewell, Eversley." Her voice was courteous, as if her husband had done no more than greet her. As if he were no more than a passing acquaintance.

The duke opened his mouth, undoubtedly to say something unkind, but his wife was too quick for him. Joan hadn't noticed that the duchess had brought a glass of red wine with her—until she threw the contents of her glass just below her husband's face.

The liquid, a deep, rich color, red as blood, hit his chest and splashed outward, staining all that snowy, rumpled silk, the white ermine, the white velvet.

"Bloody hell!" the duke bellowed.

Joan jumped to her feet and began to clap. "Brava!" she called. "A fitting close to a melodrama!" Beside her, Joan heard a choke, a suppressed laugh, from Thaddeus.

The duchess turned back to the table. Joan grinned at her; Lavinia jumped to her feet and clapped wildly as well; along the table the women rose and applauded, Aunt Knowe adding another "Brava!" for good measure. The duchess blushed, and smiled directly at Sir Reginald.

Behind her, the duke was clutching his chest and wheezing a demand for smelling salts. "You! Butler!" he shrilled.

Prism walked, very slowly, toward the door, ignoring him.

Joan was happy to see the smile on the Duchess of Eversley's face.

"If you would all please excuse me," she said, nodding.

"Of course!" Aunt Knowe said, bounding around the end of the table. "I shall retire with you." She paused by the bier. "You always were a numbskull, Eversley. Now you've become a raving lunatic, and you don't even have old age as an excuse."

The duke gave a crack of laughter that was more breath than sound. "If you think I care for the opinion of an unsightly, overgrown shrew—"

The Duke of Lindow cut him off. "Insult my sister at your peril, Eversley. I will not hesitate to put a rapier through what's left of your withered heart."

Joan met Lavinia's eyes, both of them full of glee. Joan's father never lost his temper, but it

was thoroughly entertaining to see him trans-
form into a menacing duke, every inch of him
outraged.

Eversley fell back on the wine-stained velvet,
panting. "Trying to kill me, I see. I see. I see the
light!"

"I only wish that was the case," Joan whispered, sitting down and pulling Thaddeus down
beside her. She turned her head to find him staring at her incredulously. "What?" she asked.

"How can you find this wretched scene funny?"

"I'm a Wilde," she said, shrugging. "Madmen
are two for tuppence around here, and we are
absurdly dramatic by nature. Miraculous saves
and brushes with death were practically a daily
occurrence when I was growing up."

Thaddeus shook his head as if to wake himself
up. Down the table, everyone was seating themselves again, chattering as they did so. Only Sir
Reginald still looked murderous.

"I told you that I wouldn't make a good duchess," Joan said, feeling that she *had* to vanquish
the bleak look in his eyes. "I might as well say
now, Thaddeus, that when I am near death, I
shall want a bier as well, and eight servants fanning me with peacock feathers."

"Fitzy's, I suppose?" he asked dryly.

"A nice touch," she said. She poked him.
"Handsome young men, mind you."

His eyes lightened. "Pillows made from a
woolly goat?"

She wrinkled her nose. "I hate to think of Gully
and Fitzy not being with us any longer."

Thaddeus leaned toward her, and before she

could stop him, he kissed her. A chaste kiss, but on the lips. At the table, where anyone could see them and undoubtedly *did*. She didn't dare glance around. Instead she frowned at him.

"We said—"

"Until matters are resolved with my father," he shot back, nodding. "I have a strong feeling that will happen before the next course arrives. Meanwhile, I'm bent on being as dramatic and scandalous as my future wife."

The bleak look in his eyes was gone, though it hadn't been her silliness that chased it away. She had the feeling that was due to the prospect of marriage. Marriage to her. The thought gave her a prickle of nerves, but Aunt Knowe hadn't raised a numbskull, to use her aunt's word.

From the moment she allowed Thaddeus through her bedchamber window, the die had been cast.

"The dukedom," she reminded him.

He smiled faintly, one of his hands closing around her thigh under the table.

Almost all the women had reseated themselves, but Joan's stepmother remained on her feet. Now she walked toward the bier. The Duchess of Lindow was a quiet woman, but with great strength of character.

"Duke," she said to Eversley. "I must ask you to leave. You have insulted one of our dearest friends, as well as my beloved sister-in-law."

"I'm not leaving until I get what I came for," Eversley said, with all the fury of Hamlet's ghost. A drop of red wine was slowly rolling down his cheek to his jaw, and he had a manic gleam in his eyes.

"What do you want from us?" the Duke of Lindow inquired, moving to put his arm around his duchess. "We have no miracle cures; you profess to have no interest in speaking to your wife."

"I need to talk to *your* eldest son," Eversley said. "As well as my own," he added.

Prism glided back into the room and offered smelling salts, which Eversley waved away. "Too slow, too late," he sighed.

"May I bring you something else, Your Grace?" Prism inquired.

"Invalid's jelly," Eversley said. "I like it made with sweet herbs and just a touch of mace."

Prism raised a finger. A footman slipped from the room.

"You'll have to get off that bed if you want to eat," the Duke of Lindow said. "Prism, have one of the brocade chairs from the library brought here."

Prism nodded and left the room.

"Sitting is difficult," Eversley said plaintively. "My lungs . . ."

"We can put you to bed; your son can visit you there."

"No, no, I don't have time," Eversley said. For the first time, Joan thought she heard a real emotion in his voice. She glanced at Thaddeus and he nodded, just the slightest move of his chin.

Eversley *was* dying, or believed himself to be dying.

Chapter Nineteen

Thaddeus could feel his heart thudding behind his chest wall. Thankfully, his mother had left, and Lady Knowe would ply her with brandy and make fun of Eversley, histrionically lying in his bier, until his mother found herself giggling, despite herself.

The foolish thing was that some ragged, small part of his soul still loved this absurd man.

The boy who thought that if he won at cricket, excelled in mathematics, took a first in astronomy *and* philosophy . . . that boy was still under his skin, straining to make his father love him.

Failing.

But now, looking at his father posed on that bier like a battered version of the god Dionysius, splattered in wine, self-indulgent lines carved into his face . . . Thaddeus realized that he'd never understood the truth of it.

He had felt he was in a competition with his father's other family. That they must be more lovable, more perfect than he.

Not true.

Eversley had never loved him, and never would.

"You indicated that you do not wish to speak to your son in private," the Duchess of Lindow said, startling Thaddeus back to the present.

"Now that my wife has made her departure, I find it easier to voice my wishes," Eversley said.

"Get on with it," the Duke of Lindow advised. "I'm hungry."

"Ah, hunger," Eversley said, sighing again. "The desires of the living are beyond me. The doctors say I will die within a day or two. I likely shall not wake from my next sleep."

"You traveled here in your condition in order to see your son?" the duke inquired. "Or my son, who doesn't know you from Adam?"

"Not I," Thaddeus intervened, putting an arm on the back of Joan's chair. "My father and I said our farewells through a series of communications between our solicitors."

"I find myself unsurprised," the Duke of Lindow told Thaddeus. He turned back to the dying man. "Well?"

"*Your* oldest son told the whole country he was going to renounce the title," Eversley began.

North, the duke of Lindow's oldest living son, cleared his throat. "I did say as much."

"My solicitors insist it is illegal," Eversley countered.

North shrugged. "More to the point, I believe *your* oldest son has no intention of indulging you."

"Indulging?" The duke's voice went up an entire octave.

Thaddeus took a sip of wine. As he put it down, Joan reached out and interlaced her fingers with his. "I'm sorry about this," he said, glancing at her.

She laughed. "Why? You know I love the theater. He's a brilliant Dionysius, Thaddeus. The god of wine, remember? And indulgence?"

"I thought the same thing." Despite the situation, he felt one side of his mouth curling into a smile.

"Are you laughing at me?" his father raged at him.

Thaddeus looked away from Joan toward his father, feeling her fingers lock even more tightly with his. He didn't answer. He had no more words for the old man who had spurned him within a week of his birth. Eversley had made periodic visits to inspect his heir, but Thaddeus had never seen him after his thirteenth birthday when the boy he considered his "real" son had been born.

"Look at you," Eversley said, apparently following the same train of thought. "You were as rigid as a starched collar as a boy, and now you look as harsh as a damned prison wall."

Jeremy slid over into the seat next to Thaddeus that had been vacated by Aunt Knowe. Thaddeus gave him a questioning glance.

"I don't want to miss anything," his friend said, chuckling. "I've always enjoyed storms, and you're the focus of this one."

"Was that your final comment?" the Duke of Lindow asked irritably from the head of the table.

The door opened and Prism entered, followed by three footmen grunting as they bore in an enormous stuffed chair. Thaddeus saw the butler hesitate for a second. The table was full.

"He can stay where he is," his master instructed.

Next to the door. The Duke of Lindow had taken a true dislike to Eversley.

"Prism, do I smell mutton? Serve the next course, if you please," the Duke of Lindow ordered.

It took most of that course for Eversley to arrange himself in the chair. The stained ermine and velvet pillows were cast to the ground; Prism directed footmen to carry them from the room. His Grace's bier was lowered carefully to the ground, and then he was drawn to his feet, groaning horribly.

Everyone at the table ate cheerfully, ignoring the performance. "Did you try the deviled lobster?" Sir Reginald asked Lavinia.

"Excellent!" she answered, raising her voice to be heard above the moaning as Eversley was hoisted into the chair. "The ragout of duck is one of the best I've ever tasted. Prism, do give my compliments to the cook."

"I shall do so, my lady," Prism said, turning from where he was supervising the tucking of a blanket around Eversley's knees.

"This is not invalid's jelly!" Eversley squeaked, recoiling from the steaming cup that Prism handed him.

"Lady Knowe's hot dandelion wine is restorative," Prism informed him.

Eversley scowled. "There's no restoring a man on the threshold of death, you fool."

"*Endive à la française?*" North asked, turning to his wife.

"Hmm, I think not," Diana replied.

"I'm dying," Thaddeus's father said loudly, once he and his many blankets were arranged. Without all the blazing white ermine and velvet, he looked small and frail, with dark smudges below his eyes.

Joan's hand closed firmly around Thaddeus's again.

"*Dust thou art, and unto dust shalt thou return,*" Jeremy commented. He met the Duke of Eversley's enraged glare with a smile. "Some of the funereal language sticks with a chap, no matter how much I'd like to forget it."

"You have acquainted us with the state of your health," the Duke of Lindow said, intervening before Eversley could respond. "You refuse to retire to a bed or privacy, therefore I assume you want an audience. You have it." He waved his hand. "My family and yours—minus your lady wife—are at attention."

"That's just it," Eversley cried, struggling to sit upright. He began to say something and fell into a series of barking coughs.

"I don't think he can manage all the verses of 'Love Divine, All Loves Excelling,'" Thaddeus said to Joan.

"Why on earth would he?" Jeremy demanded, overhearing.

"My father considers the hymn an accurate accounting of his feelings toward his mistress," Thaddeus said. "Lady Bumtrinket was treated to a solo."

Jeremy grinned. "There are times when I think that I married into the daftest family in England, so I am truly enjoying the reminder that the Wildes are not as mad as others."

"I feel as if I'm at a farce," Joan observed.

"Your father did describe us as an audience," Thaddeus replied.

Over by the door, Eversley had taken a gulp of Aunt Knowe's wine, which managed to quiet his breathing to mere wheezing. "I count not one person under this castle roof as my family," he croaked.

"Were I a poet, I'd say you had a face like thunder," Joan whispered to Thaddeus. Her hand curled tighter around his. "Just remember that he isn't your family either."

The duke was coughing again, so Thaddeus turned to her. "Unfortunately, he is."

"Some people lose their right to be termed a parent," Joan said.

"Your mother and father."

She nodded. "Remember that."

"We are all aware of the heights to which you have elevated your mistress and her children," the Duke of Lindow said, once Eversley had caught his breath.

Thaddeus's heart had slowed to a normal rate. No one was throwing him sympathetic looks, or even looking particularly scandalized. All down the table, the Wildes looked disapproving and vaguely disgusted. They didn't care that his father was a duke, and while other people had found Eversley's "other family" titillating or scandalous, the Wildes were . . . bored.

"Rum sort of fellow," he distinctly heard from farther down the table. Sir Reginald at his driest.

"Irksome," someone else said.

"My wife is the love of my life!" Eversley said defiantly.

"All appearances to the contrary," the Duke of Lindow commented.

Thaddeus's father barked, "Not that wife!"

"One has only one at a time," Lindow responded. "I'm an expert on that particular subject."

Jeremy audibly choked back a laugh, but the duke's own children felt no reluctance and snickers broke out down the table. For his part, Thaddeus felt as if his face were frozen into a blank slate, impassive and stony.

Beside him, Joan shifted until her left pannier pushed against his hip—and then collapsed. "Crickets," she murmured, and slid her chair across the resulting gap between them. "Back up," she murmured. She positioned herself in such a way that she was slightly before him.

Thaddeus felt a germ of amusement stealing into his chest as he glanced down. It seemed he had a defender, a slender warrior in a wig rather than armor.

"I married my dear Florence before I married the woman you think of as my wife," the Duke of Eversley announced, having caught his breath. "I have tried to encourage my elder son to behave like a man of honor, to renounce the dukedom, so that his mother need never know that she bore a child out of wedlock."

"You have offered no record of this supposed

wedding, nor wedding license," Thaddeus said. "My mother *was* legally married to you, for all that she undoubtedly wishes she could undo her vows."

"An illicit marriage as I had already married Florence!" his father insisted, his voice rising.

"You have no evidence," Thaddeus said. He wrapped an arm around the waist of the woman who would be the Duchess of Eversley someday. Joan leaned back against his shoulder, her expression a mix of curious and disapproving.

"You shouldn't be such a stickler for certificates!" Eversley spat. "It's part and parcel with the bloodless, tedious man you've grown to be."

"The *law* is a stickler for certificates," Thaddeus pointed out. "Your marriage to my mother is inscribed in the records of St. Paul's Cathedral."

"I don't wish to humiliate her. I came here to ask you one more time: Will you renounce the dukedom so that I need not publicly disgrace your mother?"

"He cannot," North said, speaking up.

Eversley swung his head in his direction, reminding Joan irresistibly of a vulture with a bony head and scrawny neck. "*You* plan to renounce the Lindow title. You're the duke's oldest living son, and all England knows you're renouncing the title. My son can do the same." He took a ragged breath and sucked down some more dandelion wine.

"At a moment of crisis, my father and aunt suggested just that," North said, a faint smile on his lips. "I subsequently learned that the action would not be legal. Quite likely, my wife and I are stuck with the dukedom." He leaned down and kissed Diana's nose.

"Nonsense! An English duke can do as he wishes. Is this your last word?" Eversley shrilled, turning to Thaddeus, his eyes bulging from the blue skin that surrounded them. "You refuse to grant your dying father's wish?"

"I do refuse," Thaddeus replied. "I shall be the Duke of Eversley within the day, if your doctor is to be believed. I intend to make Lady Joan Wilde my duchess."

Eversley's eyes sharpened. "I know who you are," he said, staring at Joan.

"Lady Joan is my daughter," the Duke of Lindow said, with chilling exactitude.

"Why should you be able to name a child legitimate when I cannot?" Eversley screeched, his eyes bright, near feverish.

"Joan is *mine* because her mother was married to me, and I have the license to prove it," Lindow stated. "Do you dare to contest me, Eversley?" The threat of immediate death lay behind his voice.

"No, no," Eversley squawked. "My point is that my real son, my true son, would make a better duke. I should have the right to choose!" He looked around the table wildly. "This—this serpent who calls himself my son refused to break the entail as well, so the family of my heart will be left destitute. The poorhouse awaits!"

"You left the duchy and estates to the care of my mother and myself over two decades ago," Thaddeus said, sounding impatient now. "Your allowance has been more than adequate to support your current household, and I shall continue it."

"Not to mention all those ermine robes," Jeremy put in. "Royal regalia is bloody expensive."

"Your other children are my half siblings," Thaddeus added. "I will not condemn them to destitution."

"This is growing tiresome," the Duchess of Lindow said in her clear, calm voice. "I believe that we have granted His Grace a sufficient audience." She raised her hand. "Prism, if you would be so kind as to escort the duke to a bedchamber. Or his carriage, if he would prefer."

Eversley's eyes kindled with rage, and his wizened hands gripped the arms of the chair as if he expected the butler to try to rip him from his seat. "I intend to send an announcement to the *Morning Post*, to be published after my death, explaining that I married Florence before my family forced me into a false union! Your mother won't be happy," he spat at Thaddeus.

He lifted a visibly shaking hand in the air and clawed inside his waistcoat before he drew out a folded piece of parchment. "Here it is!" he screeched. "It'll be in all the stationery shops in London. I closed it with the ducal seal, so no one can question it."

"Oh, they'll question it," the Duke of Lindow said. "I don't know where you got the idea that the ducal seal is more than a picture pressed into wax."

"I can eliminate that threat," Viola's husband, Devin, said. "I keep a sharp eye on all the printing presses in London since my wife is not fond of seeing her image in stationery shops' windows. It's the work of a moment to send a groom around to each. I'll have a man in London by noon tomorrow."

"That's right!" the Duke of Lindow said. "I'll send along a man as well, with instructions for my solicitor. They will inform every newspaper in London that publication of such an announcement will result in immediate and expensive legal challenges. Financial ruin will follow any such publication." He turned to Thaddeus. "My wedding present to you."

Thaddeus let go of Joan and stood, smiling at Devin and the Duke of Lindow. "Thank you both." Then he turned to his father. "Eversley, your cruelty to my mother has been documented in the press. Should this publication happen, she would be pained, but unsurprised. The rest of England would be disgusted, but also unsurprised."

"The Wildes will support the rightful heir to the Eversley dukedom," the Duke of Lindow said, standing as well. Then he added, "The heir who plans to marry my daughter, although he has unaccountably neglected to ask me for her hand."

Joan rose and leaned against Thaddeus's shoulder, winding an arm around his waist. "As a matter of fact, I have not yet agreed to marry him."

Around the table the family jumped to their feet in a clamor of congratulations, completely ignoring her disavowal.

Thaddeus met the Duke of Lindow's eyes, nodding, before he turned back to his own father.

Eversley gave Thaddeus a burning look, closed his eyes, and slumped back in his chair, rubbing his heart. "The newspapers won't be able to resist it." He closed his eyes. "Sharper than a serpent's tooth is a thankless child." He gasped for breath and managed to bellow, "You are no longer a son of mine!" before he collapsed back against his chair, eyes closed.

Prism stepped forward. Six footmen arranged themselves around Eversley's chair.

"Out," the Duke of Lindow said, unemotionally.

Without ceremony, they hoisted the invalid into the air and whisked him out the door.

"I can't decide whether your father's side whiskers, his ermine, or his arrogance is more objectionable," the Duchess of Lindow said, giving Thaddeus a wry smile. "I am glad that your mother missed this distasteful performance." She turned to the butler. "Prism, we have always taken comfort in the fact that our household has never betrayed us to the press. I must ask you to make it clear that Lord Greywick is a member of the family and should be protected as if he were a Wilde."

"On that front, I gather you have something to ask me," the Duke of Lindow said to Thaddeus, throwing a meaningful look at Joan.

"No, he doesn't," his daughter retorted. "I haven't accepted his proposal. Perhaps I shan't."

Thaddeus consciously relaxed his jaw, the anger

spurred by his father's behavior coursing through him, making it difficult to engage in the Wildes' version of light badinage.

Joan glanced up at him and slid her arm from around his waist. "If you please, Thaddeus, escort me on a visit to Percy."

"Percy?" Thaddeus ripped his attention from the memory of his father—his *father*—renouncing him. He had never been a true son of Eversley's. As a child, he couldn't understand his father's languid disdain, any more than he could understand why his parents lived separately. Thaddeus had consequently devoted his life to the pursuit of perfection, the perfect son, the perfect athlete, the perfect scholar.

To no avail.

"Our piglet," Joan clarified, slipping a hand in his arm and guiding him toward the door. "If you'll excuse us," she called behind her.

They walked into the corridor and out of the castle without another word.

Chapter Twenty

*J*oan loved to act; ergo, she ought to enjoy drama when it came her way.

That was not the case. She felt ill at the revelation of Eversley's hard heart and selfish demands. "How did your mother ever bear living with him?" she asked Thaddeus, as they walked around the side of the castle, heading for the cowshed where Percy resided.

"They weren't in the same household for long," he replied. "Only until she gave birth to a son. I believe that his parents managed to exert some sort of promise that he would remain at Eversley Court until an heir was born, but no one ever spoke of it."

The night was lit by a near-harvest moon that cast a silvery glow over the grass. To their left, light shone from a few windows in the castle, but most were dark. A breeze was rustling the poplar trees, and somewhere an owl announced the start of a hunt.

Percy had been housed in a fine shed built for

Viola's two beloved cows. Thaddeus hung the lantern he had brought with him from a nail in a beam, so it could light the small room.

Joan walked straight over to the pen. Percy was nestled against the side of a sleeping heifer, but he bounded to his feet and came over to sniff her hand, his mouth curled in an eternal grin. "You're growing up, Percy old fellow. He's losing his fuzz," she added, over her shoulder.

The only answer was a hard thump behind her that caused the shed timbers to shiver. Percy gave a squeal and ran back across the pen to press his body against his friendly bedmate.

Joan turned to find Thaddeus with his head resting against his fists, braced on the shed wall. She walked over and put a hand on his raised biceps. "I'm sorry," she said simply.

Thaddeus made a rough sound in the back of his throat. "I haven't lost control, in case you are frightened."

"You could never frighten me," Joan said. She turned just enough so she could wiggle between his body and the rough wood of the shed. Then she looped her arms around his neck. "My father always says that there are people whom the law supports, and those whom the law slights, such as a destitute child thrown into a prison for stealing a loaf of bread. Those who have, and those who have not."

Thaddeus shifted his head to look down at her.

Joan knew enough about him now to interpret his look as willingness to listen, if not precisely encouragement to keep talking.

"Your father is the sort whom the law inevitably favors, and yet it's never enough for him. You see what he's doing, don't you? He was born a duke, the highest nobility in the land below royalty, and that's not good enough."

"My mother—"

"It has nothing to do with your mother or you not being good enough, for all Eversley squealed about that. He *has*, and yet he wants more. He wants to be king, to set the law himself. I don't believe he cares so much for his other family. He just wants to make law himself."

Thaddeus stared down at her, his eyes shadowed.

"Ermine," she reminded him, going up on her toes to kiss his chin, because it wasn't like her future husband to be slow on the uptake, but after all, it was a painful subject. "When's the last time you saw someone with an ermine throw—in the end of August, moreover? Ermine is the fur of kings. In Shakespeare's time only royalty was allowed to wear ermine."

Thaddeus's brows drew together. "Interesting."

Joan's hands slid down his shoulders. He was built like a Roman gladiator. This was a serious moment, and yet she felt a pulse of liquid heat that went straight down to her knees with a significant pause on the way.

Thaddeus had no idea that his mouth was sensual, or that the muscled ridges of his body were utterly delectable. She was ogling him shamelessly, even as frustration and banked rage shone from his eyes.

Unable to help herself, to be honest.

She swallowed hard and pulled her mind back

to the subject at hand. "To sum it up, your father is morally corrupt and worthless."

To her relief, he gave a reluctant bark of laughter. "Worthless. I like it."

"If you'd like an elaborated version: He is a rotter who wishes to be king. I also think he's annoyed by the fact he's turned out to be a member of the human race and thereby vulnerable to death."

"He's always been half cracked," Thaddeus said slowly. "He's grown significantly worse."

"The nonsense about sending a notice to the papers is just a pathetic way to ensure that he isn't silenced by death," Joan said, easing back against the shed wall because his hard body was very distracting.

She glanced down. Her low bodice wasn't doing much to disguise the fact her nipples felt as desperate for attention as the rest of her.

"I see," Thaddeus said. He didn't sound angry any longer, but his voice rasped all the same.

Joan's eyes flew to his face and saw not anger, but raw, hungry need. "Oh," she said with a gasp. "I see."

"We have settled the question of my title," Thaddeus stated. "My father has no proof; the newspapers will not publish his nonsense. I will be the duke."

"I do think that we should wrangle that letter away from him, if only so no servant gets hold of it," Joan said, bringing her hands around to fiddle with one of the buttons on his waistcoat. She felt shy, an emotion uncommon for her. "I have an idea how to do so, not the angel, a different idea."

"I promise you that Eversley is no danger to us," Thaddeus said.

She nodded.

His hands came down from the wall, and he took a step back. Her hands slid from his waistcoat. "You make sense of my life, Joan," Thaddeus said. His face was impassive, but that didn't matter. He said enough with his eyes.

"Are you going to make sense of my life as well?" Joan asked, suddenly enjoying herself enormously.

"I don't see people clearly, as you do. I spent a great part of my childhood trying to excel in order to please a man who didn't care. But if you point out a problem, I will take care of it. I will be there for you, Joan. I will never leave you. You and your family will be the family of my heart."

Joan managed a wobbly smile. "That's lovely," she whispered.

He thrust a hand in his pocket and then sank to his knees.

"You can't do that," Joan gasped. "We're in Percy's sty. A pigsty! Your breeches!"

Thaddeus grinned at her, and Joan saw longing and joy in his eyes. Her heart thumped in response.

"I love you," Thaddeus said, taking her hand in his. "Last night my mother gave me a ring that belonged to my grandmother, one that was untainted by my father. My grandmother and grandfather lived long, cheerful lives, though saddened to witness their daughter's unhappy marriage."

Joan sank down on her knees before him, her

gown puddling over fresh straw. "Are you certain? I'm not legitimate, and all England knows it. I'm always causing scandals. If you had given me a chance, I would have kissed you before an entire ballroom."

He looked back at her, his eyes sure and calm. "I trust you. You will never have to kiss a man to get my attention again."

There was a moment of silence. Joan bit her lip. "How did you guess? Because I didn't like you then; I truly didn't."

"I didn't like you either. But I always knew where you were in a room. I loathe gossip, and yet somehow I always knew who was courting you, and who you were flirting with."

"I didn't like it when you courted my sisters," Joan whispered.

The straw rustled behind them, as Percy settled himself back against his bedmate with a contented grunt.

"May I give you this ring?" Thaddeus asked. He looked at Joan the way her father looked at her stepmother, the way Devin looked at Viola, the way she never thought anyone . . .

Joan felt a tear slide down her cheek. "Are you truly certain?" she asked in an aching whisper. "I won't run away to the stage, or ever play Hamlet again. But—"

"If you run away to the stage, I will run after you." His voice was deep and certain. "If you want to perform Hamlet, I'll be your Ophelia, albeit in breeches. I won't like it, but I'll do it."

In his large hand, an emerald winked in the lamplight, its glossy shine surrounded by diamonds. "How lovely," Joan said. She looked up. "Yes, I will marry you." The words hung in the air.

He slid the smooth gold over her finger. The emerald looked as if it had always encircled her finger. As if she could wear it for the rest of her life.

"It fits perfectly," she said, hearing wonder in her own voice.

"A sign," Thaddeus said. His voice had dropped from a rasp to a rumble. "Joan."

"I love emeralds more than any other stone," she said, turning the ring.

"Joan."

She looked up, and heat shot through her again. "Oh." And then: "Yes."

"We're in a pigsty. A duchess, a future duchess, in a pigsty," Thaddeus said, a dark thread of humor in his voice.

"The moon is up. We could . . ." Her voice faltered. Now that she'd promised to become a duchess, perhaps she should be more circumspect. Hadn't she promised not to cause scandals? Not that anyone in Lindow would know.

Or care, some devil inside her prompted.

But Thaddeus—her future husband—was prudent, gentlemanly. Not a Wilde.

"We could take the rowboat," Thaddeus growled, completing her suggestion. His eyes were burning hot. "We could go to the island, and you could lie back on my coat, Joan, naked under the moon except for this ring, and let me love you."

He brought her to her feet. They paused to say good night to Percy, who opened one sleepy eye, and set out into the night.

Through the apple orchard, down the meadow slope.

Thaddeus put the lantern down and with a wicked smile, stripped off his coat.

Joan couldn't find any words because her heart leapt for joy.

Thaddeus threw his clothes on the grass. Joan waited, forcing her lungs to fill with air, marshaling all her resources to wait patiently. She needed help. A lady could not unclothe herself without assistance. She toed off her shoes; she could do that. She pulled the pins from her hair and shook it free, letting sweet-smelling powder float into the air. It fell below her shoulders, the thick, golden evidence of her parentage.

Tonight, that felt like a joyful fact, rather than a complicated one.

After that, she just watched Thaddeus, reminding herself that his body would be *hers*. Hers to touch, explore, delight.

For life.

He took off everything except his breeches and turned back to her, hands on his hips, moonlight emphasizing every dip and shadow carved by his muscles. Joan took another hard breath. "You're beautiful."

He laughed, and suddenly Joan had the feeling that Thaddeus was meant to be a person for whom laughter wasn't rare. He had compressed himself into the form of a perfect gentleman, the exquisite duke, the somber man.

But the real Thaddeus stood on the bank, eyes lit by fierce lust—and laughter.

"My lady," he said, striding to her. "May I?"

She nodded.

"Turn around," he commanded.

Obediently, she turned, picking up the heavy fall of her hair and bringing it forward over her shoulder.

He was nimble, twice as fast as her maid, twirling her when needed, plucking knots before she fumbled to untie them. Showing a remarkable knowledge of women's clothing, she noticed. And then thought, with a happy wiggle, that Thaddeus would never again undress any woman other than herself.

Her corset fell onto the grass, leaving only her light chemise. Thaddeus leaned in and kissed her lightly on the lips. His hands settled on her waist, making her feel encompassed, encircled. He kissed her again, on her nose, her cheekbones. His fingers spread into a caress, and she shivered, swaying closer.

"The island," he rasped.

Joan opened her eyes. "There's a very nice patch of grass underneath our feet."

Thaddeus shook his head. "You told me that you would bring your future husband to the island." He kissed her. "Vixen," he whispered. "I couldn't sleep that night."

Her smile felt as if it lightened her soul with pure joy. Thaddeus handed Joan the lantern and operated the oars with such force that the boat shot across the lake, splitting a sea of sweet-smelling flowers and leaving a wake behind them.

Joan was content to watch his arms bunch as Thaddeus rowed. Her body tingled all over, but more than that, she felt a soul-deep connection with a man who was her opposite in almost every way.

Except the ways in which he wasn't, because when he shook back his hair and leapt to the bank, turning to hold out a hand, she knew that in the only ways that truly matter, they were as close as two humans could be.

Over the years, they would grow even closer.

The little clearing looked different at night: The air was gently scented, and the white jasmine blossoms caught moonlight and reflected it. When Thaddeus put down the lantern, the light created a small room bathed in gold, and yet over their heads the vast moon sailed on.

Eyes on her face, Thaddeus undid his breeches and shoved them down his legs. Then he stood before her, naked.

"May I?" he asked, reaching to her chemise. At her nod, he drew the cloth slowly, torturously slowly, up her body and over her head. Joan could feel her heart pounding as if she were looking at herself along with him, purposefully uncovering her body bit by bit, making the pleasure last.

Her chemise flew to the side, and she stood there, naked, the lamplight washing over her skin. The sight of his naked body made pleasure ripple through her.

"May *I*?" she echoed. Without waiting for an answer, she reached down and wrapped his cock in one hand.

Thaddeus sucked in a rough breath, and his hands fell from his hips. He didn't move. Her fingers closed tightly and then slid . . . He made a harsh sound in the back of his throat. He was hard and thick, and his hips arched toward her. "Hell," he groaned.

Joan grinned at him, tightened, and added a gentle twist, watching as a flicker of heat lit in his eyes. She tightened her hand even more, and his head fell back. She tried a slower stroke and his eyes opened . . . She brought her other hand there too, tentatively touching what she had seen but not caressed.

"Wait," he choked, and removed her hands. "Joan."

She smiled at him, impish, pleased with herself and the world. "Yes, Thaddeus? This is so Adam-and-Eve-ish." She rearranged her hair so that her breasts were almost hidden, cocked a hip, and held out a hand. "Surely you have an apple for me, Your Lordship?"

He caught her against him, all his heat and strength against her softness. "I'm no devil."

Joan tipped back her head. "You're devilish. Taking me to an island to have your way with me."

"Only with you," he said hoarsely, one hand running forcefully down her shoulder and curving over her bottom.

"I certainly don't mind if you leave the perfect duke behind on the shore." She shivered, her tongue shaping his bottom lip. His hand dipped lower, between her legs, and she forgot what she was saying. "*Thaddeus.*"

"Perfect dukes keep their wives happy," he murmured. His fingers were everywhere, caressing, rubbing. "Are you happy, Joan?" One finger dipped inside.

"Yes," she gasped into his mouth, because he was kissing her openmouthed, hungry, insistent, while his fingers . . . She pulled back just enough to see what he was doing. One hand circled a breast, his thumb rubbing over her nipple.

The other maddened her, two fingers plunging inside, filling her.

"More," she whimpered, absently registering that she sounded like a wanton. Not a duchess.

Thaddeus didn't seem to mind. "You're more beautiful than Eve," he said, his voice raw.

She didn't like compliments; she never had. They were always, in her mind at least, barbed. But with Thaddeus's dark eyes staring into hers, the word had a different meaning.

"Not just your hair," he said, guessing what she was thinking. "All of you, Joan, including the fact you laugh in a moment when many women are self-conscious." He caught her in his arms, picking her up as if she weighed nothing, turning to put her gently on the bed formed from his breeches and her chemise.

Those clever fingers slid down Joan's stomach, and she found she was shaking, waiting for his caress, desperate for that touch to sear her with pleasure.

He stopped.

She whimpered, despite herself. Words spilled from her mouth, "Please," but other words too, unladylike ones, commands, pleas. Thaddeus was laughing against her breast, his teeth teasing her nipple, his hands stroking her between the legs so lightly that it felt like torment rather than pleasure.

She twisted underneath him, desperate. "Thaddeus!" she cried, loving the fact that no one could hear them. "I need . . . I need more."

He laughed again, low and hoarse. His fingers breached her wet folds, finally filling her, sending a sweep of heat and relief through her.

But he withdrew and before she could complain, he was over her, kissing her, poised at her entrance, eyes catching hers. "Joan?"

"Oh, for God's sake," she cried. "Please, Thaddeus. *Now, please!*"

He thrust inside, the blunt head of his shaft not at all like his fingers. She froze, but then her body quivered and somehow accommodated his girth, squeezing him tighter, drawing him in.

It was Thaddeus's turn to groan incoherent curses. Joan was concentrating on the greedy heat she felt, but she heard fragments. "Inside you," he groaned, and thrust again, and again.

She had the odd feeling that they were on an ocean, his motion as steady as waves coming inexorably to the shore.

Every wave, every thrust, made her arch higher, grind against him, trying to get, trying to feel—

He shifted, and she shrieked. Thaddeus braced himself on one arm, stopping.

"No," Joan begged, clutching his arms. "Don't stop now, that was it, that was . . ."

"Perfect?" he demanded, eyebrow raised.

She moaned.

"Joan?"

"Yes," she breathed.

He rewarded her with a thrust from just the right angle, one that sent heat pulsing through her. "More?" He was in control, his voice strained but amused.

Joan nodded, her eyes on his. "No jesting," she whispered. "Not now."

He dipped his head and kissed her, his cock pulsing inside her but his hips still. "Thaddeus," she sobbed.

Amusement left his face. He was taut with desire, his jaw tight. "I love you, Joan," he said, caught her left thigh and pulled her to just the right position.

Joan meant to say *I love you too*, but she couldn't speak a word. Pleasure burst through her and exploded in her veins. He flexed his hips, plunging deep, and every movement seemed to cause him to swell inside her until she lost all coherence and just babbled.

Screamed.

Sobbed, "I love you."

"Yes," Thaddeus breathed.

His forehead dipped to hers as his hips bucked uncontrollably, and he gave her everything he had, all the love he had pouring into her warm body.

Chapter Twenty-one

$\mathcal{T}$haddeus rowed back to the shore an hour or so later, his body exhausted, his mind exhilarated.

Joan sat in the other end of the boat, wearing her chemise again, likely not realizing that her nipples cast dark incantatory shadows, that the shadow between her legs was a delicious intoxication. Her voice was happy, no longer drenched in lust. She hadn't noticed that his cock was tenting his breeches again.

"Do you want to hear my idea for heading off your father's nefarious plan for that letter?" she asked.

He tried to make a sound that wasn't an animalistic grunt and failed.

Joan was trailing a hand in the water, watching the ripples that spread from it, creating a moon trail instantly covered by drifting lily pads. Rather than give the oars a hard pull that would land them on the shore, he stilled.

"Or will you trust me to just give it a try?" she asked, looking up at him.

"I don't think that my father will succumb to the pleas of a guardian angel," Thaddeus said apologetically. "I believe you're correct; he considers himself the ultimate justice."

"You're right about the angel," Joan conceded. "I have a new idea."

He raised an eyebrow.

"A secret," she told him. "It may fail, but I'd love to try, if you'll allow it."

Thaddeus nodded. "Of course. Do you need any help?"

"No help needed. If I fail, I don't believe it will hurt anything," Joan said, her eyes shining with mischief. "But if I succeed, I will leave his bedchamber with his blasted letter."

To be completely honest, Thaddeus no longer gave a damn about the letter. The power of the Wildes would stifle publication: The duke's solicitors would threaten the papers; Devin would threaten the printing presses. Moreover, he was convinced that his mother would become Lady Murgatroyd as soon as she threw off mourning garments.

Neither of them would truly mourn his father, and the world would forget the cracked Duke of Eversley soon enough.

He slipped the oars into the lake and slowly paddled back. Joan was leaning over the side, greeting small frogs who plopped into the water rather than reply.

Most of England would consider him fortunate, and Thaddeus had always agreed. But in this moment, on this moonlit night, he felt as if he had only just discovered what it meant to be truly blessed.

It was to be loved.

He was still thinking about that as they emerged from the woods. Joan clutched his arm, and his head jerked up. The castle had been peacefully asleep, windows mostly darkened when they left. Now the family wing shone with light.

"The baby!" Joan cried, speeding up.

He strode after her, across the lawn, up the stairs . . . but when she burst into a bedchamber that presumably held a laboring mother, he remained in the corridor with the Duke of Lindow, who was leaning against the wall, eyes heavy-lidded with exhaustion.

"I tell myself everything will be well," His Grace said, glancing at him. "Yet I know that women die in childbirth across the country. One of my children is in danger."

"Your sister, Lady Knowe, is a better doctor than those who study for years," Thaddeus offered, propping himself against the wall next to His Grace. The doors of the old castle were so thick that nothing could be heard from within the chamber. "Do you have any idea how long the . . . the event might take?"

"It differs for each woman," Lindow said. His eyes narrowed, and he looked Thaddeus up and down.

Thaddeus couldn't stop himself from grinning, even as he tucked in the trailing edge of his shirt. "She said yes," he told Joan's father. "She finally said yes."

The duke grunted and bumped him with his shoulder. "Excellent." They both looked up when the door swung open. "Take this!" Joan commanded, holding up a glass of golden liquid.

"What is it?" Thaddeus asked.

"Is the baby here?" the duke demanded, at the same moment.

"Almost," Joan said. "Thaddeus, the soothing tonic is for your father. Aunt Knowe visited him earlier. She didn't want to give him the drink until you had a chance to say goodbye." She darted forward and kissed him on the cheek. "I'm sorry."

Behind her, the sound of excited voices rose. Joan pushed the glass into his hand and ducked back in, the door swinging shut behind her.

Thaddeus looked down at the glass, dumbfounded.

"I'll take you to Eversley's bedchamber," the duke said. "I won't enter with you because I don't want to strangle a man on his own deathbed."

"I don't give a damn about saying goodbye," Thaddeus stated.

"Better do it anyway," His Grace advised. "When my sister recommends something, she's usually right. If that drink will soothe your father on his way, then it would be well that he drank it."

They walked through several corridors and over to another wing of the castle. The duke paused outside a door. "Your father had delusions of grandeur, so we put him in a chamber that once housed King Henry VIII. Will you remember how to make your way back?"

"I believe I shall retire for the night."

His Grace looked surprised. "The family will all wait up for the baby. The men are in the billiard room, if you'd like to join them there."

Thaddeus absorbed his words: He was part of a family now.

"Except for Devin," the duke continued, "who insisted on staying by his wife's bedside. It's by way of a family tradition."

Thaddeus flinched, and the duke guffawed. "No need to follow suit! I will say, though, that the memories of seeing my last three be brought into the world are among my most treasured."

"Right," Thaddeus said.

"No need to consider it now. Death first, then life."

Thaddeus took a breath and pushed open the door.

Henry VIII's bedchamber was papered in strawberry-colored silk. Squarely in the middle of the room was a large bed, topped with a cupola, not unlike that of the monopteron on the island, except that was shaped from marble and this was gilt, decorated with spiky turrets. Fringed strawberry-colored silk cascaded from the cupola, easily twice the amount of fabric that surrounded his own bed.

His father lay facing the door on a pile of white pillows, the wine-stained ermine throw covering his feet.

A footman in Lindow livery sat in the corner; as Thaddeus entered he rose, nodded, and quietly left the room.

"Who's there?" his father called in a scratchy voice.

"It is I, Father," Thaddeus said, coming to stand at his right side.

The room was blazing with lit candelabra, but his father squinted. "I can't see well." He pointed a shaking hand. "Is that the syrup I'm supposed to drink?"

"Yes," Thaddeus said. "A soothing tonic, I understand."

"That poker of a woman said it would ease the way. I'm dying, blast take it," his father growled. "Might as well go out drunk."

Thaddeus held the glass steady at his father's mouth.

"Off with you," the duke growled after he finished. "I'll not have you stealing my letter if I close my eyes. I've left instructions with my valet. I can't breathe with you standing over me like a vulture waiting to pick clean my corpse."

"I would never steal your letter," Thaddeus told him. He laid his hand over his father's thin, veined one. "I respect the fact that you traveled here, in your last days, in an effort to ensure the well-being of your family."

His father began coughing, the hacking noises softer than earlier in the evening. He was losing strength.

"I will take care of my siblings," Thaddeus said. "I swear it. The boy will go to Eton."

"They don't take ba-bastards," his father panted. His eyes were closed. "I can't *breathe* with you here, with all your rectitude and honor."

Thaddeus nodded, even though the duke couldn't see it, and removed his hand. "Eton will accept *my* half brother, no matter his parentage. Goodbye, Father."

The duke opened his eyes and cast such a look of flickering dislike that Thaddeus almost recoiled. "You never understood, did you?"

"No," Thaddeus said. "No, I never did."

"You're so bloody perfect," he growled. "A shining example of English honor, that's what they all tell me. The best man—pah! You never faced a true challenge. You never failed, so how hard could it have been for you to succeed?"

The room fell into silence, with only the man's belabored breathing to be heard.

"You were my greatest challenge so far," Thaddeus said, finally. "And I failed. From my childhood, you made it clear that I had failed."

The duke didn't open his eyes, so after another moment or two, Thaddeus left.

He was surprised to find the Duke of Lindow waiting for him, leaning against the wall.

"Said your last words?" His Grace asked.

Thaddeus nodded. He wasn't able to speak; his father's last, bitter speech was stuck to him like a cobweb one blunders into in the dark.

Lindow scowled at him. "A contemptible bastard to the end, was he?"

"I gather he resented my accomplishments, such as they are," Thaddeus said. "Which I attained in order to please him."

"You are true gold," Lindow said. "A man, an honorable man, and he wasn't. Never was, even when he was a boy. I remember him as a peevish lad who could scarcely ride a horse and never showed interest in anyone other than himself."

"I see," Thaddeus said.

The duke's shoulder bumped against his and an arm curved around his shoulders. "Hate to say it about a man's father, but you're better off without him. For one thing, your mother can marry Murgatroyd, who *is* a good man."

"I agree."

"Couldn't do better," His Grace confirmed. "Neither could you, with my Joan." There was just the faintest emphasis in his voice.

Thaddeus met his eyes. "I know that."

Chapter Twenty-two

*S*o far this year, Joan had witnessed the birth of two babies, since Aunt Knowe served as midwife for all those living in and around the castle. In neither case did she feel more than desperate sympathy for the mother and a slight aversion to the ugly little human who caused all the pain and mess.

Viola's baby was the exception.

Birth was very different when you loved every person in the room, and the birthing mother was your dearest sister. She grew misty-eyed watching Devin embrace his wife, tears standing unashamedly in his eyes. She hugged her stepmother, who was sobbing with happiness. When Aunt Knowe brought back little Otis, washed and sleepy, Viola beckoned to her, and Joan crawled onto the bed to admire him.

"He's lovely, Joan," Viola whispered. "Just look at how perfect his toes are!"

"Oh, Viola, he looks just like you," Joan said. "That's your bottom lip."

Devin bent over and kissed his son's forehead. "Otis," he said softly, running a finger down his cheek. "Hello, my boy."

"Named after my Ophelia?" Joan asked. "Lucky Otis!" She rolled off the bed and nudged her brother-in-law to take her place.

Viola nodded. "Your Otis talked Devin into courting me, you know."

"I didn't need convincing," Devin said, a hint of a growl in his voice. "But Otis is a brother to me."

"Of course you didn't need convincing," Viola said, leaning over to rub her cheek against her husband's shoulder. "You were dazzled by my mouselike self, popping out from behind the curtains."

"No, I was dazzled by the sudden appearance of the funniest, most beautiful woman in the world," Devin responded, his voice deep with love. "My future wife and mother of my son."

"May I fetch your stepfather, dear?" the duchess asked. "Hugo has been waiting in the corridor."

"Is Thaddeus with him?" Joan asked.

Aunt Knowe bustled forward. "Neither are in the hallway any longer; my brother sent a message that they retired to the billiard room. Devin will bring little Otis downstairs to meet the men in his family in good time."

"Thaddeus is with them?" Joan asked.

Aunt Knowe nodded. "He made his goodbyes to his father. Perhaps you should join him, dear."

Joan glanced back at the bed where Viola and Devin leaned over a little scrap of humanity, their eyes shining. "Baby Otis is perfect, isn't he?"

Aunt Knowe put a hand on her cheek. "Just as

beautiful as your baby will be." She leaned in. "The clocks on your right stocking are running up the inside of your leg. Correct that before you visit the billiard room, unless you want your brothers to tease you for the next decade or so."

Her rich laughter drifted into the corridor. Joan paused and then ran toward her own bedchamber. To be blunt, she had to beat Death himself to the Duke of Eversley's bed if she wanted to carry through her plan and retrieve that horrible letter.

Thankfully, her maid was in her chamber and helped her quickly undress. "I need my prince's costume," Joan explained, hopping on one foot to pull off her stocking before her maid noticed her disheveled clothing.

Sometime later, she glanced at the mirror. A young prince stared back at her, regal from the top of his hat with its fashionable green feather, to the exquisite silver embroidery on his cuffs, to the diamonds on his shoe buckles.

She turned to the jewelry box on her dressing table, selecting a circlet of diamonds that she had been given by Aunt Knowe when she turned eighteen. She draped it over her neck cloth.

"That's right odd looking, given as you're dressed as a man," her maid objected.

"I need to sparkle," Joan told her. "Could you please hand me the diamond pin?"

"The one your aunt said was garish?" her maid asked.

"Yes, that one," Joan said. She pinned it onto her hat, directly in front where it couldn't be overlooked.

"Odd," her maid muttered.

"Should I pin more diamonds to my coat?" Joan asked. "I need to look regal. I could run next door and borrow something from Viola."

"The only thing left is to put a crown on top of your hat," her maid said. "You look as if you'd emptied out of one of the goldsmiths' shops in Cheapside."

"Regal?" Joan insisted.

"Not that I've ever seen a king, but I suppose."

Joan dropped a kiss on her cheek. "Thank you! You needn't stay up. I can shed this coat without any help."

She set out at a gallop for Henry VIII's bed-chamber, only slowing when she reached the right corridor. She pushed open the door and found the chamber empty but for the patient. It was blazing with candlelight, and the Duke of Eversley looked gaunt and gray against his white pillows.

He was still alive; she could hear his breathing. As Joan walked over to him, his eyes opened.

Joan held her breath, but he showed no sign of recognizing her. Instead, he craned his neck and wheezed, "Who are you?"

"Recognize us not?" she said, dropping her voice several octaves and putting on her Prince Hamlet expression.

"Said that I didn't," Eversley replied querulously. "There's a cold glitter about you. Have you come to take my soul? Forgot your black cloak and scythe?"

"No, no," Joan said hastily.

"Your coat's old-fashioned," he said nastily.

"What are you doing in my chamber if you're not hiding a scythe behind your back?"

"You are in *our* chamber," she intoned, pitching her voice even lower.

"A ghost," the duke exclaimed. "I never believed in 'em. Not sure I do now, even with the outdated coat. I can't see through you."

"At this moment, we exist on the same plane, between life and death," Joan told him. "I am as alive as you, and as dead as you."

"Bollocks," the duke said. He squinted again. "You're never Bluff Hal, are you?"

Joan had never been any good at history. She was playing a young Henry VIII, but she had no idea what his nicknames might have been.

"Old Coppernosed Harry, the eighth by that name," Eversley clarified.

"Names that must have been given to us in later years," she said.

"How old are you?"

"Seventeen," Joan told him. "On a wedding trip with Catherine." That was when the real Henry VIII visited Lindow, his older bride in tow.

"You didn't die for years after your first wedding," Eversley pointed out, his eyes closing as if he were losing interest. "Can't imagine why you bother to haunt this place. The current Duke of Lindow is a bastard, a virile bastard at that, with enough sons to populate a village. Given your deficits in that respect, I'd expect you to avoid this place like the plague."

"We are here because you are not a king and yet kinglike," Joan said, improvising madly. "Not royal and yet royalty. You are alone. We know all . . . for example, that you would prefer to be with your real family, the family of your heart."

Eversley's shaded eyes flickered at her, and for a moment, Joan saw the wicked mischief of Bacchus shining at her. But he reeled into a series of painful coughs.

"She . . ." the duke mumbled, once he caught his breath. "Can't let them see me like this, dying. Spitting and pissing in the bed. Said my goodbyes."

Joan's mouth fell open for a moment before she snapped it shut. "It's estimable that you traveled to Lindow Castle in your last day on this earth to ensure that your second family will be well cared for."

Eversley's laugh was more of a bark than a laugh. "Revenge," he said savagely. "It can keep a dying man alive." He fumbled under his pillow. "See this?"

Joan's heart thumped. Crumpled now, it was the paper that Eversley had waved about at dinner. "We do."

"It's my revenge." The parchment fell from his hands. "Read it. *If* you can. I never heard of a ghost who did more than throw dishes around when aggravated. I assume those are females."

"At this moment, we are on the same plane of existence," Joan reminded him.

"Balderdash," the duke mumbled. His eyes seemed to be glazing over.

Joan ripped open the seal and unfolded the letter. Her eyes skimmed it quickly: "In the name of God, Amen. I, Andrew Cornelius Erskine Shaw, Duke of Eversley, of Eversley Court, declare that

I married the woman known as my duchess only under duress and the threat of bodily harm, after having already wed the love of my heart in solemn ceremony. I declare my second marriage a farce and a desecration of the ritual of marriage; the man known as my son is a bastard, and my dukedom should be inherited by my legitimate son, Henry."

"I see," Joan said, folding the sheet again.

The duke's eyes opened again, but only halfway. "Make certain it gets to . . ." The words were lost in a mumble.

"You can trust me to do the right thing with this document," Joan told him.

"*The croaking raven doth bellow for revenge*," Eversley said, his voice clear, if only a thread.

"*Hamlet*," Joan exclaimed. "That's from *Hamlet*."

"I'll be revenged on the whole pack of them." His voice grated to a halt.

Joan waited for five minutes, but he didn't open his eyes again, and his breathing was hardly audible. She touched his hand lightly. "Goodbye, Your Grace."

She picked up the paper, tucked it in her coat, and walked out.

Chapter Twenty-three

The billiard room was crowded with tall, powerful gentlemen doing what comes naturally to men when they find themselves in company with limitless brandy: gossiping. For his part, Thaddeus had trounced Jeremy at billiards—a rare event—and retired to a deep armchair. He and the duke sat together in a comfortable silence.

Thaddeus occupied himself by staring up at the wooden tracery of the ceiling, where all the coats of arms of the Wildes were painstakingly detailed with gilt accents. A few others appeared there as well: that of the Duke of Wynter, for example. Since he was married to Viola, the new father was presumably no blood relation.

The duke followed his eyes. "We'll add yours, the Eversley arms."

"True or not?" Jeremy demanded of Parth on the other side of the billiard table, waving a glass of whiskey.

"True," Parth said. He made a shot that ricocheted off three rails and rolled into the corner bag.

Jeremy gave a crack of laughter and turned around. "Lavinia has turned an entire chamber in their house into a museum for her gowns."

Parth's brows drew together. "My wife adores clothing. If she wants to turn our entire house into a museum, I will support her." He considered. "Perhaps not the nursery."

The door opened. Devin, Duke of Wynter and father of the newest Wilde offspring, stood there, his hair tousled, his eyes glowing. In his arms was a tiny, wrapped bundle. "Otis has arrived," he announced, happiness visible in every lineament of his body.

The Duke of Lindow was the first at the door and took Otis in his arms. "Beloved boy," His Grace said softly, kissing the child. "Welcome."

Thaddeus moved to Devin's side as the baby was handed from arm to arm, grown men cooing over the child with no respect for manliness. The Wildes were like that, Thaddeus had noticed. Fearless and unashamed when it came to emotion.

"Congratulations," he told Devin.

Devin's eyes never left his son, but he nodded. "I gather congratulations are in order for you as well."

"Yes," Thaddeus said.

Devin flashed a look at him before watching, narrow-eyed, as Otis was transferred from one uncle to another. "Here," he said, starting forward, "watch his neck, you lobcock."

Thaddeus melted into the corridor. Someday he would feel comfortable in the Wilde family, but not just yet. He turned left, intending to go to his chamber, and looked up in time to see a slender figure in green hurtling toward him. A smile curled his mouth as Joan melted into his embrace, talking so fast that he couldn't understand.

"My father?" he asked, tucking her against him.

She pulled back enough so that he could see her face. "I have it, Thaddeus. I have it." She caught her breath, panting. "See?" She stuck her hand inside her velvet coat and pulled out a folded sheet.

Thaddeus blinked. "How did you get it? You didn't—"

"No, I didn't steal it from a dying man!" she cried. "I'm not dressed as an angel either, so I didn't frighten your father with tales of brimstone, though I have to say that he's a horrid old man, Thaddeus, and he deserves whatever happens to him!"

Thaddeus gave her a wry smile. "I still hope he doesn't encounter brimstone."

"Of course," Joan said repentantly. "Me too. I mean, so do I. But honestly, Thaddeus, he is *not* a nice man. I don't think he'd repent his sins, not even if the Archbishop of Canterbury were to lay hands on him."

Thaddeus looked about. "Perhaps we shouldn't carry on this conversation in the corridor." He couldn't hear any sound from the billiard room, but at any moment the family might wash into the corridor, baby in tow.

"Let's go to the turret," Joan said. "I'd invite you to my chamber, but Aunt Knowe gave me a frightful scold earlier about not being scandalous. By which she meant, *Don't be caught in your bedchamber by the maids."*

She gave him an impish smile.

"Does your aunt know you're wandering around the castle at night dressed in breeches?" Thaddeus took in her appearance. "And studded with jewels? If diamonds were raisins, you'd be a tasty cake." Thaddeus wrapped his arms around her and nipped her earlobe. "*Very* tasty." He felt himself harden against her thigh.

"We need to discuss this." Joan held up the letter, crumpled after being caught between them.

Thaddeus allowed himself to be drawn down one corridor and up another, until they ducked under an archway and started up a winding stairway.

"We used to come here often," Joan said over her shoulder.

"Why did you stop?"

"Aunt Knowe thinks it's too dangerous with side panniers."

Thaddeus agreed with her. The narrow walls turned with the stairs, and he couldn't even stretch out both his arms.

"Breeches are so much better than panniers for climbing stairs!" Joan called happily, and skipped up a few steps.

They finally emerged on the turret that topped the family wing of the castle. Like everything at Lindow, the stones that made up the crenellations were massive, so heavy that it was difficult to imagine how they could have been levered into place. The gaps weren't there to create a pretty border either. This was a battlement turret, built at just the right width to allow a man to launch a stone or pour some boiling oil over the edge.

Thaddeus walked to the edge to take a look. Looking out over the moonlit country, the acres that surrounded Lindow, including the dark mire that was Lindow Moss, Thaddeus had a sense of time and continuity. His father wanted to break the rules of primogeniture . . . but there was sense to it, unfair though it seemed. The Lindow duchy represented the achievement of generations marshaling their wealth and power.

His father, on the other hand, had tried to bankrupt Eversley Court. Perhaps the Duke of Eversley was so enraged at his parents that he wanted to destroy his heritage. It was a strange thought, but it made sense.

Joan was on the other side of the parapet. "Over here!" she called.

Thaddeus rounded the parapet and discovered his future wife sitting on a mattress tucked under a covered walkway. The moonlight was full in her face; she'd taken off her hat, and beams struck light from the diamonds around her neck.

But most of all, from her.

She shimmered.

Thaddeus sank to his knees before her. "Joan." The word was so full of longing and love that he was almost embarrassed, but he pushed the thought away. "I love you."

"I love you too," she said, dimpling. She leaned forward and brushed her lips over his. "Now read this." She pushed the letter into his hands.

"I needn't read it," Thaddeus said. "The Wilde solicitors will forestall attempts to publish if there are other copies somewhere. How on earth did you get it?"

"Your father thought I was the ghost of Henry VIII." She struck a royal posture. "You didn't know this, but spectral royalty carries out a kind of visiting deathbed service for men who are kingly. He gave the letter to me of his own free will."

Thaddeus grinned. Even holding his father's despicable letter in his hand, he found himself grinning. "My understanding is that Henry was a great deal larger around the middle than you are."

"I played Henry as a boy, silly," Joan said. "That's when His Majesty visited Lindow. Admittedly, there's not much sense to his ghost lurking about. I forgot to use the royal 'we' a few times. Oh, and by the way, your father knew he was dying when he traveled here."

"He said as much," Thaddeus said.

"He didn't want his other family to have to experience the indignities of his death." Joan nodded at his hands. "Open it."

Thaddeus looked down, feeling a pulse of deep rage at his father. Wasn't it enough that the man had destroyed his legal family, tried to ruin his wife's life, and left his heir scrambling to please a father who loathed him?

"I could just rip it into shreds and throw it to the winds," he suggested.

"You could," Joan said.

Thaddeus turned it over. "I don't understand. I don't bloody understand the man. I suppose he wanted to ensure that I'd support his family, but this idiocy makes it equally likely that I'd spurn their claim."

"He babbled about revenge," Joan said. "Even quoted Hamlet on the subject."

"One of the most self-destructive emotions a person can have," Thaddeus said. "This ends *here*." Methodically he ripped the letter, unread, into tiny pieces and launched it into the air. The breeze caught the tiny scraps and carried them over the parapets and away.

Thaddeus leaned forward to brush a kiss on Joan's lips the way she had on his, but that wasn't enough. He lifted her into his lap and found himself in that happy place that existed only when they were alone together, whether on an island or a turret.

His entire body soaked in the happiness of having her in his arms. The world, lying in shards at his feet, knit itself together. She was the glue, the one thing that made his father's petty cruelty irrelevant.

Sometime later, he murmured, "My father taught me something about love."

Joan blinked up at him, her eyes dark with desire. "What?"

He could just see the sweep of her lashes and one rosy cheek. "He loved his second family. I told him I'd send my half brother to Eton."

"He scorned you for being honorable, yet he depended on that very quality," Joan pointed out. "He came to you, at the end. He could have sent the letter to London without you knowing it had been written. I think the letter was a pretext.

He knew no one would send it on to the newspapers."

She turned her head and kissed his chest. "Would you like to take off your coat, perhaps?"

Thaddeus choked. "No, I would not like to unclothe myself on a mattress that's been here God knows how long."

"Since April," Joan said helpfully. "New ticking and a cover every spring."

Thaddeus could just imagine how many of his soon-to-be brothers-in-law had taken advantage of the mattress since April. "No," he said firmly. "Picnic with ants, yes. This mattress, no."

"Such a duke," Joan grumbled. She kissed his chin.

Thaddeus drew her to her feet. "Much though I would love to escort you to your bedchamber, despite Aunt Knowe's admonishments, there is something I have to do."

Which was how the Duke of Eversley—vengeful and embittered as he was—left this mortal coil with one hand firmly held by his son and heir, and the other by a young Henry VIII.

He sank into that final darkness with a germ of joy in his heart. A king had attended his deathbed. He had breathed his last under an ermine throw.

Finally, his worth had been recognized.

Chapter Twenty-four

$\mathcal{A}$t the breakfast table the next morning, Joan carefully spread Aunt Knowe's marmalade onto her toast, keeping her gaze far from Thaddeus. Every time their eyes met, she found herself trembling like a ninny, pink color rushing into her cheeks.

Yesterday . . .

Yesterday had been marvelous.

Oh, not the death of the Duke of Eversley. But the rest added up to the happiest day of her life: Thaddeus's proposal in Percy's sty, making love on the island, the birth of little Otis, their conversation on the turret . . .

Afterward, in her bedchamber, when Thaddeus made love to her so tenderly that she started crying, and then burst into laughter at the dismay on his face.

She had woken to find Thaddeus propped on one elbow, warm eyes smiling at her. His jaw still had an arrogant slant, but it was part of him, and she adored everything about him.

Even after an illicit night in which they slept only in snatches, he looked elegantly composed, whereas her hair fell a tangled cloud around her shoulders. The white sheet draped over his flat stomach as if it had been carved from marble by a master sculptor. His hair was rumpled just the right amount to make a woman's breath catch; his eyes burned with emotion.

Truth be told, it wasn't the fact that she'd spent the night in a man's arms that was making Joan blush over her toast. It was the emotion she saw in that man's eyes.

A growl at the other table made her head jerk up. Her father was staring down at the post just delivered by Prism. Joan's heart sank when she saw what he was holding.

The Duke of Lindow was rarely enraged, but the one thing certain to drive him to a fury was the proliferation of prints depicting the "wild Wildes" that continued to circulate throughout England. They were collected by kitchen maids and countesses, and unfortunately, the more outrageous prints sold like hotcakes.

In the last couple of years, she had often been the subject of the best-selling print in the kingdom, a dubious honor at best. She tilted her head, but from her viewpoint, it didn't appear to be a sketch of her, thank goodness. The last thing she wanted to do was remind Thaddeus just how much the gossip columns relied on her for material.

"Look at this!" His Grace said, holding up the print contemptuously by one corner. "Sent to me straight from one of the stationers."

"What does it depict, darling?" his wife inquired,

looking completely unconcerned. When the third duchess first married, she had disliked being a subject of entertainment for the popular press. Now she was inured to it.

He crumpled the print and tossed it on the table, where it bounced and ended up beside Jeremy's glass. "It depicts me buying wedding licenses by the dozen," he grated.

Parth was the first to laugh, but everyone in the room followed.

"There's more than a grain of truth to it," North chortled. "You did marry three times."

"North, dearest, I believe that the etching refers to the duke's children, referring to the family's reluctance to wait for the calling of the banns," the duchess said serenely. "My husband is depicted as buying licenses for his children."

"Should have told me before I paid a fortune for mine," Jeremy said, laughing.

"Buying licenses in bulk is actually doing godly work, brother," Aunt Knowe said gleefully. "The Book of Common Prayer says it all. Marriage is ordained as a remedy against sin and to avoid fornication, if you don't mind my bluntness at the breakfast table."

The duke groaned.

"An inauspicious moment for this announcement," Thaddeus said with a distinct thread of humor in his voice. "Joan has agreed to marry me immediately."

"She has?" the duchess asked, her brows drawing together.

"Due to my father's death," Thaddeus went on smoothly. "The Duke of Eversley left explicit instructions that his body was to be removed to Eversley Court, there to lie in state until a funeral one week later, at night, with his ermine throw as a pall for the coffin, fourteen torchbearers, and silk crepe scarves given to all mourners."

Joan's stepfather narrowed his eyes at Thaddeus. "You'll meet me in my study after this meal, Duke."

"Certainly," Thaddeus said, unruffled.

"Only as his wife could I attend the funeral," Joan pointed out. "I'm certain that Aunt Knowe wouldn't want to chaperone me, since baby Otis is here."

"Among other reasons to miss that particular funeral," her aunt said.

"Would it be crass to say that it sounds like the kind of theatrical event you'll enjoy?" North asked Joan.

"Yes, it would," Aunt Knowe said.

Joan stuck out her tongue at her older brother, who burst into laughter. "You don't look like someone deserving of 'Your Grace' at the moment, sis!"

"I, for one, am deeply grateful that Joan has agreed to marry my son straightaway," Thaddeus's mother announced. "I feel quite ill." The Duchess of Eversley was the picture of rosy-cheeked health. "I shall not be able to attend my husband's funeral. Instead, I shall remain in the company of my dear Lady Knowe, with deep gratitude to all of you for sheltering me in this time of mourning and . . . illness."

"Excellent!" Aunt Knowe cried.

"I gather that the late duke threatened to send

a letter to the newspapers announcing that our marriage was illegitimate," Thaddeus's mother added, looking remarkably unconcerned.

"The letter has been destroyed," Joan told her quickly.

"If it leaks out, it won't matter to me," she said, patting Thaddeus's hand. "Shortly after my marriage, my father confessed that he knew of Eversley's love affair. His mistress was still living with her father when we wed."

Thaddeus was stunned to hear that.

"My grandfather married you to a man whose heart was . . . was claimed elsewhere?"

"My father was confident that their love would prove a triviality. After it became clear that was not the case, he apologized to me repeatedly." The duchess smiled at her son. "Your grandfather left a thorough account, Thaddeus. No court in the land would overturn my marriage. You are the Duke of Eversley."

Thaddeus had no doubt about his legal claim to the dukedom, but his mother's affirmation was still welcome.

"I believe that the late duke knew perfectly well that his letter wouldn't be dispatched to London," Joan said. "After all, he waved it in the air last night, so that all of us would know it existed. And he didn't give it to the household staff; the letter had no address."

"That's true," her stepfather said, nodding.

"The late duke knew that his elder son would take care of his other family, take care of the funeral, take care of the letter too." Joan smiled at

Thaddeus. "That's what honor is, after all. The duke scorned it, but in the end, he relied on it."

"Hear, hear," Aunt Knowe said, putting down her fork to clap.

The family picked up her cue, and "hear, hear" resounded around the breakfast room.

Thaddeus forced his mouth to ease into a smile. His heart clenched, but it was a good feeling. Joan's fingers curled around his.

At the head of the table, the Duke of Lindow nodded to Prism, and footmen stepped forward to put glasses of champagne before each person.

Thaddeus looked around the room, at the faces—from the duke's to the butler's—all of them smiling at him with admiration, his mother among them. He turned his head and there was Joan, his beloved Joan, beaming at him.

The Duke of Lindow rose, holding his glass of champagne. "We welcomed two new members to the Wilde family last night: Otis and Thaddeus. I am blessed to call both my relatives. And Thaddeus, since Otis is upstairs in his mother's arms, I'll address this to you: I hope that we, your family, will in time fill the space left by your father's passing."

Thaddeus nodded. Words spilled into his head regarding his father. But that didn't matter.

He stood up, letting go of Joan's hand, looking from face to face. "My future wife has already filled the space left by my father's disregard. Becoming one of this vast tribe makes me very happy, but my true joy is that you are giving me Joan. Her love is the greatest gift I've ever been offered, and I promise you, her family, that I will treasure her for all the days of my life."

He nodded to Joan's father, sipped his champagne, and looked down at his future duchess.

She was laughing, of course. And the table was laughing with her. Then she sprang to her feet next to him, glass in hand.

"I think we should all toast the new Duke of Eversley," Joan cried. "Not because he is devilishly handsome and brilliant, but because he has showed himself a Wilde in three ways. Number one!" She raised a finger.

Her eyes were sparkling with mischief. "He brought us Percy the piglet. Who has raised the tone of the cattle shed with his very fine pleated collar and is beloved by the Lindow nursery."

This point was met by much clapping. Thaddeus wrapped his arm around Joan, and she leaned against his shoulder.

"Number two: He just announced that we're marrying by special license, as did most of my brothers, not to mention my dearest sister Viola!"

Roars of laughter and more applause.

Joan paused and waited for silence. "And number three. I say this with great love, dear ones, but I will say it: I longed my entire life to be an actress, to walk across a public stage, to hear applause from strangers, to test my acting skills. Father, you allowed me to perform here at Lindow Castle. But Thaddeus—"

He frowned at her, and she put a fleeting finger on his lips before she turned back to the table.

"Thaddeus no sooner heard my wishes than he arranged for me to act on the Wilmslow stage, which I did. Two nights ago, Otis and I recouped our roles as Hamlet and Ophelia."

"*What?*" the duke roared.

"Oh, darling." The duchess sighed.

Thaddeus was interested to see that the other Wildes were not only unsurprised; they mostly seemed cross to have missed the performance.

"I wasn't good," Joan said flatly.

The duke's face darkened even more. "Of course you were!"

"You were undoubtedly the best actress ever to appear in Wilmslow!" Lavinia cried.

"No, I wasn't," Joan said. She smiled around the table, still leaning on Thaddeus, who wound both arms around her. "I was funny in a part that is supposed to be serious. The audience roared with laughter as Hamlet died. My point is that Thaddeus *heard* me. And he did something about it. He gave me my dream."

Joan raised her glass of champagne. "That is why Thaddeus is truly a Wilde, not an Eversley. Because when push came to shove, the most law-abiding man in all the kingdom threw away the rules and made sure that the woman he loved would be happy for the rest of her life."

Thaddeus's heart thumped. He turned her about and began kissing her, irrespective of his audience.

If any Wilde still thought that Thaddeus Erskine Shaw, Duke of Eversley, was as rigid as a starched collar, as his father had described him?

They knew better now.

He didn't stop kissing his future duchess, even when a crumpled print depicting the head of the

Wilde family buying marriage licenses by the dozen flew over the table and bounced on the patriarch's dish.

"Got a license to spare?" Jeremy asked his father-in-law, laughter in his voice. "Something tells me that the new Duke of Eversley would prefer not to wait until a license arrives from London!"

Epilogue

Nine years later

The pond had that summer afternoon feeling; the water was so warm that Horatius could feel it on all his limbs like a blanket. His mom and dad and baby Lou were back on the island, but he was lying on his back in the pond, his hands paddling now and then to keep him afloat. On all sides, flat cool lily pads bumped against him and then slid out of the way to let him pass.

Back in the castle, his cousins would be shrieking and running about the nursery; every one of his grandfather's children was home for the first time in two years, and the castle was filling up with sound. But at nearly eight years old, Horatius was too old for most of the games. Not all, but definitely too old for the screaming.

He would have been playing with Otis, but his favorite cousin just turned nine years old, and the uncles took him off to choose a pony of his own. His family had a picnic instead, eating a fish that he and his father had caught by themselves. He could still taste the clean white flavor of it.

A rustle in the water told him that one of the frogs had just launched into the pond to cool himself off. Horatius turned over lazily, letting the sun hit his back. Face down, he opened his eyes to an underwater world, a complex maze of water lily stalks with small fish slipping between them. The surface glowed just out of his eyesight, at his shoulder.

A deep breath, and he looked back down, cataloguing all the various colors of green he could see. His father said that exactitude was important, and he agreed, so he summed up: verdigris, absinthe, terre verte, celadon, emerald . . . lots of emerald.

Another breath, and the tapestry of the world under the lake was his again. Off to his right, a great carp slid through two weedy stalks, its dorsal fin fluttering like a sail, the curved line of silver scales starting at his gills. The carp almost came face-to-face with Horatius, and his mouth gaped open with surprise.

Horatius drifted along, letting the sun heat his neck. When his father, the duke, cleaned the carp they ate for luncheon, scales had flown into the air like flecks of silver. His little sister, Lou, for Louisa, because she was named for his great-aunt Knowe, clapped her hands and screamed to hold one. But then she put it in her mouth and spat it back out indignantly.

"She's learning," his mother had said.

The duchess was the most beautiful lady in the whole world, but she said looks didn't matter and

Horatius agreed. What was truly beautiful was the world under the surface of the water, with stalks moving gently, the lily pads like a forest of skinny trees, thickest near the shore.

Dimly, when he came up for air, he heard his mother call, "Horatius!" He put his face back down, though, because it wouldn't do to waste that deep breath. His father's bellow penetrated the water, and he spluttered upright.

Not that his father was angry. He was never angry; he said that a gentleman, especially a duke, had to learn to control himself because too many people could be harmed if he said something irresponsible.

His family was standing on the shore looking for him, the three of them, so Horatius started swimming toward them carefully, so he didn't rip water lilies from their stems. All around him, small frogs plopped into the water, annoyed by the noise he was making. A dragonfly whizzed past his ear, its sapphire-blue wings almost transparent, heavy head bobbing.

His sister wasn't unlike a dragonfly, now he thought of it. Her head was too big for her body, even though his mother said she was absolutely perfect.

By the time he reached the shore, the family was in the punt, waiting for him.

The duke stood in the rear, manning the pole that they used to get across the lake. There were too many lily pads to row properly these days, so the rowboat stayed under the willow tree. Horatius clambered into the punt, water sheeting off his breeches.

His mother smiled and chucked him a cloth so he could wipe his face. Thankfully, she wasn't at all like his friends' mothers. He hadn't started Eton yet because his parents said they couldn't do without him, but he already had friends who were there, and one of them said that his mother didn't remember his name.

Horatius had kept quiet, because his parents definitely knew his name; he was named for one of his mother's brothers. But mostly, they loved him. A future duke doesn't boast about stuff like that, about anything, really. There were lots of things a duke couldn't do, but that was all right.

His father reached out and tousled his hair; it was a silly golden color, starting to curl up in a way he loathed. "Everything all right under the water?"

"Always," Horatius said.

Lou reached out her hands to him, cooing, but he knew that she'd squawk if he actually took her. She didn't like chilly water. "I got something for you," he said, remembering. He shifted his hip so that he could dig into the wet bag he strung around his waist.

"It isn't another snail, is it?" his mother asked.

"No," Horatius said with a touch of indignation. Lou hadn't even paused to think that he was giving her something *alive*; she just popped it in her mouth and swallowed it before anyone could stop her. He hated to think what that poor snail thought as it bounced down into her fat tummy.

"I saw this glinting, so I dove to the bottom." He wrestled open the bag and pulled out a silver spoon, a little mucky. Reaching over, he doused it in the water a few times and then handed it over.

Lou gave an approving squawk and stuck the thin end in her mouth and chomped on it. Like a puppy, she was growing teeth and liked to chew.

His mother gently turned the spoon over to see the insignia.

"Lindow Castle crest," Horatius said. "That makes sense, right?"

"Thaddeus!" his mother gasped.

"The treasure," his father said, giving Horatius a big smile. "You found the lost Lindow Castle treasure."

"It's only a spoon," Horatius pointed out, but then he brightened. "I can go back down and find more!"

"That will be up to your grandfather. Your uncles spent many hours trying to find that treasure, so they'll be jealous."

Mother was looking up at his father with that daft expression that they both got now and then. Sure enough, his father jammed the pole into the bottom of the pool and leaned down to kiss her, so Horatius jumped overboard before they could tell him no. They were halfway across the pond anyway.

He splashed his way to shore and tore up the slope and through the apple orchard looking for the castle billy goat. Gully had to be a hundred years old, with a white beard and all, but Horatius knew he loved company.

Sometime later, when the Duke and Duchess of Eversley made their way through the orchard, they found the future duke lying in the grass, his arms wound around an elderly goat, face buried in Gully's malodorous fur, both snoring.

"Do you suppose Horatius will be a naturalist?" Joan asked, leaning against Thaddeus's shoulder.

"He already is a naturalist," Thaddeus said. "A brilliant one. He has a very good idea there."

Joan looked up, laughing. "Napping?"

Her daughter's curls were nodding on her father's broad shoulder, the silver spoon clutched in her chubby hand.

"Or something," Thaddeus said, bending down to kiss her.